Readers love
J.S. COOK

The Quality of Mercy

"This is a short and sweet story with a bit of mystery, a little suspense, tossed into a snowstorm."

—MM Good Book Reviews

"JS Cook delivers with skilled, vivid, evocative writing that pulled me right in, had me reading to the end, and left me very moved."

—It's About the Book

Famous Last Words

"Short, Sexy, and Steamy, that is what this book was."

—MM Good Book reviews

A Little Night Murder

"...a wonderful noir-style read, perfect for a rainy afternoon."

—Romancing the Book

Come to Dust

"Dark and intense, J.S. Cook will have you guessing until the very end."

—Sensual Reads

By J.S. COOK

But Not For Me
Come to Dust
Famous Last Words
A Little Night Murder
The Lovely Beast
Oasis of Night
The Quality of Mercy
Sixteen Songs About Regret
The Stranger at My Door
Valley of the Dead
The Winter Dark

Published by DREAMSPINNER PRESS
http://www.dreamspinnerpress.com

OASIS
OF NIGHT

J.S. COOK

Published by
DREAMSPINNER PRESS

5032 Capital Circle SW, Suite 2, PMB# 279, Tallahassee, FL 32305-7886 USA
http://www.dreamspinnerpress.com/

Oasis of Night
© 2015 J.S. Cook.

Cover Art
© 2015 Maria Fanning.
Cover content is for illustrative purposes only and any person depicted on the cover is a model.

ISBN: 978-1-63476-132-1
Digital ISBN: 978-1-63476-133-8
Library of Congress Control Number: 2015905071
Second Edition June 2015

First Edition of Valley of the Dead published by Dreamspinner Press, 2013.
First Edition of Heartache Café published by MLR Press, 2009.

Printed in the United States of America
∞
This paper meets the requirements of
ANSI/NISO Z39.48-1992 (Permanence of Paper).

To my husband, Paul: Don't let the bastards grind you down.

Acknowledgments

MANY THANKS to Tricia, Linda, and Anastasia for their editorial expertise, and Sue and Camiele for making it look pretty.
Thanks to Elizabeth, and to Paul and Janet for the cover art.

Heartache Café

PROLOGUE

It was freezing cold, with an icy wind out of the northwest and snowflakes swirling in the gusts—the kind of day that made you want to find someplace warm and stay there. I still don't know how I got where I was. I don't remember all that much about it, only the minor details, a few things here and there. It was like I'd been afflicted with some strange sort of amnesia. I'd been up all night—hell, I'd been up the past few nights, going over and over things in my mind, trying to make it come out different, but it never would. No matter what I did, it wasn't going to change, and for the rest of my life, I'd see it every time I closed my eyes.

My discharge papers lay where I'd tossed them, next to the empty whisky bottle and the ash tray overflowing with cigarette butts on the coffee table in the squalid little living room that sat to one side of the kitchen. I didn't have to read them to know what was written there; I'd always known it, just like I knew that I had brown eyes and brown hair, that I tended to put on weight around my gut and had to watch it, and that I couldn't play football worth a damn but I could drink my weight in whisky, no questions asked.

It hardly even mattered anymore. I finally had my fill, and when it got light enough to see, I got in my car and drove—anywhere, it didn't matter, and it wasn't like I had any of it planned. Maybe I'd just drive into the Delaware, or maybe find a nice dead-end street and ram my car into a cement wall—anything to make the pain stop, to get the goddamn voices and the pictures out of my head.

There was a smell in my nostrils, the ashy scent of something burning, or maybe it was blood. I'd been somewhere, somewhere else, and there was a woman there, and we'd had words.

1

I'll tell everyone you forced me. I'll tell everyone you raped me. You'd better help me or I will.

He wasn't even a doctor, not really. Maybe he'd been one once, but he'd long since lost his license and no longer had the right to even hang a sign. I drove her there and wanted to go in with her, but she wouldn't have it.

Let's not make this any harder than it has to be, okay, Jack?

So I waited in the car, but it seemed to take an awful long time, and while I was waiting, I had a little drink, just to pass the time. I had a drink, and then another one, and what the hell, I might as well finish the bottle, so I did. And then I fell asleep.

I fell asleep.

It was dark when I woke up, and the face looking back at me from the rearview mirror had a five o'clock shadow and then some. A little warning voice in the back of my brain told me this was bad, this was really bad, this was worse than anything, and maybe I shouldn't get out of the car, maybe I should just call the cops.

I didn't listen. I never do. I went up that filthy, stinking little alley and opened his office door, but I was much too late, and he was gone.

There was blood everywhere.

I stopped my car just before the bridge and walked on. The sun was rising, the first rays creeping over the city a little at a time. I looked up at the great steel span of the bridge and began to climb. The cables cut into my bare hands, and I was almost weeping with the cold, but I kept climbing. I'd climb so far that it would never touch me. I'd climb until I could forget that awful little room and the stink of blood and all the rest of this sordid mess. I'd climb up till I was free.

I stood there looking down into the icy water, wondering if the drop would be enough to kill me or if I'd drown first or die of cold. I saw the weirdest thing, a small sailboat coming down the river. A ridiculous little thing, no bigger than a minute, sailing down the Delaware like it had every right to be there and then some. I thought about pictures I'd seen of graceful feluccas on the Nile River in Egypt, and as I watched the little boat tacking into the wind, something occurred to me.

I climbed down off the bridge, walked to where my car was parked, and drove away.

CHAPTER ONE

YOU WOULDN'T think it even gets hot in a place like this, but let me tell you, brother—it does. Around about the middle of July, the fog clears away and the sun comes out, hot enough—as they say around these parts—to split the rocks. It's a different sort of place, not like anywhere I'd ever been before, but when you have to leave home as suddenly as I did, you don't much care. You just pick a direction on the map and head out, hoping things turn out okay. Twelve hundred miles as the crow flies to St. John's, Newfoundland, from my hometown of Philadelphia. I slept nearly the whole way, never mind the roaring of the airplane engines. Some things hit harder than others, and I'd been dealt a knockout punch.

When we landed at the airstrip in the little town called Torbay, I felt like I'd come to the end of the world. Nothing much to see except trees—black spruce and tamarack and scrub pines—and the red gravel airstrip. I got out of my seat and climbed down, stiff and sore and feeling like I'd been run down by a truck. I guess I was still in shock a little bit. The air was colder than I was used to—even Philadelphia winters didn't have this kind of soggy bite. All I wanted was to get inside the little terminal and maybe get a cup of coffee. I had five hundred bucks, American, in my wallet, a passport, and a copy of my discharge papers from the Army. I guess I should have felt ashamed, because here was Hitler, stomping his jack-booted way across Europe, and there was nothing I could do about it. *Unfit for active service.* Yeah, that's me, thirty-eight years old and already broken beyond repair.

This—all of this—was just a blur to me. I was seeing other streets and hearing a different accent, and I was walking into Moe's first thing in the morning for a cup of joe, sitting down at the counter to look over the newspaper before I went outside and took a sharp left toward the waterfront. Maybe that's what drew me to this place, the promise of cold salt air and the tang of the sea in my nostrils, the bustle of the waterfront, and ships coming and going at all hours of the day and night. I loved the idea that I could do the same, just go whenever I wanted to, anywhere I liked, and not have to answer to anybody. If I felt like it, I could hop a freighter to some other place and work my way across the world.

It was something Moe and I had talked a lot about, whenever I was in there. *You thinking of going somewhere?* He'd always refill my coffee cup without my having to ask, and I'd always leave a tip. *Thinking of leaving old Philly, huh?*

Right up until the last of it, I wasn't sure. Even after it happened, I figured I could just keep on the way I was, doing all the things I'd been doing. I figured I was strong enough to take it, right up until I stood on the Delaware River Bridge one morning, looking down into the swirling water and wondering if I had the nerve.

You want to know what stopped me?

Egypt. Yeah, you heard me, Egypt. See, I'd always wanted to go, and standing there on the bridge with the wind whipping me around, I figured if I followed through with what I had in mind, I'd never get to go. I'd never get to see the pyramids and ride a camel and do all that stupid, touristy stuff that people do. Pretty dumb, huh? Maybe, but it was enough to get me down off the bridge before the cops came, and it was enough to make me understand that if I ever wanted to see the pyramids at Giza or stroll the native quarter in Cairo, I had to get out of Philly. I had to go somewhere far away and try my best to forget.

"Passport?" She was young and pretty, the girl behind the counter, with dark red hair worn in rolls at the sides of her head. She smiled at me like she meant it. "Welcome to Newfoundland, Mr. Stoyles. If you follow that corridor and turn right, there are taxis out front to take you into town."

"Is it...." Goddammit, it was starting again. I took a deep breath and tried to get ahold of myself. "Is it far, into town? I have a room booked at the hotel, I just...." I fumbled in my pockets and found the scrap of paper. "Yeah, I have a room at this hotel downtown."

She looked it—and me—over and smiled again. She sure was pretty—and nice, in that way women hardly ever are anymore. She looked at me like she was interested in more than how much money I had on me or where I was likely to go in life, once the war was over. That was something I didn't even know myself.

Listen, Jack—why don't you come up to Newfoundland with me? They're building all kinds of stuff up there, and the whole place is ripe for the picking. Frankie Missalo, an old Army buddy of mine; we'd both joined up long before the whole thing went to hell at Pearl Harbor. Only thing was, he'd stayed in while I'd gotten kind of… waylaid. *Lots of Army contractors up there, and lots of Yanks like us needing somewhere to get a proper cup of coffee. Come on! Ain't you always said you wanted to have your own place?*

So I did what he said and bought my ticket, and here I was. All I wanted now was to live a quiet life, waiting out the war to the best of my ability and minding my own business. I wasn't interested in anything but that.

I SPENT three days at the hotel while Frankie and I scouted around for an empty space downtown. I'd just about given up hope when a real gem came on the market, a little storefront with lots of room for chairs and tables and a piano. The space was longer than it was broad, and flared out nicely toward the back. Already I was making mental nips and tucks, adding a pot of flowers here, some ornaments and paintings there, and over here, the bar, with its rows of bottles and a big mirror behind it. I found a cash register for cheap at a consignment store, and when Frankie showed up with a truckload of cafe chairs and tables, I didn't ask him any unnecessary questions. I just got busy moving in.

"Whatcha gonna call it, Jack?" Frankie spread his hands out in front of him and squinted. "Whatcha want's a big sign, neon lettering. Jack's Cafe."

"Naw, that's been done. I want something that people are gonna stop for, something that'll really bring 'em in." I slung a towel over my shoulder and came out from behind the bar. "Something catchy, you know?"

"Yeah." Frankie shook his head and then lit a cigarette. "Something like Moe's Place?"

I faked a punch at his jaw. "Keep it up, mug." We both laughed. "How about a beer?" I couldn't stop touching the shiny brass taps; it was hard for me to believe this was my place, my very own.

"You, ah…." Frankie's eyes skidded away from mine. "You having one, Jack?"

"Nope." I got a glass for him. "What'll it be?"

"Whatever you got's none too good for me." He sat at a table near the bar and stretched his long legs out in front of him. "So here you are, Jack! Lock, stock, and barrel, huh? An honest-to-God property owner." He thanked me for the beer as I sat down. "How much trouble they give you about the license?"

"You kidding me?" I sipped from the glass of ice water I'd poured for myself. "They couldn't give it to me fast enough. Anybody woulda thought I was the Second Coming or something."

Frankie, a lifelong Catholic, grimaced. "Yeah, cut that, okay?" He glanced around and nervously raked a hand through his sandy hair. "Don't be bringing bad luck on yourself before you've even started."

I didn't answer him. Yeah, I'd been brought up in the Church too, but it never stuck on me the way it stuck to Frankie. I've known him since we were kids, when he was serving at mass and singing in the choir. He wasn't what I'd call superstitious, but he sure had a healthy respect for the church.

"So tomorrow's the big day?" He set the beer glass down.

"Yeah. Tomorrow's the big day." I spread my arms wide. "Welcome to the Heartache Cafe."

CHAPTER TWO

THE COLD, wet winter of 1941 wore on into spring, and I began to loosen up and enjoy myself a little bit. What Frankie had said was true, I'd always wanted to have my own place, and it was fun being lord of my own little manor, such as it was.

I spent that whole winter making improvements to the Cafe, the kinds of little touches customers appreciate, the things that keep them coming back. I put in a piano so anyone who wanted to play could, and refurbished the tiny kitchen at the rear so I could serve hot sandwiches, fries, hamburgers, and things like that. I stocked the jukebox in the corner with all the latest tunes, and I made sure to get new records in as soon as they came out.

St. John's was a small city compared to Philadelphia, and word began to get around that there was a place downtown on Water Street to get a genuine cup of real American coffee. Pretty soon every Yank in the place was making it a habit to pile into the Cafe after work, sometimes for a bite to eat, sometimes for just a glass of beer.

I opened at noon each day, and the Cafe stayed open until midnight or sometimes later, depending on how business was going. On Mondays and Wednesdays, I offered a lunchtime special, and that got quite a few of the office girls in the door for a cup of coffee and a sandwich. Friday usually meant the best business of the week, because all the wartime contractors working in the city were turned loose with plenty of money in their pockets and an itch to spend it, and I was only too happy to take their dough. I didn't mind the work, and I didn't mind staying late. It wasn't like I had to go far to get home. I'd furnished the nice little suite of rooms above the Cafe with everything I needed, and it was plenty cozy up there. Maybe I wasn't exactly happy, but I was content, and brother, that was good enough for me.

Pretty soon, though, the trickle of customers increased, and what had once been a nice, steady pace soon became too much for me to handle. It got so busy that I didn't even have time to go to the bathroom, and most nights I didn't get out of there till well after midnight. I put a Help Wanted sign in the Cafe window and hoped for the best. I had a few tentative inquiries, mostly from local boys, eager to try the bar trade but just as eager for the free booze they figured was a fringe benefit—nobody I'd trust to watch the place while I took a lunch break or ran to the bank with the day's deposits. I'd just about given up hope of finding anybody at all.

I was sitting at a front table by the windows one day, taking advantage of some spare time to square away the books and settle my accounts for the week. What I resented about accounting work—everything—was nicely balanced by my sense of satisfaction. The Heartache Cafe had finally begun to turn a real profit, and my bank account was starting to bulk up a little. It seemed like things might turn around for me, that leaving Philadelphia wasn't such a bad idea after all, and maybe I could make a life for myself in this strange place. The town was even starting to grow on me. The people were really friendly, kind beyond what I expected, and if their odd accents made me guess a little at what they were trying to say, I didn't mind so much. Hell, my Philly accent wasn't exactly kosher either.

I didn't hear the tap on the front door until it reached a certain volume. I was nursing a headache, the result of too little sleep. Around two I'd awakened with a scream dying in my throat and the last vestiges of a nightmare clinging to my back like some hellish succubus. I'd come downstairs to the Cafe and sat for a while in the dark, sipping a cup of coffee and shivering. The row of bottles behind the bar winked at me in the moonlight, and maybe I considered it—hell yeah, I considered it. I'd even gone behind there and touched them all, read their names out loud. I selected a glass and held it underneath the spigot before I came to my senses.

"Hey! Anybody home?"

I got the door unlocked and let him in. He was about my height, maybe thirty years old, with a lean, pale face and the kind of big, dark eyes that hinted at all kinds of secrets. He was ridiculously good-looking, the kind of guy that'd set the hearts of office girls aflutter for miles around, and there were dimples in his cheeks.

"Nice to meet you, Mr. Stoyles. I'm Chris—Chris DuBois. From New Orleans, although you probably can't tell. I been gone awhile." His hands were big, warm, and very clean, and when he shook my hand, his grip was just right—not so weak as to be effeminate, but he didn't try to strong-arm me either. I can't stand a guy who shakes hands like he's trying to break my wrist. Mr. DuBois tossed his jacket over a chair and looked around the place, and already it seemed like he belonged. He wore his clothes like he'd been born in them, but it wasn't cocky self-assurance. He was simply… comfortable. "How many taps you got?"

"Uh, four for right now. I'm planning on expanding later on."

"Good." He went behind the bar and examined the rows of liquor bottles, counted the glasses. "You need more highball glasses, especially if you got girls coming in here. Women like them kinds of drinks with cherries and stuff." He opened the refrigerator and looked over the contents, murmuring to himself. "Not bad, not bad. You serve food?"

"Uh, sandwiches, french fries, that sort of thing. The kitchen's in back."

"Uh-huh." He opened and closed cupboard doors, rang open the till drawer, and tried the hot and cold running water. "Ice?"

"Every day. There's a truck. Let me show you the delivery entrance." I took him through the back and showed him the door that let onto a narrow alley the locals called a lane way. Built on the slope of the hill, it descended through several steps and platforms, but the whole city was like that, a series of terraces and inclines rising up in a northwesterly direction from the waterfront.

"Kinda like Frisco, huh?" He smiled at me; his teeth were very white, his bottom lip soft and sensuous and full. I wondered what kind of a kisser he was, and just as quickly accepted I'd maybe never find out. "You ever been to Frisco?"

"Yeah, I been to Frisco." I hoped he'd leave it at that. I wasn't interested in some guy who'd make my personal business his own. "A while back." I couldn't get a read on him. On the one hand, he seemed interested in working at the Cafe, but on the other, he didn't seem to care one way or the other if he got the job or not. "I can't afford to pay you very much, Mr. DuBois."

"Chris." He grinned. "I ain't standing on no ceremony, and whatever you're offering is fine by me." He glanced around once more and reached for my hand. "Sold, Mr. Stoyles."

"Jack." I maybe held on to his hand a moment longer than was strictly necessary. "Just Jack."

CHRIS AND I worked together like the proverbial well-oiled machine, and as much as I hate clichés, it was true. He made it clear I could depend on him, and I returned the favor by letting him have the run of the kitchen and the bar. He talked me into hiring a part-time cook to handle the lunch crowd, and found me Dave Chan, a quiet Chinese kid from around the corner, whose family had been here for at least a hundred years and who could cook like nobody's business. I let Chris supervise Dave, not that Dave needed much in the way of supervision; he was a good kid, quiet and polite and very clean, and he always left the kitchen spotless at the end of the day, which impressed me. I tried to stay out of Chris's way and let him do his thing, so when I wasn't in my office at the back, I confined myself to waiting tables and filling up the coffee cups. Things might have gone along all right until the first Tuesday after Easter, the day the redhead came in.

"Hey, Jack!" Chris called to me from behind the bar. "There's a phone call for you. I think it's Frankie." Too bad Frankie wasn't the redhead in question; it might have saved Chris a world of grief if he had been, but neither my luck nor his ever tended to go that way.

She came in through the front door like she owned the place, towing an expensive-looking suitcase behind her and wearing a fur stole. She was maybe twenty-nine or thirty, with the kind of creamy-pale complexion some women are just born with, and intelligent green eyes. Her lips were full and painted bright red to match her hair. The suit she wore was wool, and I could tell by looking that her stockings weren't exactly wartime surplus. It had been ages since I'd seen a dame with real silk on her legs, but she wore it like she deserved it, and maybe she did. She stopped at a table near the window and looked around, then sat carefully, smoothing her skirt under her behind. It was a real nice behind—yeah, I noticed—and the rest of her went with it. She was classy all the way through, the kind of dame that makes you work for it.

But don't you understand? There's no way! I couldn't possibly. I'll tell them that you forced me. I will. I promise.

I shook off the bad memory and turned back to the phone. Frankie was giving me directions to a poker game that night in the city's East End

10

and telling me to bring enough to cover all my bets. We joked a bit about his awful luck and how I always beat him in the end, and by the time he rang off, Chris was at the redhead's table, taking down her order. As I watched, she reached out and ran one long red fingernail down his arm, right where his rolled-up shirtsleeve left it bare, and I felt something then that I hadn't felt in a long, long time.

I got over there double-quick. "Anything I can get for you, Chris?"

"Aw, no thanks, Jack. It's okay. I got it covered."

The redhead sized me up and stuck out her hand. "Chris tells me you own this place. I'm Julie—Julie Fayre. Isn't it funny? Everybody thinks I made it up, but it's my real name. I just got in from Montreal. It's so good to be home." Her voice was low and throaty, the accent more Canadian than local, that kind of neutral, midcontinent sound that might be Upper Manhattan or Toronto, you're never really sure.

"Jack Stoyles." I dropped her hand like it had burned me. "Chris, can I have a word with you?"

The redhead caught Chris's eye and winked. "He's afraid I'm going to corrupt you." She turned her gaze on me and let it play over me, taking her time. Obviously she liked what she saw. "I think I'm going to like this place. Such big, strong, handsome men to look out for me." She took out a compact and a lipstick, and suddenly all I could think about was Miss Julie Fayre with Chris—touching him, kissing him, running her long red fingernails up the inside of his thigh, pausing to cup the bulge at his crotch, rubbing him through his clothes… making love with him in some cheap hotel room, taking off her clothes and opening her legs to him, running her hands over his body, touching his mouth, his closed eyelids, his cock.

I broke away and went to the bar and made like I was busy with a phone call. I knew a guy, a reporter at the local newspaper, the St. John's *Telegram*, by the name of Dan O'Hagan. He and I sometimes got together to drink coffee and play dominoes—he claimed to be addicted to the game and kept a set of tiles in his desk at work. If things were quiet at the Cafe, I'd sometimes go over to his office on Duckworth Street and play a game or two. Dan knew everything about everybody in town, from the oldest founder families to the lowliest "corner boy" busking for pennies in front of the train station. He could recite the lineages of the great merchant families, like the Bowrings and the Ayres, and whistle every single one of Johnny Burke's tunes from start to finish.

He knew what ships came in and when, and what they might be carrying. He kept track of troop movements into and out of the city, and how many Americans, Canadians, British, and others were in temporary residence at any given time. I suspected Dan's day job was just a front. Where I came from, any guy who knows that much about everything has some other racket on the side.

I wasn't really interested in Dan's covert connections, though. Right now I wanted to find out what he knew about Miss Julie Fayre, who she was and where she came from.

"Julie Fayre?" It was hard to mistake the astonishment in his voice. "Julie Fayre, she of the silken, russet hair? Jack, Jack, my son, you're killing me here." She was the daughter of one of the oldest construction families in the country, and her family was responsible for the bulk of the work being done on the new Army base at Fort Pepperrell. Julie had gone to college in Boston, where she had excelled. She was beautiful, she was rich, she was educated and intelligent. She was everything a guy like Chris could want, dammit. "What's Julie Fayre doing in your place? She slumming, or what?"

"Thanks a lot, Dan."

"Jesus, boy, that's the quality, sure. Tell her to stay there. I'll be wanting a whack at that myself."

"That's okay, Dan. I think Chris and I can handle it from here." I rang off.

Chris was waiting for me. "Did you want me for something, Jack?"

"Naw, it can wait. Get Miss Fayre's order, will you?"

He stayed where he was, the tray clasped in his arms, his beautiful face wearing a puzzled, slightly hurt expression. "Did I do something wrong, Jack?"

"No." *I'll tell everyone you forced me. I will. I'll tell them.* "No, it's fine." I pressed my hand against my forehead, willing it away, but the damned memory stuck, embedded in my brain like some weird music you hear once and can never get rid of.

"We'll talk later, huh?" His palm was warm on my shoulder, burning heat through my shirt.

I gazed into his dark eyes, pulled as ever toward him. It would be so easy some night, when both of us were alone in the Cafe, to lean over and kiss him, to feel the slow, sweet burn of his tongue in my mouth and his hands on my body, but some part of me knew it was no good. None of this was any good. I didn't even know if Chris went that way, and as for me, I'd be damned if I'd start anything. Oh no, that wasn't for me. Jack Stoyles was good and finished with that whole love routine.

"Yeah, Chris. We'll talk later." I pretended an itch on my shoulder, an excuse to shrug him off, and went back to my office.

Around midafternoon, the cafe's traffic slacked off, but Julie Fayre stayed on, drinking endless cups of coffee and flirting with Chris. Once I looked out and he was sitting next to her, and her hand was lying casually on his lap. It wasn't hard to imagine where things were going between them, and I'd be willing to lay bets that Miss Julie Fayre intended to get her hooks in him. I wondered how that would go over with her family— according to Dan, her old man was plenty rich and plenty starchy, and maybe he wouldn't want some daughter of his getting cozy with a mere bartender. Nuts to both of them. If she wanted Chris so bad, she could have him, and good luck to her.

Did you ever notice how, when you're preoccupied with something you think is really big, something even bigger walks in the door?

I didn't even see him until he was standing in front of me, waiting patiently, his hands folded, an expensive raincoat draped over his arm. I had bent down to fiddle with a tap, and as I straightened, I caught a whiff of his cologne: warm and spicy, with something kind of citrusy low, underneath. And then I was looking into dark eyes with long, thick eyelashes and asking him if I could help him, while my heart pounded in my chest and my stomach spawned its own little butterfly air force.

Maybe he said something; I don't know. It seemed like the world around me, the Cafe and the street outside, all vanished into meaningless noise, and there was only him: his eyes, the curve of his mouth, his beautiful hands. His expression was one of gentle curiosity, tempered with a subtle sadness, and he seemed like somebody whose patience was very probably infinite.

"I wonder if you might help me." At first I couldn't place the accent. He was definitely not local, but he didn't sound like anybody I had ever heard either. There was something English in his voice, but that influence had been laid down long ago and had since been superseded by other tones, mellifluous and almost Mediterranean, with their liquid vowels and careful voicing of the consonants.

"Sure thing, mister. I'll do what I can." My mouth was moving, sound was coming out, but I might have been telling him giant spiders had

13

broken through the ceiling of the Cafe and were eating their way toward me. I couldn't stop looking at him. I wanted to stay near him because he would understand me, and he would give me what I needed; I was certain of it.

"I am looking for a particular building, which I believe is somewhere around here. The museum building, I believe it is. They told me it has an arch on the front. It is a red brick and sandstone building. Do you know it?" He unfolded a travelers' map from the inside pocket of his jacket and spread it open on the bar. "Now, here is a bus stop, and here is another road, leading down towards the water. Don't you think it smells absolutely awful down here? It's like the Nile."

Yes. That was it. Now I knew, and the minute I realized it, all the hairs on the back of my neck stood up straight. I was back on the Delaware River Bridge, the wind whistling in my ears and my knuckles white, trying to work up the nerve to jump. "Egypt?" I could hardly speak. "You're Egyptian."

"Oh, yes—forgive my bad manners." He extended a hand across the bar. "I am Samuel Halim, assistant to the British consul, and you?"

I managed to croak out my name and give him the directions he needed. He thanked me and left, and that was it. As stupid and crazy as it sounds, it took everything I had not to run out the door after him. I didn't even notice Julie Fayre had gone, or Chris was standing by the bar, looking at me like I'd just gone nuts.

"Jack?" He leaned in and touched my arm. "You okay?"

"Yeah." I forced myself to breathe. "Yeah, Chris, I'm okay."

"You don't look okay." He squinted at me. "You look kinda sick."

"Did you see that man?"

He glanced over the cafe. "What man?"

"Guy that was just in here, Egyptian guy. He had a map, he asked me...." Like a dream that can't survive the light of day, the memory of him was leaving me. Maybe no one had come in. Maybe I had merely imagined him—his big, soft eyes and his gentle hands, and that sculpted mouth. Maybe he wasn't real at all. I reached behind the bar for my jacket and slipped into it. "I'm going for a walk. Can you keep an eye on the place?"

"Sure, Jack. Anything at all." He reached out and caught hold of my elbow. "You sure you're okay?"

"Yeah, just fine," I lied. I wasn't sure of anything. I wasn't sure at all.

"By the way, the afternoon paper's here." He tossed it on the bar. "Jeez, I thought this place was supposed to be safe." The headline screamed it loud and clear: ENGINEER DEAD OF GUNSHOT WOUNDS. "Somebody killed the poor bastard first thing this morning. Can you believe that?"

CHAPTER THREE

THERE'S A river that runs through the city, arising somewhere to the west and emptying eventually into the Atlantic Ocean. At the extreme east end of the river are the shipyards, busy now in wartime, working nearly nonstop. Like most displaced Americans, I liked to spend my free time at the railway station, watching the trains, or on the waterfront, trying to ignore the harbor's stench while the great warships came and went. If I was really preoccupied with something big and dangerous, I'd walk for a while, usually down by the river, but sometimes I'd go uptown, heading north toward the city's widening sprawl. It got so that I knew the city better than I'd known my old home town of Philadelphia. People here were friendly, and they'd often call a greeting to me or sound their car horns if they saw me walking by. More than once some customer of my cafe would stop and offer me a lift; even the streetcar drivers knew me by sight.

I was walking by myself one day, maybe six weeks after Julie Fayre had first come into the Heartache, and when a dark blue late-model car pulled level with me on Duckworth Street, I didn't think anything of it.

"Mr. Stoyles. I wonder if we might have a word?" It was the accent—not to mention the precise diction—that made me look up. I didn't recognize the man behind the wheel, but he apparently knew me. The car slid to a stop just in front of me, and he reached across to open the passenger side door. "Would you get in?"

Growing up in Philly, you learn a thing or two—and my mother told me never to accept car rides from strangers. "Don't think so, pal, but thanks all the same."

"Why ever not? I am headed your way." The smile was silkily accommodating. He gestured at the seat with one gloved hand. "Please. I will take only a few moments of your time, and it is very important that I talk to you."

"What for?"

"You have heard about the murdered engineer?"

"Yeah. So?"

"I have reason to believe that the man who was murdered might somehow be connected to you, Mr. Stoyles." He sat back. "Please. I have information. You will find it to your benefit to hear me out."

"All right." I slid in and shut the door; the car pulled smoothly away from the curb. "You know my name. How about returning the favor?"

He reached a hand across. "Jonah Octavian." He must have seen my expression. "Yes, I agree. As far as names go, it invites incredulity, but it is my name." He turned the car north and headed uptown, away from the waterfront, toward the dark green hills that press against the horizon.

I watched him out of the corner of my eye as he drove. He was older than me, maybe fifty, with black hair graying at the temples and a neat moustache. There were laugh lines fanning out from the corners of his eyes, and his thin, rather cruel mouth was bracketed by wrinkles. Apart from the moustache, he was clean-shaven, but he wore no cologne or aftershave lotion. His clothes were—as far as I could tell—expensive. He seemed in no hurry to talk, so I left him alone. I figured he'd tell me whatever it was as soon as he was ready.

"Your bartender, Mr. Stoyles." He was ready sooner than I thought.

"Yeah. What about him?"

"He's been with you how long?"

"Few months. Why?"

"What do you know of his background?"

"Enough."

Octavian smirked. "But not everything."

I was beginning to lose patience with this guy. "Look, Octavian, you got something to say to me, you better say it."

"I have it on good authority that Mr. DuBois—your bartender—was recently handed a check in the amount of… well, let's say it was a sizable amount. This check was written by a young lady of his acquaintance. Perhaps you know her? A Miss Julie Fayre. I've no doubt you've heard of her family. They're in charge of the new Army base that's being built out here."

That's where he was taking me; I saw it as soon as we crested the hill. It wasn't much to look at right now, just mounds of displaced earth and heaps of metal and concrete. Eventually, however, it would form an important link in a very strategic chain.

"Just what are you getting at, Octavian?"

He stopped the car and threw it into park, turned to face me. "Did you ever stop to wonder who might have killed that engineer? This is a very peaceful place. You've been here long enough to see that. These lovely people, these very friendly neighbors of yours, they go about their own business and never harm a fly." He reached into the glove box and took out a manila envelope, which he tossed into my lap. "Ken Cartwright was the civil engineer hired by the United States Army to oversee this project. The contract that he signed stipulated that, in the event of debilitating injury or accidental death, Mr. Cartwright would be automatically replaced as project overseer."

I was starting to see what he was getting at, and it bothered me. "Go on."

"Since Fayre Construction Limited is the contractor in this case, Mr. Cartwright's duties would automatically default to them."

I tore open the manila envelope and took a quick scan of the contents. The pieces suddenly fell into place. "I see. So what's your interest in all this? Why should you care about some murdered engineer?"

"I run a construction company, Octavian and Weiss—you may have heard of us. When your country declared war on Japan—and subsequently decided to set up military bases here—I decided that I would bid on the various construction contracts that were offered." His black eyes were deep and cold as obsidian. "Time and again, I was outbid. I thought it an unusual situation, and so I did a little investigating of my own. Do you know who the winning bidder was, Mr. Stoyles, in every single case?"

"I think I can guess." I wondered where Julie might fit in all of this.

"Fayre Construction."

"So you're saying that Fayre Construction had Cartwright killed? But why?"

"A civil engineer's duties and responsibilities are many, Mr. Stoyles. Paramount among these is determining the safety of a site and the structural integrity of any buildings that go on it."

It felt like somebody was pouring cold water down my back. "Yeah?"

"Naturally, safety costs money—money that must be factored in with other costs. Most engineers—most professionals—know better than to cut corners. Others do it in the hopes that nothing will go wrong. Most of the time, Mr. Stoyles, nothing does, and the unscrupulous contractor need not fear either exposure or reprisals."

"You sound like you know what you're talking about."

"Indeed. I learned my profession in Athens, Mr. Stoyles, and I have been here for many years. Many of the beautiful modern buildings you see around this… fledgling city… were built by me." He reached into his coat and took out a gold cigarette case, offered me one, and lit one for himself. "Ken Cartwright submitted a report to the United States Army, stipulating certain site conditions. The report never reached its destination. Instead, a doctored version of it was submitted and construction went ahead. Once Ken Cartwright discovered what had happened…." He shrugged.

"So who doctored the report? And what happened to the original?"

"I have told you all I know." Octavian reached across me and opened the door. "Good-bye, Mr. Stoyles, and if ever I can be of some use to you, do let me know."

I STOOD for a while after Octavian had gone, watching the steady progress of men and machines, and then I turned south and headed back to my cafe. I wanted to discount everything Octavian had said, but couldn't. After all, how well did I really know Chris? How well did I really know anybody? If what Octavian had said was true, then maybe Julie Fayre was in on it, and maybe she had convinced Chris it was worth his while to come over to her side. Yeah, I could see Julie Fayre making it worth his while, but it wasn't something I wanted to think about. Thinking about Julie Fayre just made me mad, but I couldn't stop thinking about her, and by the time I made it back to my Heartache, I was fit to be tied.

We were in between the lunch crowd and the afternoon rush, so the place was pretty empty. A couple of vagrants lounging on the front steps asked me for spare change when I went by, but I ignored them and barged inside.

Chris was wiping down the bar and looked up when he saw me. "Hi there, Jack. Anything I can get for you?"

I opened my office door and threw my coat at the hook. The things I was thinking were making me crazy. I had to sit down, get some perspective. "Chris!"

He appeared in the doorway. "Yeah, Jack?"

"Come in and close the door."

"There's nobody—"

"I said come in and close the goddamn door!" My fists were clenched so hard my knuckles were white.

"I do something wrong, Jack?" He was visibly shaken. "If it's about that broken tap, I swear, you can take it out of my paycheck, I didn't think—"

"How well do you know Julie Fayre?"

"Julie?"

"I know you've been seeing a lot of her since that day she came into the cafe." I struck a match and lit a cigarette. "Show me the check she gave you."

"What check? Jack, are you feeling all right? I dunno what you're talking about."

I stood up so fast my chair fell over backward. "Did your little girlfriend give you a check to keep your mouth shut?"

"My… what? Check?" His dark brows furrowed. "You drunk?"

I hit him so hard he staggered back against the wall and nearly fell. "Don't you ever say that, you hear me? You will never see me drunk. Never."

I made for the door, but Chris was quicker and barred my way. He caught me by the upper arms and held on to me. "Jack, what the hell is wrong with you, huh?"

"Let go of me."

"Not until you tell me." His long fingers locked around my arms. We were standing ridiculously close, so close I could make out the tiny spray of freckles across his nose and the lush curve of his lower lip. The heat of his body pressed against me like a living thing.

"Julie."

"What about Julie?"

He released me, and I dragged out the manila envelope and shoved it at him. "Tell me you didn't know about this."

He dumped the contents into his hand and gazed at it for a moment, his face expressionless. "She said she worked in an office."

20

"Show me the check, or have you cashed it already?"

"Jack, I don't know anything about any check."

"Ever hear of a guy named Octavian?"

"No." He thought for a moment. "Wait… he's some kinda contractor, isn't he?"

"Yeah, Chris. He's some kind of contractor." I went back and sat at my desk, my head in my hands. I didn't know who to believe, Octavian—who had no reason to lie to me, or at least not any reason I could think of—or Chris.

"Jack." Chris's voice was at my ear. I opened my eyes. He was crouched beside my desk. "Julie's nice and all that, but I don't want a dame to come between us." His hand rubbed small circles on my back, heat burning through the thin cotton of my shirt. "I'd hate it if that happened. You and me, we got a good thing going here."

"You don't know nothin' about me." I shook my head.

Chris's hand moved to my forearm, gripping gently. "I know as much as I need to."

The tip of his tongue slid out, moistening his lips, and it was all I could do not to grab his head and press my mouth against his. I wanted him so bad it was a physical ache, pounding down my bones and leaving me weak and shaken.

"You better get back behind the bar." I sounded like I'd just run a marathon. "It might get busy."

"Sure, Jack."

As soon as he left, I closed my office door. The bottle was where I'd left it, in the desk drawer. I took it out and handled it awhile, turning it, feeling the slosh of liquid, pressing my thumbs against the uncracked seal. I knew what that first sip would feel like: the acrid burn of poison, settling into heat. Then another sip and then another, and what the hell, I'd get a glass and fill it to the brim.

I put the bottle back, shut the drawer, and locked it.

I waited until Chris had left for the night and then I went to the till. I lifted up the cash drawer and ran my hand underneath. There was nothing but dust. I put the drawer back and straightened a stack of twenties, and as I did, my fingers caught the texture of a different kind of paper. I pulled it out and looked at it.

It was a check made out to Chris DuBois for twenty thousand dollars.

SERGEANT BILLY Ricketts was about as much cop as anybody could stand, and that included me. I'd had some dealings with him since coming to town—nothing very serious—and he always made it very clear that the recent influx of what he called "Murrycans" had brought nothing but trouble. Ricketts was a cop from the old school, and he liked to beat the hell out of suspects first and ask questions later. If something didn't square with the way he thought it should be, he'd hammer on it until it fit. He wasn't very subtle, but he could be remarkably effective, and despite his prejudices, he'd always been very fair to me. When vandals had broken out both front windows of my cafe, Ricketts's men had combed the streets for days until they found them. He was a good cop—just not a very polite one.

When I showed up at the Royal Newfoundland Constabulary headquarters the next morning, Ricketts was anything but pleased.

"Stoyles, I haven't got time this morning for you and your bloody foolishness, so whatever it is, leave it with the desk and I'll get back to ye." The phone on his desk rang, and Ricketts picked it up, hollered into it, and put it down again. "Bloody arseholes." He realized I was still there. "What?"

I laid the check on his desk. "If you can slow down long enough to take a look at this, I'd like your opinion on it."

"Would ye?" Ricketts reached across and picked up the check. He peered at it, smelled it, rubbed it between his fingers, held it up to the light, crumpled it, and smoothed it out again. "Mm."

"My bartender claims no knowledge of it, nor does he have any idea why Fayre Construction wrote him a check for such an ungodly amount. He has never worked for them. His only connection is his… a woman he's seeing."

Ricketts looked at me. "The Fayre girl?"

"The same."

"Mm. Used to know her mother. Judy Blanchard, she was. Knew her in school. Stuck-up as they come. Figured her shit didn't—" The phone rang; Ricketts picked it up and shouted something unintelligible into it. "So Fayre Construction wrote your bartender a check for nothing. Is that what you're telling me?"

"Yeah. Add that to what Octavian told me—"

"Octavian?" He spat it out like it tasted bad. "You been listening to that fool? Sure, he's as stun as my arse and then some."

"Not about this, he isn't." I showed him the contents of the envelope Octavian had given me and laid the whole thing out for him. To Ricketts's credit he listened carefully, his beady blue eyes searching my face while his thick, blunt fingers scratched at his desk blotter or fiddled with his pens and pencils, his lapels, the unbuttoned flaps on the pockets of his uniform—anything else within reach.

"I'll put a man on it." He picked up the phone and spoke; the door to his office opened almost instantly, and a thin young man with pale gray eyes and hungry features stood there like he'd been starched into his clothes.

"You called me, Sergeant?"

"Constable Picco, you remember Mr. Stoyles. You've been into his cafe a few times, haven't you? Mr. Stoyles is a Yank."

Picco's lean face fell. "Oh. Mr. Stoyles." He said my name like it left a bad taste in his mouth.

"Mr. Stoyles would like our help. Take a good look at him, Constable Picco. From now on, you are working for Mr. Stoyles."

Picco's expression was something less than ecstatic. "Your orders, Sergeant?"

"I'll have Doreen bring you the file in half an hour."

Picco nodded. "Very good." He inclined his head as much as the uniform's stiff collar would allow—or maybe that was only my wishful thinking. "Good day, Mr. Stoyles." He went out and shut the door behind him.

"He must be a real hit at parties."

"Don't be foolish. He don't go to parties. He's in with that Mission crowd—one of them Pentecostals." Ricketts shoved his handwritten notes into a file folder. "Is there anything else, Mr. Stoyles, or can I let ye get back to pouring coffee?"

"I'll get back to pouring coffee. Will Picco… will he get in touch with me, or should I call you, or…?" I imagined Picco stomping into the Heartache Cafe and declaiming the results of his investigation to anybody within earshot.

"I'll call you. You needn't worry about that." The phone at his elbow rang, and I was effectively dismissed.

I got back to the Heartache Cafe right before the lunchtime rush. Chris was already busy taking orders, so I grabbed an apron to help him out. I was serving a tray of Cokes with limes and iced tea to a table full of school teachers when the front door of the Cafe came open with such force that the bell was nearly torn off the frame. A small man wearing a too-big overcoat staggered in, holding his arms out in front of him like he was trying to push something away. I recognized him as one of the vagrants who usually sat outside my cafe, begging passersby for change and sometimes venturing inside to buy a glass of beer. He saw me and started forward, but he never made it. He fell flat on his face, the handle of a knife protruding from the space between his shoulder blades.

CHAPTER FOUR

CONSTABLE PICCO had closed my cafe down, pending an investigation; some men in clean white coats had come with an ambulance and taken the dead vagrant away. Picco's men made a thorough sweep of my place while he detained my customers for questioning, but it was useless. Nobody knew anything, but that didn't seem to deter Picco. He kept Chris and me in my office for over an hour after the last of the customers had left.

"Did you know this man, Mr. Stoyles?" Picco stood as erectly as ever, his gray eyes taking in everything. "Had you seen him before today?"

"I already told you, he's usually out there, in front of the Cafe. Sometimes, if the weather's cold, I'll bring him out a hot cup of coffee."

Picco did something with his eyebrows. "I see. Have you ever given him money?"

"Sometimes. What's wrong with that?"

He gave me an unfathomable look before turning back to his notebook. "Are there any knives missing from your kitchen, Mr. Stoyles?"

This was beginning to get on my nerves. "I told you already, no."

"And where is your cook?"

"It's his day off. Chris handles the cooking when he's not here."

Picco looked Chris up and down with an air of patent disapproval. "You are an American also, Mr. DuBois?" He pronounced it "DuBoys."

"Actually, it's DuBois. I'm from New Orleans."

"New Orleans, Louisiana. Also in the United States." Picco jotted something in his notebook and flipped the cover closed. He glanced

25

around the Cafe with an expression of profound distaste. "Hopefully my investigation will not take too long. In the meantime, this… place… will remain closed."

I started forward. "Are you sure that's necessary?"

"Very, Mr. Stoyles. It is vital that everything remain exactly as it is."

"Why, you—" I felt the blood throbbing in my temples and made for him, but Chris caught me around the waist and hauled me back. "You've got no reason to close me down, Picco! Just you wait till I get Ricketts on the phone!"

Picco raised one eyebrow. "Sergeant Ricketts is attending a police conference in Nova Scotia and will not be back until next week. I am overseeing matters until his return."

"I just bet you are."

Chris held on to me until Picco left, and then he went and locked the door behind the departing constable. "That guy really loves his job, doesn't he?"

I muttered something about Picco's mother and left it at that.

Chris chuckled. "Still, you gotta admire his dedication. Cup of coffee?"

"Sure." I walked over to where the group of school teachers had been sitting. They had overturned the table in their haste to get away, and the floor underneath was a wet, sticky mess. I took a tray and started picking up the pieces of broken glass, piling them together for the trash.

What was Picco's problem, anyway? If this was Philly, they'd come and cart away the dead guy and business would go on as usual. People would be thronging the place, for chrissakes, to see for themselves. I couldn't afford to be closed, not even for a day. Sure, the Heartache did good business, but I wasn't so successful that I could stand a loss of profits.

A shard of broken glass sliced into the index finger of my right hand and cut deep. "Dammit!"

"Whoa there, Jack." Chris's clean, strong hands closed over mine. "You cut yourself."

"Aww, it's nothing."

"Sure it is." He held my injured hand gently. "Come into the kitchen, I'll get that cleaned up for you."

I waited while he ran the hot water and fetched the first aid kit from the shelf over the sink. "How is it that Dave can slice and dice in here for hours and never get so much as a scratch?" I wondered.

"He's had a lot more practice." Chris rubbed my cut finger with a little soap and rinsed my hand under the water. "Cafe's a mess, huh?"

I remembered the tumult after the vagrant had been stabbed. "They tore out of here like a herd of goddamn elephants."

He held my hand clear as he reached to turn off the taps. "Aw, customers!" He flashed me a grin. "Who needs 'em?"

In spite of myself, I laughed. "Last time I checked, we do." I watched as he wrapped a clean dish towel around my hand. "Unless you've got some private source of wealth?" Too late, I realized what I'd said, and his face closed down.

"No, Jack." He concentrated on ripping open a clean dressing. "I ain't got no private wealth."

There was silence between us for several long moments. "Chris, I'm sorry."

He wouldn't look at me. "Why do you have to keep bringing it up? I told you before. I don't know anything about that check. I don't know how it got in the till. I damn well didn't put it there." He wrapped my cut finger and tied off the dressing. "How's that? Too tight?"

"No, it's fine." The tap was dripping; I reached around him to turn it off, and he caught hold of my arm on the way back.

"What's really going on here, huh?" His grip softened, and he slid his palm up my arm. "What's eating you, Jack?"

"Nothing. I'm just sore about the Cafe being closed." I was lying and we both knew it. "Having a guy stagger in and die in the middle of the lunchtime rush isn't my idea of a good time, you know?" Maybe it wouldn't be such a bad thing to confide in Chris. It had been a very long time since I'd confided in anybody, since I'd allowed myself to get close to another person, to lean on someone else. Oh, I knew lots of people around town—nodding acquaintances, mostly, no real friends—but here was someone offering to be there for me, for real. It was a novel sensation.

"Yeah. The Cafe keeps you busy, right? Keeps you from thinking too much." His other hand slid gently up my left arm, skin against skin, and the casual contact was almost more than I could stand.

"You shouldn't touch me." I tried in vain to pull away from him.

"Why's that, Jack?" His eyes sought my gaze. "Why shouldn't I touch you? Guys touch each other all the time. Didn't you ever play sports?"

"I can't—dammit, Chris, I can't handle it." I pulled away, turned my back to him. My heart was going a mile a minute, and I felt dizzy, like if I took one step in any direction, I'd fall flat on my face. Hell, maybe it was loss of blood or something.

"You can't handle me touching you?" He came up behind me and squeezed my shoulders, leaned into me so close I could smell his aftershave. I couldn't help myself. I swayed back against him, and as I did, his arms went around my waist so he was hugging me from behind.

It was a real nice feeling, being held like that, having someone's arms around me, and I'll admit I gave in to it, but only for a minute. Any more than that would just be making things worse, and I didn't want to go through that whole thing again—getting, having, only to lose that love and eventually the lover. I couldn't take it anymore. Another episode like the last one and I'd crawl inside a bottle and stay there, and that would be disastrous. One good drunk would kill me.

I pulled away from him and walked out of the kitchen, but he caught up with me in the middle of the Cafe. Suddenly his arms were around me and I was gazing into soft brown eyes and his warm hands were cupping my face and he was kissing me. His mouth opened over mine, the gentle suction pulling me in to him while his strong arms held me tight against his body. The tip of his tongue teased my lips apart, and a flush of heat bloomed at the base of my belly. I forgot the spilled drinks and the broken glass, forgot everything except the man in whose strong arms I was held, the man who was kissing me with such fervent expertise.

"How did you know?" I pulled back far enough to look at him. "About me, I mean."

His thumb stroked my bottom lip. "It took a while. You don't exactly open up, you know?"

"Chris, what are we doing?" I groaned as his mouth pressed into my neck; my hands slid down to cup his backside and squeezed him gently. God, he was beautiful! What the hell was I thinking? "Maybe we better stop." I forced myself to step away from him. "Anybody could come along and see us." I smiled at the picture he made: his hair was disheveled from where I'd had my fingers in it, and the pressure of my mouth had turned his lips dark red.

"Yeah, I guess you're right." He stroked my cheek. "You're a right guy, Jack."

It was a strange thing to say. "What do you mean by that?"

"I can trust you. That's not something you can say about a lot of guys these days." He smiled. "There's a war on—haven't you heard?"

I laughed. "You're crazy."

"Jack… you believe me about the check, don't you?" He was asking me for something, something I wasn't sure I could give him. "I swear to you, I had nothing to do with it."

"Yeah?" There was a heavy feeling in my gut. I didn't like it. "What about Julie?"

"We're friends. Jack, you know how it is. It helps to have a woman on your arm, especially in this town."

"Yeah." What he said made sense to me, but something about it didn't ring true. "Yeah, I guess it does."

"What's between us stays between us, huh, Jack?" He touched my arm, needing confirmation.

"Sure, Chris. It stays between us." I moved to clean up the broken glass, and Chris followed me.

"Think Picco's going to find anything?"

"I don't know." I tried to answer his questions, but my mind wasn't really on the things he said. I was too busy processing the feeling I had deep down in my gut—the feeling that something wasn't right.

IT TOOK me a long time to get to sleep that night. Usually I slept with the bedroom window open, but now it seemed to amplify even the slightest noises from the street below and all the little creaks and groans the building made when the wind blew. Then I was too hot, so I got up to open the window again; then too cold, so I went to the linen cupboard to fetch an extra blanket. The events of the day kept going around and around in my head like some demented carousel, with people's faces and voices all mixed together while I drifted in that weird, in-between space that isn't quite sleep and isn't really waking. It seemed like Constable Picco was behind the bar, opening all the taps at once, and Chris was walking a beat outside the Cafe door, dressed in a cop's uniform and swinging a nightstick. Twice I woke up suddenly, convinced someone was standing at the foot of my bed, and toward dawn I could have sworn someone held me in their arms while I slept. They vanished as soon as I woke up.

There were dreams: the kiss replayed itself, over and over, from different angles and different points of view; Chris was holding me too tight, the tips of his fingers digging into my upper arms, hurting me; the Cafe was on fire, flames licking up the walls, liquor bottles exploding in the heat.

I turned over in my sleep and was on a boat, lying on the deck with my arm thrown across my face to shield my eyes from the strong rays of the sun. Someone else was there, another man. I opened my eyes and saw a slender figure, vaguely familiar to me, wearing sandals and a pair of shorts. I watched him haul on the ropes, the muscles in his back working as he unfurled the sails. His skin was smooth and tanned, and a bead of sweat was sliding down the valley of his spine; something told me it was a body I knew intimately, as intimately as I knew my own, and this made me happy. "We are sailing down the Nile, just as you wished." He tied off the ropes and stretched out on the deck beside me. "The least you could do is pay attention."

I took my arm down and smiled at him, reached for him, and pulled him into my arms. The kiss went on and on, growing more heated, more torrid, and my hands pressed flat against his back. I wanted to feel all of him against me. I wanted to press him into me, to join our bodies. "Yes," he whispered, "yes, this is what I want as well as you." A wild current of pleasure rose up from my belly and shuddered me apart, and I gave in to it, sobbing aloud.

IT WAS full daylight when I again opened my eyes. The bedside clock said it was a little after nine. I lay there for a few moments, wondering what the hell it all meant, and just then the phone rang.

It was Chris. "Ricketts called you yet?"

"Ricketts? No, why?" Picco had said Ricketts was in Nova Scotia. Was that right?

"Just how much do you hate Picco?"

He wasn't making any sense. "What?"

"Ricketts is looking for you. He says he called your place, but you didn't answer. The upshot is, Picco's in some kind of trouble and Ricketts wants to see you."

"He wants to see me? What for? I didn't do anything to Picco." Maybe Picco blamed me for the dead vagrant. It wasn't beyond the realm of possibility. From what I'd seen of Picco, he wasn't too interested in doing me any favors.

"He just asked me to find you and get you down to headquarters." There was a pause, and I could hear the smile in his voice. "You still in bed?"

"Yes, I'm still in bed."

"You a man who wears pajamas, Jack?"

"Chris, you like working at the Heartache Cafe?"

"I sure do, boss." He chuckled. "I sure do. Say, you want me to go down to headquarters with you?"

I thought about it for a moment. If Ricketts intended to ream me out, maybe having Chris along as backup wouldn't be a bad idea. On the other hand, if there really was something up with Picco, Ricketts was liable to close up like a clam when he saw I'd brought an audience. "Naw, I think I'll be okay. Listen, if I'm late, can you open up for me?"

"I thought Picco said to leave the place closed. What's he gonna do if he walks by and you're open?"

"Unless Picco's going to make up the difference in lost profits, the Cafe stays open." A part of me relished the idea of going up against the flat-eyed constable. "He wants to get a court order, let him."

"Okay." Chris didn't sound convinced. "Will do. Call me if you need me."

"Thanks, Chris." I threw back the sheets and put my feet on the floor. My shorts were wet and sticking to me.

"Hey, Jack?"

"Yeah?" I pulled the cotton away from my skin. Obviously the things I'd dreamed had felt real enough for me to reach the ultimate conclusion. That hadn't happened in a long time—longer than I could remember. After what had happened in Philly, that part of me had just gone to sleep, seemingly for good.

"Was it a good dream?"

"Will you mind your own damn business?" I put the phone down, but not before I heard him laughing on the other end.

I got showered and shaved as quickly as I could, and dressed without bothering to eat or even have a cup of coffee. I half hoped Chris might

31

show up early and have a pot waiting for me when I got back from headquarters.

I found Ricketts in his office, sitting behind a huge stack of file folders, which he was paging through in his usual, methodical way. He grunted at me when I came in and waved me to a chair, and I waited till he had finished whatever it was he was doing.

"Stoyles. Something wrong with your phone, is there?"

"Sorry about that. I didn't sleep well last night. I guess I must have really hit hard." The remnants of my dream were still with me: the sun's heat, the man on the sailboat, and that cascading wave of pleasure that had flooded my body. "Thought you were in Nova Scotia."

"I was. I'm not, now." Ricketts huffed out an exasperated breath. "Well, I won't bother trying to dress it up, because what I got to say isn't pretty." He handed me a pair of photographs, the usual mug-shot type familiar to police departments all over the world. "Seen either of them before?"

I studied the photographs carefully. The man on the left was almost certainly the vagrant who'd been knifed in my cafe the day before; I didn't recognize the other one. "Who are they?"

"The dead one was called Johnny Mahoney. Been hanging around Water Street as long as I can remember. His father used to fish up on the Labrador. Had a big schooner, the *Three Bells*, it was called."

The face that stared out at me from the photograph was empty-eyed and sullen, the unshaven cheeks hollow with deprivation. "What happened to Johnny?"

"Got into the drink. Well, that would have been just fine if only he'd stuck to plain rum, but he didn't. People fell on hard times here in the thirties. Lot of these lushes like Johnny couldn't afford the real thing, so they started drinking whatever they could get."

It was a story I'd heard all too often, and one I knew intimately. "Like what? Aftershave lotion?"

"Yeah, sometimes. Sometimes it was wood alcohol, or stuff they brewed up in the basement out of God-knows-what."

I handed the photograph back to Sergeant Ricketts. "Who's the other one?"

"That's Billy Parsons—Bull Parsons, they calls him. Ever seen a mug like that before?"

Parsons was stocky, with a head shaped like a potato and no discernible neck. His nose had been broken, obviously more than once, and his thick, blubbery lips did nothing for his overall appearance. The expression in his eyes was pure, straightforward viciousness.

"No, he doesn't look familiar."

"Bull Parsons and Johnny Mahoney spend their time downtown, pestering people for spare change. Once they got enough for a bottle or a few drinks in a pub, they're gone for the rest of the day. Usually they're on Water Street, and ever since you showed up, they like to hang around your place. Maybe there's a lot of foot traffic down that way, or maybe you're a soft touch."

I had admitted to giving Mahoney the occasional hot cup of coffee in cold weather, and a few coins when I had it to spare. What was wrong with that?

"Parsons and Mahoney were doing great until Parsons got the bright idea that they could make a lot more money and buy a lot more booze if they took their little racket one step further."

I didn't have to ask what he meant; Ricketts's expression told me everything I needed to know. "Armed robbery."

"Armed robbery. Now, Stoyles, you know as well as I do that nowadays we got all kinds coming here—oh, present company excepted, of course."

I tried hard not to laugh. "Skip it."

"And some people who come here—especially by way of the waterfront—might not enjoy having two bloody stupid layabouts like Parsons and Mahoney sticking them up and taking all their money. You follow me?"

"Sure. So they got in over their heads and somebody stuck a knife in Johnny Mahoney." Chances were, whoever had murdered Mahoney was long gone by now, back out to sea.

"Right you are."

I was confused. "Sergeant, you called me down here because of something to do with Constable Picco."

"I'm getting to that, just hold your horses." Ricketts laid the mug shots side by side on his desk. "Parsons and Mahoney had a nice little racket going. Then Mahoney gets killed. Parsons was picked up the next night, walking down Queen's Road, dead drunk and completely witless. Grieving for his friend, he was—or so he said. Overcome with sorrow.

Constable Picco happened to be in the lockup when Parsons was brought in, and the officers who booked Bull Parsons reported a really strange little incident."

"I'm listening."

"Have another smoke—do you good." Ricketts lit it for me before continuing. "In order to reach the cells, Parsons had to walk past Picco, who was standing by the wall. Why he was down there, I have no idea. Anyway, Parsons and Picco looked at one another, and Parsons nodded."

"So?"

"What I'm going to say to you, Stoyles, isn't for general consumption. So far I've managed to keep most of this out of the papers, but it won't last forever. Before I say anything, I need to know that you won't go around shooting off your mouth as soon as you're out of my sight." I assured him I'd keep quiet. "What I got to say has to do with Picco."

"Uh-huh." Maybe Picco had complained about me. "What's he done?"

"Constable Picco is in trouble." Ricketts's gaze was more intense than usual. "The worst possible kind."

"I see." Around here that usually meant he'd gotten some girl pregnant and would have to marry her, but with my history, I could hardly judge a guy for that. "Who's the girl?"

"What?" Ricketts stared at me like I was nuts. "What girl? Picco? You honestly think Picco's after getting into some girl's drawers?"

Probably not. "Well… what is it, then?"

"Picco…. Picco got mixed up in something… something well in line with his duties, but which makes it look like he's been involved in a certain… matter."

"So don't you guys usually take care of that yourselves? I'm not a cop."

"Yes, I realize you're not a cop, Stoyles, but that's not the point." The tone of Ricketts's voice could probably peel paint. "If you'd keep your trap shut for a minute and let me get on with it?"

I sat back and folded my arms.

"As Bull Parsons passed by Constable Picco, he and Picco nodded at each other. Now, normally, that wouldn't bother me. Picco grew up on Brazil Street and so did Parsons, they're around about the same age, and I don't know, maybe they were pals when they were little boys. The point is, at a quarter to twelve last night, Bull Parsons walked out of the lockup as easy as you please."

"You mean he escaped?" I was astonished. "What about Picco?"

"Picco's gone." Ricketts got up from his chair and paced over to the window. His office overlooked the street with a view of the Narrows just beyond. The morning sun pierced the venetian blinds and laid paler strips of light against the dark tiles on Ricketts's floor. "At five o'clock this morning—no doubt while you were still sleeping the sleep of the just—a Greek seaman named... er, Pano-something-populous—I got his name right here—turned up dead. We found his body floating in the harbor, not far from the American docks."

"But Picco... just gone?"

"He's disappeared. Didn't show up for duty this morning. Nobody's seen him since he left last night. Maybe he realizes what's after happening, and he's hiding away—or maybe the friends of that Greek merchant seaman think he's part of the reason why their pal was killed." Ricketts lifted the blinds and peered through them for a moment, then let them drop back into place again. "His sister said he didn't come home, and she hasn't heard one blessed word from him since yesterday dinnertime."

"When Mahoney was killed in my cafe."

Ricketts turned his eyes on me with renewed interest. "In your cafe? You said he came in with the knife already in him—or are you after changing your story?" He lowered himself into his chair with an audible grunt.

I shook my head. "No, that's what happened. Dammit, you know what I mean."

"Just checking." Ricketts rocked back in his chair, peering at me like he was thinking of asking me for something. I couldn't help but think this whole conversation was merely a prelude. "Stoyles, you know this town pretty well—almost as good as me, and I was born and brought up here."

"Uh-oh."

He ignored me. "You're not, as you already told me, a cop, so you can go places and... do things that my office doesn't allow me to do. Are you following me so far?"

"Yeah, I'm with you. I don't like where this is going, but I'm with you."

"I'm wondering if you mightn't have a look for him."

"For Picco."

"Yes."

"You want me to look for Constable Picco."

Ricketts lifted the telephone and spoke some words into it. A secretary appeared with a pot of coffee on a tray. It smelled heavenly. "Doreen makes a fresh pot every morning at ten thirty on the dot." He poured for us both; it tasted as good as it smelled.

"Why do I think this is a bribe?" I added an extra lump of sugar to mine and sipped it gratefully.

"I can't pay you—departmental budget doesn't allow for it—and I can't even congratulate you publicly." Ricketts's chair squeaked alarmingly as he leaned forward. "Stoyles, I wouldn't even be asking if I didn't think you were the man for the job. This can't become public knowledge. You know how that would look. 'Rogue Policeman Loose in City' and all that garbage."

"Where do you think he might be?"

"Could be anywhere. The only family he's got is his sister. He lives with her over there on Long's Hill. He's got no social life as far as anybody can tell, and he runs as regular as the trains. What I'm saying, Stoyles, is that he shouldn't be too hard to find. What I am also saying, Stoyles—" Ricketts paused to refill our cups. "—is that you will have my eternal gratitude if you can manage to find Constable Picco and bring him here before the newspapers blow this way out of proportion."

I MADE my way back to the Heartache by my usual route, and my familiarity with St. John's stood me in good stead, because I didn't see a thing. What Sergeant Ricketts had told me had me intrigued, but I wondered what, exactly, he expected out of me. Sure, I knew the town, but I didn't have the foggiest where someone like Picco might be, or even where to look. It wasn't like we were friends. Picco couldn't stand me, and he considered my cafe a den of vice. He showed up at my door at least once a week, looking for some excuse—any excuse—to close me down.

Chris had, as I'd predicted, a pot of coffee waiting for me when I got in, and fresh bread from the bakery around the corner. The Cafe wouldn't open till later, so we had the place to ourselves for a little while, and we made the most of it with french toast and hot coffee and a little conversation. I'd promised Ricketts I wouldn't say anything about what he'd told me, but Chris wasn't just anybody.

"So these Greek guys—Ricketts thinks maybe Picco's indirectly responsible for getting their guy killed?" Chris reached over to refill my coffee cup.

"That's the theory, and Ricketts wants me to find Picco before this whole thing blows sky-high."

"Are you going to?"

I caught his gaze and held it. "Would you be okay running the place by yourself for a few hours?"

"Yeah." His eyes slid away. "Julie called. She said she might come by later on… if that's okay?"

"It's okay." I remembered what he'd said about camouflage, but it still hurt a little bit. "She's welcome any time." I took my cup and plate to the sink. "I'll try and get back before the lunch rush gets too hairy."

"Jack." He caught me by the wrist and pulled me toward him. "Be careful, huh?" His thumb brushed my bottom lip. "I… just watch yourself, all right?"

"I will." I wondered if I should kiss him, but I decided not to push my luck. Maybe he'd mentioned Julie on purpose, as a way of telling me something like *don't take things for granted* or *don't get too comfortable.* That was fine by me. I still didn't know how I really felt about that kiss, and I needed some time to sort it out.

I decided to try Picco's sister over on Long's Hill. The hill slopes down off the more-or-less main drag of Harvey Road, home to numerous fish-and-chip shops, the Knights of Columbus Serviceman's Leave Centre, and a couple small mom-and-pop stores. At the bottom of the hill, there's the Theatre Pharmacy, a bunch of churches, and the usual stuff you'd expect to find in a city of this size.

Picco's house was near the bottom of the hill, one of those triple-decker Victorians that seem to make up the greater part of the city. I knocked on the door and waited, knocked again, and was just about to leave when the door opened and a face peered out. "Oh, excuse me. I'm looking for Alphonsus Picco's house. I must have the wrong place."

The girl couldn't have been more than fifteen or sixteen years old, tentative and skinny, wearing a faded print dress and a cardigan sweater. "This is Phonse's house. I'm his sister." She had the same gray eyes as her brother, the same narrow, pale face. "Do you want to come in, or what?"

"If that's okay with you, sure." I didn't want to presume too much on the girl's hospitality, so I stood in the porch. "Miss Picco, I'm a... friend of your brother."

Her pale eyes examined my face. She was chewing on a strand of her dark hair. "Phonse got no friends. He keeps to his self."

This wasn't getting off to a great start. "Uh... I wonder if I could speak to your mother or father?"

"Mom's dead. Dad's overseas. How come you wants Phonse?"

"Well, I can't really say."

"He never came home last night." She sucked on the wet strand of hair, then drew it across her pale cheek. "You married?"

"No. Uh, no, I'm not married. You say Alphonsus didn't come home last night. Have you heard from him at all?"

"No, only some fellow came here this morning and dropped off a parcel for him."

"A parcel. Does he get many parcels?"

She shook her head vigorously, her stringy, dark hair slapping back and forth. "Come in, look, I shows ye."

I wiped my shoes carefully on the mat and followed her down the narrow, dark corridor to the kitchen. To one side of the passageway, there was a sitting room filled with some unmatched pieces of furniture: a couch, an easy chair, a telephone table. The furniture was threadbare and had seen better days, but everything in the room was spotlessly clean. A cabinet radio sat near the window, and there were some books on a table near the door. Obviously someone in this house was a reader, but I couldn't see it being the girl. There was something about her that was just a little bit... off. There was something odd about her, something that didn't quite fit. She reminded me of a girl I'd known back in Philadelphia named Nettie. She lived up the street from me and earned her living cleaning houses for people. She always had a wash bucket with a variety of mops and cleaning implements protruding from it. She said the same thing to anyone she met, regardless of the day or the circumstances: *It's a great day, ain't it?* I never heard her say anything else.

"I opened the parcel. I didn't know what was in it. I suppose he'll get mad at me now." She showed me a brown-paper package she'd left on the kitchen table, next to a stack of utility bills, some of them bearing the ominous stamp FINAL NOTICE. The parcel had been neatly slit along one side. "I cut it open."

"So you don't know who left this for Alphonsus?"

"No. He wouldn't want me taking parcels from strange men. Phonse wouldn't want that. Do you think he'll get mad because I opened it?"

I smiled at her. "I don't think so." There were five hundred dollars inside, all in American greenbacks, but no note, except for a tiny slip of paper, on which were scrawled the words PAID IN FULL. "Did Alphonsus loan anyone any money that you know of?"

"No. He don't make that much. He got to take care of us, pay the electric, and stuff like that."

"The man who brought this parcel—what did he look like?"

She didn't really remember, she said, except he talked funny, like some of the sailors. "He wasn't from here." She tugged at my sleeve. "Do you want to see his room?"

"Alphonsus's room?" It couldn't hurt. Maybe he'd left something behind that might yield a clue; you never knew about these things.

I followed the girl up the narrow, creaking staircase to the second floor landing. She led me to the first door on the left and opened it. There was nothing unusual about the room. It was your typical bedroom, with a single bed placed against the wall, a chest of drawers with a mirror, and a rug on the floor.

"You can have a look around." She started down the stairs, calling back over her shoulder as she went. "I got to finish cleaning the vegetables for dinner. Phonse might be home then."

I went through Picco's room methodically and left nothing untouched. It felt kind of funny to be up here, searching through his underwear drawer, but I told myself it was for a good cause. If Picco really had gone missing—whether of his own accord or otherwise—it was important to get to him as quickly as possible, for a lot of reasons. If he'd gone into hiding, he needed to be coaxed out, and if he'd been snatched, they probably didn't intend to keep him as a house guest.

I turned over his pillows and lifted the mattress, but found nothing. I half hoped I'd come across a girlie magazine or maybe even some dirty postcards, but if his bedroom was anything to go by, Picco was almost monastic in his habits, and then some. I found a Bible on the table by the bed and a handful of religious tracts in the drawer. There was some sort of devotional booklet laid on the windowsill and, directly opposite Picco's bed, a framed picture of Jesus gazed down sorrowfully from where it was mounted on the wall.

No—not sorrowfully, not sorrowfully at all. I moved closer and took a good look at it, then reeled back a little. It was a crucifixion scene, but it had to be the weirdest one I'd ever laid eyes on. The man on the cross was naked except for a brief loincloth, and his contorted body rippled with muscle. His head was thrown back, but the facial expression was all wrong. His features were taut with erotic anticipation and his mouth was open. Moving closer, I could clearly see the outline of an erect phallus through the loincloth. The image was that of a man mere seconds away from sexual completion.

Oh, Constable Picco, you naughty boy.

I was still smiling when I descended to the kitchen and said my good-byes to Picco's sister. She was engrossed in cutting up the largest mound of carrots I'd ever seen, and barely looked up when I left. I wondered what would happen to her if Picco wasn't found—or if he wasn't found in time.

I stopped into the Theatre Pharmacy to use the phone. Chris picked up on the first ring, and I told him I was going to ask around a few of the George Street pubs to see if anyone knew anything. I wasn't hopeful—lowlifes tend to be close-mouthed, in this or any town—but it was worth a try.

Picco was well-known around downtown, but nobody in any of the bars I visited had seen him in a couple of days. I dropped word that I was looking for him, hinted darkly that he was in some kind of serious trouble, and left it at that. I would let the underground network do the rest for me.

I got back to the Heartache around three in the afternoon, long after the lunch rush had come and gone. Chris was mopping up the bar and tidying things away when I got there. "I'm sorry." I sat down on a bar stool. "I honestly didn't mean to be gone so long."

"It's okay." His grin didn't reach his eyes, and I figured maybe he was pretty mad at me.

"No, it isn't. I promised I'd be back in time to help out. I had no right leaving you here to mind the shop all by yourself. I'm sorry and it won't happen again."

He raised his soft brown eyes to mine. "You got dirt on your nose."

I raised my hand reflexively. "Yeah?"

He swiped at it with a towel. "And there's a guy waiting to see you in your office. I offered him a drink on the house, but he didn't want anything."

"What guy?"

"One of these foreign-types. Wearing a real nice suit. He showed up around two o'clock, and when I told him you were out, he asked if he could wait."

"Huh. Okay." I slid off the bar stool. "You want the night off?"

His cloth moved in slow, meditative circles. "Nope."

I went back to my office and opened the door, and he was there—the Egyptian—and all of a sudden the air went out of my lungs. *We are sailing down the Nile, just as you wished… the least you can do is pay attention.* "You." My mouth was dry. "It's you. You came back."

"Yes, I came back." He extended his hand to me and I grasped it gladly. We held on to one another for a few moments, merely looking and smiling. "You seem very glad to see me." That same humor was there in his voice, just under the surface, warm and gentle.

"I am very glad to see you. Some coffee? Tea? Can I offer you a drink?"

"I am a Moslem, Mr. Stoyles. My religion forbids the consumption of alcohol—but thank you. Perhaps we can have coffee another time?"

"Yeah, sure." I couldn't believe he was actually here, in my cafe, in my office. "Jeez, the last time you left here, I didn't think I'd ever see you again. You were asking for directions."

"You seem surprised that I came back. Did you not expect to see me again?"

"I, ah… yeah! I mean, no, I didn't—Mr. Halim, I don't want to seem—"

"Sam." He smiled and my heart started beating double time. "Please, call me Sam. May I call you Jack?"

"Yeah." *Yes, this is what I want as well as you.* I wondered if it showed there, on my face, and then I decided I didn't care.

"You were so kind to me when I came in here that I decided to return." He reached into the pocket of his suit. "I have been away for a while, visiting my country, and I puzzled over what would be an appropriate present. Are you familiar with the Egyptian cartouche, Jack?"

"Yeah, I've heard something about it. They used to draw these circle things around kings' names—so people would know who they were, right?"

41

"Quite correct. It is also considered by my people to be a symbol of eternity." He handed me a small velvet pouch. "There. I give you a cartouche of your own, Jack."

I opened the bag and tipped the contents out into my hand. The small, lozenge-shaped ornament gleamed with its own inner fire: real gold, of a very high carat value, unmistakably luxurious. "Sam, this is too much. I only gave you directions—"

"It is inappropriate to refuse a gift." He cleared his throat in an ostentatious manner, but he was trying hard not to smile. "Please, take it. Those hieroglyphs spell out your name, you know."

"Thank you." I was overcome.

He rose and folded his coat over his arm. "And now I must go. Here—" He handed me a small card. "Call me sometime this week, if you like. I should very much like to see this town. Are you up to playing guide?" His eyelashes were ridiculously long, fanning out from those huge, gentle brown eyes. The curve of his mouth under his tightly groomed moustache was beautiful. He smelled like pine and citrus and sunshine.

I felt like a goddamn schoolboy in his presence. "Uh, sure. Yeah, I'd like that, Sam."

He bowed slightly. "It is time I made my afternoon prayers. Good-bye."

I watched him go, and I was back there with him, sailing on the Nile.

Yes, this is what I want, I thought, *as well as you.*

CHAPTER FIVE

I DID nothing for the next few days except wait while the local underground did its work. I knew if I was patient, eventually word of Picco's whereabouts would filter back to me. I only hoped it wouldn't take too long. I might have plenty of time, but Alphonsus Picco didn't.

It was a sultry Wednesday in mid-July, and I had just opened the Heartache for the day. I poured myself a soda with lots of ice and went to sit at a back table where I could keep an eye on the door while I did some paperwork. I could have just as easily stayed in my office, but from this vantage point, I could see not only the entire cafe, but also anyone who might be loitering on the sidewalk, trying to work up the nerve to come inside.

Chris was behind the bar, taking a quick count of the liquor bottles for me. We'd had an unusually thirsty group of customers the day before, and some of our supplies were running low. I told Chris to let me know if we needed anything and I'd go down in the basement to fetch it.

Just then he called to me from across the room. "I think we might be running low on bourbon, Jack."

"Okay." I laid my glass down for a paperweight and went downstairs. The basement was reached by a set of narrow stairs to the rear of the cafe. It was a damp underground space dimly lit by one light bulb dangling from a cord in the ceiling. I'm not a guy that takes fright easily but that damn basement gave me the creeps. Maybe it was the layout of the place, thin and narrow like the rest of the Cafe, the thick walls set around with whitewashed local stone. There was always a weird smell down there, not the usual sort of thing, but something acrid and faintly sweet, like medicine. It reminded me of Judy. It reminded me of that horrible dark alley, and the little room....

She was still alive, that day in Philadelphia. He was gone, the fake doctor, and there was an awful lot of blood, and in the midst of it, she lay there on the table, naked from the waist down, her legs in stirrups like she was being tortured—like she was being murdered. She was still alive when I got there, and she held on to my hand and whispered something, but I'll be damned if I know what it was. I've spent a lot of sleepless nights since then, trying to remember, and sometimes, just as I'm slipping into unconsciousness, I'll get a thread of it, a whisper that sounds something like her voice, but then it's gone.

"Jack?"

I turned so fast I nearly dropped the bottles I was holding. I could barely make her out, only the white curve of her cheek, the soft sweep of her auburn hair. "Julie? How'd you get down here?"

She laughed and came toward me. "I parked around the corner and I saw the door. I thought it might be the back way into the Cafe, and suddenly I'm down here in this... *labyrinth*." She was wearing a light summer dress and her hair was pulled back off her face. She was beautiful and rich and she knew it. "Thank God you got here in time. I thought I was about to start sprouting mushrooms."

"Julie, how'd you get down here?"

She blinked. "I told you. I parked around—"

"There's no other door."

"What? Of course there is. Don't be silly." She took a couple of the bottles from me. "My grandfather was the original owner of this building, did you know? At the time, it was used to warehouse port. The company who leased it from us claimed that overwintering the port down here gave it a certain unmistakable bouquet that was impossible to produce elsewhere, even under similar conditions."

"You seem to know something about wine." What else, I wondered, did she know?

"Oh, Jack, don't look so sour! Have I spoiled your party, showing up unannounced?" She reached up and patted my cheek. "I'm here to see Chris, and I'm sorry if I've ruined your little boys' club. Next time I'll call, okay?"

"Julie, where's the other door?"

Just then Chris bellowed from upstairs: could I please bring up the bottles? I guess that was what saved Julie from having to answer me—lucky for her. I wondered what it was about her that repulsed me. Yes, I was jealous—it didn't take a genius to figure that out—but there was more to it than that. There was just something... *rotten* about her, something dark and depraved and wrong. Knowing what I knew about the Fayre family and their affairs disposed me to dislike her even more. I didn't want her near Chris; I didn't want her to have anything to do with him. "Chris didn't say you were coming by today." I pointed her ahead of me up the stairs.

"He didn't? I guess it must have slipped his mind."

We emerged into the Cafe, and Julie made a beeline for the bar. A few people were beginning to filter in, and Chris was busy mixing and serving drinks. He drew off several pints of beer and set them up on the bar for Anita, one of the waitresses I'd recently hired to help cover the lunchtime rush, turned, and saw Julie. "Hey, Julie! What are you doing here?"

She laid the bottles on the bar. "Well! That's a fine welcome."

Chris leaned over to kiss her cheek. "Hiya, baby. When'd you get here?"

"I found her wandering in the basement." I handed my bottles across the bar to him.

"Yes, Jack was kind enough to rescue me. I parked around back and got myself lost coming in the wrong door."

Chris raised his eyebrows at me. "There's another door?"

Julie ignored the question. "Are you free for lunch, darling?"

Chris stared at her. "Take a look around, baby—I can't pick up and leave."

"Oh?" She smiled brightly at me. "I don't think Jack would mind so much, would you, Jack? I mean, these girls are here, and Jack's a big, strong man."

Chris mixed two whiskey sours and lined the glasses up for Anita's pickup. A group of twelve or so government office workers filed in and arranged themselves around two tables near the window. "Naw, sorry, baby. Can't do it right now. You're welcome to wait for me if you want to."

"Maybe I'll do that." She saw an empty table by the wall. "Jack, an iced tea when you have a minute?"

I forced myself to smile at her. "Chris, give the lady anything she wants."

"Jack, you darling!" She flounced off and settled herself behind the table.

Chris caught my look and was quick to defend himself. "Jack, before you say anything, I didn't invite her here. I never said a word. She just showed up."

Anita wiggled in beside me and laid her tray on the bar. "Four gin and tonics, three white wine cocktails, and five iced teas, Chris, when you're ready." Anita was maybe five feet tall and about eighty-five pounds soaking wet and carrying an anvil, with a mop of curly dark hair and big blue eyes. "You're after raising the tone of this place, are you, Jack?"

"What do you mean?"

Anita nodded toward Julie, reapplying lipstick at her table by the wall. "She's not the type usually comes in a place like this. What's she, slumming or something?"

"Thanks a lot," I said.

"Sure, where'd you dig her up to? Down the basement?"

I blinked. "How'd you know?"

"What the frig was she doing down the basement?"

"Julie's grandfather used to own this building," I said. "He leased it out to someone else, though. They used to store wines downstairs in the basement."

Anita put one hand on her hip and treated me to the sort of look she usually reserved for drunken sailors. "Go away, boy. That what she told you?"

I was more confused than ever.

"Wish O'Dwyer owned this building, sure. His grandfather owned it before him. He used to make headstones—you know, for graves—and he kept a lot of his marble down there. Sure, the O'Dwyers have always owned this building—most of this street, if you want to know." Anita picked up her laden tray and, with a final shake of her head, disappeared into the mass of tables.

I went back to my table and sat, keeping an eye on Julie. Even if I didn't trust Jonah Octavian, the things he had told me about the Fayre family business—and their manipulation of the Fort Pepperell job—rang true, and Julie's weird behavior just now did nothing to allay whatever suspicions I might have had about her. What was she doing in the basement? I didn't honestly believe she'd simply wandered in there, and gotten herself lost in the dark. Julie was hardly helpless. I wondered what would happen if she was cornered, good and proper—if, say, I got between her and something she really wanted.

I went back to my paperwork, but something at the door of the Cafe caught my eye. Jonah Octavian, in a light-weight summer suit, wearing a straw panama on his head and mopping his face with a large white handkerchief. He spied me sitting in the back and started forward, and then a strange thing happened: Julie Fayre, still sitting at her table by the wall, saw Octavian at the same moment he saw her. It was like two strange cats meeting in an alley, all unsheathed claws and ruffled fur. Julie rose from her chair and fixed her gaze on Octavian, her eyes dark with something that looked an awful lot like rage. She continued watching Octavian as he strolled back to where I was, her top lip drawn back over her teeth in an unmistakable gesture of disgust, her head swiveling to follow his every move.

"Mr. Stoyles, I hope you will forgive my unannounced appearance in your cafe."

"It's open to the public." I pulled out a chair for him. "You look warm and thirsty. Sit down, take a load off." I signaled Chris to bring us a couple of Cokes.

"Thank you." He laid his hat on a nearby chair. "You are most kind."

"Not at all. What can I do for you?" I didn't mention Julie's odd reaction to him. I hoped he might tell me what it was all about himself.

"It has come to my attention that you are looking for someone." Octavian stowed his handkerchief in his pocket. "A young police constable."

"Okay—obviously you're situated somewhere along the pipeline."

Octavian paused to light a smoke. "Whether I am or not is of no concern to you, Mr. Stoyles."

"Right. Did you pay him the five hundred, or was that a gift from one of your cronies?"

Octavian stared at me incredulously and began to laugh. "Oh, Mr. Stoyles. Oh dear, me. You are such a literalist." He looked up as Chris laid a cold soda down in front of him. "Why would I be handing large sums of money to the police?"

"Good question. Why would you?" I took a long drink of my soda. The heat had invaded the Cafe like a living thing, and it was all the ceiling fans could do to keep up with it.

"It must be, or else you wouldn't have bothered mentioning it." Octavian took a sip of his drink. "Mr. Stoyles, I have information. What you do with it is up to you."

"Why should I trust you?"

"There is no reason why you should, except that you might recall my information has been good in the past." He nodded toward Julie's table. "Why is the Fayre girl in here, anyway?"

"My cafe is open to anybody who can pay for the privilege of sitting at a table. I have no reason to keep her out." Not strictly true, but I'd be damned if I'd let him know that.

"And your bartender?"

"Is none of your business."

"Ah." He smiled faintly and applied himself to his soda. "So it is as I suspected." He shrugged. "I cannot fault his reasoning. The Fayre girl makes a wonderful screen, but I would caution you, Mr. Stoyles, against keeping dangerous pets."

He was beginning to irritate me. "You got something to say, or did you just come in here to play word games?"

"The young policeman, Constable Picco."

"Yeah."

"He is much closer than you think."

"So he's still alive."

"Without a doubt, Mr. Stoyles. The... parties to whom he gave offense are merely keeping him out of circulation for a little while. For his own good, you might say."

That made me laugh out loud. "The last time I checked, Bull Parsons couldn't lay hands on five hundred bucks even in his wildest dreams."

"I never mentioned Mr. Parsons." Octavian took a look at his watch. "As a newcomer to the city, you probably don't know about the caves that exist at various points in the Southside Hills. I can say nothing for certain, Mr. Stoyles, but if you chose to look there, it might lead you in an interesting direction." He stood and put on his hat. "Good day." He bowed once and was gone, weaving his way through the tables to the door.

A shadow fell over my table: Julie Fayre. "Mind if I join you, Jack?"

"By all means."

She eased into the chair and spent several moments arranging herself, moving her chair so we were sitting at right angles to each other and close enough to touch. "I can't thank you enough for introducing me to Chris. He really is something, Jack."

I pretended not to understand. "Yeah, he's a great bartender. I'm lucky to have found him. Most guys his age are overseas."

"Mm." She leaned close to me, her hair brushing my shoulder. "You're quite the fortress of solitude, aren't you?"

"I don't follow you."

"Well…." She smiled faintly and stroked my forearm. It seemed to be her main party piece. "You work here in the cafe all day, you're alone all night. I just think it must get a little lonely." She laid her hand over mine and interlaced our fingers. "I'm not so bad once you get to know me, Jack."

"Is that so?" I pretended to scratch an imaginary itch on my neck— anything to get free of her.

"You don't like me very much, do you?"

"Oh, I wouldn't say that."

Her hand began stroking my leg, smoothing the fabric of my pants, crawling up my thigh. "You and I should be friends, Jack. After all, we have the same objectives."

"Do we—Miss Fayre, could you not do that?"

"Do what?" She tilted her head close to me, just as her hand closed around my balls, squeezing gently. Her tongue slid out to wet her lips. "Oh, Jack, I think we could be such close friends." She was good with her mitts, I'd give her that. In seconds she had me completely unzipped and her hand was in my shorts. The tablecloth hid what she was doing, and it's not like I could have moved, anyway. Every molecule of blood I owned had gone straight to my cock. "It's important that we understand each other, you and I." Her hand worked me, her thumb slipping over and under, spreading my body's moisture.

I ducked my head to hide my expression, the taut anticipation in my face. Come to think of it, I probably looked like Alphonsus Picco's crucifixion picture right about then. "I don't… mmm… follow you."

"It would be a shame—" Her mouth was close to my ear, and her tongue flicked out, spreading heat. "—if something horrible happened to Chris DuBois."

THE ONE question that kept going around and around in my mind had to do with Johnny Mahoney; why was he killed? It made sense that the

Greeks would have knifed him in retaliation for the death of their shipmate, sure—but where did Bull Parsons fit into all of this? And what about Alphonsus Picco? It was likely the five hundred dollars was given to him as payment for letting Bull Parsons walk free, except that made no sense either. Picco was the kind of cop who would write a ticket if he saw you spitting on the sidewalk; it was highly unlikely he'd simply look the other way while Parsons walked. The only explanation was that Picco *hadn't* looked the other way—that Picco might have been in the lockup when Parsons was brought in, but that he wasn't there when Parsons escaped. I decided to pay a call on Billy Ricketts to get some further information.

I found him standing near the water cooler in the Constabulary headquarters, refilling paper cups and downing the contents as quickly as he could. All the windows in the place were open, but there was hardly a breeze to stir the blinds, and the several electric fans in evidence were trying and failing to stem the heat.

"I don't know why people think this is a cold place." Ricketts waved me ahead of him into his office.

"Maybe because they've been here in February?" I couldn't help grinning.

"It's hot enough to split the goddamn rocks out there today." He mopped his forehead with his sleeve and collapsed into his chair with palpable relief. "What can I do for you?"

I explained what I knew about Picco and the money, and I asked Ricketts point-blank, did Picco seem the sort of officer to take a bribe in return for letting someone walk?

"No. Don't get me wrong, Stoyles. On his good days Picco would try the patience of a saint. He's snotty, arrogant, and he thinks he knows better than anybody else. But he's a good cop, and I don't believe for a minute that he'd take money to let someone like Bull Parsons walk."

"So someone is trying to make us think that Picco is crooked."

"Might be." Stoyles reached behind him and took down a thick ledger, which he spread open on the desk and turned so I could see it. "Picco has been on the force for five years. He's had a fair few arrests. He keeps his nose clean and he's always on time. Never misses a day, not for sickness nor nothing else." Stoyles pointed to a ledger entry, his thick finger underlining where he wanted me to look. "July 24th of last year, we had an incident. Young fellow off one of the boats had too much liquor and climbed up on top of the courthouse with a loaded rifle. How he got up there, God only knows."

I'd seen the courthouse and I had to agree. "What happened?"

"Few of my men spent the afternoon and a good part of the night staked out, waiting for him to come down. Must have gone on like that for hours. It was Picco who finally did what nobody else had the balls to do." Ricketts shook his head. "He climbed up and talked the fellow down. I don't know what he said. I asked him and he wouldn't tell me. Went up and got him down, not even a shot fired. I offered him a commendation for that, but he didn't want it." Ricketts closed the ledger, and for a moment, perhaps not even that, I had the strange sense that he was close to tears, and it was weird. Ricketts wasn't the kind who went in for theatrics, and the whole thing had that kind of feel for me, like he was putting it on. "He's hard to get along with. He's as stubborn as a mule. There's times when I'd like to knock him arse over teakettle just for being such a bloody pain in my backside, and if he's got a goddamn friend in the world, I've yet to meet him." Ricketts sighed deeply. "He's a good cop, Stoyles. I'd hate for anything to happen to him."

"Do you have any idea where he might be?" I told him what Octavian had said, about the caves in the Southside Hills. "Could he be there? Is there anywhere in the city where someone would hide him, if they wanted to keep him on ice?"

"Oh, there's lots of places." Ricketts leaned forward, elbows on the desk. "Stoyles, there are houses up there on Temperance Street that have tunnels leading out of the basement and down to the waterfront. There's old buildings down on Water Street with false walls and ceilings in them, and crawl spaces underground. Picco could be anywhere. I certainly wouldn't take the word of Jonah Octavian as gospel—but it wouldn't hurt to take a look."

A constable knocked at Ricketts's door, then stuck his head inside the office. "Someone here to see you, Sergeant. Picco's sister. She says someone broke into their house overnight and stole some money."

I FIGURED it would be best to wait for cover of darkness before venturing over to the south side of town. The last thing I needed was for some overzealous neighbor to come snooping around before I got a decent chance to check things out. I didn't necessarily trust Octavian any more than I trusted anyone, really, but I didn't see the harm in having a look around.

I got lucky with more than just the dark, because as soon as the sun went down, a thick, fishy-smelling fog, the likes of which is legendary in these parts, dropped to the ground like a big wet curtain. You couldn't see a hand in front of your face—let alone an ex-pat American poking around the waterfront.

I didn't want to risk my car being seen and identified, so I packed a few things into a rucksack and made the journey on foot, heading west on Water Street toward the South Side. What Octavian had called caves were actually storage bunkers for ammunition to feed the great guns at Fort Amherst, located at the harbor's mouth. Each bunker was equipped with a set of double doors, and each had a full complement of locks. In short, it was the perfect place to hide someone, at least in the short term. Nobody ever went in there unless the city was under direct attack. These days, the threat was much more likely to come from the roving U-boat packs that roamed the coastline, looking for a gap in the island's defenses, but the *Kriegsmarine* rarely came too close to the harbor, at least not since the installation of an antisubmarine net across the Narrows.

Ricketts had provided me with a rough, hand-drawn map showing the approximate location of the caves. I knew Picco could be in any one of them, or somewhere else entirely. The best thing to do under the circumstances was to check each one in turn, so I did, while the fog turned into a kind of misting drizzle that soon soaked me to the skin. The doors gave me surprisingly little trouble, especially given the lock-picking skills I'd learned from Packy Burns back in Philadelphia. I held my breath in hopes that the military police wouldn't take a sudden interest, and prayed the beam of my tiny flashlight wasn't visible beyond a couple feet. The last thing I needed was a full military escort, arriving with sirens roaring and guns blazing, just as I was breaking into a munitions bunker. I'd be out of Newfoundland so fast my head would spin.

The first three bunkers yielded nothing but the smell of mold and gun grease; the fourth bunker had been sealed some time ago, the entranceway bricked over. I hit luck on the fifth. The door was wooden and, thanks to the rivulet of water cascading down the cliff face, had rotted nicely. I popped open the padlock with a screwdriver and kicked a hole in the door big enough to get my fist in. There was some business with deadbolts, and I swore a blue streak for a couple minutes while I fiddled around with that, but finally I was in.

The place was as dark as the proverbial tomb, so I had no idea how far back it went. I reached out my arms, but I couldn't feel the walls, and I couldn't feel anything else either—clearly it was empty of munitions. I shuffled my feet along the floor, but it was slow going. My small flashlight didn't penetrate very far into the darkness ahead, and the absence of sound was disorienting.

I stopped and looked at my watch, and then I heard it: a small noise, a sound like someone clearing their throat. "Hello?" There was a scuffling noise to the rear of the cave, and I moved toward it. "Picco, is that you? It's Stoyles, Jack Stoyles. Where are you?" No one answered, but I heard that same sound again, deep and guttural. On a hunch I shone my flashlight toward the back of the cave, and that's when I saw him, Alphonsus Picco, bound hand and foot and gagged, lying slumped against the damp rock wall. His uniform was gone, and he was wearing civilian-style trousers and a long-sleeved shirt. When I reached to undo his gag he scooted backward on his heels, the fear in his eyes unmistakable. "I'm not going to hurt you, I swear." I reached out for him and untied the knot at the back of his head, then moved to undo the bonds holding his hands and feet. His wrists were raw from the pressure of the ropes; he yelped in pain when he tried to stretch his legs out to their normal extension. "How long have you been here?" I handed him my canteen full of cold water, and he drank thirstily.

"Is my sister all right? She doesn't know where I am. She needs to know I'm all right."

I assured him she was fine and got busy tending to his wounds. The weals on his wrists weren't as deep as they'd initially appeared, and I was able to clean them with a little water and apply a dressing. I filled Picco in on the situation, and when he was finished, I asked the question I'd be dreading: who had given him the money?

"I don't know nothing about no money. If that was dropped off at the house, it's got nothing to do with me."

"Your sister said that your mother was dead, but could the money have come from your father?"

Picco stared at me like I was insane. "My father's dead, boy. There's just me and Norma." And, when I told him what his sister had said, he explained, "Yes, well—my father was a drunk. He worked down there at the rail yard. He went to work drunk, and he came home drunk. One day he stepped in front of a locomotive that never had time to stop." Picco's gaze slid away from mine. "We told Norma he went overseas in the war."

"I'm sorry. I didn't know."

He made a dismissive noise. "There's lots that you don't know. Keep that to yourself." He nodded at the canteen. "Thanks." It must have galled him to say it.

"You're welcome. Picco, who brought you here? Did you see their faces?"

"No. I was on duty in the lockup when they brought Bull Parsons in. He was drunk. Then Willie Harris never showed up for his shift, so I told the sergeant I'd go in his place. I was walking up Baird's Cove, headed towards the courthouse, when these two fellows were walking one on either side of me."

"Did you notice anything about them?"

"They had accents—not like yours, I mean. I can't describe it." When I asked him if he remembered what they'd been wearing, he could only say they were nicely dressed—they didn't seem like normal dock workers or laborers, but more like businessmen. "Them fellows that were on the boat, the day Johnny Mahoney got killed—well, these two talked like that."

"They were Greek."

"Could be." He wrapped his arms around himself and shivered. I took off my jacket and draped it around his shoulders. "Thanks. I suppose you'll be throwing this in my face forever now, hey?"

"What are you talking about?"

He jerked his chin at me. "Coming over here to get me, bringing me a drop of water and giving me your coat. You won't let me forget this, will you?"

Like most Newfoundlanders, Picco hated the idea of charity, and given our history, hated it even more when it came from me. The idea that he might somehow owe me something was repugnant to him. "Oh, I'm sure you'd do the same for me, right?"

He huddled farther into the coat. "Yeah. I suppose."

I laughed in spite of myself. "Come on, let's get out of here. Think you can walk all right?"

"I very much doubt, Mr. Stoyles, that either of you will be walking anywhere." A dark form, rendered strange and insubstantial by the shifting fog, stood silhouetted in the doorway; the gun he held trained on us was entirely real and solid. "Backs against the wall, the both of you, and please don't make me shoot you. It would make a deafening repercussion in such a space as this, and my ears are really very delicate."

The man was Jonah Octavian.

CHAPTER SIX

I FELT Picco tense up against me, and I reached out a hand to steady him. In the semidarkness of the cave, his face was white and scared-looking. "Octavian, I don't know what's going on here. How about you give me something to go on?"

He laughed. "I am not required, Mr. Stoyles, to give you anything besides a bullet—which I will, all in due time." He turned his attention on Picco. "Constable, I wonder if you would mind handing over my five hundred dollars?"

Picco's eyes narrowed. "I haven't got your money."

"Then perhaps you could tell me where it is?"

"I don't know where it is."

Octavian was a moving blur; his gun hand came up with frightening swiftness and clubbed Picco in the side of the head. The young policeman dropped like a rock.

"What the hell did you do that for?" Everything in me wanted to charge him, knock the smarmy bastard to the ground, and beat the hell out of him, but he had a gun and I had nothing. I wasn't that suicidal, and I knew Octavian was cold-blooded enough to pull the trigger.

"I dislike being lied to, Mr. Stoyles."

"He's telling you the truth! His sister came into headquarters—she told Ricketts that someone broke into their house overnight and stole the money."

"Stole the money?" He advanced on me, reached out, and grabbed my collar. "Stole the money? Mr. Stoyles, do you think me feeble-minded?"

Picco groaned from somewhere behind me. "He's telling you the truth, boy."

"Maybe it was you." Octavian waved the gun, covering both of us. "Maybe you broke in and stole the money, hm? Perhaps it was Constable Picco's friend, Mr. Parsons. Was that why you let him go, Constable?"

Picco managed to drag himself to his hands and knees; he wavered there for a moment, then spat out a mouthful of blood. His voice, when he spoke, was pure venom. "Go fuck yourself."

Octavian rushed at him and kicked him in the ribs; Picco yelped and lay still. I told myself to keep calm. Octavian probably wanted a reason to smack me around, and I wasn't about to give it to him. "We don't know where your money is. I suggest you ask your buddies for that information."

"I think I will leave the two of you here until your memories improve. Yes, I believe that is what I will do. Perhaps a day or so, perhaps longer."

"I don't get you, Octavian—why'd you bother telling me where Picco was?"

Octavian's eyebrows rose. "Because I knew you would go there. I know your type, Stoyles: if there is even the slightest possibility of hope, you do not hesitate. There is something in you that has to be a hero. I find this quality often in Americans." He shrugged. "I suspect you know much more than you are telling, but I could not walk into your cafe on a weekday afternoon and force you to tell me where my money is. I am not a barbarian. But here, in this—" He gestured at the dripping walls of the cave. "—*place*, deprived of food and water and eventually of air, you will soon be eager to tell all." He reached for my rucksack and took out the tools I'd brought with me. The canteen was still somewhere to the rear of the cave. With luck he wouldn't see it, and we could use it to catch the water dripping off the walls. "I will take your screwdriver and all your other little toys. I should hate for you to hurt yourselves while I am away."

"You son of a bitch. Is this why you tried to frame Julie Fayre? To get her out of the way so your company could swoop in and gobble up the goodies?"

Octavian gazed at me for a moment, the black eyes empty and flat. Then he laughed, stretching his lips over his teeth and opening his mouth wide. "Julie Fayre? If you believe her to be innocent, you are an even bigger fool than I supposed." Octavian settled the gun butt against his palm. "The money, Mr. Stoyles. I will be back for you in... let us say a day or two. Good-bye."

I watched him back away until he was swallowed up by darkness, and after a moment, I heard him throw the padlock on the door. Even with the hole I'd made on my way in, there was no way I could get us out without tools. That damned padlock would stay on the door until someone came and took it off.

I went to where Picco was and helped him up. "Did he hurt you bad?"

"Not the first time I've been smacked in the mouth." He allowed me to clean the blood from his face with the tail of my shirt. He was obviously feeling that kick in the ribs Octavian had given him, because he didn't fight me when I rewrapped my coat around his shoulders.

Since there was nothing much else to do, we settled down to wait. With any luck, someone—hopefully Ricketts or his men—would find us. Without luck? I preferred not to think about it.

OCTAVIAN HAD taken my flashlight, so I couldn't see my watch. Time gets strange when you're locked up in a place without any lights. Picco slept for a while, curled up on the floor and hugging his knees, while I sat with my back against the stone and listened to the sound of dripping water. After a while, all the little noises blurred together, and there was a strange sound underneath, almost like a voice.

Shall I let the sails out, or does this satisfy you? His voice was close, almost whispering in my ear, and his warm hands smoothed the naked skin of my back. *I do believe you would be perfectly content to drift forever.* His lips touched my nape; he was kissing his way down my body, and the heat of the sun soaked into my bones, blissfully warm. I rolled onto my back and he came into my arms and we were kissing one another. I wanted him so bad it was like a taste in my mouth. *I love you, I love you, I love you—*

A noise yanked me out of my dream, jarring me awake, and I sat bolt upright, forgetting for a moment where I was. The darkness of the ammunition bunker pressed on me from all sides; the sun was gone and someone was sobbing in their sleep.

"Picco." I groped my way to him and shook his shoulder.

He woke, grabbing my arm. "Stoyles."

"Yeah, I'm right here."

"Can't see a frigging thing." His voice was groggy, clouded with sleep. "Wonder what time it is."

"I dunno."

Picco sounded like he was shivering. "Why is it so cold?"

"Cold?" The air was damp, but it wasn't unpleasant, not exactly. "Are you cold?"

"I'm freezing." He seemed reluctant to admit any weakness, especially to me.

"Come over here."

"Why?" I couldn't see him, but I could easily imagine the gleam of suspicion in his pale eyes. "What are you going to do?"

"Will you shut up and come over here?" The rock formed a natural ledge big enough for both of us; the cave wall sloped backward. I fashioned a makeshift cushion out of my rucksack and put it behind his head, then pulled him up so he was lying against me.

"Right on—this is nice and fruity. Well, you can forget about it. I'm not your bum chum—"

He made to crawl away, but I pulled him back, wrapped my arms around him, and nestled his head against my shoulder. "Stay put. You have a fever, probably from that smack Octavian gave you." I laid my palm against his forehead. He was burning up. This was bad; this was very, very bad, especially since an untended fever could fry his brains. As much as I disliked Picco, I wouldn't have wished such a fate on anyone.

I held him in my arms as the hours passed and his fever mounted; he clung to me and whispered nonsense while I drifted in and out of sleep. I dreamed Picco's crucifixion picture came to life and stood over me, all sinew and throbbing muscle. The figure reached for me and pulled me into his embrace and kissed me hungrily, his tongue delving into my mouth. Then I was back on the sailboat, lying under the Egyptian sun, touching and being touched by the man from my dream, his long, graceful fingers cupped around my balls, rubbing and squeezing, dragging me deliciously to climax.

There was a mouth at my neck and Picco's hand was cupped around the bulge at my crotch. I woke with a gasp and caught hold of his wrist, but he twisted away from me.

"Please. I've never had—" He licked his dry lips.

An invisible hand squeezed my heart. I traced the curve of his bottom lip with the pad of my thumb. "You're not well," I whispered. "It wouldn't be right. I'd be taking advantage of you." He was beautiful—how had I never noticed? That narrow, clever face, lean and pale, and his strange gray eyes with their long lashes, his taut, slender body, well-muscled and erect. Maybe it really was as people said. Maybe the other side of hatred was... something pretty damn erotic.

"I don't *care*." He held tight to me, sobbing with want. "Please. I'll never tell a soul. I swear. I swear it on the Bible—"

His mouth was fever-hot and his kiss was eager but clumsy, but Constable Picco was a very fast learner, and he felt real good in my arms. His body's heat burned into me. I felt him unbuttoning my shirt, but in the complete darkness of the cave, it was impossible to see what he was doing. His mouth pressed against my bare chest, tongue flickering briefly on each of my nipples, and my body jerked forward, grinding itself against him, and I listened to myself groaning. It wasn't enough. Lying in this filthy cave with him wasn't nearly enough. I wanted to lie naked with him on clean sheets, our bodies sliding deliciously against each other, speaking with hands and tongues. I all but tore the buttons off his shirt as I stripped him, but the buckle of his belt was a little easier. His cock was hard, blood-warm, and filled my hand; he groaned at the touch, a ragged, anguished sound.

I bent and took him into my mouth and sucked him, working him with my lips and my tongue while his fingers beat an agonized tattoo against my scalp. His lean young body heaved, his breathing ragged and uneven as I sucked harder, drawing him closer and closer to his climax, and then his fists clenched and he gave in to it, shouting something unintelligible. I drew back and stroked him as the orgasm shuddered through him, leaving him limp and voiceless. He came into my arms, and we found each other's mouths in the dark.

His hand slid into my fly and his long fingers closed around my cock. I grunted as he rubbed me, smoothing the warm, elastic skin of my shaft, his thumb flickering over my cockhead, spreading heat. I thrust into his hand, every muscle tense, my breath coming almost painfully in my chest, and I was there, the climax rushing through me in throbbing waves, leaving me spent and empty. I reached out in the dark and touched Picco's face. "Thank you."

He took my hand and kissed the palm. "Jack—perhaps we shouldn't say anything."

"No, of course not." Something occurred to me. "Was this—I mean, have you ever…?"

I couldn't see him, but his voice, when he spoke, was shy and boyish. "This was the first time."

This knowledge humbled me, and I was quiet for a long time. When I could speak, I reached out and drew his face to mine and kissed him.

"I don't expect anything of ye." The native brogue—a subtle mixture of English and Irish—was strong in his voice. "I can't let meself get involved with anybody, and not like this. No, sir, not like this. You knows what people are like. They'll talk, and I don't—Norma—I'm all Norma's got. I got to watch myself."

I hugged him, this strange, prickly young man, and kissed him. "I understand. You don't need to explain yourself."

I heard him sigh. "You knows why we're in here, don't ye?" He wrapped his arm around my waist and laid his head on my shoulder.

"Octavian?"

"That's part of it. Mind you, that's a big part of it. There's not a lot of Greek people in Newfoundland, Jack—"

"Wait a minute." I drew my fingers down his face. "You called me Jack, but what am I supposed to call you? Alphonsus?"

I couldn't tell for certain, but I think he was smiling. "Norma calls me Phonse."

"Would it be all right if I called you Phonse?"

"I suppose—only not when I'm on duty."

I nodded, grateful he couldn't see my smile. "Of course. Constable Picco all the way."

"Octavian is Greek. The boys that Johnny Mahoney and Bull Parsons tangled with were Greek. I've seen Octavian down around the waterfront more than once—hanging out on the harbor apron, looking at the boats. I've seen him going on boats and coming off them."

I understood what he was driving at. "So you think the Greek that knifed Johnny Mahoney is one of Octavian's pals?"

"Yeah, that's what I'm saying. Wouldn't be hard for Octavian to get aboard one of them ships, now, would it?"

"But what about the money? The five hundred dollars? The only reason to plant that money in your house was to make it seem like you were involved in Parsons's escape, and you weren't. So somebody—

Octavian, if your hunches are correct—had a reason to make you seem like a dirty cop."

"Jack." He reached out and laid his fingers against my mouth. "I'm awful tired."

I held him in my arms, and maybe we both slept, I don't know. The next thing I knew, someone was standing over me, shining a light in my face, and I was wide awake. "Over here, boys!" The voice belonged to Billy Ricketts. If he thought it strange that Picco and I were lying in each other's embrace, he didn't say anything, and within half an hour, I was safe at home in the Heartache Cafe.

IT WAS late by the time I finished filling Chris in on what had happened, and business was pretty slow, so I closed up early and told him to go on home. I had a hot shower and made some coffee and went to sit in my office, the back door open to let some air flow through. After what I'd just endured, I wasn't sure I could stand being corked up in an enclosed space. Alphonsus Picco would never know how his presence and the quiet comfort of his body had kept me from going crazy in that cave. Maybe someday I'd get around to telling him.

There was a warm breeze tonight, and through the darkened windows of the Heartache, I could see a thin rind of silvery moon rising over the harbor. There was a pressure in my head and my temples were pounding, but the coffee tasted good, and after a while I rested my head in my hands and tried to relax. Maybe I'd sleep with the windows open tonight, and the bedroom door, and let the sounds of the city lull me to rest.

I sensed his presence before he touched me, his warm hands kneading the tension out of my shoulders, caressing the back of my neck. "I wonder if I might be of some small assistance at this time?" His breath ghosted against my cheek as he leaned down to speak to me, and he smelled of incense and patchouli and salt sea air.

It was all I could do not to turn and wrap my arms around him. "Hello, Sam."

"Your head hurts?"

"Yeah. I spent a few hours in a cave. I guess you could say it's an occupational hazard."

His laughter was deep and rich, and it warmed me. "Wherever there is trouble, you are surely to be found?"

"Mmm, something like that." Perhaps if I kept him talking, he would stay. If he stayed, he might keep touching me. That was what I wanted. "What brings you to the Heartache at this hour?"

"I wanted to talk to you about Jonah Octavian."

I turned and showed him an exaggerated sad face. "You wound me, Sam. Here I thought this was a social call."

He patted my shoulders, then came around to face me, moving to lean against my desk. He looked worried, but it didn't detract one iota from his essential attractiveness. He was wearing casual trousers and a dark blue, short-sleeved shirt, open at the neck; it exposed the strong column of his throat and the hollow at its base, dusted with dark hairs. I couldn't stop looking at that tiny patch of skin. I wanted to kiss him there. I wondered what it took to make him cry out, to bring him to completion, and what he looked like, sounded like, at that moment. It must have showed in my face. "Jack, are you quite all right?"

"Huh? Oh, yeah, Sam, I'm just fine." I sipped at my coffee and realized too late that the cup was empty. "Would you, uh—would you like some coffee?"

"I would. Perhaps you would, as well?"

"Come on into the kitchen. I'll put a pot on." The service light was on over the stove, so I didn't bother to cut on any other lights. I filled the percolator with water and added coffee in the right amount, all the time acutely aware of his presence.

"Your cook keeps this place remarkably clean. I have always found that to be the mark of a satisfied worker." He leaned against the counter, watching me with those long-lashed brown eyes of his. "Are all your employees so satisfied?"

I hadn't honestly thought about it. "I guess so. Why?"

"I was merely wondering. You seem the type of man that has no trouble giving… satisfaction when it suits him." His gaze was frank and open and very, very suggestive, and I wondered what he would do if I said to hell with convention and kissed him. He was standing so close, I could feel the heat of his body and smell that damnable cologne he was wearing. He was shorter than me by maybe four or five inches, but there was an unmistakable force just underneath the surface, and he embodied the automatic authority of a man used to being in charge of other men. He had, I was sure of it, known power at some point in his life, and I wondered about his cover story.

"Are you really the assistant to the British Consul?" I fetched some cups down from a shelf above.

The corners of his lips curved up, but he wasn't quite smiling. "Of course." I got the distinct impression he was humoring me. "Is that not what I told you?"

I leaned my elbow on the counter and gazed into his eyes. It was like gazing into the swirling heart of a newborn star. His lips were soft, not overly full, and sharply defined, and there was a shallow dimple in his chin. A tiny pulse beat in the hollow of his throat. He had, I saw, nicked himself shaving. "Mmm-hmm."

This time he did smile. "I never really know what it means when an American makes that particular sound." He reached into his hip pocket and took out his wallet. "Here is my identification card, with my photograph, as you can see. There, it says Samuel Abdelleh Halim. That is my name." He flipped through to another section. "This woman is my wife. These are my four children: Samuel, Hanbal, Stamos, and Tabia. They live in Cairo with my wife, Tareenah."

Disappointment settled in my gut like a stone. "Your… wife?" It was ridiculous to feel this way. I had no claim on him.

"Every Moslem man is married as soon as he comes of age to take a wife. Tareenah and I were married when I was twenty and she eighteen. It is the way of our people." He folded the wallet away. "You seem surprised."

"No, it's just… you don't seem the type." The percolator bubbled merrily, and I lifted it onto a tray, along with the cups. I felt compelled to make small talk. Maybe I was trying to cover my disappointment. "Stamos, huh? That's a Greek name."

"My mother was Greek." He held my wrist. "Does my being married disturb you, Jack? If I knew it would have this effect, I would not have mentioned it."

"It's fine." My face felt frozen, and I had the absurd feeling I might burst into tears any minute. "Let's go sit in the Cafe. It's nice and cool out there with the windows open."

"Sure, if you like."

For a while we sat there, drinking coffee and talking of nothing much, which was good, because my mind certainly wasn't on the conversation. I watched his mouth as he talked, and the flutter of his long lashes, and his graceful hands, reaching to pour coffee or add sugar, and I reminded myself that he was married, with four children. "You said you wanted to talk about Jonah Octavian."

He didn't waste time with preamble. "You believe Jonah Octavian was behind the abduction of Constable Picco and yourself. You also believe he is responsible for the murder of the beggar Johnny Mahoney in front of your cafe."

"I never thought of him that way." But the word "beggar" fit Mahoney and all the others like him.

"Forgive me if I offend you. In my country there are a great many beggars, and what we call *baksheesh* boys, always with their hands out, eager to exploit all possible sources. Some consider it an honorable profession." He tilted his head to the side, regarding me. "What would you have called him?"

"I dunno. A pain in the ass?"

Sam laughed long and hard at this, and I was glad. I liked to see him laugh. It did wonderful things to his lean, tanned face and the sculpted lines of his mouth. "Such colloquialisms! You are a funny man, Jack." He clasped my forearm and then he was leaning down and our faces were close together in the dark. "Does it really matter that I am married?"

My heartbeat speeded up, thumping double-time in my chest, and maybe I made some little sound in my throat, I don't know for sure. His lips ghosted over mine as the very tip of his tongue slipped into my mouth, and the night and the Cafe swirled into nothing as I gave myself to the kiss. When I opened my eyes, my hands were clenched in the front of his shirt, several of his buttons were undone, and he was breathing heavily, his eyes closed and his long, thick lashes fanned against his cheeks.

He swallowed hard and drew back, and we looked at each other in silence until he broke the gaze to take a hurried sip of his coffee. "I came here to ask you if you might not allow Jonah Octavian his freedom—at least for a little while longer."

I rubbed the ball of my thumb against his lips. "Why would the British Consulate care about Jonah Octavian?"

"You know I can't tell you that." He captured my hand in his, drew my thumb into his mouth, and sucked on it.

"Oh, Sam… for the love of God, stop that."

He disengaged my thumb and drew my index finger briefly into his mouth, sucked it strongly, and the motion of his lips set up an answering pulse deep inside my belly. "Your people are too hasty, Jack. You are always in a hurry." His mouth hovered over mine, our breaths mingling in the space above my lips. "You do not allow yourself to understand the enormous debt you owe to pleasure, nor the many barriers you have erected against it." He kissed me again, a slow caress that deepened gradually. "You need to be shown how to love." He stroked my cheek with a raw tenderness as sublime as it was painful; his long, agile fingers traced the contours of my face till I was drowning in sensation. *"Out beyond ideas of wrongdoing and rightdoing, there is a field. I will meet you there."*

"What is that?" My whisper sounded abnormally loud. "That's from something, isn't it? What is it?"

"An old poet, long dead—a Sufi mystic named Rumi." He kissed my mouth gently and rose to go. "Good night, Jack."

"Good night, Sam."

I stood at the back door of my cafe and watched him disappear into the night, and I thought about old stories of fairies, ghosts, and djinn as his slight figure moved in and out of the pools of pale light cast by streetlamps and the moon.

CHAPTER SEVEN

SERGEANT RICK Callan was in charge of the building project that would eventually be Fort Pepperrell. He was the sort of guy you think of whenever somebody says "solid." About my height, but absolutely massive through the chest and shoulders, and with that no-nonsense attitude that is inevitably a feature of military men everywhere. He had an office in a temporary trailer set up at the edge of the building site. A flight of rough wooden stairs led up to a windowless metal door, which in turn opened onto a small room with barely enough space for Callan's desk, his files, and his clerk—a tall, handsome young private named Thomas. Thomas's job seemed to involve all the typing in the world, because the whole time I was there, he never stopped, except to answer the phone and once to direct a nearly wordless query to Callan.

Callan offered me a cup of coffee out of a thermos on his desk and I accepted. It was hot and delicious and very welcome. A cold, misting drizzle had come down the night before, borne upon a fog bank the size of Pennsylvania. I'd been told to expect such weather around here, but after the recent spate of hot days and balmy nights, it was a nasty surprise.

"You in the service, Mr. Stoyles?"

"Discharged, Sergeant."

His dark eyes flickered over me, examined me, and then dismissed me, all in the space of a few seconds. "Discharged?" He said it like the word left a bad taste in his mouth. "Honorably?"

"Yes—for medical reasons."

He smirked. "Medical reasons? You telling me you are a Section Eight, Mr. Stoyles?"

"No, Sergeant." I fought back the urge to tell him what he could do with himself. "I'm not insane—at least not as far as the Army is concerned."

"You cannot know how that comforts me, Mr. Stoyles. You see, I am a very curious man, and when you called me the other day, requesting an interview—what day was it that Mr. Stoyles called, Private Thomas?"

Thomas didn't look up from his typewriter. "Wednesday, Sergeant."

"When you called on Wednesday, requesting an interview, I took the liberty of looking up your service record." Callan indicated a folder on his desk. "It says here that you originally enlisted yourself in the British Army way back in 1939, and attempted to transfer to the United States Army shortly thereafter." He sat back and looked at me, his big hands clasped across his abdomen. "Now why would you do a thing like that?"

I wondered why my private convictions were anybody else's business. "I came here for information, Sergeant. Last time I checked, that didn't involve filling you in on my background." I stood, prepared to leave. "If I'd known this would turn into a court martial, I would have stayed home." I started for the door and had my hand on the knob when Callan spoke.

"I apologize, Mr. Stoyles, if I seem unduly forthright." He took a breath and tugged at his uniform jacket. "Please, sit down. Thomas here will tell you that I am curious about all aspects of the military. Nowadays, with the war going on, that curiosity extends to military personnel past and present." He gestured at his makeshift office. "Spending my days in here as I do, with only sweet young Thomas for company, I tend to forget the social niceties. I do hope you can forgive me for what must seem like an unnecessary intrusion into your personal affairs. If I were back home right now, I can assure you my dear mother would be only too glad to whale the tar out of me." His grin was spontaneous and genuine, and it transformed him into a sudden small boy. I realized, too, that he was really good-looking.

"There's a hint of an accent there." I sat and accepted a second cup of coffee. "What part of the States are you from, Sergeant?"

"That would be Mississippi." He shifted in his chair. "You're from Philadelphia—a Yankee."

I laughed. "Yeah, that's right."

"Philly is a great town, even if it is full of Yankees." He closed the folder and sat back. "You asked me to give you some information on the project we are building here—isn't that so, Lieutenant Stoyles?"

It had been a while since anybody had called me that. "Please—just Jack is fine by me."

"Well, just Jack, right now this whole damn place, as you can see, is nothing but a row of big tents. We are in the midst of building ourselves some barracks and getting the place outfitted, but it's slow going. Even with the number of ships that come and go from this place, we've had some trouble getting hold of the building materials we need."

I told him I was interested in all the contractors who had submitted bids for the project, specifically those contractors involved with the construction of the physical buildings that would make up the site. I understood the tendering process in principal, but I wondered if Callan had received any unusual bids for the construction work.

"Now that you mention it, Jack, there's something that's been going around in my mind since we started this whole barn dance." He went to the filing cabinet and pulled out a manila folder bulging with papers. "We understood from the beginning that this here island has been through some rough economic times, and they've had just about as much trouble with their various governments as ever a people ought to have." He flipped through the folder until he came to a sheaf of pale blue paper, the type used to print forms. "This here is the totality of bids on all the various aspects of this project. Why don't you go on and take a look at that, tell me what you see."

There was a flush of sudden recognition as I paged through the documents. Without exception every single bid was from Fayre Construction. In almost every case, for just about every job, Fayre Construction was the only bidder. Despite Octavian's insistence that his company had placed numerous bids, no other tenders had even been submitted, which meant Octavian had probably been warned off. I mentioned this to Callan, certain he'd already noticed it.

"Oh yeah." He grinned. "That's not all, Mr. Stoyles." He reached across and flipped through the pages until he came to a carbon copy of a typed page: an engineer's report on the building site. "We allow our contractors to subcontract engineering services as they see fit. It saves us the trouble of having to weed through the local applicants. We figure that a construction company that's been doing business here in the city will know who the best engineers are, anyway. That was how we hired Mr. Cartwright."

I flashed on Jonah Octavian's conversation with me, that day in his car. *Ken Cartwright submitted a report to the United States Army, stipulating certain site conditions. The report never reached its destination.* "This report is signed by Ken Cartwright."

"Yeah. Whether he wrote it or not is open to debate." Callan lit a cigarette. "Mr. Cartwright's report states outright that this building site is free of any abnormalities that might cause a structural compromise. Do you know what happened when we started to build here, Mr. Stoyles?" I confessed I didn't. "Some workers began excavating an area on the north side of the site in preparation for the erection of a barracks. Mr. Cartwright's report stated that the soil in the area lay upon good, solid bedrock—mostly granite, some shale. Recent heavy rains had destabilized the ground, which wasn't granite or shale or anything like it—I swear to God, Mr. Stoyles, it must be the one place on this whole goddamn island that isn't solid rock—and the trench collapsed, killing three men."

I let out a breath I didn't realize I'd been holding. "Jesus."

"Yeah."

It was more than an engineer's professional reputation was worth to make a mistake like that, and I said as much to Callan.

"That's just it, Mr. Stoyles. An engineer wouldn't make that sort of mistake. Hell, my old grandpa could go up there with nothing but a pointy stick and know there wasn't no rock underneath that soil!" He closed the folder and slapped it with the palm of his hand. "There's no way Mr. Cartwright wrote that report. His name's on it, but you and I both know it's not hard to forge a signature, especially if it's one that you're familiar with—if it's a signature that you see every day of your life and could probably copy in your sleep. Do you see what I am driving at, Mr. Stoyles?"

There was a long silence in the trailer, save for Thomas's typewriter. "Julie Fayre." I knew why Octavian had given me the manila envelope that day, containing Julie Fayre's employee identification card, among other things.

"Got herself a job working for Ken Cartwright, typing his reports and letters and things." Callan took a drag off his cigarette and crushed it in the ashtray at his elbow.

"Do you think she altered the report? Submitted one of her own in its place—a report that said there were no problems with the site?"

"That is exactly what I think, Mr. Stoyles—and I believe it is what you think as well."

It explained a lot: Julie's odd behavior, the check made out to Chris. "Where's the original?"

Callan leaned back in his chair. "I am not a policeman, Mr. Stoyles, and I certainly am not a private investigator, no sir, but I am willing to bet a week's pay that young Miss Fayre still has the original report and has either destroyed it or hidden it somewhere she thinks it will never be found."

Like the basement of the Heartache Cafe.

I thanked Callan and said my good-byes to him and Private Thomas. He'd given me a lot to think about, and I wanted some time to mull it over. I walked from Fort Pepperrell along the wide street simply called the Boulevard, which ran along the shores of Quidi Vidi Lake. It wasn't a lake as such—more like a large pond—but it was pretty, with its wide expanse of calm, blue water and the wildflowers and tall reeds that grew along its banks. I was glad I'd had a conversation with Sergeant Callan, but his probing questions about my past had made me very nervous. I'd come here to get away from that part of my life, from the sense of shame I felt at something that wasn't my fault, which I could neither control nor subdue, but which under military rules and discipline might as well have been painted on my forehead.

Do you understand the term "blue ticket," Lieutenant Stoyles?

Yes, sir.

Do you understand why you are getting one?

Yes, sir, I do.

Then get your pansy ass out of my office.

Maybe that was why I'd taken up with Judy in the first place, to prove something to myself—to prove I was a man in the commonly accepted sense, that I could perform with a woman, that I could be "normal," that I would no longer want the kinds of things I'd wanted all my life. But it all went south and I was left with nothing: no career, no job, no way to avail of any of the benefits so readily available to veterans whose discharge—unlike my own—was free of taint or suspicion. I told myself I'd come here to escape the things I felt after Judy died, but that wasn't the whole truth. I'd come here because it was as far away as I could get from everything.

JULIE FAYRE lived in one of the more venerable parts of the city, an area known simply as Georgestown, home to ponderous Victorian mansions built by the sorts of men whose fortunes rose and fell according to the mating habits of the northern codfish. I found Julie's place on Maxse Street, a narrow lane populated with wooden-framed houses; she lived in a large white house on the corner of Maxse and Monkstown Road. I didn't expect to find her at home, so I was surprised when she answered my knock—wearing a housecoat and not much else. "Well, hello, Jack! What brings you here?"

"I have some questions I want to ask you. Mind if I come in?"

"Well, I was just—"

I pushed past her into the house. An open suitcase sat on the sofa in the living room, and two smaller cases were stacked in the hallway near the front door. "You going someplace, Julie?"

"I thought I'd take a little vacation, perhaps go out to Gander for a few days. You know, my family has relatives out that way." She stroked the neckline of her housecoat, probably hoping to draw my gaze, but I ignored her. "Now that you're here, why don't you make yourself comfortable? I can fix us a couple of drinks." She turned to go into the kitchen, and I followed her.

"Where's the original report, Julie?"

"What?" She reached into the cupboard and took down a couple of highball glasses. There was some business with the liquor cabinet and more fiddling in the icebox. "What are you talking about, Jack?"

"The engineering report on Fort Pepperrell, the one you typed for Ken Cartwright, when you worked for him. What'd you do with it?"

She passed me my drink and raised her glass to me. "To the most handsome man in town."

"Stop avoiding the question." I thought about it for maybe half a second—then took a healthy slug of whiskey, and another. Predictably, it was good quality, and probably very expensive, but I didn't think a little thing like money would bother someone like Julie. "What'd you do with the report? Did you burn it? Tear it up?" The taste was mellow, smooth, and smoky, with a faintly bitter tang—just the kind of whiskey I'd expect in a place like this. I drank the rest of it off and set the glass down on the countertop. It was a measure of my agitation that I'd downed that drink without even the slightest hesitation—well, they say you're never really cured, and I guess that was true.

"I haven't the faintest clue what you're talking about." She laid her hand against her hip, and something in the pocket of her robe crackled.

I lunged forward, but she was too quick for me. She darted out of the kitchen and down the hall, and she was nearly at the front door when I finally caught up with her. I slammed her back against the wall and held her there while I delved into her pocket and came out with a long white envelope, addressed *poste restante* to a mail bureau in Athens.

"Thought you said you were going to Gander." There was a pain starting behind my eyes and I suddenly didn't feel too good. It had been ages since I'd eaten breakfast, and maybe that was it. "This says Greece. Jonah Octavian's Greek—from Athens."

"Give me that!" She struggled against me, fighting to get her leg up so she could knee me in the groin, but I used my body's weight to keep her pressed against the wall.

"Is this why Octavian's company didn't bother to put in a tender for the Pepperrell job? Because he figured banging you was worth it?"

"Give me that envelope! You have no business taking it. It's mine!" She flailed at me with clawed hands, her polished red fingernails just missing my eyes.

I grabbed the front of her robe and slammed her into the wall. "Just what kind of twisted game are you and Octavian playing, Julie? You want to tell me that?" Hell, I was enjoying this, or would be if it weren't for the headache throbbing at the back of my eyes. I held her hands above her head with one hand and ripped open the envelope with my teeth. "Ken Cartwright's original report." It was getting hard to see her. A subtle mist had begun to stain the edges of my vision. "So this seals the deal, huh? You're sending Cartwright's report to yourself in Athens. I suppose you know Greece is in Nazi-occupied territory?" I reached around her and put my palms flat against the wall. It was becoming difficult to speak, and I knew without a doubt that something was horribly wrong. "Nazi-occupied territory, Julie, but I can't say I'm surprised. That's what this has been about all along, hasn't it? Where've you been hiding this?"

"In the basement of the Heartache Cafe, Jack." She smiled sweetly and stroked my mouth. "Poor Jack. When's the last time you took a drink?" She poked her finger into the center of my chest and shoved. It felt like a steel spike being driven into my body. "You stupid, stupid man. You think you can manipulate me?"

"Julie...." There was a roaring, ringing noise in my ears like the sound of a dozen telephones all going off at once. "What did you put in my drink?" The wallpaper had a pattern of intertwining leaves and flowers, and it was sliding past me. I was slipping down the wall, and I couldn't stop myself from falling. The carpet rushed up to meet me, and the roaring in my ears intensified, shutting out all sound.

The last thing I heard was the sound of a woman's laughter.

I DIDN'T know too much for a while after that, and it was the feeling of cool water on my face that brought me out of it. I blinked a couple times and saw Sam Halim looking down at me. He was crouched beside me, bathing my face, and I was lying on the floor in Julie Fayre's Victorian house.

"Sam." It was hard to talk. My tongue felt swollen to about twenty times its normal size. "How'd you know...?"

"Lie still, Jack. The ambulance is on its way." I made to get up, but he pushed me back again. "Lie *still*. You have been poisoned."

"What? Poison?"

"Yes. Judging by the symptoms, I suspect it may have been quinine. Please, lie still."

"Sam, I'm so stupid. I knew there was something wrong with her." I reached out for his hand and held on to it. "You gotta get to Billy Ricketts. Tell him to get Octavian, and don't let Julie leave town! They're in it together, Octavian and Julie—"

"Jack, if you do not lie still and stop talking, I am going to have to gag you." Sam's brown eyes were full of genuine concern, and it touched me. "Please stay quiet. It is really very important." I felt the momentary impress of his lips against my cheek. "Do you trust me, Jack?"

"Yeah."

"If ever you have cause to question me—now, or in the coming days—remember that I am your friend."

"Okay, Sam. Okay." I couldn't keep my eyes open, but it didn't really matter. Whatever she had given me—quinine or something just as bad—was messing with my eyesight. There was a misty veil over everything, like looking through a steamed-up window, and the headache was making me nauseous.

Sam sat with my head in his lap until the ambulance arrived and they loaded me in.

I woke up in hospital several hours later with a sore throat, certain I'd spent the night throwing my guts up into some kind of tube or funnel while a doctor and two nurses watched.

Chris was sitting in the chair beside my bed, sound asleep with his chin on his chest. From the little I could see, he looked awful: pale and exhausted, with a day's growth of beard. I didn't want to wake him, but just then he opened his eyes. He reached out and laid his hand on my arm, his face close to mine. "Jack. Listen, don't ever pull a stunt like that again, huh?" He stroked my cheek, gently. "I mean, I get that you've been feeling bad, but bumping yourself off ain't the way to go about it."

"Bumping myself off?" As soon as I said it, I remembered Sam Halim's face, back there in Julie's house: *If you do not lie still and stop talking, I am going to have to gag you.*

"That Egyptian friend of yours, Sam Halim, told me all about it. He called the ambulance for you—don't you remember?"

"Yeah, the ambulance." The mist in front of my eyes was as disorienting as hell, and I found it hard to think straight, but for Chris's sake, I figured I'd better make an effort. "All's well that ends well, huh?" As far as jokes went—especially about something like this—it was pretty feeble.

"Yeah." His voice sounded flat, expressionless, like he didn't really believe me, but there was something else there too. "Jack, there's no easy way to say this, so I'm just gonna come right out and let you have it." He clenched his fists, then smoothed his palms against his thighs. "Sam's gone."

The declaration rang in the hospital room like the clanging of a bell. For a moment or two, I couldn't really comprehend what he was saying. It made no sense at all. "Gone? What do you mean, gone? Where? How could he—where would he go? I mean, why would he—"

"No." Chris caught hold of my hand and held on, and the sound of his voice filled me with dread. "He—there was a car accident." His fingers tightened on mine. "He was driving back to the Consulate. I guess he'd been on some business, and, ah...." He swallowed hard. "Some guy was driving a Packard down Duckworth Street—maybe he had a snoot-full, I don't know. He hit Sam's car. They took Sam to the hospital, but he, ah... he didn't make it, Jack." He patted my hand. "He didn't make it."

CHAPTER EIGHT

I SPENT the next four days lying in my hospital bed and wondering what the hell had happened. I still couldn't get it through my head that Sam was gone—that he'd been killed by a drunk driver and that was that. It didn't make any sense to me, and nothing fit together. I couldn't shake my gut feeling that there was a lot more to this, and as soon as my eyesight cleared enough for me to dial a telephone, I got busy finding out what was really going on. I called the number on the card Sam had given me, the one connected to his direct line, but all I got was some lady telling me it had been disconnected. Next I tried the main reception desk of the Consulate. They weren't exactly thrilled to talk to me, and it showed.

"British Consulate, Alexander Somerset speaking. How may I direct your inquiry?" The voice was young, snotty, and upper-class, with hints of the private hunt club, Eton and Savile Row.

"Listen, Alexander, I'm looking for someone."

"I suggest you contact the local police department or the American Consulate."

"No, you don't understand—you have a consular official working there, an Egyptian named Samuel Halim. I've been trying his direct line, but all I get is a recording saying that it's been disconnected."

"Samuel Hamel, did you say?"

"Halim. Samuel Halim." You idiot. "He's originally from Cairo. He's been here for a while now. He's an assistant to the British Consul."

There was a long pause on the other end, during which I could practically hear Somerset rolling his eyes. "I'm terribly sorry, sir, but

77

you must be mistaken. There are no Egyptian nationals employed here. Good day."

"Wait!" This was insane. I felt like I'd fallen through the looking glass. "His name is Samuel Halim. He's about five feet eight inches tall. He has brown hair and brown eyes. His wife's name is Tareenah and he has four children."

"I'm terribly sorry, sir. We have no one—"

"Goddammit, he drinks a lot of coffee! He likes to sail. They said he was killed in a car accident a few days ago, but that's wrong. He's not dead."

"Sir, I really cannot help you. We have never had any Egyptian nationals working here, and I know of no one with the surname Halim. Good day." His tone was final, and so was the click at the end of the line.

I fell back on my pillow and ground my teeth together in frustration. I picked up the phone again and called Dan O'Hagan at the *Telegram*.

"Jack! Jesus, boy, how are you? I haven't heard from you in donkey's ages. How are you getting on?"

Dan listened while I told him about Sam, but I was careful not to say anything about Julie or that little scene at her house the other day. I figured some things were better kept out of the papers.

"So you're telling me that this Halim fellow, this African—"

"Egyptian."

"Right, this Egyptian fellow was killed in a car accident, only he wasn't." There was a pause, and I could hear his pencil scratching away at the other end. "When was the accident and where?" I told him. "Any other casualties? No? Okay." His chair creaked, and I knew he was settling back in it, probably lighting a cigarette. "I'll have a look through what we got and let you know, but I can tell you, Jack, I don't remember any accident here on Duckworth Street, not recently anyway. If somebody was killed, I'm sure we'd know about it."

"One more thing, Dan—if you're not too busy?"

"Shoot."

"Jonah Octavian—he's been in the city awhile, hasn't he? For a few years now?" I wondered if he knew who Octavian was.

"Oh, *him*." He chuckled. "Octavian's so full of sh—look, Jack, don't believe too much of anything Octavian says. He showed up here about six months ago, from Athens. He says he's some kind of contractor, but he's never built much of anything that I can see. As far as I know, Octavian's real good at flapping his gums, making everybody think he's some kind of big deal."

Octavian had lied about Fayre Construction, saying Fayre had repeatedly outbid his company for the Fort Pepperrell project. He had even supplied evidence that Julie was involved with Ken Cartwright's murder somehow. If Julie and Octavian were in bed together—metaphorically or otherwise—why was he undercutting her?

Maybe sabotaging her—or at least, appearing to sabotage her—was a good ploy if his intentions were to deflect suspicion. He and Julie acted like they hated each other's guts, and maybe that was Octavian's way of playing it, to keep the heat off. It wasn't real original, but I'd seen it work before.

I thanked Dan and hung up. I knew the newspaperman couldn't promise me anything, but he'd never led me wrong before, and if he said there hadn't been any such accident, I believed him.

I called the Heartache and Chris picked up. It sounded pretty busy there, judging by the noises in the background. He seemed glad to hear from me, but he had nothing much to tell me. "Picco was in here the other day, asking for you. I told him you'd had a little accident, and he said he might come up to see you."

"Constable Picco?"

"Oh, yeah, that's the other thing, he's Sergeant Picco now."

"A promotion?"

"Yeah, can you beat that? I guess Ricketts was pretty impressed with him." He lowered his voice. "I got another piece of information that might interest you, Jack. Jonah Octavian's left town. Yeah, sold his business, the whole shot, and lit out for parts unknown." I wondered if Julie had gone with him, but I kept my mouth shut—and then Chris answered even that question for me. "Julie's coming over later today. We figured we might go have lunch in the park if it's not too busy. Anita and Janice said they can cover, but I wanted to check it out with you."

Everything in me wanted to warn him, but I knew that was something I'd have to do in person. I couldn't figure out why Julie had stayed in town after our little episode. She had to know her scheme with Octavian was running on borrowed time, that it was only a matter of days until I was released from the hospital and then I'd be coming after her. She'd killed Cartwright and she had tried to kill me, and in this country, murder was still a hanging offence. What kind of inducement or twisted loyalty tied her to Octavian to the degree that she'd risk her own neck? She'd planned to go to Greece with him—but Greece was occupied by the Nazis, and nobody in their right mind intended to go there, unless they had a damn good reason. Julie knew I'd found her out—that was the reason for the quinine in my drink—and she had likely surmised that I'd told Chris what I knew. Whether I actually had or not was immaterial. The possibility that Chris knew the truth about her was enough to make him a threat. More than likely she was sticking around on Octavian's orders, to take care of Chris and me.

"I think I'd feel better if you stayed put." I knew he'd resent me for cutting in on him and Julie like this, but I was doing him a favor. "Dave's got to stay in the kitchen, and I'm not sure Janice and Anita could handle themselves if something serious broke out."

"Okay."

"I'll make it up to you, Chris, I promise."

"Yeah, sure, Jack. It's no big deal." We spent a couple minutes making small talk, but I could tell he was in a hurry to get off the phone. Yeah, he'd be sore at me for a while, but I'd rather have him angry than dead.

I got Sergeant Ricketts on the first try, and he seemed glad to hear from me. "I never got the chance to thank you properly, Stoyles, for helping out young Picco."

"Never mind that. If you really want to thank me, you can buy me a cup of coffee at the Heartache sometime. Chris tells me Picco got himself promoted?"

"Don't spread this around, Stoyles, but I figured it was the least I could do. The lad's proved himself time and again, and what we were paying him was poor enough to begin with. God knows none of us are rolling in it, but he's got the full charge of his sister, and you know, she's a bit simple in the head." He coughed and changed the subject. "Something tells me this isn't a social call. What's on your mind?"

"The guy who knifed Johnny Mahoney—what was his name?"

"Yorgus Panodopolous." There was pride in Ricketts's voice. "Only took me three bloody weeks to learn to pronounce it. What are you worrying about him, for? Bull Parsons took care of him, or don't you remember?"

"How long have the Germans been in Greece? Do you remember?"

"What? Germans? Are you feeling all right?" He huffed out a breath. "Of course you're not feeling all right, but you know what I mean. April—they went in there in April, only the Bulgarians and the Italians were already—Lord Jesus, Stoyles, what are you asking me for? It was in all the papers."

"Stamos, huh? That's a Greek name."

"My mother was Greek."

Sam Halim wasn't dead. Every instinct I had said it wasn't true, that there was something more here, something bigger than I figured on, something really important. "Ricketts, did you ever catch up with Bull Parsons?"

"No. Why?"

"It's just a hunch I have, but I need to talk to Parsons. Any idea where I might find him?"

"Going to drag your hospital bed behind you?"

I ignored him. "Where does he usually drink?"

Ricketts grunted. "On the waterfront, but sometimes you can find him in Lottie's Pub. Good luck—you bloody idiot."

LOTTIE'S PUB was one of those places that, if you have any sense at all, you keep away from. It was located in a row of squat brick buildings on the extreme eastern end of Water Street, not far from Steele's Fine China and Silver. There was nothing like fine china or silver inside of Lottie's, which was as dark, dank, and filthy as spilled beer and a lifetime's worth of cigarette smoke could make it.

Lottie herself was somewhere between forty and older than dirt, a sloppy dame with huge, sagging breasts and a potbelly. Her dyed red hair was piled up on top of her head and secured with whatever might be handy—pencils, cocktail straws, bobby pins if you were lucky—and her hands were like the claws of some dead, rotting animal. Everybody said Lottie was crazy, that she had a real bad temper, that she once beat a woman's head in with a flatiron, but I'd seen her kind before: a cheap floozy with the personality of battery acid and a face to match.

"What are you doing in here, Stoyles?" Lottie was standing behind the bar, separating dirty glasses from dirtier ones. "Get going before I calls the cops on ye."

"I'll go when I'm good and ready. You seen Bull Parsons in here lately?"

She lit a cigarette and stuck it in the gap made by a missing tooth. "Who wants to frigging know?"

"I do." I took out a twenty and laid it on the bar, careful to keep my hand on it. "I'll make it worth your while."

"Will ye?" She sneered at the money. "I've seen twenty dollars before."

"Sure you have, but not for a long time. How much can a dame like you pull in these days? Five bucks, but only if he's drunk and legally blind?"

"You get out of here!"

She grabbed for the hammer she kept under the bar and made a swing at me, but I stepped back out of her reach. "Twenty dollars, Lottie, and I know you can use it. Hell, you spend that much on smokes. Where is he?"

She didn't need to answer. A huge, shaggy form disengaged itself from a table near the back and shuffled toward the bar: Billy "Bull" Parsons. "What the Jesus do you want?"

"Some information." I held the twenty up in front of him. "There somewhere we can talk?"

He jerked his head toward the back of the room. "Come on, then."

We walked past shadowy men sitting in the dark, and half-drunk locals; Patsy Mullins, the prostitute, sat crouched against a wall, slurping up whiskey and whispering to herself. I knew enough to keep well out of her reach. I'd heard stories of her temper and how she'd once clobbered a big, strong cop in the foyer of the General Hospital—hit him so hard he went down like a torpedoed battleship and didn't wake up for a week.

"What's on your mind?" Parsons levered his bulk into a chair and peered at me out of hooded eyes. I decided to get straight to the point.

"Did you kill a Greek merchant seaman named Yorgus Panodopolous? He's the one who knifed your friend Johnny Mahoney, isn't he?"

"Did I kill him?" He laughed, but it wasn't a nice sound. "Why would I tell you?"

"No reason, but I'm figuring you didn't. Or if you did, you'd have to be the dumbest palooka this side of the dirt to stick around here after bumping some guy off. So—did you kill him? Maybe to get him back for knifing Johnny Mahoney?"

"I don't know nothing about it." He sucked back some beer and made a face. "Me and Johnny were down on the waterfront one night, following some fellows what came off a boat. They always got money. Johnny said we should stick 'em up and take their money, and we did. Three or four of 'em came after us, but we got away. Then Johnny got killed that day. I don't know who did it."

"Was it you?"

"Fuck off."

"Do you have any idea? About anything?"

Either he was too drunk to understand the implied slight, or too stupid. "No."

He made a grab for the twenty, but I held it out of his reach. "One more question. Who let you out of the lockup the night Phonse Picco went missing?"

"Nobody let me out. I let meself out. The key was right there, in the door."

I wasn't sure I'd heard him right. "In the door."

"Yeah."

"Do you remember who put the key in the door?"

"Some cop—big fellow with a red face. Ricketts, his name is."

"Ricketts."

It was conceivable that Ricketts had, in an extraordinarily busy moment or a lapse of memory, left the key in the cell door—conceivable, but not very likely.

I suddenly wished Sam Halim were here.

I GUESS I was still feeling the effects of the quinine, because by the time I got back to the Heartache Cafe, I was weak and sweaty. I barely made it in the door before I collapsed into a chair, my heart going like a trip hammer. Luckily the place was nearly empty, except for a dock worker sitting by the wall, reading the newspaper, and a slick corner boy with oiled hair, sipping a Coke and chewing on a toothpick.

Chris saw me and came hurrying over. "Jack! What the hell are you doing? I called the hospital and they said you took off." He crouched down and mopped my face with the towel he habitually carried over his shoulder. "You shouldn't be out of bed."

"I'll be okay." I smiled to reassure him I wasn't going to drop dead on the spot. "How about a cold glass of water?"

"Sure, Jack, anything."

I stood. "Bring it back to my office, huh?"

"Aw, Jack, why don't you go upstairs and lie down? You look like you were run down by a truck." He suddenly couldn't look at me. "Whatever you took, it's probably… what I mean is—"

I interrupted him. "Chris, I didn't try to kill myself."

"What?" He blinked. "But Mr. Halim said—"

"I think you maybe misunderstood." Perhaps now wasn't the time to tell him the whole truth, but it would have to be soon. Chris was in as much danger from Julie as I was. It wasn't right to keep him in the dark. "Chris, I was poisoned."

"Poisoned."

"Come on back to my office." I ushered him in ahead of me and closed the door. It felt good to sink into my own chair, behind my own desk, in my own place. "Chris, this is gonna be hard for you to hear, but I figure I gotta tell you sometime." He was still standing by the door, so I told him to sit. He sank onto the couch and gazed at me expectantly. I struck a match and lit myself a cigarette. "Julie Fayre poisoned me with an overdose of quinine."

His face smoothed out, becoming strangely expressionless. "Julie did it."

"Yes. Chris, she's not who you think she is. Julie Fayre is in it up to her pretty little neck with Jonah Octavian—they're business partners and probably lovers—and that means you can't trust her. She came after me, and you can be damn sure she'll come after you."

His fists clenched. "Jack…."

"Chris, listen to me! Julie's tying up loose ends, and then she's going to meet Octavian in Greece. He's already gone. That's why he sold his—"

He was over the desk, fists clenched in the front of my shirt. I had never seen him so angry. His face was flushed and sweating, veins throbbing in his forehead. "You don't know what you're talking about! You hate Julie! You've always hated Julie—you're jealous of her! You think I don't know—"

I slapped him just hard enough to make him fall back.

He stared at me, then raised a hand to his mouth. "Okay." His voice was shaky. "Okay, Jack, if that's the way you want it."

"Chris, listen to me!"

"Why should I listen to you, huh?" He tore off his apron and tossed it onto the couch. "I ain't gonna listen to you anymore. Nothing you say makes sense to me, Jack." He yanked the door open.

"Where are you going?" I came out from behind the desk and grabbed his arm.

"None of your business where I'm going."

"Chris, you can't be out wandering around. Julie's looking for you. If you get in her way, she'll put a bullet in you!"

He yanked his arm away. "I'm going! Don't try to stop me, Jack. I'm going."

IT WAS harder to find Alphonsus Picco now that he had been promoted, but I managed to track him down, thanks to his sister, Norma, and a helpful dispatcher at Constabulary headquarters. Picco was in charge of the west end of Water Street, an area populated by large department stores—Ayres and Sons, the Bowring Brothers—and inhabited by a strange mix of shoppers, petty thieves, servicemen, and the ubiquitous "corner boys" in their shabby coats and flat tweed caps.

Picco supervised a division of ten other policemen, and I found him on the corner of Water Street and Ayres Cove, looking westward and writing something in his notebook. His uniform was new, and his buttons had been polished to within an inch of their lives. His boots shone with an unnatural brightness, and the crease in his trousers could have sliced paper. He greeted me with his customary enmity. "Stoyles, what do you want?"

"I need your help, Sergeant. Oh, by the way, congratulations on the promotion."

"Mm." His gray eyes flickered over me, his gaze dismissive, but I wasn't bothered. It's hard to really hate a man when you've had his cock in your mouth. "Someone stole your spoons?" He jotted something in the notebook. "Let me guess. The printer misspelled your name on the menus."

I yanked the notebook out of his hands. "My name isn't on the menu, Sergeant, and if you don't mind, I'd like you to pay attention."

He crossed his arms on his chest. "What?"

"I need you to find somebody." I explained, as quickly as I could, about Julie and her deal with Octavian. I told him what my suspicions were and why he needed to act quickly, before she skipped town.

"Why didn't you ask Ricketts?" There was suspicion in his eyes. "You and him are chums, aren't you?"

I grinned. "Not like you and me." I couldn't tell him that I no longer trusted Ricketts, or that I suspected Ricketts was on Octavian's payroll. If Bull Parsons hadn't walked out of the lockup that night, I would have never suspected Ricketts—the idea would have never entered my mind—but the evidence against him was mounting. Sure, Parsons could have lied to me, and maybe he would have, if he had any reason. But my gut insisted Parsons was telling the truth.

"All right." To his credit, Picco didn't hesitate or even blink. I walked with him to a public phone and waited while he called up the dispatcher. "There you are, Mr. Stoyles." He grabbed his notebook back and tucked it into the breast pocket of his tunic. "Is there anything else?"

"I think that's it." I put out my hand, not quite touching him. "Thank you."

"Right." He nodded curtly and turned to go.

"Hey, Picco?"

"Yes?"

"You look damn sexy in that uniform." It was a bit too flip, so I amended it. "What I mean is, the promotion looks good on you."

He raised an eyebrow. "Good day, Mr. Stoyles."

When I got back to the Heartache, Chris was gone, but Dave Chan said there was a message for me from Dan O'Hagan at the *Telegram*. I called O'Hagan's direct number and got him right away.

"Jack, listen—you won't believe this." He cleared his throat. "That accident you asked about? Never happened. There was no accident anywhere near downtown—hasn't been for a while now, which is pretty bloody surprising, considering the way they drive around here."

He isn't dead, he isn't dead, he isn't dead. "No accident."

"Nope. No accidents downtown. I dunno who told you that, but they gave you a wrong number."

"Thanks, Dan." I hung up and thought about what Dan had just told me. There was no accident and Sam Halim hadn't been killed downtown.

So where was he?

CHAPTER NINE

I WAITED at the Heartache Cafe while Picco and his men scoured the city for Julie. It wasn't inconceivable that she would try to skip town like she'd done before, working her way across country by rail or hopping a Greek freighter to Athens to meet up with Octavian. There were a dozen different ways she could escape, and Picco's men couldn't be everywhere. There was nothing I could do about it, not with Chris gone and nobody to mind the store, so I stayed put, gnawing my fingernails and waiting for the phone to ring.

It was well past four that afternoon when something finally broke. The Cafe was nearly empty and I had just brought a load of dirty dishes to the kitchen when the phone at the end of the bar went off. "Heartache Cafe, this is Jack."

"This is Sergeant Picco. Miss Fayre is in custody." The line went dead.

"Wait, Picco—where did—ahhhh!" I hung up. I wondered where they'd caught her—at the railway station, waiting to board a train, or maybe hanging around the waterfront, hoping to catch the attention of some unwary Greek willing to give her passage to Europe?

I didn't have time to do too much musing, because just then Chris came in. His clothes were rumpled and dirty, like he'd been rolling in the gutter, and there was a cut over one eye. His lip was bleeding. He threw himself into a chair and buried his face in his hands.

"Hey… you okay?" I pried his hands away from his face. "What happened? Did a runaway truck do this?"

He laughed mirthlessly. "Sergeant Picco's fist did it."

"Oh, boy. Chris, don't you know you can get jail time for assaulting a police officer?"

"I was there when they brought her in. I was at the desk, asking for Picco, and he comes in with Julie in handcuffs."

"Stay here. I'm gonna get a wet cloth for your face." I ushered out the single remaining customer and turned the Open sign to Closed on the door, then went through to the kitchen to get a wet cloth. Dave was finishing the clean-up from lunch, but I told him to go on and gave him the rest of the day off with pay. I figured Chris wouldn't want an audience for this sort of thing.

"You should have seen her, Jack." He submitted to my inept ministrations and let me clean the blood off his mouth. "She looked at me like she never saw me before."

"It's not your fault, Chris." It sounded weak and stupid, but what else could I say? I wasn't about to launch into a big speech about how some people are just sick and wrong inside. He was already a victim.

"Was it true?" He caught hold of my hand, the one holding the cloth. "What you told me about Julie—about the poison and all that stuff—was it true, Jack?"

The expression in his eyes cut me to the heart, but it was better that he heard the truth from me. It was all going to come out at the trial anyway. "Yeah, Chris. It's all true."

He nodded. "She's no good. She was never any good." He let go of my hand. "Jack, do you think… I mean, there's going to be a trial, right?"

"Yeah, Chris. There's going to be a trial."

"But what about Octavian? He put her up to this! If it wasn't for him, Julie would have never done—" He stopped. "Yeah. Maybe I should keep telling myself that, huh?"

I laid my hand on his shoulder and squeezed gently. "It isn't your fault. Chris, you gotta believe me." I cupped his cheek in my hand. "Don't crucify yourself because of this. You didn't know. Nobody knew about Julie. She had everybody fooled."

I invited Chris to stay with me for a few days, but he said he'd rather go on home, and I let him. I offered to drive him the couple of blocks to his apartment, but he said the walk would do him good. Watching him like this, seeing him tear himself up inside because of a no-good dame, was doing a number on me. I figured the best thing to do was go upstairs and lie down.

I passed by the bar on my way upstairs, and I lingered for a minute, looking at the bottles. Maybe one drink wouldn't be so bad? It would help me sleep, for sure. I could mix in a little sugar and some hot water and make myself a toddy—a nice hot drink would send me right off into dreamland, and anyway, it was only one, so where was the harm in that? I unscrewed the top of a bottle of Gordon's London Dry Gin and sniffed it. A green smell like trees and turpentine. The taste would be astringent on the tongue, and it would burn as it went down, a subtle flame that glistened on the lips....

My nostrils filled with the scent of hospitals and medicine, and in my mind, I saw it all again: the small room with its white walls, the gleaming metal stirrups, the crackling white paper on the examination bed, and the lingering smell of blood. *Judy, oh God! Judy.* I took hold of her hand, but she was already cold, and her vacant face gazed up at the ceiling with an expression of astonishment and wonder, whispering to me as the life drained out of her. Above the waist, she might have been a worshipful sylph gazing upon the faces of her gods; below the waist was a mess of congealed blood, rotting tissue, and death.

I put the bottle back and went upstairs.

I UNDRESSED and lay down on the bed, staring into the artificial darkness of the afternoon, the ceiling fan turning slow arabesques above my sweating head. A slight breeze from the harbor teased the window blinds, allowing sudden, unexpected shafts of light to peer into the room. My thoughts went around in my head like a Coney Island carousel. I had just managed to drift off when I heard someone banging on the Cafe door downstairs. The banging got louder and more insistent, so I threw on some clothes and went to see who it was.

"We're closed! Go away!"

"Open the door, Stoyles!"

I recognized that voice. "Picco." I threw open the door, and the young sergeant stood there in civilian clothes. "What the hell do you want?"

"Can I come in?" He seemed to be trying his best to be civil.

"Yeah, sure, come on in." The spectacle of Picco politely wiping his feet on the Cafe's welcome mat made me smile. I ushered him to a chair and put on a pot of coffee. "What time is it?"

"Nine thirty."

The proximity of his voice nearly sent me out of my skin. He'd trailed me into the kitchen. "Picco! Goddammit, don't do that."

"I daresay he told you—Chris."

"That you and him had a dust-up? Yeah, he told me."

"I wanted to make sure you knew I didn't want to get into it with him." Picco sighed. "We brought her in to headquarters, and he was there, waiting. I told him to get out of the way, but he wouldn't move." Picco's pale eyes were troubled. "I think he wanted me to hit him. He came at me and I had to defend myself."

I believed him. "Yeah. Chris is pretty broken up about the whole thing." I took a long look at him. "That's not why you came here, though, is it?"

"No." He leaned against the counter. "Julie Fayre already pleaded guilty. She doesn't want a trial."

"She doesn't want a trial." I knew immediately what he was getting at. "So she'll be sentenced."

Picco nodded. "As soon as possible." He nodded toward the percolator. "Your coffee is boiling over, Jack."

I snatched up the pot and fetched two cups. "She's looking at murder… and that means the death penalty."

"That's exactly what it means." He accepted a cup of coffee from me and added cream and sugar. "I wanted to let you know. Maybe you can tell Chris. I don't… I'm not sure if there's anything I can do to…." He shook his head. "Sorry."

"Phonse, when they… what do…." I gazed into my coffee. "I guess nobody's been stoned to death here for a while, huh?" It wasn't even funny, but it was the best I could do.

Picco's face was carefully expressionless. "She will be executed according to the prescribed method."

"Jesus, Phonse."

He put down his cup. "I'd better be going. Jack, I only came by to tell you—I didn't want you to hear it from the papers, seeing how Chris knew her and everything."

I saw him to the door and locked it behind him. The Cafe suddenly seemed stark and empty.

How the hell could I tell Chris his girlfriend would die by hanging?

FROM ARREST to admission of guilt to summary judgment didn't take very long at all, and by the end of August, Julie Fayre was set to climb the scaffold. They don't hang people in public anymore—at least not around here—but it still had that tang of subtle horror to it.

I didn't open the Heartache on the morning of Julie's execution. I figured Chris had enough to deal with. Since neither Chris nor I were related to Julie, we weren't allowed to attend her execution, which would take place inside the prison walls. We weren't even allowed to be present in the waiting room, and no matter how much I pleaded, the warden refused to reconsider.

"I'm not an unkind man, Mr. Stoyles, but look at it from my point of view. What do you think would happen if every man jack who wanted to could come and watch an execution?"

Julie was due to be executed at exactly midnight, and since I figured Chris could use the company, I picked him up at his place late in the afternoon and brought him home with me. He was more animated than I'd ever seen him, talking loud and waving his hands around—maybe that was his way of coping with the situation. He wasn't making much sense, but I let him talk if that was what he needed to do.

Dave had come by earlier in the day to see if I needed anything. He'd left a cold supper in the fridge for us, and I made a mental note to let Chris have whatever he wanted to drink, and as much of it as he needed.

There wasn't really anything to say, and we both knew what we were waiting for, so we passed the time listening to the radio and playing cards, but it didn't help much. The hours seemed to crawl by while we pretended interest in *The Doyle Bulletin* or our poker hands.

Around ten thirty, Chris suddenly got up from his chair, walked to the bar, and stopped, both hands pressed flat on the polished wooden surface. "I can't take it, Jack."

I approached him and laid my hand on his back. "I know." I smoothed the taut muscles. "I know."

"She deserves it—I know she does—but I can't—Jesus Christ, none of this seems real!"

I fished out a bottle and poured him a double scotch, straight up. "Here. Get outside of that."

He stared at the whiskey like he'd never seen it before. "Jack, do you think it hurts?" He picked up the glass, his hand shaking, and downed the whole thing in one go. "When they—you know, the trap door there—they drop the bottom out—"

"Chris." I didn't want to answer him. I'd seen a guy hanged once, back in 1937 at San Quentin. As far as deaths went, it was messy, shocking, and unpleasant. "Don't do this to yourself."

"Will it be quick?" He kept his gaze focused on the polished surface of the bar. "They just sort of jerk the thing out from under you, right? And you fall through?"

I refilled his glass and pressed it gently into his hand. "That's right. You just fall through."

"Do they die right away?"

I rubbed the back of his neck; the muscles felt like knotted cords. "Yeah," I lied, "of course they do. It's over quick. She won't feel a thing."

He turned around, eyes full of tears. "You promise?"

"I promise, baby." I took him in my arms and just held on to him. "I promise."

At eleven thirty we checked that all the doors were locked and went upstairs to my apartment. Chris wasn't saying much. He'd only had two drinks, but he stumbled on his way up the stairs, clinging to my arm. By then I think he was so far gone in grief that he couldn't really see or feel much of anything.

I sat beside him on the bed, and pretty soon we both got really quiet. He asked me if I could turn out the light, so I did. We sat there in the dark, listening. The city noises filtered into the room through the open window: passing cars, a bicycle, a man whistling a sea chanty. The clock ticked closer to the appointed hour, and I remembered it: San Quentin, midnight, and a cold mist from the Bay clinging to everything.

I'd come up from Frisco just for it, and I was grateful for the chance to walk with him as far as they would let me go. We'd grown up together, he and I, had gone into the service as young men just out of school, but somewhere along the way, I'd lost track of him. He got down on his luck, took to drinking heavily, and beat his young wife to death one night in a fit of drunken rage. Yeah, it was the same old story. At the foot of the scaffold, he reached to shake my hand, but I dragged him close to me, holding him. In the back of my brain, I had some weird idea that if they saw how much I loved him, they would turn him loose. He hugged me and made some kind of joke, and then the guards were taking him away and he put his hand on the railing and started the climb.

Everybody says there are ten steps to the gallows, and when a man walks up those ten steps, he thinks about all the things that he's ever done wrong in his life—repents of his sins, I guess you could say. I think that's a load of bull. I watched him walk it and I saw his face, and there was nothing there but naked horror. He didn't mind dying—I knew him—but he was afraid of pain, and worse, he was afraid of making a fool of himself, of crying out or begging them for mercy that wasn't theirs to give.

And we were at midnight. The clock on the Basilica tower chimed, and Chris made a strangled noise and started up. I caught him at the bedroom door; he fought me but I held on.

"Goddammit, Jack, let me go!"

"I can't do that, Chris. You know I can't do that." I wrapped my arms around him, and he sagged against me, all the fight gone out of him.

If the initial drop breaks the condemned person's neck, a hanging death is quick, almost instantaneous. If the neck doesn't break, the death can take as long as twenty minutes. The tolling of the cathedral's bells seemed to measure out the end of Julie Fayre's life.

I held Chris in my arms while he cried, and when he turned his head to seek my mouth, I didn't refuse him. We lay together on my bed, kissing and touching, and when he took my hand and guided it to the warm bulge of his clothed erection, I didn't refuse him that either.

I wasn't stupid, I knew this wasn't love or anything like it. I knew it was comfort, and I knew he needed something from me, something I was glad to give. I stripped him tenderly and laid him down and smoothed my palms down the warm expanse of his beautiful body, following those caresses with warm kisses and murmured words. I pressed my mouth to the center of his chest and licked each of his nipples gently, teasing each tiny nub to hardness. I parted his thighs and took his swollen cock into my mouth and sucked him, while he shivered and wept above me, his hands clenched in my hair. His body rode the swelling tide of pleasure, strong thighs contracting, hips pumping, and I reached around to cup his tight buttocks, holding him close to me.

His breathing quickened and his hands slid out of my hair to clench at his sides. "Jack... oh Jack, I'm gonna come... you come with me, Jack...."

I let his cock slip out of my mouth. I lay on top of him and kissed him, and we rocked together, rubbing ourselves on each other, bodies shuddering toward the end. Then a bright light burst inside my head and I came so hard I saw stars. In a stroke or two, he was there too, crying out as his cock pulsed his hot seed over my belly and chest. He shivered down to sanity, and we lay there for a long time, the breeze from the window cooling our bodies.

"You said his name."

"Huh?" I turned my head and gazed into Chris's eyes. There were tears clinging to his lashes.

"You said Sam Halim's name, Jack."

"No, Chris, you're wrong. I couldn't have." Sam Halim, with his big, dark eyes and his gentle hands and his voice—Sam Halim, who was missing and presumed dead, except I didn't really believe that.

"You did." He traced the outline of my lips, consummately gentle. "Any idea where he is?"

"No." I sighed. "No, I... have some ideas, but... no, Chris. I don't know where he is." Maybe he had gone back to Cairo.

Chris's gaze was steady. "Then you should go and look for him, Jack."

He didn't need to say the rest. I knew exactly what he meant.

I knew.

WHEN I woke up the next morning, Chris was gone, but he'd left a note on the pillow: *Thanks for everything. You're a true friend.* I knew he would be all right. It would take a while and he'd feel pretty rotten in the meantime, but he would be okay in the end. That's the thing about people. We're resilient because, really, when you get right down to it, we don't have any other choice.

I made a pot of coffee and took a cup to one of the tables in the back. A boy had already been around with the morning papers. I made a mental note to stash them as soon as I'd finished reading them—the last thing Chris needed was to see the news of Julie's execution splattered all over the front page—but when I unfolded *The Daily News*, I got the shock of my life: RICKETTS FIRED, RESULTS OF POLICE PROBE, and underneath, in smaller type, *Constabulary sergeant took bribes, freed prisoners.*

I'd hardly had time to digest it when someone knocked at the door. Dave looked out from the kitchen, but I told him I'd get it. I threw off the lock, and there was Sergeant Picco, spit-shined and as neat as a pin. He was almost civil, for a change. "Stoyles."

"Don't stand in the doorway, Picco. Come on in."

He grimaced. "Thank you." He stepped across the threshold and looked around him with an expression of distaste. By now I knew it was just something he did—a part he was playing, a way of pretending he was above all this sin and transgression.

"Something I can get for you?"

"I… came to see your bartender, Mr. DuBois."

I noticed the small package under his arm. "You brought him a present."

Picco's gaze was full of anguish. Clearly he was torn between doing the right thing and doing the human thing. "What happened to Mr. DuBois's lady friend wasn't his fault. He must be feeling horrible right now." He thrust the parcel at me like he was afraid it might explode. "Please give this to him when he comes in." He made to turn away, but I caught his arm.

"Sergeant, I wanted to thank you for your help. I'm afraid I haven't been as… polite to you as I could have been, other circumstances notwithstanding."

He understood immediately what I meant, and a slight smile curved his lips. He blushed and ducked his head. "If you ever tell anybody about that, I'll kill you."

I crossed my heart and hoped to die. "You're a good cop, Picco—a real good cop—and as you know, I tend to get into scrapes. I'm hoping I can call on you to help me out sometime."

He fixed me with a glance. "You heard about Ricketts?"

"Yeah."

He sucked in his breath and made the tutting noise that, around here, is shorthand for acute disapproval. "He was taking money from Octavian. Octavian and Ricketts had that money delivered to my house to try and make me look bad."

"That diverted suspicion away from Ricketts and onto you."

"Yes. Once Octavian had Ricketts where he wanted him, he needed to get me out of the way for a while—so Octavian's men hauled me off the street and stuffed me in that cave over on the Southside."

I gave him the benefit of my biggest grin. "Yeah… that cave."

"I meant what I said." He narrowed his eyes, and his accent was suddenly very strong. "I'll kill ye. I'll break your fuckin' legs, I will."

I couldn't help but laugh. "Take it easy, Picco." Something occurred to me. "So Octavian turned on Julie Fayre, is that it?"

"I don't know. Octavian almost certainly had something to do with Johnny Mahoney's murder. I think him and Parsons got too close to that Greek ship down there in the harbor. Octavian was probably bringing something in here, but he couldn't offload whatever it was with Mahoney and Parsons hanging around all the time, so he stuck a knife in Johnny Mahoney—or paid someone to do it. Lots of people around here are hard up for a dollar."

"So Octavian, Ricketts, and Julie Fayre were probably splitting the Fort Pepperrell money three ways. Octavian's company didn't bother to bid on the project because it was easier to have a dummy corporation—or a stand-in like Fayre Construction—do it, and he could control matters behind the scenes."

Picco nodded. "You're not half bad at this, Stoyles. What I mean is, you got a brain. You ever think about being a police officer?"

I waved it off. "There's more to this—Octavian, the Greek ship, Johnny Mahoney, Fort Pepperrell—it all points to something more than just skimming money off various construction projects. Julie killed Ken Cartwright to shut him up about the site problems—that meant more money for Octavian and his buddies. She poisoned me and was coming after Chris because we caught on to her, and she couldn't have that. But what else is Octavian doing? There's more to this—that Greek ship, for one thing."

"Stamos, huh? That's a Greek name."

"My mother was Greek."

I knew why Sam Halim had disappeared. Consular attaché, my ass.

I must have looked like I was having some kind of seizure or something, because Picco grabbed my forearm. "Hey! You all right?"

"Phonse, you're a goddamn genius." I grabbed him by the shoulders and planted one on him, right there in the middle of the Cafe.

THE YOUNG lady behind the counter at Western Union was pretty, polite, and seemed genuinely interested in helping me when I explained what I wanted to do. "But, Mr. Stoyles, sir, what if there's no one by that name to receive your cable? You'll have wasted your money."

"Oh, someone will receive it," I said. "They're the police, right? They're always looking for information."

"All right, Mr. Stoyles, if that's what you want." She handed me the message form. "Write your message here."

I knew exactly what I wanted to say, just two words: I KNOW.

I paid the lady and walked away smiling.

WHEN I got back to my cafe, the lunch rush was in full swing and Dave was busy in the kitchen. I had given Chris the day off, but Anita and Janice were busy serving customers, and my other bartender—a silent Dutchman named Piet—was busy mixing drinks.

Anita unloaded a tray of sandwiches and Cokes to a table in the corner and came over. "Jack, there's a fellow over there waiting to see you." She nodded at a thin, somber-looking gent in a pale gray suit. "He says he's from the government."

Great. Tax trouble was all I needed. I went over and introduced myself and offered him a drink, hoping to lessen the blow—but he wasn't from the tax department. He was from the museum.

He offered me a thin, dry hand to shake. "Morris Blount, Mr. Stoyles. I'm from the Newfoundland Museum. Is there somewhere we can talk privately?"

"Uh, sure. Step into my office." I showed him to a chair and shut the door. "So, what am I in for? Did I steal something from one of the exhibits?"

He gazed at me, expressionless and flat-eyed, and I felt like a minnow right before it's eaten by a shark. "Last week we were moving one of our exhibits, and we found something that doesn't belong." He reached into his briefcase and brought out a small wooden box. He placed the box on my desk and opened it to reveal a little bowl, about as large in diameter as the palm of a man's hand and seemingly carved out of a single piece of speckled, gray-and-pink stone. "This is a diorite bowl, Mr. Stoyles. It is Egyptian, late third dynasty, and was unearthed in an area about two kilometers south of the Giza Plateau, near Cairo." He lifted it out reverently and laid it on my desk.

"Pretty." I didn't dare touch it. I had an idea how much a thing like that was worth, and I was terrified I'd break it. "So this was in... your museum?"

"Correct, and that is not all." He reached again into his briefcase and brought out a plain manila envelope, the contents of which he dumped onto my desk: a slip of folded paper, a book of matches from the Heartache Cafe....

...and the gold cartouche given to me by Sam Halim.

"I don't understand." *If ever you have cause to question me—now, or in the coming days—remember that I am your friend.*

"The bowl was located at the rear of our exhibit dealing with the early peoples—the Thule, the Dorset Eskimo—on a ledge that is normally inaccessible to museum visitors." Blount folded his hands and regarded me quizzically. "Why someone should leave an ancient Egyptian artifact in such a place is, frankly, inconceivable, but it was the addition of the items which you now hold in your hands that puzzles us the most."

"The gold cartouche was a gift from a... dear friend." *There. I give you a cartouche of your own....* "I guess he left the book of matches too. I'll be honest, Mr. Blount. I don't have any idea where the bowl comes into it."

He gestured at me. "A thread, Mr. Stoyles."

"Huh?" I glanced down at my shirt, thinking maybe I had a button loose. "What do you mean?"

"Are you familiar with the legend of the Minotaur?"

"Yeah—Greek or something, isn't it?" *My mother was Greek.... Stamos is a Greek name....*

"When the Athenian hero Theseus went into the labyrinth to fight the Minotaur, the goddess Ariadne gave him a ball of string."

"Uh-huh."

Blount's lips tightened. If I didn't know better, I could have sworn he was fighting off a smile. "So he might find his way *back*."

I sat there staring at him while the clock above my desk counted off the moments. "A ball of string." I reached out and touched the bowl with just the tips of my fingers, and found it cool and smooth.

"Diorite is an extremely hard stone, Mr. Stoyles, and very difficult to work with, but ancient artisans recognized its innate beauty. Even the most unpromising chunk of diorite could be shaped into something beautiful, something... useful." He placed the bowl back into its protective box and handed the box to me. "There you are, Mr. Stoyles." He rose to go.

"Wait just a minute! You just said this was—you said this was valuable—and now you're just gonna leave it here?"

Blount put on his hat. "Unfortunately, Mr. Stoyles, the museum does not have the financial resources to send someone to Cairo, and yet the bowl must be returned to its rightful owner." He fished an old-fashioned pocket watch out of his vest and peered at it. "Oh dear, I must be going. Mr. Stoyles, thank you, and if ever I can be of any service to you, please don't hesitate to call. I'll just show myself out."

He slipped past me and was out the back door, moving faster than a guy like him ought to. I went after him, but I was too slow. He had vanished, probably into any one of the narrow laneways that crisscrossed this part of the city.

I went back to my office and got on the horn to the museum. "Look here, some guy called Mr. Blount just left a valuable piece of Egyptian... uh... stuff here. I can't be responsible for everything that people leave in my cafe, so you better send somebody to come and pick it up, okay?"

The young man at the other end of the phone seemed genuinely puzzled. "Mr. Blount, did you say?"

"Yeah, Blount—skinny guy with a light suit and a briefcase."

"Would you mind waiting for a moment, Mr. Stoyles?"

There was a thump as he laid the phone down and the sound of people talking in the background and things being moved around on the desk. I waited for five minutes, then ten, and I was just about to hang up when there was a click—and the low hum of the dial tone filled my ear.

When I called back, the line was busy. It was busy every time I called, and I spent the better part of the afternoon calling. It was nearly six when I remembered the slip of paper Blount had given me. I fished it out of my pocket and looked at it.

There were two words, printed in block letters, in black ink: I KNOW.

I understood what I had to do.

CHAPTER TEN

IT TOOK a few days to tie things up around the Heartache. I called my local suppliers and advised them that all deliveries would go to Chris and that he would be responsible for ordering and for taking possession of whatever the Heartache needed to keep going in my absence.

I got hold of Frankie Missalo and explained about Julie, and I asked him if he'd keep an eye on Chris, sort of look out for him.

"You sure this is what you want to do, Jack? Egypt's neutral, but maybe you don't want to be heading out into the unknown like this. Case you haven't heard, there's a war on."

"I know there's a war on." I pretended to sock him in the jaw—it was an old joke between the two of us—and he laughed. "It's just something I have to do, Frankie—you know?"

He laughed. "Is it a dame?"

"No. No, it's not a dame... it's a little stone bowl, actually."

Frankie looked at me like I'd lost my mind. "A bowl." He shook his head. "I never could figure you out, Jack, but hey, if it makes you happy...." He stuck out his hand and I took it. "Send me a postcard with the pyramids on it, huh?"

"Thanks, Frankie. You'll, uh...." Chris was tidying up behind the bar so I lowered my voice. "You'll keep an eye on him?"

"Till you get back." He tilted his head and peered at me. "You are coming back, aren't you?"

"Yeah, Frankie. I'm coming back." I walked him to the door and waved good-bye as he ran to catch his bus. It was late afternoon and the Heartache was empty of customers. The radio was playing softly, and dust motes spun in the stray shafts of sunlight shining through the plate glass windows at the front. Everything was as it should be. Leaving was going to be so strange—it seemed like I'd just arrived here five minutes ago—but at the same time, it felt right, like something I had to do.

My suitcases were packed and the diorite bowl was resting in its wooden box, wrapped in several layers of cloth for the long overseas voyage. I had purchased a flat gold chain from a local jeweler and had the cartouche Sam had given me mounted on it like a pendant. I wore it inside my clothes, the gold warming to my skin, and whenever I was alone, I'd pull it out and smooth the inscription between my fingertips, remembering. He'd been so formal that day, but there was a kindness underneath the affectation of ceremony.

It is inappropriate to refuse a gift....

Things had fallen into place for me almost from the start—at least as far as this trip was concerned. When I'd explained things to Chris, he had immediately volunteered to look after the Cafe while I was gone, and urged me to get started as soon as possible. Frankie Missalo had turned up one afternoon with twenty bucks he owed me, and as soon as he heard the story of Sam, the museum, and the diorite bowl, offered to find me a seat on a military flight—something that's only ever done for really important people, ambassadors and politicians and other high-ranking officials. My passport was updated, and the special visas I needed to enter the country were pushed through much faster than I would have ever thought possible. I was going to Egypt.

I was actually going to Egypt.

"JACK? GOT a minute?" Chris poked his head around the door of my apartment, his jacket in one hand.

"Sure, Chris. Come on in." I cast around for somewhere to sit. My suitcases, some of them still open, were laid across every available flat surface, and the various maps and guidebooks I had been staring at for days were scattered everywhere. "Sit down, if you can find a place."

"Jack, I just wanted to say good-bye and wish you a good trip." He stuck his hand out, but I dragged him into a hug. "I'm gonna miss you." He pressed his face into my shoulder and hugged me hard. "Place won't be the same without you."

"I'll be back." I pulled away a bit and looked at him. He'd lost weight in recent days, and his eyes were shadowed with dark circles, probably from lack of sleep. "I asked Frankie Missalo to look in on you while I'm gone." He opened his mouth to protest, but I interrupted. "Humor me, Chris. Huh?"

"Sure, Jack." There was a noise from downstairs, and a voice calling his name. "I gotta go."

I looked out over the banister and down into the Cafe. Alphonsus Picco was standing by the bar, waiting for Chris. He looked as nervous as a bridegroom. "Picco, huh?"

Chris was blushing and I was glad. Goddammit, I wanted him to be happy. I wanted us all to be happy. "Yeah. He, uh… well, after that whole thing with Julie, I…."

"No need to explain."

"I really like him. He really likes me. We just go for walks and stuff. We talk."

I grinned. "You kissed him yet?"

"Yeah." He wouldn't look at me.

"Is he a good kisser?"

"Jack!"

"Okay, okay…." I made a gesture of surrender. "You're happy, I'm happy."

"Jack, don't spread it around, okay? He's a cop. It could cause trouble if people knew."

"I'll be as silent as the grave." I shook his hand. "Take care of the Heartache till I get back, huh? And Chris?"

"Yeah?"

"Take care of yourself."

I watched him go down the stairs and out the door with Alphonsus Picco, and I'll admit I felt a little bit sad—but I always get that way when things change, even if the change is for the better. When it comes to the past—especially my own—it's like I have selective amnesia.

I checked my suitcases and closed them up, and laid my passport and my visas on the table where I'd find them as I went out the door. I wound my watch and set my alarm for six in the morning and turned out all the lights in my apartment.

It was nearly midnight when the telephone rang, and I'd been asleep for about half an hour. I groped for the light, turned it on, and jiggled the receiver off the hook. "Yeah?"

"Hello, Jack. Did I wake you?" His voice was as warm and rich as I remembered.

"Sam. Sam, where are you?" I clutched the receiver till my knuckles hurt. "Where are you calling from?"

"I am in Cairo." A long sigh, and silence before he spoke again. "Something curious has happened to me, Jack. I'm afraid I don't remember anything. I don't remember how I got here, or why I came." He began to weep, and the sound of it nearly broke my heart.

I clutched the phone as if I could will myself to him through the wires.

"Hold on, Sam. Just hold on. I'll be there in the morning."

Valley of the Dead

CHAPTER ONE

AUGUST, 1942, and the sun was just rising over the Nile when we arrived in Cairo. I'd slept most of the way over, lulled into insensibility by the droning of the big plane's engines, waking only once when a grinning blond kid in an Air Corps uniform offered me a hot cup of coffee. I didn't know what Frankie Missalo had told them, but none of the other guys spoke to or even looked at me. Maybe they figured I was on some covert spying mission, trying to slip into Egypt on the QT or something. Either way, I was grateful for the quiet and the chance to catch up on my sleep, but every time my eyes closed, I ended up dreaming about Sam.

You ever have one of those ordinary days when it seems like nothing interesting is going to happen to you? I mean the sort of day where you just disappear into your work until the whole world goes away? Sam Halim walked into my life that way, on a day so ordinary it could have been any one of a thousand others. By the time he walked back out, I was hooked, brother, but good.

I'd been in agony ever since the day he'd disappeared from Newfoundland. It was hard to believe he'd only been missing for two weeks. When I'd heard his voice on the telephone the night before I left, it was all I could do to hold on. *I'll be there in the morning*, I'd told him. We were pushing it with everything we had, to fly from Newfoundland to North Africa in just one night, but that didn't matter to me. They could burn the engines out, just as long as I made it into Cairo in one piece.

That was the other thing, I'm originally from Philadelphia, but a lot of things happened back in Philly that would make it pretty hard for me to go back there anytime soon. For a while, I just drifted, rootless, wondering what the hell I was going to do with myself.

Then my old pal Frankie Missalo had come along. *"Listen, Jack, why don't you come up to Newfoundland with me? They're building all kinds of stuff up there and the whole place is ripe for the picking."*

Frankie and I had grown up together, roaming the mean and dirty streets of Kensington, earning a place for ourselves with our wits, as well as our fists. How we managed to stay out of real trouble is beyond me. By then the Irish mob had much of Philly under its thumb and boys like us were easy targets for guys like Dean O'Banion, fellas who wouldn't hesitate to enlist us as runners or worse. Maybe it was because of the church—Frankie was an altar boy and my old lady made sure I went to mass almost as often as I brushed my teeth—or because Father Danny O'Keefe patrolled the streets like a modern day knight errant, but we managed to escape our early days in Philly more or less unscathed. It was said that Father O'Keefe carried a blackjack hidden underneath his cassock, and if he caught you swearing, chewing, smoking, or taking the Lord's name in vain, he'd let you have it—and if the Father let you have it, you'd get it again when you got home, sure as shooting. Even Frankie's old lady, who was crippled with arthritis, wasn't above cutting him a few sharp cuffs about the ears when he deserved it.

There wasn't all that much to do in Philly when we were young men, apart from running guns or illegal whiskey or both. Frankie and I both said we'd probably go into the army; we joined up long before the whole thing went to hell at Pearl Harbor. Only thing was, he stayed in while I got kind of... waylaid. You'd think that with a war on, they'd want as many able-bodied men as they could get, but I guess that didn't extend to my kind. When Frankie suggested we light out for Newfoundland, I was game—not that I'd ever heard of the place. *"Lots of Army contractors up there, and lots of Yanks like us needing somewhere to get a proper cup of coffee. Come on! Ain't you always said you wanted to have your own place?"*

It sure started that way. And then Sam walked in, and after a while I figured, hey, this is getting kind of cozy, maybe there's something more here than meets the eye. I let myself believe that he was something I could count on—that this handsome, debonair Egyptian had come into my life to save me from myself. All that was before Sam disappeared.

I got a late-night phone call, the way people do in the movies. *"Where are you calling from?"*

"I am in Cairo." A long sigh, and silence before he spoke again. *"Something curious has happened to me, Jack. I'm afraid I don't remember anything. I don't remember how I got here or why I came."* He began to weep, and the sound of it nearly broke my heart; I clutched the phone as if I could will myself to him through the wires.

"Hold on, Sam. Just hold on. I'll be there in the morning."

Before he disappeared, Sam had given me a gold cartouche on a chain. I was wearing it around my neck. In my suitcase was the tiny diorite bowl handed off to me by the mysterious man known only as Mr. Blount. He'd made a point of contacting me at my cafe just so he could give me the artifact.

"Last week, we were moving one of our exhibits, and we found something that doesn't belong. This is a diorite bowl, Mr. Stoyles. It is Egyptian, late third dynasty. The Museum does not have the financial resources to send someone to Cairo, and yet the bowl must be returned."

Why me? He'd said the bowl was found in the Newfoundland Museum, along with the gold cartouche that Sam had given me; that either of these items ended up there was incredible. I had a strange feeling that this was just the beginning, that there was much, much more to Sam's disappearance than merely bad luck or the satisfaction of some wartime grudge.

"Normally we'd land at the airport in Heliopolis, but you know how things are these days." The blond kid was back with another cup of coffee, which I gratefully accepted. It was strong and hot, just the thing to clear the clinging web of sleep from my mind. "We'll be putting down at a little airstrip just outside of town. I hope that's okay with you."

I laughed. "Yeah, that's just fine. It's not like you guys need my personal permission." I knew they had to be careful. It was only a few weeks ago that Rommel's brazen push toward Cairo had been stopped at El Alamein, and it was pretty much guaranteed that he'd try it again. Things weren't going so well for the Nazis in North Africa, and we all hoped that if Rommel made a second assault, Monty's boys would stop him in his tracks.

The level rays of the rising sun glanced off the wing as the pilot banked the plane sharply, and suddenly the city of Cairo seemed to spring up out of the earth like one of those pop-up books they sell for children. I forgot everything—the blond kid, my coffee, the fact that I was even in an airplane. I'd never seen anything like it. I had expected a dusty desert landscape, but what I saw instead was the broad sweep of the Nile River, with lush green plains stretching north as far as the eye could see. On the other side, there was the Sahara, with its miles and miles of gently rolling dunes colored golden by the rising sun. It was more beautiful than I had imagined, and I remembered a daydream I'd had one day, standing on a bridge straddling the Delaware River. I was sailing on the Nile, borne away and drifting before the prevailing winds, serene and unencumbered.

I'd climbed that bridge to kill myself, but there had been a tiny sailboat tacking before the wind, venturing down the Delaware like it had every right to be there and then some. It had stopped me cold, and the sight of it reminded me of a picture I'd seen somewhere, of graceful feluccas sailing on the Nile. Right then, I had wanted to go to Egypt more than I'd ever wanted anything in my life. I didn't know how I'd get there or when. I just knew that I was going to Egypt. It was fate. I hadn't counted on any of the things that had happened to me the past few months: my spur-of-the-moment move to Newfoundland, the cafe, a new life. I'd been miserable in Philadelphia, caught up in something dark and horrible and ugly, something I figured I could never escape—and before I even knew what was happening, I had a cafe of my own in downtown St. John's, a sexy Louisiana bartender named Chris, and a brand-new lease on life. And Sam Halim.

I met Sam when he came into my cafe looking for directions. That wasn't so unusual; tourists did it all the time. But Sam had been different. After the hard time I'd had back in Philadelphia, I wasn't looking to fall in love with anybody. No, sir, I'd had my fill of love and everything that went with it.

"I am looking for a particular building, which I believe is somewhere around here. They told me it has an arch on the front. It is a red brick and sandstone building. Do you know it?" I'd never heard a voice so deep and rich, full of sun and desert heat and exotic sensuality. He wasn't particularly tall—maybe five eight or so. But, my God, he was beautiful: huge, long-lashed brown eyes in a lean face, a sensuous mouth under his tightly groomed mustache. I'd felt my knees go weak just looking at him. All it took was a glance, brother, and I was gone for good.

"There's the airstrip." The blond kid nudged me with his elbow. "We'll be on the ground in a minute. Better buckle in."

I fastened the safety belt and tried to quell the jumping in my stomach. It wasn't the flight or the prospect of our imminent landing that was doing it to me, but that finally I was in Egypt. Finally, I was going to find Sam and help him remember.

I HAILED a cab outside the little terminal building and climbed inside. The heat, even this early in the morning, was incredible; it rose off the ground in shimmering waves, and the air felt like a hot, dry blanket. "You ever get used to the heat around these parts?"

The driver was a young fellow perhaps twenty years of age, wearing native dress. "The heat? I do not notice, effendi. My name is Shiva." His English was excellent. "Where might I be taking you today?"

I gave him directions to Shepheard Hotel on the Shari' Muski in the Ezbekieh district. Frankie Missalo had given it the thumbs-up as far as hotels went. I knew nothing about Cairo, and I hadn't wanted to take a chance on ending up in some fleabag buried out in the native quarter. If Frankie thought Shepheard's was the best place to stay in Cairo, I believed him.

The Cairo streets were absolutely jam-packed with vehicles, people, and animals, all seemingly intent on getting ahead with little regard for anyone or anything. Shiva merged fearlessly into what appeared to be a never ending swarm of traffic and, horn blaring, blasted through an intersection with utter disregard for other cars, many of which were forced to a screeching halt to avoid us. A donkey cart, piled high with fresh produce, swerved in front of us, mounting the sidewalk in a last-ditch bid to avoid a motorcycle carrying two young men and a goat. Two blocks later, Shiva executed a right-hand turn that involved multiple hand signals (some of the offensive variety) and a sudden and unexpected slalom across three lanes of traffic.

"Hey, maybe you should slow down there, Shiva." I was suddenly glad I'd opted to sit in the back seat instead of the front. "You're liable to hit somebody."

"It is fine." He smiled over his shoulder at me. "In Cairo, everybody understands the way the traffic works."

There were no stop signs or traffic signals that I could see, and I figured the lines painted on the road were there for decoration, since nobody seemed to care what lane he was—or wasn't—in. Add to that the sheer confusion created by people, vehicles, and animals, and by the time Shiva dropped me at the front entrance of my hotel, I was ready to fall on my knees and kiss the ground. I even tipped him extra, as thanks for getting me there alive.

Shepheard's was incredible. I'd seen luxury in my time, but this was something else completely. I could have shaved using only my reflection in the marble floors. I wasn't sure what sort of picture I made, standing there grimy and unshaven from endless hours in an airplane, with my duffel bag slung over one shoulder and my luggage heaped up in a pile around me. I'd also brought my .45 Colt automatic with me, but unless they specifically asked, I was keeping that particular bit of info to myself. "Jack Stoyles. I have a reservation."

The young woman at the desk was one of several clerks who were busy being officious.

"Mr. Stoyles, of course. North Atlantic Command advised us to expect you. Your room is ready. Please, follow me."

North Atlantic Command? She had me all wrong, but the thought of a hot shower and clean clothes overrode my innate honesty, so I kept my mouth shut. She showed me to a suite decorated in cream and gold and blue, dominated by a huge bed that you had to walk up a flight of steps to get to. "Wow." I dropped my bag on the floor. "This is really nice."

She handed me my key. "My name is Tania. Should you need anything at all during your stay, Mr. Stoyles, please call down to the front desk, and we will be happy to oblige."

I reached into my pocket for a tip, but she held up a beautifully manicured hand. "All costs have been taken care of, including gratuities." She handed me a small, buff-colored envelope. "This message was left for you at the desk." And before I could thank her, she was gone. I closed the door and tore open the envelope, expecting to find a note from my old pal Frankie. A slip of yellow paper, neatly folded in half, fell out onto the floor. I bent to pick it up. The handwriting didn't look at all familiar to me. *Mr. Stoyles,* it read, *you will please meet me on the terrace for tea at four o'clock this afternoon. Observe the red flower.*

Red flower? What was that all about? I turned the note over, but there was nothing written on the back. Whoever had sent it hadn't bothered to sign it. Frankie had told me how, in the old days, people would make appointments to have tea on the terrace at Shepheard's, that it was a kind of see-and-be-seen ritual. You knew you were somebody if you took afternoon tea in the English tradition on the terrace. Well, I didn't know if I was somebody, but if Red Flower wanted to meet on the terrace, I was game.

I stripped off my grimy clothes and went into the bathroom. The tub was huge, as lavish as everything else, and I was hoping there was plenty of hot water. I turned the shower on full and just stood under the spray for a while, letting the water wash away the dust of my journey. Maybe it was the heat, or maybe I was just missing him, but I found myself thinking about Sam. I closed my eyes and let my imagination run wild, and pretty soon the water started to feel like somebody's hands on my body….

…like Sam Halim's hands on my body. Oh yeah, now there was one hot fantasy: naked with Sam under a blood-warm stream of water, touching him and being touched in return, smoothing my palms over his wet skin, his mouth on mine. It was like those dreams I'd started having right after I met him, of sailing on the Nile and making love under the hot Egyptian sun. We'd never done anything, had never gone any further than a kiss, but I somehow knew the things he'd like, the way he'd want to be touched and the caresses that would make him cry out, make him forget himself, make him come.

I wrapped one hand around my cock and let the other slide across my chest, touching, teasing my nipples and the flat of my belly. The hot water thundered down on my nape and shoulders as I stroked myself, and somehow it seemed like Sam's hand was covering mine, and his arm was around my waist, holding me. I came like a freight train, my knees almost buckling from the force of my orgasm. And through my half-closed eyes, I could almost see him standing there in front of me, water dripping down his face and beading on his lashes. *This is what I want, as well as you.*

I turned off the water, staggered to the bed, and was almost instantly asleep.

WHEN I stepped out onto the terrace at five minutes to four that afternoon, the waiters were wearing native dress and the typically inscrutable expressions you see in all those desert movies. I'd slept for what seemed like days and woken with a raging appetite. I hoped that the tea here was a full English affair, with sandwiches and pastries. I felt like I could eat the proverbial horse, dressed with a little mayonnaise and nestled between two thick slices of San Francisco sourdough.

I wondered when Red Flower would show up and introduce himself. It turned out I didn't have long to wait. Someone brushed against my elbow in passing, and I smelled a hint of some exotic perfume. The red flower was a giant hibiscus pinned to the lapel of a pink dress.

Red Flower was a woman.

"Mr. Stoyles." She wore a broad brimmed hat that partially shielded her face, but I could see that she was beautiful—dark-haired and dark-eyed with a neat figure. I wondered who she was and who had sent her, and I wondered if I needed to worry. "I have taken the liberty of reserving a table away from the crowd. If you would care to follow me?" She led me to a tiny table already set for two, located behind a group of potted palms. A silent waiter appeared to seat us. Red Flower said something to him in Arabic, and he disappeared.

"Doesn't this sort of ruin the effect?" I gestured at our surroundings. "I thought the point of having tea on the terrace was to be seen."

"Is that why you came here?" She leaned over the table. "To be seen?"

"Maybe I should be asking you the same question." It felt like being interrogated, and I didn't like it.

"Mr. Stoyles"—she looked up as the waiter reappeared, bearing a pot of tea and a three-tiered tray loaded with dainties—"will you take tea?"

I was more than capable of fixing my own plate or anybody else's, but I reminded myself that this was their country, and they did things differently here. She selected sandwiches and tiny cakes and poured the tea.

"Thank you."

"You no doubt are wondering who I am and why I have summoned you here." She gazed at me with her beautiful liquid eyes, and I figured this was some kind of ploy. I'm naturally suspicious, and I'd heard about all the different tricks your average Egyptian employs to get himself a little of your tourist baksheesh, but she didn't seem the type.

"Yeah, you could say I'm a little curious." I sipped my tea. It was excellent. "Maybe you can tell me what your game is."

A muscle twitched at the corner of her mouth. "Mr. Stoyles, I know you are here looking for Samuel Halim."

I'd been buttering a scone; I stopped. "Yeah?" There was something not right about this. No. Strike that. Everything about this wasn't right. I had the distinct feeling I was being set up.

"I, too, am very interested in finding Samuel Halim."

I put my knife down with a *clang*. "Is that so? Suppose you tell me what for."

Her dark eyes were suddenly full of tears. "My name is Tareenah, Mr. Stoyles. Samuel Halim is... my husband."

I was glad I hadn't taken a bite of my scone because I'm pretty sure I would have choked. Yeah, I knew Sam was married; it was one of the first things he'd told me once we got to know each other. I just couldn't figure out what she was doing here, or how she knew about me. "I'm... pleased to meet you, Mrs. Halim."

She covered her face with her hands and cried, and something inside me just crumbled. Call me a sap if you like, but I can't handle seeing a dame cry. I pulled out my handkerchief and offered it to her, mumbling what I hoped were comforting words. But I didn't dare touch her. I knew better. Your average Egyptian male doesn't take too kindly to a foreigner looking at, never mind pawing over, a native woman. I'd end up beaten to a pulp and dumped in an alley somewhere—if I were lucky.

"Thank you." She accepted my handkerchief and dabbed at her tears. She really was the most astonishingly beautiful woman I'd ever seen. I could tell she hated losing her composure like that, and in front of a foreigner. "Mr. Stoyles, you are wondering how I came to know about your... friendship with my husband." She pleated the damp handkerchief in her hands as she talked. "You are wondering why a woman like me would take such chances, meeting you in a public place."

"Yeah, I wondered about that." I didn't know a whole lot about Egyptian customs. Not every woman chose to wear the veil, and I understood it was a matter of religious devotion to those who did. Religious or not, however, an Egyptian woman was expected to observe certain behavioral conventions, and if Mrs. Halim had seen fit to meet me—a foreigner and an unmarried man—in public, her reasons must be pretty important.

"When I married Sam, I knew that his work was very important to him and also very dangerous." She picked up her cup and sipped her tea. "I knew that he would be called upon to travel, and that I might not hear from him for weeks at a time." She shrugged. "Such is the nature of his profession, that there is often physical danger."

"Physical danger?" She'd lost me. "Wait a minute. He's the assistant to the British Consul in Newfoundland. How dangerous could it be?"

She raised her eyebrows. "Assistant to.... Oh, Mr. Stoyles, no. I imagine Sam told you that as a covering tale, as you Americans say."

This was getting more and more confusing. "He's not the assistant to the British Consul in Newfoundland?"

"Mr. Stoyles, my husband is a captain with the Cairo police."

You could have blown up a fifty-story building right in front of me then, and I wouldn't have even noticed. "He... did you say... he's a cop?" I'd always figured there was more to his story than Sam had originally told me, but I hadn't counted on this. Sam, a cop? It explained a lot of things, though, come to think of it: his intelligence, his excellent physical shape, and his air of eternal watchfulness.

"You did not know."

I gulped down some tea. "No. No, I didn't."

A waiter passed by, and I stopped talking, but he was merely conveying a tray of dainties to a table in the far corner. Two blonde American girls, maybe sixteen years old, sat with a gray-haired man who was probably their father. The girls wore pastel dresses in some light fabric, with hats and gloves to match; the older man was smiling—a little painfully—as both girls chattered at him.

"So if he's a Cairo policeman, what was he doing in Newfoundland?"

She shook her head, lips pressed together. "I don't know. There are aspects of my husband's work that have to do with the war, and he is not free to discuss things with me or with anyone else. Mr. Stoyles, I am afraid. Sam was to have returned home several weeks ago. Since then, I have heard nothing from him. I question the police almost daily, but they always tell me the same story: they have no information, and even if they did, they could not divulge anything for reasons of national security."

I helped myself to a tiny square of something that seemed made entirely of nuts and honey. "Mrs. Halim, I'm not sure what I can do to help."

She extended her hand across the table, but did not allow herself to touch me. "Find him, Mr. Stoyles. *Please.* I have some money of my own. I will pay you what I can."

"Oh, no." I stopped her as she was opening her purse. "Not a chance, lady. I never take money from women."

"You will not help me." Her shoulders sagged. "You have no intention of helping me to find my husband."

"Mrs. Halim, the only reason I came here was to find Sam, so you can bet I'm going to help you." I smiled, but I was careful not to look directly at her; that kind of thing doesn't go over too well in Egypt. "I'll stay here as long as I can. I can't promise you anything. I'm a restaurateur, not a detective."

"Oh, thank you!" She clasped her hands together. "Thank you so much. Thank you. *Shukran Gidann!*"

I FIGURED the first place to start my search would be the Cairo Police Department, so first thing the next morning, I went down to find a taxi. As luck would have it, Shiva was waiting in front of Shepheard's with his engine already running. If I didn't know better, I could have sworn he was following me. "Not at all, effendi, but I make it my business to anticipate your needs." When I told him to take me to the Cairo police, he didn't even ask questions, just shifted into gear and pulled out into the noisy, smoky chaos of the Cairo street. "You know, effendi, I am not any ordinary taxi driver."

"Uh-huh." What was Tareenah Halim's angle anyway? How much did she know about Sam and me? She knew we were friends, but I somehow doubted she'd understand if I told her Sam and I had kissed—or maybe she would. I'd heard from more than one person that open and public displays of affection between men were quite common in Arabic societies, even encouraged, as a kind of bonding ritual. All the same, I found it hard to believe that any devout Moslem would cotton to the idea of two men kissing in anything other than friendship. It was kind of hard to tell what Mrs. Halim would think; she was difficult to read. Sure, she'd started crying on the terrace at Shepheard's, but maybe that was calculated, designed to make me open up and tell her everything I knew. I'd seen dames use that kind of manipulation before, so I wouldn't put it past her. In spite of her careful efforts to make me think she was harmless and delicate, I sensed there was steel in there somewhere, hidden underneath her pretty pink dress and red hibiscus flower.

"I anticipate and fill your every need, effendi Stoyles." Shiva grinned at me in the rearview mirror. His teeth were white and very even. "I am your friend."

"Hey. How do you know my name?"

"I had only to inquire at the hotel." But he sounded uneasy, and his gaze slid away from mine.

I didn't believe him, and I wasn't about to let it go, but right now my main concern was getting some answers. Luckily, Shiva knew the city well, and before too long, we were pulling up in front of the police station—how he knew which police station, I couldn't figure, and this made me really uneasy. Ever since I'd arrived in Egypt, I'd been besieged by people who seemed to know why I was there, and I didn't like it. What happened if some knife-wielding crazy decided to take exception to me? Was there anybody I could call for help? Come to think of it, was anybody in Cairo what he or she seemed to be? I felt in my pocket for the tiny diorite bowl, making sure it was still there; I'd get Shiva to take me to the museum after I'd been to the police station.

"Uh, look—"

"I will wait for the effendi Stoyles." He produced a folded newspaper from between the seats and sat back.

The inside of the police station was pretty much what you'd expect: a chaos of ringing telephones and conversation, the continuous movement of people up and down the corridors and in and out of the building. I approached the main desk, where a tall, skinny guy with great big ears was leaning on his elbows, staring down at the contents of an open file folder. My Arabic wasn't the best, but I'd gone to the trouble of buying a phrasebook; on the long plane ride over I'd amused myself by learning the half-dozen or so that I figured I'd need. I approached the desk. "*Salam alekum. Sabah el-kheir.*"

Big Ears looked up. "Peace be with you, also, and good morning." He had a faintly British accent, and I felt more than a little foolish. English seemed to be the *lingua franca* around here, what with the war and so many different nations all trying to score one for their side.

"You speak English, huh?"

"So it would seem." The arch of his right eyebrow could slice through flesh. "What can I do for the Americani?"

"I'm looking for—" I figured there was no point in being coy about it; best to just come right out and say. "I'm looking for Sam Halim."

His attention shifted back to his file folder. "Captain Halim is out of the country on important business. Good-bye." The telephone rang, and he reached behind himself to pick up the receiver. "*Aiwa? Assif. Mish fahiim.*" He placed his palm over the receiver and looked down his nose at me. "I cannot help you. Good day."

"No, you don't understand. It's very important that I see Captain Halim."

"Captain Halim is out of the country on—" He snapped to taut attention as a slightly older officer with sergeant's chevrons on his sleeve approached the desk.

"What is going on here?" The sergeant picked up the file folder and flicked a glance over it, then turned to scrutinize me. "I heard you asking about Captain Halim." His eyes were huge black pools of utter contempt. "He is out of the country on important police business." His voice was sharp and slightly nasal, and he struck me as one of those people who always sounded irritated. You know, the kind of guy who thinks talking to you is a waste of his time.

"Yes, I know, but it is very important that I speak to someone connected with him." I did my best to look desperate. "Please. This can't wait."

"I am Sergeant Ibrahim Samir, Captain Halim's second-in-command." He lifted a hinged section of the counter and summoned me forward. "Come with me." I followed Sergeant Samir's elegantly trousered and beautifully shaped behind down a narrow corridor and into a room marked PRIVATE. He closed the door behind us and gestured at a small table and chairs. "Sit."

"Sergeant Samir, I appreciate your seeing me on such short notice—"

"You will produce appropriate identification. Failure to do so will result in immediate incarceration." He leaned against another table with his arms folded on his chest, while his big, black eyes bored into me like a pair of diamond-tipped drills.

"Like to play hardball, huh?" I took out my wallet and laid it open on the table. "There. Knock yourself out."

He didn't smile. "The American style of humor has never appealed to me." He picked up the wallet, and I couldn't help noticing that his hands were lean and tanned, and that the forearms left bare by the rolled-up sleeves of his shirt rippled with muscle. The same shirt was open at the neck, offering me tantalizing glimpses of his throat's smooth hollow, sprinkled with dark hairs. Like many of the Egyptians I'd seen in the streets, he wasn't real tall, but he sure made up for it. His face was square-jawed, lean and tanned, with full lips, a straight nose, and beautifully arched brows framing liquid black eyes. He was clean-shaven, albeit with a faint dusting of beard, and I wondered whether Sergeant Samir was just coming off the night shift—maybe that would account for his sour disposition—or if he just really needed to get laid. "Jonathan Stoyles." He read the name off my driver's license, drawing out the syllables. "Jonathan Stoyles."

I tried to lighten the mood. "Most people call me Jack."

The black eyes fastened on me. "I am not most people."

"Look, Sergeant. I'm not looking to cause trouble. I just need to find Captain Halim."

"Captain Halim is out of the country." He flicked through my wallet with palpable disdain. "You are not to go around Cairo asking questions about Captain Halim, is that clear?"

"Now, wait just a minute—" I started up out of my chair, and before I could blink, I was pinned against the wall, his arm across my throat. We stood there like that, just staring at each other in the silence, and somewhere outside that little room there were other noises: phones ringing and people talking and footsteps walking up and down. He smelled like clean linen and incense, and he gave off a radiant heat. His eyelashes were long and thick and very black, and there was a tiny scar at the corner of his mouth. His gaze played over my face, and he slowly dropped his arm in favor of pinning me to the wall with his chest. It was suddenly hard to breathe, but not for the reasons you might think. We were lined up and pressed together, and I was painfully aware of him not merely as a police officer, but as a man. His gaze flickered over my face, committing my features to memory, and his hands moved to clasp my elbows. His tongue slid out to wet his lower lip, and I nearly groaned out loud. Dammit, I thought feverishly, *I* need to get laid.

"You will not ask about Captain Halim. If I find that you have done so, I will not hesitate to arrest you." His fingers tightened on my elbows. "Resist, and I will have no choice but to take you. By force." If this were any other situation, and he was any other guy, I'd be convinced that he was teasing me, flirting with me, trying to get me hot and bothered. It wasn't real hard to imagine, except I had a hard time picturing this guy letting his guard down long enough to get horizontal. He was wound as tight as a cheap watch. "Do you understand?"

I nodded, not trusting myself to speak.

He stepped back and handed me my wallet. "You may go."

Shiva was napping in his taxi, head back and mouth open, when I rapped on his window. He snapped instantly awake and turned the key in the ignition. "Where does the effendi Stoyles wish to go now?"

"The Egyptian Museum." It was time I returned the diorite bowl. Maybe somebody there could shed some light on this business.

THE MAIN entrance to the Egyptian Museum was big and red and arched, and reminded me of the Newfoundland Museum in these respects, although the latter was on a much smaller scale. The main hall was an enormous, vaulted space, set about with precious artifacts from Egypt's long and illustrious history. The curator in charge of antiquities, Mr. Hassan, was one of the most imposing men I'd ever seen. Well over six feet tall, he dominated the museum's main hall like some great, ancient colossus come to life. He was maybe fifty years old, with graying hair and piercing green eyes. When he took my hand to shake it, I felt as if half my arm were being enfolded in a bear's paw. When he told me to step into his office, I obeyed.

I unwrapped the little diorite bowl from the nest of cotton that I'd packed it in and explained how it had been entrusted to me by the mysterious Mr. Blount on behalf of the Newfoundland Museum. I was glad to have the opportunity to return so rare an artifact to its original home.

Hassan listened politely as I related my tale, but when I tried to hand the bowl over to him, he refused. "Mr. Stoyles, I fear you have been misled. This bowl is very beautiful and, at first glance, I am inclined to say it is genuine. I regret to say, however, that it does not belong to us."

"It doesn't belong to you." Maybe the long overseas flight was still wearing on me, but for a moment I thought he was joking. "This bowl doesn't belong to you."

"It does not." He smiled. "It is the law in Egypt that any ancient artifacts must be immediately turned over to the government. We pay fair market value for them, and the artifact in question becomes part of our permanent exhibit." He ran a careful finger around the bowl's rim. "This is lovely, and as I said, on first glance I would say it is genuine, but alas, it is not." He shrugged. "It would seem you have been… misled."

"Not your bowl, huh?" I pressed my fingers to my eyes and made a mental note to find a good Turkish bath. Maybe a soak and steam, followed by a good hard pummeling, would clear my head. "Mr. Hassan, I'm very sorry."

"Not at all." He took a key out of his desk drawer and stood up. "Come with me." We went down a wide, open hallway to where a series of glass cases were set into the wall. Hassan stopped in front of a display of stone vessels and unlocked the cabinet. He took out a small, pink bowl and handed it to me. "This is a diorite bowl, recently unearthed at Giza. It is consistent with a style of stone carving that dates to the Old Kingdom. You can see it is identical to the bowl you hold in your hand." He smiled indulgently. "Perhaps a little too identical."

"Yeah." The little bowl was smooth and pleasantly cool to the touch. "Yeah, too identical." I shook my head. "Mr. Hassan, I don't know what's going on. I'm sorry to have wasted your time." I handed him back the museum's small bowl, feeling slightly foolish and more than a little irritated. Maybe Blount figured it would be a fine joke to send me halfway around the world, but I didn't think it was funny.

"You haven't wasted my time, Mr. Stoyles. Any time I have an opportunity to share our nation's culture with a visitor, that is time well spent." He walked me back to the main door and shook my hand. "If you have any further questions, I am at your disposal."

Shiva tucked his newspaper away between the seats. "No luck, effendi?"

"No luck, Shiva. You might as well take me back to the hotel."

We eased out into the traffic, and I laid my head back on the seat and closed my eyes. I was bone weary, and the arousal I'd felt earlier with Sergeant Samir had dissolved, leaving nothing behind except faint irritation. What the hell was I doing here? I must be out of my mind, traipsing the world on what amounted to some imaginary goodwill mission. Maybe Sam Halim didn't want to be found; maybe Mrs. Halim had no business asking me to help her find him. Maybe I should have stayed in Newfoundland, running my cafe and minding my own business.

"The effendi is weary?" Shiva's dark eyes sought mine in the rearview mirror. His tone was kind, and his expression said he was willing to listen if I wanted to talk.

"Shiva, you have no idea." It was barely three o'clock in the afternoon, but I was bushed. Somehow, in the midst of all my running around Cairo, I'd forgotten to eat, my body's internal rhythms still messed up from the long overseas flight. I felt headachy and thirsty, out of sorts.

"Might I make a suggestion, effendi Stoyles?"

"Sure, suggest away."

"A cleansing bath, followed by a massage, often works wonders for the body and the spirit."

For a moment I wondered if he was offering me his services. Maybe he wasn't just a cab driver? "Uh-huh."

"There is a very fine masseur at the Shepheard Hotel. He is an American from Texas. If you ring the front desk and ask for Nick, you will not be disappointed."

Shiva dropped me at the hotel, and I decided to do as he suggested. After a long, cool shower, I called down to the front desk and got Tania, the same girl who had checked me in the day before. I felt a little foolish even asking, but she was all business. "I'd like a massage. Uh, I heard you have an American working here, a man named Nick?"

There was the sound of papers rustling. "Of course, Mr. Stoyles. Nick is a favorite with our guests. Shall I send him up to your room straight away?"

"Yeah, that would be great. Thanks." I waited in my white hotel bathrobe, feeling a bit ridiculous and wondering if all this luxury was really necessary. Out there in the world, a war was raging, and the Nazis were doing their level best to capture North Africa, while somewhere, Sam Halim was caught up in it. Was this why I'd come to Egypt, so I could enjoy myself, sitting here in this fine hotel and soaking up the lush life? I didn't have time to contemplate further because there was a polite tapping at my door, and I opened it to find six feet of lean, redheaded Texan gazing back at me. He had the well-developed arms and chest of a swimmer, and a swimmer's narrow waist. His coppery hair was vaguely crew cut, but disheveled in a way that suggested somebody'd had their fingers in it recently. As soon as he saw me, he put down the portable massage table and reached to shake my hand.

His accent was pure San Antonio. "Mr. Stoyles, it sure is good to meet another American. How's about I come in and get set up?"

"Sure, Nick."

"Most people call me Tex." He grinned, the kind of smile that made me think some pretty dangerous thoughts. "Ain't nobody but my grandma ever calls me Nick."

I stood back as he snapped open the massage bed and spread clean towels on it. A couple of minutes later, he was inviting me to strip off and lie down.

If you've never had a real massage performed by a professional, let me be the first to recommend it. And if the idea of a perfect stranger rubbing and stroking you seems a bit much, trust me, you don't know what you're missing. Within ten minutes, I was relaxed to within an inch of my life. Within twenty, I was almost melting off the table as his strong, capable hands kneaded every ounce of tension out of my back and shoulders.

The more relaxed I got, the more I found myself thinking of Sam and wondering where he was. The telephone call I'd received from him, back home in Newfoundland, confused me. *Something curious has happened to me, Jack. I'm afraid I don't remember anything. I don't remember how I got here, or why I came.* What did that mean? Was somebody messing with his memory? I understood why everybody was so tight-lipped. If Sam really was out of the country on secret wartime business, a misdirected word in the wrong quarters could get him killed. Then there was Sergeant Samir, a guy I was pretty sure had hated me on sight; I couldn't figure it, since he didn't know me from a bucket of rocks. Why the antagonism? Maybe he hadn't liked me asking about Sam, or maybe Sam had entrusted him with secret information. That would tend to make him a bit twitchy. And that whole scene in the police station, pinning me to the wall like that. It wasn't just my imagination. Something had passed between us, something that had nothing to do with police work.

"You wanna turn over, Mr. Stoyles, and I'll do your arms and legs?" Tex tapped the bottom of my foot, and I did as he requested. I figured he'd offer me a towel or something, but he didn't, and then I wondered if maybe I wasn't making too big a thing of it. I'd been naked in front of other men before. In high school, I'd run track, and played some baseball in college. I'd seen my share of locker rooms and what went on in them. You'd think I wouldn't care one way or another, except Tex was really gorgeous, and he was looking me over now with frank appreciation. "You keep yourself in good shape, Mr. Stoyles."

"Everybody calls me Jack."

"You keep yourself in good shape, Jack." He took my right hand in his and rubbed oil into my palm, gently squeezing and pressing. At first it hurt a little, but he kept it up and pretty soon it started to feel real good. "Most people hold a lot of tension in their hands. Nobody ever realizes how much time they spend clenching their fists." He rubbed the tight web of flesh between my index finger and thumb, gently distributing the oil until warmth spread up my arm, dispersing into my chest. "Don't mind if I chat, do you?"

"No, go ahead."

"It's just that I don't get much of a chance these days to talk to another American." His grin did wonderful things to that gorgeous face. "I miss it."

"I see what you mean." I grunted as his fingers dug into the tight muscles of my forearm. "How long you been in Cairo?"

"Since before the war, but I bummed around quite a bit before that. You here on vacation?"

"Something like that."

"Where you from?"

"I'm living in Newfoundland now, but I'm originally from Philly."

"Philly, huh? My sister moved to Philly a few years back." He started in on the other arm. "She was engaged to a guy there, but it didn't work out." He swept his thumbs in broad circles from my wrist to my elbow and back again.

"Where is she now?"

"She's dead." His hands stopped moving and my guts twisted into a knot. "Yeah, she uh…." He went very still and very quiet, and when next he spoke, his voice was full of sorrow. "She wrote my mother she was coming home, and then we didn't hear anything from her. It was kind of weird, because Judy—that's what we called her; her name was Judith but she hated that name—Judy was real good about keeping her promises." He leaned over me and began playing his hands down my torso in long, sweeping strokes. "That wasn't too long ago… last year, in fact." Something must have shown in my face, because all of a sudden, he was looking at me intently. "I'm sorry. I didn't mean to give you my whole life story."

"It's okay." I sounded like my throat was stuffed with cotton. "Was she… in an accident?"

He shook his head. "No. She went to see one of these doctors. She was gonna have a baby, and I guess maybe she didn't want that." He smoothed warm circles into my hipbones. "Turns out he wasn't really a doctor at all… not anymore."

"Jesus." I'd driven Judy there that day and waited for her outside in my car. I offered to go in with her, but she didn't want that. Maybe he'd been a doctor once, before the state medical board took away his license. Now he couldn't even write a prescription, let alone perform abortions on women scared and desperate enough to go to him. Christ, I remembered it like it was yesterday, every sordid detail, and thinking about it now was making me sick. It was some kind of screwy odds that I'd ended up meeting Judy's brother in a place like this, or maybe what they say about running from your past is true. No matter where you go, there you are. Yeah, maybe that was it.

Tex's hands spread more oil on my hips, his long fingers roaming toward my cock. I knew I didn't want that. I gently caught one of his hands and smiled at him. "What say we skip the happy ending, huh? You don't have to do that." His face registered a subtle hurt, and I rushed to reassure him. "It's not you. It's me."

"Oh." He turned away to wipe his hands on a towel. "I'm sorry. I just assumed…."

"Not your fault." I rolled off the table and went to get my wallet. I guess I was ashamed of myself, because I tipped him a lot more than the going rate. "Is it okay if I request your services again?"

He looked at the money, then nodded and slid the bills into his pocket. "You're a right guy, Jack."

No, I'm not, but you don't need to know that. "Thanks, Tex. I'll see you around, huh?"

Tex had hardly gone before the phone in my hotel room opened up. It was Mrs. Halim. "I am hosting a small gathering this evening with a few of my husband's friends from the community. I would like it very much if you were there. Someone else will be attending as well. I am hoping you might be able to… discuss some things with him." She didn't say it, but I knew she wanted me to come so I could size up the other guests. She was hoping this evening's little shindig might provide me with some ammunition in my search for Sam. "I have just one request, Mr. Stoyles."

"Name it."

"You must not tell anyone you know my husband. Do you understand? Under no circumstances are you to mention you and my husband have met or tell anyone the purpose of your visit to Cairo."

CHAPTER TWO

S HIVA'S TAXI let me out in front of an all white house in a residential district of Cairo. The house was the traditional, flat-roofed design, with the outer door opening first into an inner courtyard, complete with a small fountain and assortment of native plants. I sensed this last was Sam's idea, and seeing the lush green aloes and Egyptian grasses made me miss him so much, it was almost a physical ache. The winding, tiled pathway leading up to the main door was accented in shades of cream and midnight blue, colors I knew he liked. Sam was the sort of man who lived life fully, with all of his senses; I'd known there was something special about him the first time I laid eyes on him. That feeling had remained, had grown and blossomed into something I hesitated to call love, but was devoted friendship for sure.

My knock was answered by a huge Egyptian in formal dress. "Good evening," I said. "Mrs. Halim invited me."

"*Masaa' al-khayr.*" He peered narrowly at me, his dark-eyed gaze moving slowly over my features, as though he were committing my face to some internal rogues' gallery. "*Ma esmouk?*"

A hot flush crawled up my neck. I didn't have the slightest clue what he was saying, or even why he was saying it to me. Was he asking for identification? A written invitation? "Uh, look buddy… sorry to disappoint, but I don't speak Arabic, or whatever that is."

He gazed at me blankly. "*Aasef! La moshkelah!*" He smiled broadly, which could have meant anything at all.

"Uh…." The heat in my neck bloomed on my cheeks and forehead, and I began to sweat. A nearby group of people stopped their discussion and drifted my way, clearly intrigued with what was going on. "Look, buddy, I don't speak Arabic. English only."

"English." His accent was thick, but understandable. "Good evening. What is your name?"

"Jack Stoyles." I was so relieved, I could have kissed him. "Mrs. Halim invited me."

"Excellent." He bowed and indicated I was to follow him. "Right this way."

He led me through a stone archway into a great room where people were talking and laughing to a background of traditional Egyptian music. I saw no one I knew. My first instinct was to go away, but at that moment, I spied Ibrahim Samir standing by himself near a small alcove just off the main room.

I stepped back into the shadows and watched him as he stood contemplating a large, framed portrait of Sam Halim in full uniform. This was a little odd. Most Moslems frowned on making images and confined their artistic efforts to such things as carpets and fine fabrics, but I was swiftly learning Sam Halim wasn't your usual Moslem. The man in the picture looked stern and a little sad, and there were a lot of medals pinned to his breast; he wasn't looking at the photographer but instead gazed off into the middle distance, absorbed in something only he could see. Samir raised his hand and touched the portrait's lips, then touched his own mouth with the same hand—a shockingly intimate gesture. He murmured something I couldn't quite hear, and I turned quickly, pretending absorption in a woven wall hanging. I figured I was already on Samir's bad side, but I wasn't interested in mixing it up with him, not here and certainly not now.

"Salam alekum."

The little voice came from somewhere down around my knees and, glancing down, I saw a small boy, perhaps seven years of age, tugging at the hem of my tunic. In deference to local customs, I'd worn Egyptian dress. I wasn't quite ready for the white, ankle-length burnoose but, acting on Shiva's advice, I'd purchased a long-sleeved, dark green tunic with gold embroidery and a pair of loose white trousers. "Yeah, salaam to you, too."

"Have you seen my father?" His round, smooth face was Tareenah Halim's, but his soft brown eyes and elegantly arched brows were all Sam. "I wish he would come home."

I crouched so we were at eye level. "Do you miss him?"

He nodded, close to tears, and I was seized with the sudden urge to fold him into a hug. "He said he will bring me a toy monkey and some books. I'm too old for toys, really, but I like it when he reads to me."

Sam had shown me his photograph, back home in Newfoundland. *These are my four children: Samuel, Hanbal, Stamos, and Tabia. They live in Cairo.* I nodded as if we two shared a confidence. "I won't tell anyone your secret."

A shadow fell between us. "Stamos, you are supposed to be in bed."

I stood up. "Mrs. Halim, good evening." She was wearing a pale pink robe edged in gold, and gold shimmered at her wrists and earlobes. She was even lovelier than I remembered.

She inclined her head. "Welcome to my home. Stamos, to bed." The boy scampered off into another part of the house. "I would extend the hospitality of my household to you. Please partake of some refreshment." She led me to a buffet table groaning with food and helped me to heap my plate with Egyptian delicacies. "I am glad you were able to attend." She placed a glass of fruit juice into my hand. "It is good you are here."

"Mrs. Halim, why am I here?" I'd puzzled over it all the way here in the taxi. "You told me what not to do, but—"

"Not now." She ducked her head. "Please. Circulate, and listen carefully. There may be some among my husband's intimates who know where he has gone."

I did as she asked, working my way slowly from room to room, pretending interest in the potted plants and the varied textures of Tareenah Halim's rugs. It wasn't hard to do: nobody knew me, I didn't know them, and most conversation was conducted in Arabic. Three men in formal Egyptian robes were standing by a window, speaking quietly together. I made my way over there, but they must have realized what I was up to because they scattered like flies in a strong wind as soon as I came close. Two men wearing the khaki drill of the Long-Range Desert Group spoke to one another in accents that sounded vaguely English, but were probably Australian; a broad-shouldered giant of a man wearing a Greek colonel's uniform came to stand nearby. A police siren sounded outside, and I went to the window, pretending curiosity. As it faded into the distance, I felt a hand on my shoulder. I turned to see Sergeant Samir. "What is it you are doing, Mr. Stoyles?" Samir wasn't in uniform, but all the same he looked real good. He was wearing a dark blue tunic over the traditional white trousers, and he smelled faintly of soap and sandalwood.

"Going to ask me for identification, Samir? Or isn't that your usual shtick?"

"I have no idea what you are babbling about." He looked me up and down disdainfully. "I am surprised to see you dressed like this."

"My cardboard box is at the cleaners." I swayed closer to him—maybe too close, because he stepped back half a pace. "Mrs. Halim invited you, too?"

"I am Captain Halim's personal assistant, and a good friend of the Halim family." He wasn't comfortable out of uniform; without a Sam Browne belt, he had nowhere to rest his hands. "I am invited to all their gatherings." He paused to let two ladies and a young boy pass by. I noticed he bowed slightly, but did not look directly at either of the women. Sergeant Samir'd had his manners drilled into him by somebody. Either that, or he was the world's biggest toady. "You still have not answered me."

"I'm not required to, but since you asked so nice, I'll tell you. Mrs. Halim invited me."

"Why did she invite you?" His tone was contemptuous. "You are… nobody."

For a second, it felt like being back at home in St. John's. If I closed my eyes to the surroundings, I could have sworn the constabulary's finest, Sergeant Alphonsus Picco, was dismissively grilling me. "Thank you very much, Sergeant Samir. Say, you wouldn't happen to know a cop named Picco, would you?"

His dark brows creased. "Pickle?"

I bit my lip to keep from laughing. "Skip it. The Halims have a nice place, huh? Too bad Sam isn't here to enjoy the party. Not like him to run away, though. I wonder what's up."

I must have struck a nerve. His back stiffened, and he stared at me like I'd just opened my fly and pissed against the wall. "*Shut* your mouth, Mr. Stoyles."

"Kind of makes you wonder where he is, why he isn't here." I lowered my voice conspiratorially. "I don't suppose he's run out on Mrs. Halim and the kids?"

Samir's hand lashed out, quick as a snake, and struck me a stinging slap across the face. Two elderly men standing nearby turned and stared. I reached out, grabbed Samir's collar, and slammed him against the wall. "Take your hands off me," he barked, "or I will—"

"You'll *what*?" I let him go, waited while he smoothed his tunic. "I've wanted to have a word with you, Samir, ever since the police station."

He raised his chin, his black eyes snapping. "I am ready whenever you are." He inclined his head. "Perhaps we might talk in the garden?"

"That suits me just fine. Lead the way."

The courtyard of the Halim house was circled by a tiled walkway that led down a forested slope toward the Nile. I followed Ibrahim Samir away from the house and toward the smooth swath of dark water; he led me to a tiny wooden structure set within a grove of trees at the water's edge, and then stopped. He turned to face me, and slammed his hands against my shoulders, knocking me back against a wooden post. It was dark, and I wasn't prepared enough to fend off his attack, which had caught me completely by surprise. And then he was close to me, his hands on my face, gentle.

"Just what the hell are you doing, Samir?"

He murmured quiet words in Arabic and drew back. "I should not have slapped you."

I floundered for a moment, dumbfounded at my reaction to him. "Still want to take me by force?" The waters of the Nile lapped gently against the wooden boards, and I held him there, my fingers digging into his biceps. "Or are we playing some other game now?" I could have him, I realized, if I wanted him. I could possess him here and now, and he'd let me do whatever I wanted.

"I very much want to take you." His grin flashed white in the darkness. "But not by force."

"That slap was a nice touch, Samir. Very effective. Mrs. Halim's guests probably think we're down here beating each other's brains out." He felt good pressed up against me like that. Yeah, Sergeant Samir was one hot little number.

"I needed to speak with you. A diversion was in order."

"Is it about Sam?"

"Yes."

I took a deep breath. "I don't think we should talk here. It's not safe. There're too many people around. I don't know who to trust." I wasn't entirely sure I could trust him, but I had to start somewhere. If Samir really was Sam's number-one man, he might have information pertaining to Sam's disappearance. "Listen, wait half an hour and then get over to

Shepheard's." I gave him my room number and key. "Let yourself in and wait for me. I'm going to sniff around and see what I can find out here."

"There will be questions when we go back to the house... speculation. If we appear together, they will think we have reconciled our differences."

"Want me to smack you around a bit?" I grinned. "Make it look real?"

"I think we might dispense with that," he said dryly. "Allow me to precede you into the house. Then, after a few minutes have passed, you may return."

"Gonna make them think you beat me senseless, Samir? Some of that good, old-fashioned police brutality?"

He offered a withering look in reply. "I have my reputation to think of." With that, he was gone. I heard him climbing the hill behind the house, then the crunch of his feet on gravel as he rounded the corner. I smoked a couple of cigarettes while I waited, gazing out over the Nile and admiring the reflections of the lights across the river. What would it be like, sitting out here with Sam, enjoying the quiet of the evening? Would I ever see him again? He once said to me: *Nothing is certain in this life.* I couldn't disagree. Since leaving Philadelphia, my life had taken some unpredictable turns, and if somebody had looked into my future and told me I'd be running a cafe in St. John's, Newfoundland, I'd have said they were screwy. Yeah, I'd figured I was done with love, too, until Sam Halim walked into my life one day and kissed me. I guess Sam was right. Nothing is certain.

Tareenah Halim met me at the door. "What is going on?" She was agitated, wringing her hands. "What have you done to Sergeant Samir?"

"I'm sorry if I caused a scene."

She pressed her hand to her forehead. Clearly, she was upset. "He is my husband's.... He and my husband.... Please, come into the house." I let her take my elbow and guide me inside. I could almost hear Sam's amused voice in my head: *Jack, my wife is a very unforgiving woman. I hope you realize what you have done.* I figured everybody would be staring at me when I came back in, and I was right. Sure, they'd seen plenty of fights in their time, but nobody quite knew what to think about the brash *Americani*. Usually, if somebody took a swing at a Cairo cop, he'd get his ass beat. They must have been wondering what the hell was going on, especially since Samir didn't have me in handcuffs and wasn't giving me the business end of his truncheon. Well, that was fine. Sometimes it's good to let people wonder: it's just the thing to shake information out of them.

Once the furor died down, I went to the buffet and got another plate of food and a glass of juice, and I nosed around a bit. There was nothing much going on, though. I was just about to call a cab when the tall guy in the Greek uniform said something that caught my ear. It wasn't so much what he said as the way he said it—with a tremor in his voice, a kind of expectation. "They ought to have known better." He nodded, and then he laughed, but it wasn't a pleasant laugh. "If they had known, they would have taken anybody else but him."

I didn't get much else, but that was enough to set me thinking. After I said my good-byes to Mrs. Halim, I went out to hail a cab and found Shiva already waiting for me. I opened the door and slid in beside him. "You tailing me?"

"Never, effendi Stoyles." He yawned and switched on the dashboard radio. "To your hotel?"

Something prickled at the back of my skull. "Why would I want to go to Shepheard's?"

He smiled. "The young policeman is waiting for you there."

I reached for the door handle. "I think I'm gonna get another cab."

"I would not advise it, effendi."

I was already out of the car and standing on the sidewalk. "Why not? I haven't got you on retainer." Something about this whole thing was weird. It seemed too much like a setup to me, and I didn't like it one little bit. This guy had been dogging me since I'd come to Cairo, for no good reason I could see. Sure, every taxi driver wanted to make baksheesh wherever he could, but this was ridiculous.

"I would strongly advise the effendi to get back into the taxi."

"Why?"

"Simply let us say it is kismet." He raised his hands and shrugged. "After all, I would be betraying a confidence if I told you that—"

He didn't get to say anything more. Gunfire opened up somewhere in the Cairo night, and two bullets shattered the windshield of Shiva's taxi. I ripped open the door and dived back inside, but it was too late. Two blue holes in his forehead told me what I already knew.

He was dead.

I WASN'T dumb enough to stick around. I knew Tareenah Halim's house was crawling with off-duty cops, so I took off out of there as fast as I could and didn't stop running till I was a good five blocks in the other direction. I found a taxi near the Bulaq Bridge. He let me out in front of Shepheard's. The night was warm, but I was freezing.

I went up to my room and knocked on the door. Samir opened it and peered out. "What is the matter?" He drew me into the room and held my shaking hands in his. "You look terrible. What has happened?"

I felt like somebody had slipped me one hell of a mickey. The more I thought about it, the harder it was to make sense of things. "Taxi driver…. Somebody shot him through the windshield."

"Are you hurt?" His quick, clever hands patted me all over.

"No, no, I'm fine. I just don't know why anybody would want to…." What the hell was I thinking? What was I doing here? This wasn't my country; I had no business being here, and maybe I was doing more harm than good. The best thing to do was go home. Get on the first flight heading away from here and make my way back to St. John's by any means necessary.

"I will telephone. One moment." Samir crossed to the phone, and I heard him speaking quietly in Arabic. I wondered what he was saying and to whom. Was this all part of the setup? Maybe he was going to turn me in, and I'd spend the rest of my life rotting away in some filthy Egyptian prison cell. "Forgive me." He glanced at me, but spoke into the phone. "I am remiss. Stoyles-bey does not speak our language. Let me continue in *Engleezhi*. A taxi driver, shot to death, two bullets. Of course. No, Mr. Stoyles was merely a bystander. I will bring him in directly to make a statement." He hung up and looked at me. "If you wish me to go, I will."

"No." Dammit, I couldn't get warm. Despite the heat outside, it felt like someone was pouring ice-cold water down my back. "No, I'll order some coffee."

He chafed my cold hands in an effort to warm them. "You're freezing. It is a delayed reaction. Come, hot water will help you more than coffee."

It was completely nuts, but then again I was hardly in a position to judge. I was ready to take whatever comfort there was about then. When Sergeant Ibrahim Samir took me into the bathroom and stripped us both naked, I didn't object—and as good as Samir looked clothed, naked, he was goddamn spectacular. He was lean and tanned, fit like you expect a cop to be, with nicely developed muscles—just enough, not too much— and a tattoo of some Arabic words on his right arm. He was lightly dusted with dark hairs, thickest on his chest, arrowing down to where his nice, thick cock lay quiescent, waiting. He stood with me under the hot water, rubbing my back and arms, warming me.

But I hadn't been touched in a long, long time and pretty soon his caresses burned like fire. I shoved him back against the wall and kissed him, our bodies pressed together like I meant to push myself right into him, then and there. I held his face and kissed him so hard our teeth knocked together. I was grinding myself against him, wanting to be near him, to be near someone, anyone. I was moving too fast, practically forcing him to do what I wanted, holding him up against the wall like I'd hired him for the evening. Sam had once said to me *"You do not allow yourself to understand the enormous debt you owe to pleasure."*

I took a breath, forced myself to slow down. "Sorry," I whispered. "I'm sorry."

"Come." Samir took my hand. "Let us lie together awhile."

He laid me down and touched me all over, warming my skin with the palms of his hands, caressing me in a way I hadn't enjoyed for a very, very long time. I was more than capable of giving pleasure to another, of holding someone in my arms to comfort and sustain them, but I had trouble accepting the same thing for myself. It had always seemed superfluous, something you did if you were involved with someone, if you were lucky enough to be in love. It wasn't something I did—yet now, every time I tried to move, Ibrahim Samir gently pushed me down and kissed me, and warmed my flesh with his mouth and hands, and with his body. Time became a fluid thing, stretching out into forever, and I was floating on it like a broad swath of subtle water that effortlessly bore me up.

He lay beside me, kissing me, murmuring gentle words and stroking me until my belly pulsed with heat and my swollen cock leaked fluid onto my thighs. I opened my legs, took him on top, and held him tightly against me as we kissed. I noticed a little of his iron control had gone; he was feeling this as much as I was. He trembled when I slid my palms down his back and stroked his perfect ass, and when I set my teeth in his shoulder and lightly bit him, he whimpered. I pushed against him, and he pushed back, his cock trapped between our bellies, subject to the delicious friction of our coupled skins.

I guess the world went away a little bit then, because it seemed like there was nothing besides the two of us, clutching at each other and rubbing ourselves together until Samir cried out, his fingers digging into my upper arms hard enough to leave marks. His head dropped forward, his dark hair touching my shoulder as he shuddered through his climax and its aftershocks.

I sought his lips and kissed him as my pleasure peaked and spread through me, a release so sudden and so violent, I shouted into his open mouth. I jerked, shivering, as the last of it dispersed itself, and lay for a long time with my eyes closed, my skin humming with a subtle pleasure.

"WHAT'S THIS say?" I traced the Arabic lettering on Ibrahim Samir's right bicep.

"It is a quote from the Holy Quran. It says 'Allah helps those who persevere.'" He took a drag off the cigarette and passed it to me. The Cairo night was very quiet outside the hotel room. Now and then, we could hear the far sound of a siren or the honking of a taxicab's horn, but that was all. The radio played quietly in the far corner of the room, and Vera Lynn was singing "We'll Meet Again." We lay in each other's arms, talking softly about nothing in particular.

"We have a similar saying." I smoked, handed the cigarette back to him. "God helps those who help themselves." I looked into his big, black eyes, and I knew I was a real son of a bitch. "Ibrahim, where is Sam?"

He stubbed out the cigarette and rolled up on his elbow so he could look at me. "You are sorry for asking it of me, and yet that is why you came to Cairo in the first place." He kissed me gently. "I am under no illusions, Jack. This is but a pleasant interlude." He was trying his best, but his expression said he was hurt, and I hated myself.

"You been real good to me." I waited for his answer. Either my guesses were way off or Samir knew something.

"Captain Halim has been my superior officer for ten years, ever since I joined the police force. I fear I am not the easiest man, yet Captain Halim has a saying he feels applies especially to me."

"I bet he does."

"Some people are controlled only with patience."

"Mm." I laughed. "I had a supervisor used to say that about me, too."

"I have had to learn patience, a great deal of patience. During our long association, I have functioned as what you Americans would call a right-hand man. Captain Halim has trusted me with things he would not normally tell anyone else. I have a special drawer in my desk, a drawer that is always locked. I have the only key. In that drawer, I keep a record of the things Captain Halim has asked me to do for him, the errands he wishes me to run, the messages he would like me to deliver."

I waited. He was going somewhere with this.

"Captain Halim is a highly respected policeman in the city of Cairo. A highly respected policeman is often the target of those less scrupulous than himself, parties who believe his influence can be purchased for a few piasters. Shortly after the outbreak of the war, back in '39, a group of Allied agents contacted the police commissioner, asking if there were any experienced officers who might like to aid the Allied cause; Sam Halim was chosen from a small pool and entrusted with certain assignments. One of these assignments involved the investigation of alleged war profiteering by a certain Greek, a man named Jonah Octavian."

"Octavian." Yeah, I knew him. Jonah Octavian had kidnapped Royal Newfoundland Constabulary sergeant Alphonsus Picco and stuffed him in a cave on the South Side of St. John's. When I went to look for Picco, Octavian showed up just in time to shove me into the cave with him. "Yeah, I know all about Jonah Octavian."

"Then you will know he is a lying, murderous dog who will do anything for profit. Captain Halim had been requested to go to Newfoundland, where Octavian's latest project was progressing. His identity would be altered so it would seem he was a member of the British Consulate."

I am Samuel Halim, assistant to the British consul.... "But he wasn't."

"No. Captain Halim often volunteers his services to the Allied cause. His mother was Greek and he attended Oxford University. The cause of the Allies is very dear to his heart."

"Sam is… very dear to your heart, isn't he, Ibrahim?"

He dropped his eyes and nodded.

"I saw you at Mrs. Halim's party, standing in front of his picture. You were touching it."

"I… Captain Halim sees me as nothing more than his… irritating inferior." His smile was sad.

I didn't believe it, but I didn't think I had the right to say so—not to Ibrahim Samir, not now. "So you know where he is?"

He shook his head. "Captain Halim left Newfoundland en route to Cairo. He was following Jonah Octavian. Octavian is a Nazi operative who uses his business connections to glean information he sells to the highest bidder. Captain Halim landed in Cairo. This much we know. After that, he disappeared. We heard nothing from him for many days. Last week, a coded message arrived at the police station. We knew by the code used it was from Captain Halim."

"You're kidding me." My heart thumped against my ribs. "So he's been in contact."

"The message was only two words. I must confess they made no sense to anyone, even to me."

I clenched my fists in the sheets. "What were they?"

"Cafe Heartache."

It must have shown in my face. "Huh."

"These words mean something to you?"

"No." I concentrated on looking blank. "Nothing."

Samir glanced over at the clock. "*Sahbi,* I must go. My shift begins very soon."

I lay there thinking while he took a shower. The night air through my hotel window was very soft, almost a gentle caress, but I couldn't rest. I couldn't stop seeing those two blue holes in Shiva's forehead, and I couldn't stop thinking about Sam. Not knowing where he was or if he was alive was killing me. Maybe Octavian's boys had gotten hold of him and were torturing him. Mrs. Halim had asked me to circulate among her guests and see if I could find out anything, which could have meant she suspected someone at the police department of having inside information. She'd even told me someone had arranged to meet me at the party. Was Ibrahim Samir the man she meant? Under normal circumstances, this would have been plenty bad enough, but there was a war on, goddammit; Sam was out there somewhere in the midst of it, and there was nothing I could do to help him.

I got up and threw on a bathrobe. The shower had stopped, and I heard Ibrahim moving around in the bathroom. I turned out the lights and stood by the window, smoking in the dark and listening to the radio. Everything I'd felt and heard and seen started to get hot inside of me, like it did sometimes. It was like the meter was running and the driver was gunning the engine, but you weren't getting anywhere.

"There is an answer." Ibrahim's arms went around me from behind, and he hugged me. I leaned back into his embrace. "Sometimes the thing to do is stop thinking about it."

"Yeah, maybe you're right." I turned so I was facing him. "Be careful out there tonight, huh?"

He stroked my cheek. "I will." His mouth was warm when he kissed me. I closed my eyes and melted into the caress. The darkness was briefly sliced by a sliver of light from the opened door, and then he was gone.

I sat down on the bed and took a few deep breaths, trying to ground myself. Was the coded message really from Sam? And why "Cafe Heartache?" Why would he reverse the name of my cafe, and what was it supposed to mean? As far as messages went, it was damned obscure, or maybe that was deliberate. The sick, empty feeling in my stomach told me Jonah Octavian was probably behind this whole thing; he'd taken off for parts unknown after his little girlfriend, Julie Fayre, had tried to poison me, leaving her to face the gallows alone. Yeah, this sort of thing had Octavian's nasty stamp all over it.

The diorite bowl Blount had given me lay on the bedside table. I picked it up and held it, instinctively seeking out its cool, stone contours. I tapped it against my palm while I thought.

And then I felt something give, almost like the bowl had split in two.

It had. The round indentation had parted along a central seam, revealing a flat panel beneath, fitted with a tiny door carved out of a separate piece of diorite. I got a fingernail under the flap and pulled it up.

There, shining like a new piaster, was a tiny brass key no bigger than my thumbnail.

I was wondering what it unlocked when the phone rang. It was Tareenah Halim, and she sounded upset. "Mr. Stoyles, I must ask you to desist in your inquiries. Please."

This was new. First, she asked me to look for Sam, and now she was telling me not to bother? "Mrs. Halim, are you sure this is what you want?"

"I cannot explain. Please." She was on the edge of tears. "Do not ask more questions about my husband. In fact, it is best if you return home as soon as possible. I can say no more than this. Good-bye."

There was a *click* and my ear was full of dial tone. But I didn't have too much time to wonder what she meant. Just then, the door of my hotel room blew in with a noise like a hundred pounds of dynamite, and everything around me was suddenly in flames.

CHAPTER THREE

I DON'T remember much after the room blew up, but the next thing I knew I was roaming the native quarter, wearing my tunic and trousers from Mrs. Halim's party, and holding that tiny brass key in my hand. It must have been well after midnight, maybe two o'clock in the morning, and the native quarter was still and quiet. I felt like people do when they're dreaming, like I was walking in an unfamiliar landscape, moving slowly through some alien dimension that had nothing to do with me one way or the other. I had no idea where I was and no clue how I'd gotten here. The important thing was to keep walking. As long as I kept walking, I would be all right.

The streets in this part of the city were narrow and very old, the buildings hanging over and forming a sort of tunnel. There weren't a lot of cars parked anywhere, and the style and general condition of the houses indicated the native Egyptians didn't fare nearly as well as the rest of Cairo. Even the flood of wartime prosperity, so abundant elsewhere, was scarcely in evidence here. This part of Cairo resisted the march of time, its face turned stolidly toward the east, its future uncertain and its present consumed with necessary day-to-day concerns. There wasn't much to hope for, not here among these shabby buildings with their tidy lines of clean laundry drifting in the warm night breeze. Hope was something that happened on the other side of town, in the imagined cultural heartland of the Ezbekieh or at Shepheard's palatial hotel, where army officers from various nations met for cocktails while their troops were dying horrific, flyblown deaths in the merciless desert.

I guess I walked for close to two hours.

How I'd managed to dress myself and flee the hotel, I didn't know. I'd taken nothing with me except the little brass key—no wallet, no passport, no valid form of identification that might help me out if I was stopped by Cairo's often overzealous police. Dawn had just begun to lighten the sky when I remembered something I'd read in one of my guidebooks, about how the muezzin would soon be making the first call to prayer.

I ducked into a doorway and sat down, resting my head against the wall and letting my tired eyes close. It seemed like weeks had passed since I'd been at Tareenah Halim's party, instead of only a few hours. I ached everywhere, my feet worst of all, and a spot over my right eyebrow throbbed painfully with my heartbeat. Who wanted me dead so bad they'd bomb my hotel room? Tareenah Halim and Ibrahim Samir knew I was in Cairo, as had Shiva, who had greeted me by name practically the first time we met. Mrs. Halim had deliberately sought me out to ask if I'd help find Sam. I'd left a trail behind me on the plane, in the taxi, in the hotel, at Sam's house. If anybody wanted to find me, they wouldn't have to look hard, I'd practically announced my presence the minute I set foot in Cairo. I figured the explosion in my hotel room wasn't some random act of violence, but a deliberate attack, set up by somebody who knew why I was here, who intended to try and stop me.

I'd brought nothing of value to Cairo. Even the diorite bowl Blount had insisted was a treasured Egyptian artifact had turned out to be a phony. Although, now I thought about it, there was something real funny about that whole thing. Egypt had a law that said any recovered artifact, regardless of its provenance, had to be handed over to the government. It was sometimes a problem getting people to turn things over, because more often than not, whoever found the thing could get more money for it on the black market. Your average farmer, or *fellah,* was going to hold out for the best deal he could get, and who could blame him? If he happened to turn up some ancient artifact with his plough, it could mean the difference between poverty and a modest increase in his personal wealth. Most people were honest enough to turn in whatever they found. And yet, when I'd brought the bowl to the Egyptian Museum, they hadn't wanted to hear about it. It didn't make any sense, unless that was the plan all along—and I had to admit, finding that little key hidden in the base of the bowl was surprising. It was very surprising. And Ibrahim Samir, he was pretty surprising, too. I hadn't expected that....

141

The muezzin's call pierced the early morning air like a klaxon, and my head snapped up. I was looking into a pair of vaguely familiar blue eyes. "Jack." He touched my shoulder. "Jack, your feet are bleeding."

Whatever I was going to say was lost for all time. I tumbled forward and the world went away.

IT WAS the feeling of cold water on my face that brought me out of it. I opened my eyes slowly and waited for the room to stop whirling. I was lying on a bed in a modest little room with all the usual furnishings: chest of drawers, bookcase, lamps. I had no idea where I was.

"Whoa there, don't try and sit up too soon." Gentle hands pushed me back down, just in time. I felt distinctly like I was about to embarrass myself.

"What happened?"

"Little explosion at Shepheard's, Jack. Don't you remember?" Tex helped me sit up and handed me a glass of water, but I couldn't imagine drinking it. My stomach felt like a bag full of bumblebees.

"Were you at the hotel when it happened?" I downed the water anyway. My mouth was parched, as dry as the Sahara.

"Just coming off my shift. Have you been back there?"

I shook my head. "All my stuff is still there. The room is probably destroyed. Tex, what the hell happened?"

"Nobody's really sure. All they know is a bomb was planted near your room, set to go off around midnight." He sat back and gazed at me. "Jack, you got any enemies in Cairo?"

"I haven't been here long enough to make enemies. Unless...." As soon as I said it, the whole thing hit me: Jonah Octavian. He was the most likely candidate for this sort of thing. There was bad blood between us, especially after that stunt he'd pulled with Picco back in St. John's. I wouldn't put it past him to bomb my hotel room. It was just the sort of thing he'd go for. I hesitated to tell any of this to Tex. I didn't want to burden him with a lot of old news that had nothing to do with him, and I didn't know him well enough to know if I could trust him.

"Tex, thanks for everything but I gotta go." I stood up and took one step, then collapsed on the floor, groaning in pain. My feet felt like they were on fire. This was a great start.

"Jack, come on. I'll get you a taxi." He helped me back to the bed, and I noticed my feet were heavily bandaged. "You were wandering around the native quarter barefoot for hours. Didn't you even notice? When I found you, your feet were bleeding. I could have tracked you all the way back to Shepheard's just by following the bloody footprints."

I didn't remember any of that. I'd been with Ibrahim Samir, and just after he left, the room blew up. I couldn't even figure out how I'd gotten dressed. When Ibrahim had left, all I was wearing was a hotel bathrobe. Who'd dressed me? How had I ended up in the native quarter? And out of all the things I might have taken with me, why had I chosen the little brass key? "I had a key in my hand." My pulse pounded in my temples, and I felt sick again. "Where is it? Did you take it?" It was conceivable I'd dressed myself and left the hotel; I just didn't remember doing it.

"Take it easy, Jack." He reached into his pocket and handed me the key. "I'm on your side, remember?"

"Sorry. I'm sorry. I'm… not myself. Look, you been awful good to me." I felt like an idiot. "I don't remember much of what happened after the blast. Do you think…?"

"I'll go with you."

We went out, and Tex hailed a cab. The morning sun cast its warm, level rays over the city, setting the Nile alight. I didn't relish the idea of going back to Shepheard's. There would be an investigation and the police would be asking questions; I would need to get my story straight.

"I'd rather not stay at Shepheard's if I can help it." I hoped Tex wouldn't ask too many questions. I wasn't up for lengthy explanations.

"Sure thing. You want somewhere off the beaten path, am I right?"

Or maybe he already knew more than I suspected.

"Uh, sure." I shrugged. "Anywhere's okay."

As it turned out, Tex was really helpful. He was familiar with Cairo, and knew where all the decent hotels were. He explained to the desk clerk at Shepheard's that I'd been in the room where the blast had occurred, and within half an hour, they had retrieved my luggage and the rest of my belongings, apologizing profusely all the while. They assured me that measures were being taken, everything was being done, the police had been called, this sort of thing would not go unpunished, and so on. I offered my good-byes to the desk clerk, and within half an hour, I was installed in a clean little room at the Acacia Court with a wonderful view of the Citadel. The Acacia Court was nowhere near as fancy or luxurious as Shepheard's, but the bed was comfortable and there was lots of hot water. "I'll be back later to check on you," Tex promised. He grinned, winking at me. "Try not to blow yourself up."

"Wait a second." I laid my hand on his arm. "There's something about this I just don't get."

He'd been about to step out into the corridor but now he came back in and closed the door. "And?"

"I order a massage at Shepheard's and you show up."

He grinned. "That's my job, Jack."

"Yeah, I know that." Christ, I wanted to trust him. I wanted to believe that this big, good-looking kid was somehow watching out for me. "But now, with everything that's happened, here you are again. Cairo is a big place. How long had I been wandering in the native quarter? And who comes to my rescue? You do."

"Jack, I—"

"It's all a bit too convenient for coincidence. That's what I'm saying." I felt like a real heel. Maybe I should have been grateful he'd found me, instead of bellyaching about it. "I don't mean—"

"I can't tell you anything." He spread his hands, a gesture of helplessness. "Jack, I wish I could."

"That sounds pretty final." Strangely enough, I didn't blame him.

"You're right about the watching out for you part, but that's all I can tell you." He reached out and squeezed my shoulder. "Why don't you get some rest? You've had a tough day." The door swished shut behind him, and I was alone.

I stripped off my scorched, filthy clothes and collapsed into bed, but I couldn't sleep. I lay there in the artificial darkness, turning the tiny key over and over in my hand. Who had put the key in the base of the bowl? Was I meant to find the key or was it meant for someone else—say, someone at the museum? Or had it been placed there before I'd left Newfoundland? I didn't understand what was going on with Tareenah Halim, either. She'd gone to a lot of trouble to secure my help and now she didn't want it. The more I thought about things, the more confused I got.

Finally I got up and, taking a pad of paper and a pen, wrote the words CAFE HEARTACHE. Samir said the decoded message from Sam had consisted of only these two words. My cafe was called the Heartache Cafe, which identified me as the intended recipient, but Sam hadn't provided much to go on. If this were a puzzle, I would assume the juxtaposition of those two words, for starters. I fiddled around with it awhile, arranging and rearranging the letters. I came up with things like A A A CHEER FETCH and A A A CHEF ETCHER and A A A EH REC FETCH—none of which helped me one little bit. On impulse, I struck off the A A A and the EH from the last one and was left with REC FETCH, which didn't mean anything to me. Then I swapped places and had FETCH REC, and that kind of gave me an idea. Was Sam trying to say "fetch records"? It was a long shot, but maybe that was what the key was for. It was too small to fit in any door I'd ever seen, but maybe a filing cabinet or a safety deposit box…?

I fingered the tiny mark stamped into one side of the key. It was the image of a bowl, with three straight, downward strokes; I'd never seen anything like it. On the opposite side was the number 28, obviously a reference to a cabinet or box. I got hold of the phone and called the concierge. "What bank uses the image of a bowl with three lines on it?"

"A bowl? Three lines?" He was clearly confused, but polite about it. "A bank, sir?"

"Yeah. It's a… what do you call it? A motif? A symbol?"

"Perhaps sir is referring to a logo?"

"Yeah, that's it. A logo. What bank uses that?"

"I do not have that information at my fingertips, but if sir would give me but a moment, I will ring back with a reply."

While I waited for him to call back, I sorted through my mostly undamaged luggage for clean clothes. Something told me to lock my passport in the wall safe in my room, but I put my wallet in my back pocket and made sure I was wearing a watch. My feet were still sore from my impromptu walking tour of the native quarter, so I dug out my shoes, the same worn, comfortable old pair I'd brought with me. I made sure I was dressed like I belonged here. I didn't want to look like a tourist; I wanted to blend in with the locals or, at the very least, come across as some anonymous expatriate in town for the war. I debated whether to have some breakfast but my stomach still felt queasy, so I decided to skip it. Five minutes later the phone rang, but it was a different voice on the line.

"Mr. Stoyles, I am pleased to help you." The accent was vaguely Greek, the voice about as soothing as an oil drum full of ball bearings. "You had a question about a logo?"

"Yeah." My intuition prickled the hairs on the back of my neck. "I think I was talking to somebody else, though."

"He is not here. He has gone on a little break. I am more than happy to help you."

Nothing about this felt right, but I didn't have a choice. "Yeah, all right. Give it to me."

"The logo you describe is that of the National Bank of Egypt. There is a branch very near here, should you require banking services."

"Thanks. I appreciate it."

I made my way to the street and had a look around, alert for trouble, but didn't see anything besides what you'd expect to see on any given weekday. I slipped around to the front and started up the street, walking approximately parallel to the Nile with the air of someone going nowhere in particular. It stood to reason I'd be followed, and I intended to make it as difficult for them as possible. The only flaw in my brilliant plan? I had absolutely no idea where I was going. The guidebook I'd brought to Cairo with me had been destroyed when my hotel room blew up, and there was nobody around to ask—at least, nobody who spoke English. I reasoned that eventually I would come across something recognizable or somebody who could give me accurate directions.

I'd just crossed the Shari' esh-Sheikh Rihan when the unmistakable sound of gunfire made me flatten against the nearest building. I looked up and down the street but didn't see anything. I was trying hard to concentrate on my surroundings, but my heart was going like a trip-hammer and the heat made it hard to breathe. I crouched behind a clump of aloes and made a quick survey of nearby rooftops. There was no way a handgun would have accurate range at that distance, which meant anybody shooting at me from up there would have to be using a rifle. I waited, counting slowly to a thousand, and then started off in the opposite direction. Again, gunfire rang out, but this time I said to hell with it and started running for all I was worth, reasoning it was harder to hit a moving target. Two or three bullets sang dangerously close to me, and flying stone chips from a building struck my cheek and drew blood.

I was within sight of the hotel when a small yellow Fiat with Cairo plates screeched to a halt beside me and the passenger door flew open. "Get in."

I didn't recognize her. She was wearing a headscarf and dark sunglasses, but so were about a hundred other women on the streets. "Get in!" She seemed to take my hesitation personally; she reached across, grabbed my sleeve and yanked me toward the car. I fell in, and the door slammed shut behind me; she shoved the car into gear and squealed away.

"Do you know who was shooting at you?" She took a corner at speed, and then cut down an alley, knocking aside trash cans and scaring half a dozen unwary chickens who had the bad luck to get in her way. "Did you see who it was?"

"Didn't see a thing, lady. By the way, who are you?"

She pulled the sunglasses off and tossed them onto the dashboard of the Fiat. "I must apologize, Mr. Stoyles. I should never have left you to your own devices. I am afraid my husband will not be very pleased with me."

"*Bismillah....*" Tareenah Halim. "You do this sort of thing on a regular basis?" She was making like Mata Hari, but I had no idea what the hell was going on. "First you tell me to find Sam, and then you tell me not to bother. You mind telling me what's going on?"

"Ibrahim Samir contacted me. I have been searching for you since last night, when the bomb exploded at the hotel. At first we thought you had been killed."

"How'd you know I wasn't?" This was getting ridiculous. "You got somebody tailing me?"

She threw me a nervous smile. "Mr. Stoyles, I am eager to have my husband returned to me safely. There are many things you do not understand."

How much did she know about Sam's other life, about the relationships he'd formed away from Cairo? It wasn't my place to tell her; that was Sam's job. "You said a mouthful, lady."

"Have you eaten breakfast?" She turned down a narrow side street and put the car in park. Her long, black hair cascaded around her shoulders as she took the scarf off and tossed it into the back seat. "I apologize if I shock you. I do not normally wear the *hijab*."

"It's fine." I couldn't take my eyes off her. She really was one of the most beautiful women I had ever seen. "I understand. So, what now?"

"Food." She put the car into drive and peeled out onto the main street. "First, a good breakfast. My Samuel would never forgive me if I let you starve to death."

I was confused, and I told her so. "What's going on? Why are you involved with all this?"

"It is complicated. Before Sam left on his most recent assignment, he took care to put certain measures into place. This included a handpicked cadre of trusted informants. One of these you have already met."

"Ibrahim Samir."

"Correct. He is much valued by my husband. A difficult and often angry young man, but faithful to a fault and completely loyal to Sam. You cannot imagine how rare a thing that is these days, with war raging throughout the world." She stopped to let a blue-robed fellah and his donkey cross the street; the donkey was so weighed down with bales of cotton as to make his species nearly unidentifiable.

"Who else?"

"A young American working at Shepheard's Hotel as a masseur. I believe you have already met him. He is also loyal to my husband, but I took the precaution of asking him to watch out for you while you were in Cairo." She rolled down the driver's side window a little. "The third is, I regret to say, no longer with us."

Shiva, the taxi driver. "Do you know who killed him?"

She shook her head, the black hair flying around her shoulders. "I do not. Probably the same person who was shooting at you this morning. He has already determined you are my husband's close companion. You are a marked man, Mr. Stoyles."

"Tell me something I don't know."

"My great-grandfather's first wife was the ugliest woman in Zaqaziq."

My head snapped around. "What?"

Her smile was luminous, as beautiful as the day. "You said to tell you something you did not know." She laughed gently. "Mr. Stoyles, I am not what you expected. I realize this. Too often, those of the West imagine the women of Egypt as creatures from some medieval caliph's *hareem* whose marriages are arranged for them by a male relative. I met Samuel at university in England, where I was studying languages." She turned down the street leading to the Halim residence. "Not all marriages are arranged, Mr. Stoyles. Some of us do marry for love."

It was like a punch in the gut. Oh, I knew I had no right to be jealous—Sam and I had never made any promises to one another—but it felt like a metaphorical door had just slammed in my face. He loved his wife and she loved him. They'd been pals in university; they had a beautiful house and four lovely kids and everything was fine. "That's nice." I tried to put some feeling behind it. "Yeah, that's real nice."

We pulled into the driveway, and she turned the car off, but she didn't get out right away. Instead she turned and put her hand in mine. There was something in her beautiful dark eyes that told me this woman knew everything. "My husband speaks very highly of you. He has said to me many times that he cherishes you as the dearest among all his companions. Indeed, he called you *habibi*."

My throat was tight. "I don't know what that means."

She squeezed my hand. "It means you are beloved of my husband."

"Did he…." A whisper was the most I could manage. "Did he say that?"

"Come inside and eat, Mr. Stoyles. You have had a very eventful morning."

A little girl in a pink dress was waiting for us inside. She had dark hair and wise, sad brown eyes; she might have been a tiny, feminine version of Sam. "Stamos won't let me have the crayons."

"Tabia, where are your manners?"

Tareenah Halim introduced us and, crouching so we were at eye level, I took the girl's soft little hand in mine. "I am very pleased to meet you, Tabia. Your father has told me about you."

Her brows creased. "Are you his friend?"

"I am."

"I wish you would tell him to come home. Stamos is completely out of control." She dipped her head and disappeared into the interior of the house.

I sat at the table while Tareenah brought bread and honey, fresh fruit, and strong coffee made as only the Egyptians can make it. She drank a cup while I ate, and she didn't waste time on small talk. "Mr. Stoyles, who do you think was shooting at you? Is there anyone in Cairo who might wish you dead?" I explained about Jonah Octavian and my theory that he was a Nazi operative involved in war profiteering. She seemed to know who I was talking about. "My husband mentioned this man. He is a *kalb*—a dog."

"I agree. Sam telephoned me the night before I left Newfoundland to come to Egypt. He said he did not remember how he got to where he is. Do you think someone might have been…." I hesitated, not wanting to alarm her unnecessarily. "I don't know… doing things that would confuse him?"

She poured another cup from the Turkish pot with a mere flick of her wrist. "Allied prisoners—that is to say, prisoners who are sympathetic to the Allied cause—are often tortured by the Nazis, who use the drug scopolamine." Her gaze did not waver. "It interferes with memory."

"Why did you tell me to stop looking for Sam?"

Her lower lip trembled, but she took a breath and squared her shoulders. "I have reason to believe that some of my husband's colleagues may not be the worthy men they appear to be. The night of the party, I overheard three of them talking, and one of them let drop a phrase that gave me great pause."

"I see."

"Mr. Stoyles, I have debated with myself for a long time. When first I met you, I wanted you to look for Sam. Then I was not so sure. I feared involving you in it." She turned her cup around and around in its saucer. "You are a foreigner; I did not want to take the risk."

"You didn't know if you could trust me."

She nodded.

"I don't blame you. Hell, the whole world's gone insane, and I have no idea where to even start. Sergeant Samir said Sam had gone to Newfoundland on an assignment, and he disappeared right after he landed in Cairo." Upon arrival, Sam would have either gone to the police station or to his home; there was nowhere else he needed to be. He hadn't come home, which meant he had gone to the station or been waylaid on his way there. "Mrs. Halim, how well do you know your husband's colleagues? The other men at the police department, I mean. Is there anybody there you don't trust?"

"Most of the men Sam works with are veterans of the force. Ibrahim Samir has been there for some ten years; Sam's superior officer, for nearly twenty-five."

"Even veterans can be seduced away from duty if the price is right."

"I don't think it is a matter of money, Mr. Stoyles. I believe whoever has kidnapped my husband has done so for ideological reasons." She sighed. "Still, it would be like Sam to get a message out if at all possible. Perhaps I should be a little jealous, Mr. Stoyles, that he chose to telephone you that night rather than his wife."

"I don't think it has anything to do with you. I doubt they'd even let him use the phone. He probably got to a telephone and only had a brief window of time to make the call." *That's why he called me instead of his wife.*

"Perhaps you are right." Her smile was forced, and I suddenly felt like I'd overstayed my welcome.

"Mrs. Halim, you've been very kind to me. That breakfast was delicious, but I think I should get going. I want to stop by the police department and see what I can find out. I don't know how much good that will do, but it's worth a try. I'll stop by my hotel first and change my clothes." It would be a good opportunity to advise the Cairo police about Shiva, not that I expected them to do very much. Whoever had plugged him was long gone by now.

She nodded. "I will drive you."

I DIDN'T tell Tareenah Halim, but I had no intention of looking for somebody who might have a reason to sell Sam out to the Nazis. My experience with thugs like that told me I only needed to make it known I was looking for him, and his captors would come crawling out of the desert like dung beetles.

I didn't bother going up to my hotel room, either. As soon as Mrs. Halim's yellow Fiat turned the corner of Shari' esh-Sheikh Rihan, I hailed a cab and directed him to the National Bank of Egypt branch on the Sharia El Madabegh. I had no real way of knowing which branch the key had come from, but this particular branch was the one featured on the tourist map I had bought to replace my guidebook. I figured I'd start there and work my way backward if necessary. Hopefully, they wouldn't raise too much of a stink when I asked to unlock the box; some banks were okay with it as long as you had the right key, but some got suspicious if just anybody waltzed in asking for admission to the vault.

The cabbie let me out practically on the doorstep, and I made sure to give him a decent tip. I've lived in cities all my life, and one thing I've learned, a savvy taxi driver is one of the best friends you can have. "You want I should wait for you, effendi?" He was young, not more than twenty years old, neatly dressed in a white, button-down shirt and khaki trousers. "I do not mind waiting."

"Yeah, why don't you? I'd appreciate it." I handed over a pound note and watched his eyes light up.

"The Americani is most generous! I will wait here."

"Thanks, pal." I tapped the passenger door. "This won't take too long." If he knew I was whistling in the dark, he didn't say anything.

I went in through the big double doors and joined the line forming to one side of the tellers' counter. The bank had opened for the day's business less than an hour ago, but already there were quite a few people ahead of me. I noticed a woman in full native garb with two little boys, and an elderly man wearing a hearing aid. There were also two men in casual trousers and long-sleeved shirts who seemed to be together; I couldn't be sure, since they were standing with their backs to me. One was taller than the other and slender in that rawboned way that suggests a familiarity with physical exercise; he was standing close behind the shorter man and seemed to be holding his companion's elbow from behind. The man in front was wearing clothes that weren't exactly pristine, and this seemed strange to me considering how many admonitions to personal cleanliness there are in the Koran. Most Egyptians, even the poorest of the poor, make an effort; the soap sellers and perfumers do a brisk business in this part of the world. The way his companion was standing was weird, too, almost reaching around the other man from behind and holding on to him. I couldn't get it out of my mind. There was something really wrong about this, something undeniably sinister.

The young man standing at the wicket looked me and my key over carefully before consenting to give me access to the vault. We passed through a doorway and into a small anteroom; the vault door was open, and I could see row upon row of safety deposit boxes, reaching from floor to ceiling. "Your number is 28." He took the key and ascended a small ladder, unlocked the box, and brought it down to me. "There are rooms out the door and to your left, should you wish privacy. Please advise someone on the staff when you are done."

I tucked the box under my arm and started out the door, but I never made it. The rawboned man was there, holding a Luger against his companion's side. "You will stop right there, Mr. Stoyles."

His companion was Samuel Halim.

CHAPTER FOUR

SAM'S FACE was pale and frightened, the skin over his cheekbones taut. There were new lines bracketing his mouth. I saw recognition in his eyes, and I was relieved; maybe the bully boys had left off with the drugs. He gazed at me and shook his head, a millimeter's shift from right to left.

"Step into this room, Mr. Stoyles." Sam's captor waved the Luger at me, directing me into one of the small booths the bank provided for the privacy of box holders. I went in first, with Sam following me. Luger-Boy came last. He had the thin, ravaged face of a fanatical ideologue, complete with the burning eyes; a long, jagged scar ran from his left eye to the corner of his mouth. He shut the door behind us and took the box from me. "If any of the contents are missing, I will kill both of you." His accent wasn't Egyptian and he wasn't an American; if I'd had to guess, I'd have said Swedish or Norwegian, one of the Scandinavian states. He flipped open the lid with one hand, while his other held the gun to cover us both. I was standing close enough to Sam that I could touch him, and I did, laying the palm of my hand on the curve of his lower back. It felt good to touch him, to feel the heat of his body burning through his dirty cotton shirt.

"Where is the list?" Luger-Boy rifled through the contents of the safety deposit box and came up with a small piece of pale blue paper. Someone had written on it in pen, both sides, but it was just long columns of numbers. "Ah. Captain Halim, you delight me."

"Made your day, huh, buddy?" I wondered what the piece of paper was that had him so interested. Maybe radio frequencies or some sort of code; I'd heard the Allies were using special routing codes to foil German code breakers, who seemed to be nicely keeping pace with Allied cryptographers. Getting hold of that sort of intelligence would be a real coup. Maybe this was what Sam had meant with his FETCH REC anagram, although I couldn't see Sam being so stupid as to leave something like that lying around in a safety deposit box. "Now that you've got what you came for, how's about letting us go, huh? We won't cause you any trouble." It only made sense they'd been tailing me ever since I'd come to Cairo; that I hadn't spotted anybody meant nothing. The city was full of taxi drivers and water sellers and beggars looking for baksheesh, and anybody could have been feeding these guys information.

"Shut up, Stoyles. If I want your opinion, you will be the first to know." He pored over the list, his expression almost gleeful. "Yes, this is perfect. We have been looking for this for ages."

"Must be your lucky day."

"It is, Mr. Stoyles." His wolfish grin came and went. "Now that I have this, Captain Halim is of no further use to me."

"What are you gonna do with him?"

"He will be disposed of. But first, you will take this box back and give it to the teller. And don't bother trying anything. I will be watching you, with this gun in Captain Halim's ribs. Trust me, Mr. Stoyles, I will shoot him right here, and then I will kill you." He shrugged. "Perhaps I will kill everyone in the bank and make you watch. It is hard to say how my mood will take me."

Sam spoke for the first time. "You are a true patriot, Errki. Your German comrades will be pleased a Finn has managed to attain what they could not." He was giving me information, and I was careful to make a mental note of it. "The name of Aaltonen will doubtless be renowned as a great one." Errki Aaltonen. Finnish. According to some people, the Finns had spent this war sitting on their hands; maybe Errki Aaltonen was trying to score points with his Nazi bosses. "You are lucky to have found it. Truly, Aaltonen, it is the only thing of value in that… *box*."

I didn't look at Sam; his tone of voice told me everything I needed to know. I took the box Aaltonen passed me and started for the door, but I was watching the Finn out of the corner of my eye. He turned his head, and I tripped myself. The box flew out of my hands, and its contents scattered everywhere. "Aw, jeez, I'm sorry!" I fell to my knees and started picking up the scraps of paper; Sam, edging toward me, placed his foot over a scrap of plain white paper and drew it toward him. While Aaltonen cursed me, I gathered up the contents and stuffed it back into the box, assuming an appropriately contrite expression. "I'm sorry. I didn't mean for that to happen. I'll just take this back to the teller."

Aaltonen's face was brick red. I'd have to say he was furious with me right then. "*Do* that, Mr. Stoyles, and attempt nothing. Remember, my gun is pressed against the dear captain's ribs."

I stepped outside, located the teller, and handed the box off to him. When I went back into the room, Aaltonen had hold of Sam's elbow again. "Leaving so soon, Errki?"

"Do nothing that you will regret, Mr. Stoyles. Turn your face to that wall and count to one hundred slowly. Then you may leave. I would caution you, however, against any… unwise ideas."

"Do as he says, Jack." Sam's face was serene, his eyes full of affection for me. "*Ana uhibbuk.*" I watched Aaltonen drag him out the door, and then I did as the Finn had ordered. Near the wall where Sam and I had been standing was that scrap of plain white paper he'd had under his foot. I bent and picked it up and read what was written there. It seemed to be a quote of some kind, poetry:

> *If anyone wants to know what "spirit" is,*
> *or what "God's fragrance" means,*
> *lean your head toward him or her.*
> *Keep your face there close.*
> *Like this.*

> *When someone quotes the old poetic image*
> *about clouds gradually uncovering the moon,*
> *slowly loosen knot by knot the strings*
> *of your robe.*
> *Like this.*

> *If anyone wonders how Jesus raised the dead,*
> *don't try to explain the miracle.*
> *Kiss me on the lips.*
> *Like this. Like this.*

I FILLED up then, and before I knew what was happening, I was blubbering like a child. I hadn't cried in ages, not even when Judy died in

Philadelphia, but I was crying now. I cried as I walked through the great foyer of the bank, past the tellers' counter, and out the great double doors. I stopped before the taxi and wiped my eyes on the tail of my shirt before I got in.

The driver gazed at me with great, dark eyes full of compassion. "You are sad, effendi?"

"Yeah, something like that." I pressed my hands against my eyelids, willing back the tears. "Can you take me to the police station?" I told him which one and gave him the address. Ibrahim Samir should be just coming off the night shift now, and I was eager to tell him what I'd found out. The little scrap of paper with the poem on it I would keep for myself... and what did that mean, the phrase Sam had used? *Ana uḥibbuk.* I had bought a new Arabic phrasebook to replace the one I'd lost in the fire, but I'd left it in my hotel room. I turned to the cab driver. "Hey, you're from here, aren't you?"

"Yes, effendi." He deftly swung his cab around a driver and two camels in the road. "My name is Khybir. I live with my brothers on the Sharia Soliman Pasha."

"What does *ana uḥibbuk* mean, huh?" We stopped at an intersection. "I don't know that one."

A subtle blush stained his cheeks, and he suddenly couldn't look at me. "I... could not say for certain."

"You don't know what it means?"

"I do know, but I am afraid the Americani might take offence."

"No, I'm asking." The light changed, and Khybir's cab darted forward. "Trust me, I won't be angry."

"It means *I love you*, when said to a man."

My heart thumped violently in my chest. "It does, huh?" I sat back and lit a cigarette, pretending nonchalance, but inside I was as jumpy as a bag of eels. "That's what it means. Great. Thanks." *It means "I love you."*

"I have answered your question?" He peered at me cautiously, out of the corner of his eye.

"Oh yeah."

I FOUND Ibrahim Samir in the locker room just as his shift ended. He looked tired and scruffy, and a fresh bruise darkened the right side of his face. "A tourist was causing difficulty near the Muski bazaar." He grinned. "He resisted my suggestion he should move along."

"Tough guy, huh?" I shook his hand warmly. I was glad to see him. I told him what had happened at the bank, how I'd seen Sam, but I left out the part about the poem. I had it folded neatly in my wallet, where I intended to keep it safe, just like I intended to keep Sam's heartfelt declaration. The poem might prove to be another encoded message. At this stage of the game, I was eager for whatever intelligence I could get. I had no guarantee Aaltonen would let Sam out of this alive.

"Our priority is to recover Captain Halim, of course, but this Aaltonen must be found." Samir led me downstairs and out the main doors of the station. "I have had a difficult night and I must sleep, at least for a while." He glanced at his wristwatch. "I will call on you at your hotel, around four?"

"Four, yeah, that's fine." I wondered what I was supposed to do till then, but Samir had that covered. He scribbled a name and an address on a slip of paper and gave it to me.

"This man knows everything about everything. He may not see you, but if he does, he will expect payment for the privilege, as well as money for any information he provides."

"Uh-huh." Yeah, I'd met guys like that before. "So I guess he does this for a living?"

Samir laughed. "He has no need to work. It is a hobby for him. Make no mistake. He is not likely to accept merely a handful of piasters; you will have to dig deep for this one. Will you be all right until I come to you?" He leaned toward me and cupped my cheek in his hand. "You have made me very happy. Captain Halim is alive. This is good news."

"Yeah, I'll be okay. As long as the Acacia Court doesn't blow up, huh?" I stepped back to let a group of American sailors go by. They were obviously the worse for drink and more than a little rowdy, but if they noticed Samir's hand on my face it obviously didn't bother them too much. It wasn't unusual for Arabic men to exchange affectionate gestures in public, so maybe they figured we were just part of the local color. If that were true, I was blending in better than I thought. "See you at four."

I thought about making a quick call to Tareenah to let her know Sam was okay, but decided against it. If, as she suspected, some of Sam's colleagues weren't kosher, it wasn't a good idea to discuss things over the telephone. No, I'd wait till I saw her in person.

The name on the slip of paper that Samir had given me was Pasha Nubar. I climbed back into the cab and directed Khybir to the Sharia Elfy Bey, near the Midan Opera. We honked our way past a lot of pedestrians, natives with donkeys, tourists, and soldiers of all stripes, before Khybir pulled up in front of an all white building with a lot of brass around the doors and windows. I went up three broad steps to a set of double doors and rang the bell. After a few minutes, the door was opened by a woman old enough to be Cleopatra's grandmother. She peered up at me out of eyes that would have looked at home on a potato and said something in Arabic.

"I'm looking for Pasha Nubar. Does he live here?"

"Ahhhhhh, *Engleezhi*! Come in, come in!" She bowed alarmingly from the waist, her skinny frame looking like it would break in half, and showed me into an opulent foyer done in gold and red. There were a lot of expensive hangings on the walls and a lot of fancy rugs underfoot, and I could smell incense from somewhere in the house, a pungent scent like sandalwood. "The Pasha Nubar will be pleased to see the honored Americani, just a moment, just a moment." It was one of those quaint acts I'd heard the locals like to put on for foreigners, so I wasn't impressed. I waited patiently, listening to the faint strains of native music wafting from another room, and a few minutes later, I heard footsteps, accompanied by heavy breathing, and then the fattest man I ever saw hove into view in front of me.

He was roughly egg-shaped and almost completely bald, with a huge, protruding stomach and tiny hands and feet. His small eyes twinkled with merriment, as if he were enjoying some private joke; all in all he reminded me of Sidney Greenstreet, and when he spoke, he sounded like him, too. "Mr. Stoyles, sir, I am so glad you have come, so very, very glad you have come."

I put out my hand as he came toward me but instead of shaking it, he took hold of it and drew my arm under his. "How did you know my name?"

"The young Samir telephoned me you might be coming. Now, then, sir, come inside and let us make ourselves comfortable." He led me down a hallway and into a large room that had been built to resemble a tent. The walls and ceiling were hung with great swaths of red silk, tasseled in gold; the floor was covered in antique carpets and a selection of lush cushions. A small table sat at one end of the room, holding a coffee pot and several cups on a tray. There was a water pipe—a *shisha*—right next to it, with multiple hoses leading off the bottle. Clearly, Pasha Nubar had expensive tastes. "Sit down, Mr. Stoyles, and tell me how you came to be in Cairo. You are not dressed as a soldier, so I do not think you come to fight. It must be love, then. Sit and have some coffee and tell me about your love."

I guess I must have looked like a camel caught in the headlights, because he laughed. It was rich and unfeigned and put me immediately at ease. I accepted a cup of strong Egyptian coffee from him and a plate full of dainties. It had been hours since I'd eaten, and I was starving. "I came looking for information, actually."

"Ah, information! The universal currency." He took a drag off the pipe and exhaled a cloud of smoke. "You are seeking the man who killed your taxi driver, Shiva El Rawy."

"You've been talking to Samir."

"Yes, but our telephone conversation was of no more than one minute's duration. He was on his way to bed and told me you would be coming." He leaned over and patted my knee. "Mr. Stoyles, the young Samir told you there is nothing in Cairo I do not know about."

"Uh-huh. Or maybe you read it in the newspapers."

He shrugged and then laughed heartily. "You have me, sir! You have me. Come, have another cup of coffee." He refilled both our cups and reclined on his cushions. "The driver, Shiva El Rawy, was not personally known to me, but I knew his father many years ago, during the last war. Shiva El Rawy was—" He started up, eyes wide and staring, and I turned to look. Just there, silhouetted head-and-shoulders in a small window, was the figure of a man with both hands held in front of his face. Pasha Nubar's enormous body jerked backward and was still, the sharp point of a blow-dart sticking out of the side of his neck. I didn't have to look to know he was dead.

I scrambled to my feet and lunged for the front door, passing the elderly housekeeper on the way; she was screaming like an air raid siren. I was out of there in the space between heartbeats, diving into Khybir's cab like my life depended on it. "Go."

Khybir blinked like he'd just woken from a long sleep. "Does the effendi wish to be taken to the hotel?"

"Just *go*, Khybir! Anywhere. Drive." This was bad. This was very, very bad. The last thing I needed was a murder rap, especially in a town like this. Once word got out a foreigner had killed a great man like Pasha Nubar, my life wouldn't be worth a handful of wooden piasters. The fact that I hadn't killed him wouldn't matter; just being in the same room with him was enough to make me the number one suspect. "Take me to the hotel, yeah." No. The guy with the blow gun would probably be waiting for me. "No, take me to the police station."

Khybir had already been en route to the Acacia Court, but he didn't turn a hair, merely slewed the cab around in the middle of the street like he did it every day. All the traffic behind and in front of us started honking their horns simultaneously, and part of an English regiment was scattered from hell to breakfast before they could finish crossing. They shook their fists in the air and cursed us, but if that was the worst of what I'd have to put up with, I didn't mind one bit. Khybir let me out in front of the police station, and I tipped him a pound note. "Don't wait for me." I glanced up at the building full of cops. "I may be here awhile."

"Indeed you may, Mr. Stoyles." A firm grip fell on my shoulder, tugging my hands behind me, and I heard the unmistakable metal *hiss* of handcuffs being fastened around my wrists. "Indeed you may."

Ibrahim Samir didn't look at all happy to see me.

THE POLICE lockup was about what you'd expect: dirty, crowded, filled with angry men of various backgrounds, some native and some not, and a member of His Majesty's Navy with the loudest, most annoying voice I'd ever heard, who seemed to be hell-bent on enraging the guards. "Let me out of here, you lot! I say, you'd best let me out. By God, I won't be having this! I can't be having this sort of thing!"

At first there was a lot of pushing and shoving as the bigger men fought for spaces at the front of the cage, where they could see what was going on, but eventually everyone subsided into silence broken only by murmured and occasional conversation. I found a spot on the floor and sat down, cradling my head in my hands. It seemed like years had passed since I'd walked off the plane; I wondered if I'd ever see St. John's or my Heartache Cafe ever again. As soon as I got out, I resolved to place a call to Chris, my bartender back at the Heartache, just to say hello and hear a friendly voice. It was strange I hadn't seen Ibrahim Samir during all of this; since he'd been the one to arrest me, surely there was paperwork to be completed, at least some of which needed my participation. But he was nowhere to be found. It sure didn't follow the kind of protocol I was used to. If you got arrested back in Philly, they'd put you through the wringer before locking you up. I was surprised I hadn't been shoved into a room with the proverbial naked light bulb and smacked around a bit.

The heat inside the cell got worse as the day went on, to the point where some men fainted. I felt especially sorry for a kid about sixteen, propped up against a wall at the back of the cell. His face was an ugly color, and he kept fainting and falling down. Two other guys who were with him would lift him back up and lean him against the wall in the same spot, and then the whole charade would start all over. When the calls for prayer were sounded, everything stopped and the natives immediately assumed the position, during which nobody disturbed them, not even the loud Englishman. Around noon, a metal can of water was handed in and got passed around, and then some kind of rough bread, bland, but still warm from the oven. Then the afternoon prayers, after which everybody— including the loud Englishman—fell into profound silence.

I was napping in the corner when the guard rattled his nightstick against the bars and summoned me over. "You, Stoyles, Americani, come here." He was the young man with the big ears I'd met the first time I'd come into the station. Obviously, he was pretending not to recognize me.

I climbed to my feet and did what I was told. "Yes?"

"You are free to go. Someone is here to meet you." He unlocked the cell door and led me out to the front desk. Khybir, the taxi driver, stood anxiously waiting for me with a worried look on his face.

"Khybir! What are you doing here?"

He reached out and touched my arm. "I have told the police all I know, effendi Stoyles. Now you are free to go."

Free to go?

"The taxi driver has come forward as a witness." The cop handed me a brown envelope containing my personal belongings, including my wallet with that precious scrap of poem in it. "His report on the murder of Pasha Nubar makes it clear you could not possibly have killed him."

I knew enough to keep my mouth shut until we were in the car. "Khybir, thank you. You're a right guy."

He blushed with pleasure. "It is my wish that the effendi Stoyles be free."

Right. What was he getting out of it, I wondered… and from whom?

I was exhausted by the time I got back to the Acacia Court, so I tipped Khybir big and headed straight for a nice, cool shower followed by a late lunch from room service. Ibrahim Samir had said he was going to meet me at four, but I wondered if that plan still held, considering the earlier debacle over Pasha Nubar's death. I didn't get Ibrahim Samir, first he was all hearts and flowers, and then next thing I knew, he had the cuffs on me and I was stuffed in a cell with a hundred other guys for something I didn't do. I was learning real quick how the justice system worked here. Obviously the testimony of one witness, biased or unbiased, was enough to damn or save.

After I ate and got comfortable, I picked up the phone and requested the long distance operator. Frankie Missalo had military connections that could have gotten me priority access, but I wasn't about to take advantage of something I wasn't entitled to. I sat on the line and waited. It was midmorning back home, and Chris would be at the Heartache.

Sure enough, he picked up almost as soon as it started to ring on the other end. "Jack! Where are you? I can't believe you're calling."

It was good to hear his voice. I hadn't realized how much I missed him. I filled him in, talking only in generalities and skipping the whole thing about me being thrown in jail. I deliberately didn't mention Ibrahim Samir, and I said nothing about Sam, knowing this was wartime and somebody, somewhere, was probably eavesdropping. Mostly, I asked how things were going at home, if there were lots of people coming into the Heartache, and how Alphonsus Picco was doing.

Sergeant Picco was a young officer of the Royal Newfoundland Constabulary who'd been instrumental in exposing corruption and graft in his department; he and Chris had gotten close after the death of Chris's girlfriend, Julie Fayre. Picco and I had been involved in an investigation of the Nazi collaborator, Jonah Octavian, who, along with Picco's superiors, was running a few side deals. When Picco had gotten too suspicious—and too close to the truth—Octavian slapped us both in a hole in the ground.

"What can I say, Chris? I guess I just needed to hear a friendly voice." I kept things general with talk about the weather and so on. Something Chris said stuck with me, though, and I found myself turning it over and over in my mind.

"Everybody's wondering what happened to Jonah Octavian."

The overseas connection was a bit crackly, and I had to ask him to repeat himself, but it still didn't make sense. "Everybody? Like who?"

"Phonse said Octavian's become what they call a person of interest."

"Octavian?"

"Something wrong with your ears, Jack? Or maybe it's the overseas connection."

"No, it's just…." Octavian? Why were the cops nosing around traces long left cold? "Skip it."

"No, Jack. Listen, Phonse said this was real. Octavian had a lot of lines in the water. Watch yourself over there, huh?"

"I will."

By the time Chris rang off, I felt real lonely and figured I'd better find some way to keep myself busy. I still didn't know anything about Shiva El Rawy, and I figured I had a good hour and a half before Samir showed—if he decided to show—so I got dressed and went downstairs to the main desk, where the registration clerk was absorbed in a Whiz comic book with Superman on the front, all tights and teeth, charging toward an unseen enemy. After I'd been standing there awhile without any sign from him that I existed, I banged on the bell a few times. "Excuse me, I wonder if you can help me with something."

He looked at me as if drawing himself back from a long way away. "Help you, sir?"

"If you don't mind."

"Superman has tracked the evil Doctor Ratoman to his lair and is extracting information from him by slowly pulling out his teeth one by one with hot pincers." He giggled behind his hand. "It's very funny."

"Yeah, sounds like a real laugh riot. Look, did you know a taxi driver by the name of Shiva El Rawy? He used to work Shepheard's, but he parked here a lot, too."

The clerk delicately licked his fingers and turned the page without looking up. "Shiva El Rawy, the driver who was murdered by an associate of the Americani Jonathan Stoyles?" He sniggered. "That Shiva El Rawy?"

It was like someone had just upended a jug of ice water down my back. "Sure, if that's the way the newspapers are playing it."

"Shiva El Rawy lived with his sister on the Sharia Eloui. His sister lives there still."

"You get that out of the newspapers?"

"Perhaps." He held out his hand, palm up, and I put a piaster in it. He glanced down at my small offering with disdain and went back to his comic book. "The Americani Jonathan Stoyles is clearly not a man of wealth."

I had just turned to go when I ran face-first into an enormous human torso clad in the khaki drill of the Long Range Desert Group. I looked up. The torso belonged to the huge Greek who'd been at Tareenah Halim's party. "Mr. Stoyles." His voice was low and surprisingly soft for a man so large; he had to be six feet six or more.

"Yeah?" I wasn't in the mood.

"You will come with me."

"That the best you guys can do? This is getting really old." I made a break for it but the big Greek caught me around the waist and held on as if I weighed no more than a child. "I dunno what your game is, buddy, but you better lay off!" I kicked and pushed but it was like trying to move a boulder. Maybe I'd be better off saving my strength. Besides, everybody in the lobby had turned to look at the commotion.

"That is much better. My name is Andros Scala. My colleagues would very much appreciate the opportunity to talk to you." He didn't bother holding a gun on me, but he didn't have to. Those big fists looked like they could pound me into hamburger with no trouble at all—either that, or he'd squeeze me to death. "You will come with me, now." We went out by the back door, where a Jeep was parked, and I got in. Scala pulled away from the hotel and turned the car in the direction of Old Cairo.

"So tell me. Who'd I piss off this time?" I fetched out my cigarettes and lit one. "You don't mind if I smoke, do you?"

He laughed. "I do not mind at all. Please, smoke as you wish, Mr. Stoyles. I am not your enemy."

"Yeah. That's what they all say." I couldn't figure his part in all this. Obviously he was military but, unless I'd attracted the attention of the Long Range Desert Group, there was no reason in the world he and I should be having this conversation. Unless…. *"North Atlantic Command advised us to expect you."* The young woman at the desk had said that to me as soon as I landed at Shepheard's, my first day in Cairo. I didn't think much of it. I just figured somebody had their memos mixed up, or maybe I looked like all the other soldiers. But what if it hadn't been a mistake? What if she'd meant it? I didn't know anybody in North Atlantic Command, and I'd surrendered my commission when I'd been booted out of the army. Why the hell would any part of the Allied command be interested in me? "You're, ah, Long Range Desert, huh? Tough bunch of guys."

Scala smiled at me. "Perhaps. If my presence requires a suitable affiliation, that one is as good as any."

"Commandos, maybe?"

His grin widened. "Relax, Lieutenant Stoyles. Enjoy the scenery."

The streets were predictably crowded at that hour of the day, but Scala handled the traffic like a pro. We drove through Giza and into the desert, past the undulating dunes that to me always looked like the breasts and thighs of a reclining nude. I sized Scala up: matinee-idol handsome, maybe forty, with black hair that was graying prematurely at the temples, and a suntanned face. His dark eyes sized up the landscape around him and dismissed it, and he struck me as a man entirely at ease in his own environment. "Do you know where we are going?"

"I'm going to take a wild guess and say the desert. Probably so you can put a bullet in my head."

This obviously amused him. "Why would I want to put a bullet in your head?"

I sat back and drew on my cigarette. "Buddy, your guess is as good as mine, but the way my life has been going lately, nothing would surprise me."

He didn't answer, just looked at me with a quizzical lift of his brows. After a while, we pulled up in front of a modest little house set in the middle of an oasis, near a clump of date palms. Two scabby goats foraged nearby and some items of laundry waved on a clothesline to one side of the house. A woman in a headscarf and with a broom in her hand came to the door and looked out. Evidently displeased by what she saw, she went away again. "This is real nice," I said. "That the little woman there?"

Scala got out of the Jeep. "You are a brave man, Lieutenant Stoyles, to joke in the face of the unknown."

His pronunciation of the word "lieutenant" was after the Commonwealth fashion: one more irritation in a seemingly never ending series of annoyances. "Just Mr. Stoyles is fine by me, buddy. I left the rank behind a long time ago."

"Do you understand the term 'blue ticket,' Lieutenant Stoyles? Then get your pansy ass out of my office."

Inside there wasn't a lot of furniture, but there sure was a lot of radio equipment. The woman in the headscarf was actually a WAC, and I saw the two other men Scala had been with at the party standing off to one side, talking quietly to a blond kid with headphones over one ear. A dark-haired, brown-eyed man with the lean, sculpted features of a star athlete got up from behind a desk and came over; like Scala, he was wearing the khaki drill of the Long Range Desert Group. "Lieutenant Jack Stoyles, isn't it?" His accent was not quite English; I couldn't place it. "I'm Captain Kevin MacBride. Welcome to our Cairo listening post. We've been expecting you."

CHAPTER FIVE

I DIDN'T know what the hell MacBride was talking about, and I had no desire to find out. "Listen, this big goon here kidnapped me from my hotel—"

"You shouldn't call Colonel Scala a goon." A third man—a gangly, sandy-haired American—appeared at MacBride's elbow. "It hurts his feelings. Maybe you ought to gimme what's in your wallet." His accent was Appalachian all the way, West Virginia or Kentucky maybe, or I missed my guess. "We've been waiting for it."

"What the hell is this, anyway? Some kind of a shakedown?" I brought out my wallet. "Here. I got ten Egyptian pounds. Take it, unless you want the piasters in my pocket as well? I dunno what your game is, MacBride, but as soon as I get hold of somebody at the American embassy...."

"The slip of paper in your wallet, Lieutenant." MacBride suppressed a smile, but only just. "If you please."

"Slip of paper?" This was confusing me all to hell.

"The one you took from the safety deposit box at the bank." MacBride held out his hand. "Quickly, man, Berlin's about to get on the wire. We haven't got all day."

"No use, MacBride. Some Finnish guy with a Luger took it from me. He's probably halfway to Helsinki by now. The only thing I got in here is this poem... part of a poem." I handed it over.

Scala and the American grinned. "Thank God," MacBride said. "Looks like Captain Halim was as good as his word."

"Wait a minute… there was another piece of paper… blue, with writing all over it, columns of numbers and stuff like that. Isn't that the one you want?"

"No, this is exactly what we want. What we've been waiting for, in fact." MacBride gave it to the blond kid with the headphones, who fiddled around with some dials on his console. "You see, for some months now, Captain Halim has been… well, he's been what you might call our point man out here."

"Wait a minute. Sam is a cop."

"True. In civilian life he is a police officer." MacBride broke off. "Look, there won't be much to shout about until Polanski here has finished eavesdropping on the Germans. Why don't we go into the muster room and wait? It's more comfortable."

A door opened onto a narrow corridor with rooms on either side, and MacBride led us into one of these: a square space crowded with desks and chairs, radio equipment, maps and charts. A row of tall windows let in plenty of bright desert light, and a long sofa at one end of the room kept company with several deep armchairs. I sank into one of these and lit a cigarette. MacBride gestured to someone at a nearby desk and presently, a pretty WAC appeared with a tea trolley.

"I've taken the liberty of ordering coffee for you and"—MacBride nodded at the gangly American next to him—"Corporal Shelton here. I've found it's usually the colonial types who drink tea."

Shelton lit a cigarette. "Goddamn horse piss."

MacBride handed me a hot cup of coffee that smelled heavenly and tasted even better. I gulped down half of it in one go. "Lieutenant Stoyles, I won't waste your time. North Africa is becoming very, very important in this war and has been ever since the summer of 1940. Like everybody else, you probably know Rommel is doing his level bloody best to gain as much ground as he can in northern Africa."

"Yeah," Shelton put in, "but so far we've been kicking his ass."

"Quite so." MacBride grinned. "As Corporal Shelton so… colorfully puts it, we've been kicking his arse. The whole point of the exercise, Lieutenant Stoyles, is not merely to secure ground, but to do so strategically."

"I still don't see where I fit in." I tapped ash off my cigarette and accepted a top-off of my coffee from MacBride. "Gentlemen, let me say for myself, and on behalf of everybody else, what you guys are doing out here is amazing and we appreciate it, but I have no idea how I fit into this." My breath caught in my throat.

"Do you understand the term 'blue ticket,' Lieutenant Stoyles?"

"I'm not allowed to serve. My commanding officer made that much very clear to me long before we ever got into this war."

"Get your pansy ass out of my office."

"In point of fact, Captain MacBride, I'm unfit for active duty."

"Yeah, we looked at all that." It was Shelton who spoke; he wasn't looking at me but at the end of his cigarette. "That don't apply in this situation. We sorta operate outside the usual parameters."

A door opened and closed somewhere along the corridor, and there was a brief flash of a bird's wing against one of the windows. MacBride sipped his tea and smoked quietly, and the big Greek, Scala, stood behind his chair, his attitude casual but watchful. I got the distinct impression he'd destroy anybody who got too close to MacBride, and I wondered what the story was with the two of them. Corporal Shelton gazed at me, drawing slowly on his cigarette, and I had the sensation of being watched very closely, as a bird of prey watches. They were not men I would ever want to cross.

"Usual parameters." I looked down into my coffee cup and saw a tiny replica of my face reflected there. "Which means…?"

MacBride sat forward. "Lieutenant, you can be eminently useful to your country and to this cause. Newfoundland is of primary strategic importance to the Allies, as I'm sure you know. Now, being a restaurateur as you are—"

"Uh-huh. So we're finally getting at it."

"You are most ably placed to hear things. And to report them."

"You want me to be a… spy?" All I could think of was the desk clerk at the hotel, hunched over his Superman comic, laughing his ass off. "Don't I get a cape or a special pair of tights or something?"

MacBride exchanged a look with Shelton. "Lieutenant Stoyles—"

"Yeah, skip it." I crushed out my cigarette and stood up. "I don't know what game you guys are playing, but count me out. I told you, I'm no longer a soldier."

Shelton looked up at me. I don't think he'd moved as much as an inch since he sat down. "You could be. If you wanted to."

"Please." MacBride stood up. There was something in his expression: humility, maybe, or desperation. "You are eminently well-placed to be extraordinarily useful."

"Okay." The hairs on the back of my neck prickled. "What are you guys getting at?"

Scala straightened. "We've already told you."

"There's a dozen other guys in Newfoundland with restaurants—cafes, bars, you name it. They've got a whole street in St. John's with nothing but bars on it! Why don't you pick one of those guys, huh?"

"Wait a minute." Shelton was lazily cleaning his fingernails with a pocket knife. "They got a whole street with nothing on it but bars?"

I blinked at him. "Yeah. It's called George Street. North America's best pub crawl outside of Bourbon, if you care."

"Lieutenant Stoyles, we chose you for two reasons." MacBride looked weary. "You are an American, and although you no longer live in the United States, your emotional connection to your home city of Philadelphia is quite strong."

My stomach clenched. "You've been talking to the wrong people."

"Also," MacBride continued, "you are a close personal friend of Captain Halim."

"Okay." I didn't bother to deny it. Obviously these guys already knew much more than they were telling. "I still don't follow you."

MacBride rubbed his forehead, and I found myself wondering when he'd slept last. There were lines fanning out from the corners of his eyes, and his mouth was bracketed with tension. "Sam Halim is an Allied operative, charged with information gathering between here and Newfoundland."

"You find it"—Shelton yawned—"and he brings it to us here."

"And the fact that I've been cashiered out of the army kind of allays any suspicions I might still be fighting the war. After all, I'm unfit." There was no point in trying to keep the bitterness out of my voice. It and a lot of other things were there, inches below the surface. "Not like you guys, who get the glorious opportunity to be heroes for Greece and Australia and the States."

MacBride coughed diplomatically. "New Zealand."

"Oh, I beg your pardon."

"You would be aiding the war effort in a way that will make an enormous difference." MacBride was deadly earnest. "And you would be making Sam Halim's work an awful lot easier for him. Your information gathering could conceivably provide us with valuable intelligence, the knowledge we need to shut down men like Jonah Octavian."

"Jonah Octavian." I nodded. "I wondered when we were going to get to him."

There was a tap on the door, and the blond kid peered in. "Got that transcript for you, Captain."

MacBride nodded. "Thank you." He dropped his cigarette butt into his teacup. "Lieutenant Stoyles, we need you. More to the point, Sam Halim needs you. For months now, we've been trying to find someone we could trust, someone to work with Sam on the other end. Cairo is crawling with Allied agents, but most of the troops who come to Newfoundland are merely passing through on their way somewhere else." His shoulders sagged. "Whether you believe it or not, the intelligence gathered by Samuel Halim is of vital importance to the war in North Africa. He needs someone he can depend on absolutely, someone who will be there for him at the other end. Someone who understands what curious acrostics mean, and who can get into bank safety deposit boxes as necessary."

What else did Kevin MacBride know that he wasn't telling? "You're talking like you know he's going to get out of this, get away from whoever's holding him."

MacBride glanced at his wristwatch. "I'm out of time for now. You'll be at the Acacia Court if I need to contact you?"

"Yeah." I couldn't frame an appropriate answer; this was all too strange for me. "Yeah, I'm not even gonna ask how you knew that, but I'll be there. Or you can get Colonel Scala here to kidnap me like he did last time." I turned to go, but was momentarily halted by MacBride.

"One more thing, Lieutenant. Be careful what you say to Tareenah Halim. I realize she's Sam Halim's wife, but at the moment, she's something of an unknown quantity."

"And Ibrahim Samir?"

"Proceed with caution, Lieutenant Stoyles." MacBride exchanged a look with the Greek. "Until we know more."

IT WAS quarter to four when Scala dropped me off in front of the Acacia Court. He dipped his head to me, smiled solemnly, and drove away. I darted a quick glance at the surrounding rooftops, just in case the blow-dart guy who'd killed Pasha Nubar was waiting for my return. The desk clerk with the comic book was gone, and in his place was a young woman in continental dress. She handed me a small yellow envelope and advised me a visitor was waiting for me in my suite. I'd been sitting all afternoon, so I didn't bother with the elevator, but climbed the stairs. I put my ear to my door, listening intently, but could hear nothing out of the ordinary, so I put the key in the lock.

Ibrahim Samir was lying naked in my bed, wearing nothing except a single sheet riding low across his hips and a look of erotic expectation. I dropped the envelope on the table, crossed the room in three strides, and sat on the bed as he moved into my embrace and kissed me. "I am so sorry." He buried his face in my neck and I shivered. He was warm and beautiful, and he smelled like cedar and sandalwood. "Believe me when I tell you the arrest was for your own good. I was acting on orders."

I captured his mouth again. "Whose orders?"

"I cannot tell you that." His eyes begged me not to ask again, and I didn't.

"You were protecting me?" I toed off my shoes and got undressed as quickly as I could. "From what?"

"It was essential we get you off the streets while we searched for the man who murdered Pasha Nubar. Nubar had a great many powerful friends, and so his killer is essentially a marked man."

"Who is he?"

"No one you know." He shrugged. "He is currently in jail, awaiting our interrogation. Perhaps he will have a trial. Perhaps not."

"That sounds kind of grim." I slipped into bed and lay down beside him. When he took me into his arms, my stomach did this weird little cave-in thing, and I got all shivery, like I was coming down with something. He leaned over and kissed me, and I gave myself to it, telling myself it didn't matter, he wanted to be here, I wasn't taking anything away from him and we hadn't made any promises to each other. We curled together, our bodies wrapped around each other, kissing until the heat between us grew too much to bear. I laid him down and took his swollen cock into my mouth and sucked him while his lean body writhed and shuddered, and he begged me to make it harder, faster, more. He whimpered in Arabic when I licked the insides of his thighs; I took his balls into my mouth and sucked them gently, and he gasped and clenched his fingers in my hair. I drew my tongue up his flat stomach to his chest and teased each of his nipples to hard points, returning again and again to kiss his mouth and suckle gently at the smooth, tanned column of his throat. He guided my hand to his erection and I stroked him, bending to flick my tongue over the head of his cock. He came with a groan, his fingers pressing hard into my shoulders.

I lay beside him, lazily kissing him, while he found my cock and stroked me, his hand sliding in a languorous rhythm, building my arousal slowly. Bright sparks formed and burst behind my eyelids, and I listened to myself moaning as he worked me, drawing me closer and closer to the edge of the precipice. It wasn't Ibrahim Samir I was seeing behind my closed lids, but Sam Halim, tanned and nude, his slim body writhing, his hands clenched into fists as I brought him to completion. My imaginary Sam came hard and so did I, panting like I'd just run a five-minute mile.

"It's all right." Samir's hand trailed down my cheek, traced the line of my lips. "I am not him. It is all right, *wahid busa bass,* just one kiss." His mouth was warm and gentle. "You are not him, either." He smiled sadly. "Now you know my secret."

And now you know mine.

He touched the gold cartouche I wore on a chain around my neck. "This was a gift?" I nodded. "From him?"

"Yes. He brought it to me. He said in times past, Egyptians would draw a circle around a name they wished to remember. They called this circle a cartouche."

"Captain Halim is a good man. I wish I were like him." He sighed. "We are looking for the man who killed the taxi driver, Shiva El Rawy. He may or may not be the same man who killed Pasha Nubar." He took a breath that to my ears sounded almost like a gasp. "Could you not love me, just a little?"

I didn't have an answer for him, and he knew it. I got out of bed and pulled on a robe, lit a cigarette. The noises in the street were quieter now, and the movement of traffic had slowed. Soon it would be dark, and the muezzin's call to prayers would be heard. I wondered where Sam was and I wondered, too, if he prayed in his confinement, or if he no longer counted on the mercies of his God. I had never seen him pray, but I imagined he did it as he did everything—carefully, deliberately, his whole attention dedicated to the moment.

Octavian had to be behind Sam's disappearance; I was sure Sam had returned to Cairo looking for him. Find Octavian and you'd find Sam, but for that, I needed someone who was infinitely acquainted with Octavian's nasty history. I needed someone who had fallen prey to Octavian's machinations before and who knew the kinds of things the Greek was capable of. "Picco—he'd know. I need to get in touch with Picco. Alphonsus Picco—how come I never thought of that before now?"

I was talking to myself. Ibrahim Samir had dressed and slipped silently away, leaving nothing behind except a rumpled bedsheet and a faint patina of hurt.

THERE WAS only the briefest of pauses for the international connection; Chris picked up after three rings, and I could hear cafe noises in the background. "Hello, Jack. Say, you must've really missed me, huh?"

"Save it, Romeo. I'm looking for your boyfriend."

"What was that? It's pretty noisy here. Say it again?"

"I'm looking for Picco. Is he around?"

"Aww, Jack, I'm hurt." Chris laughed. "He's on duty right now, but he's coming by later on. There something maybe I can help you with?"

I told him I needed intelligence on Jonah Octavian: if he was in Cairo, and, if he wasn't, where else he might be. Maybe Octavian had seen me coming and gone in the other direction, back to Newfoundland. I told Chris I strongly suspected Octavian had something to do with Sam's disappearance, but I left out my impromptu desert interview with MacBride's band of commandos. "See if the Newfie police have any information on him. I know they were itching to get hold of him, so maybe I can do us both a favor."

"Will do. Anything else?"

"Tell him to cable me whatever they have. I'm still at the Acacia Court hotel." It was risky, asking him to cable me, since a cable could be interrupted, but I didn't think it wise to tie up the international telephone exchange, especially not during wartime.

"Gotcha."

"Say, Chris, how's the old place running?"

"It's running swell, Jack, although everybody keeps asking where you are. I'm getting sick of telling them, and Phonse thinks you've found yourself some rich Egyptian guy to keep you company. He says you're probably floating down the Nile on a boat, eating figs while some pretty slave boys fan you with big palm fronds."

I laughed in spite of myself. "Yeah, skip that. Picco's been watching too many movies. Remind me, Chris, What did I ever do without you?"

"Jack, I haven't got it in me." I could practically hear his grin. "The subject's just too painful."

He rang off, and I went into the bathroom to start the shower running. On my way back, I noticed the yellow envelope the desk clerk had handed me on my way in. I tore it open and scanned it quickly. The message had been hastily written in pencil on a scrap of rough paper that looked like it had been torn out of a book. *THE AMERICANI CAN HAVE INFORMATION IF HE GOES TO 17 SHARIA EMAD EL DINE AND ASKS FOR MUKBAR.*

I showered as quickly as I could, dressed in fresh clothes, and was at the front door of the hotel in ten minutes. I hailed a cab and directed the driver to the Sharia Emad El Dine. I'd taken a few Egyptian pounds with me and removed a little insurance from the wall safe in my room—the Colt .45 automatic I'd brought to Cairo. I tucked it into the waistband of my trousers, under the hanging tail of my short-sleeved shirt.

SEVENTEEN SHARIA Emad El Dine was a drab gray building next door to a large Welsh department store carrying everything from a needle to the proverbial anchor. It was occupied by a wholesaler, so I assumed Mukbar, whoever he might be, would be waiting for me upstairs. As I got out of the cab, I noticed a thin man in native dress standing across the street, pretending to examine something in a nearby window. I didn't hang around to see what the hell he wanted. After my experience with the Pasha, I wasn't taking any unnecessary chances with strangers and dark doorways.

There was no buzzer at number seventeen to announce my arrival, but maybe Mukbar wasn't the type to stand on ceremony. I went up three flights of rickety stairs made of wood so old even the termites had given up on it. At the top, there was a narrow corridor of open doorways. I chose the one closed door in the bunch and tapped on it. It swung open to reveal a small man in continental dress, with a pale, round face and the biggest eyes I'd ever seen outside of a Betty Boop cartoon. He was smoking a thin Egyptian cigarette, holding it between the tips of his thumb and finger in a very particular gesture. "Yes? How am I able to help you?" His voice was soft but not feminine, and I couldn't readily place his accent. Austrian? Swiss? He might even be German, except it was hard to believe any German would be brazen enough to advertise his presence in Cairo these days.

"I'm looking for a guy called Mukbar. Are you him?"

He smiled, and twin dimples appeared in the round, smooth cheeks. "Yes, I call myself Mukbar. Do come in. The heat of the day is most oppressive." He stood back to allow me entry, and I saw that every interior wall was covered with pages of newspaper. He had even pasted newspaper on the ceilings. "You must be Stoyles, or Stoyles-bey as the locals would have it. Some coffee?" He lifted the pot and poured deftly. "One cannot forget civilities even in a time of war. Sit down, Mr. Stoyles, and be comfortable. We have much to discuss, you and I."

"Yeah. You said you had information." I chose a wingback chair and sat down. There was an ashtray on a small table at my elbow, precariously positioned atop a stack of news magazines, all of recent vintage, including quite a few scandal sheets. Some of these had passages marked off in violet pencil. These same passages were annotated in a spidery hand: *telephoned, no reply; send telegram; denial; research further.* "You know something?"

He tucked himself into a narrow, high-backed chair and crossed his legs delicately. "I am in a business, Mr. Stoyles, that makes information my"—he simpered—"business." He sipped his coffee and took a drag off his cigarette. "Several days ago, you arrived from Newfoundland in search of Captain Samuel Halim of the Cairo police. He, in turn, came to Cairo on the trail of...."

"Yeah?" The walls of the little room seemed to press in on me, a narrow prison made of black-and-white print. Mukbar watched me carefully, his huge eyes still and penetrating. It felt as if his gaze were somehow dissecting me.

"I cannot merely *say*, Mr. Stoyles. That is not how I do business." He arched an immaculately groomed brow. "You would suggest an appropriate price?"

I dug out my wallet and thumbed through my stack of American dollars. "Just say when, pal." He let me get to fifty before he said anything, and I got the feeling this was just for starters.

Mukbar took the money and counted it, then folded the bills away. "Captain Halim came to Cairo on the trail of one Jonah Octavian."

"Does it have anything to do with war profiteering?" Picco and I had gotten onto something in this line, and Octavian had tried to take us down for it. Odds were he was up to his old tricks on this side of the globe.

176

"I cannot say. I do not have that information."

I wasn't in the mood. "Yeah? Well you better have some kind of information, or I swear to God, I'll break you like you've never been broken." I clenched my fists. "Now stop wasting my goddamn time, or I'll go over there and smear that sick smile all over your face."

"Hm." It wasn't quite a laugh. "Clearly you are a man for whom violence is a ready solution. How disappointing." He sighed. "Ah, well. Jonah Octavian is the son of Captain Halim's aunt. That is to say, Mr. Stoyles, he is Captain Halim's first cousin. In fact, I believe they were boyhood playmates." He flicked the fingers of his free hand and a white card appeared in his palm; as he turned it over, I saw it was a photograph.

"Is this… Sam?" The boys were about eight or nine years old, and it was one of those photographs you might see in anybody's family album: two kids in swimming suits, standing with their arms round each other's shoulders, grinning into the camera. The background was all beach and sky, the image of a perfect summer's day. "How do I know you're telling the truth?"

"You wish further proof?" The same sleight of hand and a second photograph appeared, this one with an adult Sam standing next to a man who was clearly Jonah Octavian. They were smiling at one another, and Octavian had a hand on Sam's shoulder.

"Okay." It was really hard to accept what the photograph was showing me, but I tried. "So Sam is related to Octavian. Maybe they were even friendly once."

"Maybe they are friendly still." He crushed out his cigarette. "Mr. Octavian is a very strange man, moving easily between the various levels of society, yet lighting nowhere. He is like the great Nile moths which hover and hum like tiny birds, but which at heart are insects."

"Skip the allegory. I just paid you fifty American dollars, so start talking."

"Or what, Mr. Stoyles?" His lips parted. "You will… beat it out of me, perhaps?"

Something inside of me snapped, and I was up out of the chair and charging toward him. Then I was suddenly on the floor, while something I realized was his knee pressed into the back of my neck. My left arm was twisted painfully behind me, and no matter how I struggled, I couldn't move.

"You see, Mr. Stoyles, like the hummingbird hawk moth, not every creature is as he initially appears." He let me up, and I rolled slowly over into a sitting position.

"How the hell did you do that?"

"A few simple movements, enacted quickly." He shrugged. "Like Mr. Octavian, and like that moth, I have learned to adapt to my environment. Come, let us have no more of these silly theatrics."

I got up and went back to my chair. "Fine."

He lit a fresh cigarette from a pack at his elbow. "Mr. Octavian keeps a country house near the oasis at El Fayoum. Few people know about it. Indeed, few people know anything about Mr. Octavian. He has been in his country home since his return to Egypt. If you follow the desert road to El Fayoum, you will find him. Good-bye, Mr. Stoyles."

"Good-bye? What the hell is this? What do you mean, good-bye? What's Octavian doing in El Fayoum? Who's there with him? And don't tell me you don't know." This whole thing left a nasty taste in my mouth. "Guys like you always know."

"Mr. Stoyles, that is all the information I have. If I were you I would not waste time here talking endlessly to one such as myself. I would be making arrangements to get to El Fayoum—before it is too late."

I felt sick when I left Mukbar's place. If the little man was right—if Sam and Octavian were relatives—it threw a whole new light on the matter. Maybe Sam hadn't been kidnapped. Maybe he'd gone because he wanted to go, because he and Octavian were in it together, for money or whatever other reason people find to betray everything they believe in.

The walk back to my hotel was more or less a straight shot with little chance of getting lost, and I reasoned the fresh air would do me good. The more I thought about it, the more things started to fall into place, and all in all, it made a pretty ugly picture. What if Sam had planted that diorite bowl in the Newfoundland Museum and enlisted Blount's help to get me to Egypt? Maybe I'd been handpicked by whoever Sam was working for, and he'd only come into my cafe that day because he was acting on orders from his superiors. It only stood to reason what I'd taken for friendship was actually a sophisticated seduction attempt, a way to secure my participation in a complicated scheme he'd hatched with his cousin Jonah Octavian. I needed to get to El Fayoum, but I didn't see how I was going to do that without a car. Asking to borrow one would attract too much attention. If I were home, the matter would be easy. I'd borrow Chris's car and drive out there myself—but Chris was in Newfoundland looking after my Heartache Cafe, and I was here in Cairo, as helpless and on my heels as if I'd been sucker-punched in the twelfth round.

And that wasn't the worst of it.

I was being followed. It was the same guy I'd seen when I'd gotten out of the cab on the Sharia Emad El Dine to see Mukbar: a small, nondescript man in native dress. So far, he hadn't done anything except follow, always staying the same distance behind me. If I were at home, I'd have ducked down a few laneways and side streets to try and shake him, but I didn't know Cairo very well, and I was afraid of ending up hopelessly lost—maybe in an unfriendly part of the city. The best I could do was keep him in my sights and hope he'd eventually lose interest.

I was wrong. I'd just passed under the awning of a building on the Sharia Ibrahim Pasha when I felt something sinewy tighten around my neck—not enough to cut off my air, but enough to keep me quiet. The man at the other end jerked me into an alley between two buildings and shoved me up against a wall. "You ought to know better, Stoyles-bey. Wandering around Cairo and asking questions is going to get you into serious trouble."

"Who are you?" I struggled to turn around, but he twisted the cord a little tighter.

"You will not talk. You will merely listen. The man calling himself Mukbar advised you incorrectly when he told you to go to El Fayoum. You would do well to stay in Cairo, for your health." The cord twisted tighter and tighter, cutting off my air, and I fought against it until I heard my own heels drumming on the ground, then everything went black.

I WOKE to the feeling of someone's hands on my face, gently slapping my cheeks. "Jack… Jack, wake up. Come on. Wake up."

I looked up into kindly blue eyes. "Tex. You got a knack for showing up, you know that?" His penchant for appearing out of nowhere just when I most needed him was deeply suspicious.

"Come on. Let's get outta here." He dragged me to my feet and walked me out of the alley. It was late, maybe some time after midnight, although I couldn't be sure. "The quicker we can get you back to your hotel, the better."

"No, I gotta go to El Fayoum."

"El Fayoum? At this time of night? What for?"

Tareenah had indicated that Tex was a secret Allied operative, just as Sam was, but MacBride's warning still rang in my ears. Maybe he was wrong and maybe he was right, but did I really know who to trust? Everywhere I turned there was treachery. Nobody was who he seemed to be, and I couldn't rely on anything anybody said. "I… want a change of scenery."

He nodded. "Uh-huh" was all he said. "I got a car you can borrow."

"Yeah? You'd let me use your car?" I massaged my neck. Whoever had been on the other end of that rope was serious about his work. I felt like I had whiplash. "You trust me?"

"Sam Halim trusted you." He reached out and dusted me down. "That's good enough for me." He took an automatic pistol out of his pocket. "Brought a little insurance, too. You never know what's waiting for you. Best to be prepared."

It might not be a bad idea to keep him close, where I could see him. "Maybe you ought to come with me."

"Maybe I ought to." He put the gun away and fell into step beside me. "El Fayoum, huh? So what's in El Fayoum that's so important to you, Jack?"

TEX'S CAR was a decommissioned army truck you could drive anywhere, including off a cliff. The dunes were no problem. It took a couple hours to get to the oasis, which meant we landed there while it was still dark. We stopped for gasoline at a rickety shack near Tirsa, and the American owner's Turkish wife knew Jonah Octavian and his house; it stood out by virtue of it being the one farthest from the road. We killed the lights as we approached and cut the motor so we wouldn't give ourselves away. The house was white—a symbol of power in Egypt—and sprawling, with lots of fancy grillwork and clumps of aloes and date palms planted out in front. Tex and I approached on foot with guns drawn, but there was nobody around. The household, it seemed, had retired for the evening.

I motioned to Tex and hammered on the door. Nobody answered. I waited a few more minutes and knocked again, but there was no response. There were no lights showing in any of the windows, so I decided to chance it. I reached for the doorknob and turned it, and the door swung open, bumping back gently against the inside wall.

Somebody was in there all right, sitting in a chair in front of the fireplace—there was just enough ambient light from the full moon to make him out—but whether he minded us being there, I didn't know. He was dead, his head bashed in, and whoever had given him the business had taken the time to make sure it was right. His face had been battered to a pulp, but the features were still recognizable, and seeing him, I got real cold and sick inside.

The dead man was my best friend, Frankie Missalo.

One of the shadows at the rear of the room detached itself and moved toward us. I brought my gun up, level with the spot between his eyes, but I knew as soon as I saw him that I couldn't—wouldn't—shoot.

Sam raised his hands in surrender. "I am so very sorry you have had to find me like this, Jack." He glanced at the dead man lolling in the chair. "I did not want to come here." His voice was slow and solemn, and very sad. "I simply had no other choice."

CHAPTER SIX

"WHAT'D HE ever do to you?" My voice trembled and I hated myself for it. "He was nothing to you; he was nobody. Goddammit, Sam—" I went weak in the knees as it all fell in on me, the whole filthy mess. "Why'd you kill him? Why?"

"I did not kill this man. Errki Aaltonen brought me here, at Jonah Octavian's request." Sam looked haggard and worn, much like the day I'd seen him at the bank. But other than that, he was basically okay. "This poor soul was already here—already dead—when I arrived." He saw Tex standing behind me. "I see you two have found each other. That is well."

"Where's Aaltonen?" I crouched beside the chair and checked Frankie for a pulse, even though I knew it was pointless. What the hell. It gave me something to do and kept my mind from sliding away into darker places than this. "Is he here?"

"No, Aaltonen has gone into Cairo on business. Jack, you must get out of here at once."

I straightened. "And leave you here to fend for yourself? Nothing doing."

"Jack...." Sam reached toward me. "My dear friend."

Tex cleared his throat. "I'm just gonna post myself as guard, Jack. Just in case somebody comes sniffing around." He disappeared down a side corridor silently.

"I'm not leaving you." I grabbed hold of Sam's shoulders and pulled him into my arms, and it was just like this nasty house and poor Frankie and the whole sorry mess no longer existed. He felt so good, so strong and whole and real. "Goddammit, Sam, I came halfway around the world looking for you, and if you think I'm gonna—" His mouth was hot, a blissful, wet caress, and I returned the kiss gladly.

"Jack, you must go." He cupped my face between his palms and gazed at me as if memorizing my features. "We will be together again very soon, but you must leave now. You must let me do this my own way. Do you hear me?"

"That's what I'm afraid of." I held him tightly against me. "If I leave you here, I might never see you again."

"Of course you will see me again." He drew back. "If not in this world, in the next one." His strong, lean hands kneaded my shoulders. "I must be free to act without restraint." His face softened. "Jack, it is so very good to see you. I am so glad you came."

"What… uh, what happened to Frankie?" I couldn't look at Frankie's body; it hurt too much, and reminded me of when we were kids together back in Philly, going to school and playing ball and serving at mass, doing all the normal kid things. It was Frankie who'd suggested I go to Newfoundland in the first place and start over. I had him to thank for my new lease on life. I could never repay him for the thousand kindnesses, large and small, that he had done for me.

"I do not know. He was… like that when I arrived. I take it you did not know he was in Cairo?"

"No. I had no idea. He set up this whole thing for me, even got me a ride on a military transport. I don't know how the hell he came to be here, of all places."

"Jack." Sam led me away from the body. "You must leave here at once. Aaltonen is due back at any moment, and I cannot take the risk."

"But surely this place is being watched! Sam, they had to have seen me coming here with Tex."

"I know. Jack, let me err on the side of caution." He caught sight of the gold cartouche on its chain around my neck. "You are wearing it… the gift I gave you."

"Yeah." I smoothed the gold until it warmed between my fingers. "I never take it off. Sam, what is this? Why won't you come back to Cairo with me? Now. Tonight?"

"I cannot. Please, go now." He smiled. "I am so grateful to have seen you, but it isn't safe for you here."

There were so many things I wanted to ask him, so much more I needed to tell him. "Okay, Sam, if that's the way you want it." I caught him to me and kissed him, just as Tex came running up and said he'd seen headlights far out on the desert and maybe we should go. I took hold of Sam's hands and hung on as long as I could. "Promise me you will come back. I'm staying at the Acacia Court, room—"

"I know where you are, Jack." He turned my right hand and kissed the palm. "I always know where you are. *Ma salaama.* Go now."

It was the hardest thing I'd ever had to do, leaving him in that place, standing there alone in the dark with Frankie Missalo's body. Tex and I hurried back to the truck and hopped aboard, spinning sand until we finally hit the road, burning rubber all the way back to Cairo.

AFTER TEX dropped me back at the hotel, I tried to get some sleep, but I couldn't rest. More than once, I picked up the phone, thinking I'd call Philly and let Frankie's mother know what had happened to her son. But I knew I couldn't do that. One word spoken out of turn would put Sam in serious jeopardy, and anyway, they couldn't hurt Frankie anymore. I had to let things be, let Sam work whatever plan he had in his mind, and hope it would come out all right in the end. When all this was over, I'd call Mrs. Missalo and tell her how her son had died bravely in the service of his country. I didn't know if that were strictly true, but it's what I intended to tell her.

At dawn, I heard the muezzin's call echoing over the rooftops, and I knelt down by my bed. I don't know what possessed me to do it—I hadn't prayed in years—and I doubted I had any faith left, but I figured it couldn't hurt. I blessed myself and said the decades of the rosary and the Lord's Prayer and after that, I sat there in the silence while the sun rose over the city. At seven thirty, I called room service to order breakfast. The waiter brought me a tray and a telegram from the Royal Newfoundland Constabulary. Alphonsus Picco had come through. The gist of it was that Octavian had gone to Cairo to meet with some unnamed contact, an American who was well-placed in the North Atlantic command. Picco didn't know why Octavian was meeting this guy, but given Octavian's record, it probably had to do with a crooked construction scheme or three. The Constabulary's special wartime division had been investigating Octavian ever since he first turned up in St. John's, about six months before the Japanese attacked Pearl Harbor. Mostly, he kept his nose clean and didn't interfere with anybody who didn't interfere with him, but that whole business with Julie Fayre—his partner in crime and erstwhile lady love—hadn't done him any good, so these days he was being more careful. Picco didn't know who Octavian's Cairo contact was, but he'd wire me with further details if he had any.

Well, that left me about where I'd been all along. No matter how I looked at this, it all came back to Octavian. I'd come to Cairo looking for Sam, and I'd found him, but I'd found a lot of other things as well. Pasha Nubar had been ready to tell me about Shiva's murder, except he never got the chance. Samir had said they had Nubar's killer in custody, so maybe the best way for me to get a little insight was to go down to the police station and take a look. I didn't know what time Samir went on duty, so I put in a call to the station and was told that no, Sergeant Samir wasn't on duty until later that evening. "You guys brought in the scum who killed Pasha Nubar, right? Do you think your chief would mind if I had a word with him?"

He wasn't sure; he said he'd have to find out and ring me back, so I gave him my room number. I'd barely hung up the phone when it rang again. This time it was Tareenah Halim. She was pretty upset. "Mr. Stoyles, please. You must…. It is…. Please come." I was left holding a dead phone.

I showered, dressed, and shaved, and caught a cab to the Halim residence, but when I got there, the house was deserted. It looked like they'd shut the place up and gone away. I rapped on the door but nobody answered, so I knocked a little bit harder, and more people didn't answer. I peered in one of the windows, but couldn't see much besides the dim shapes of the Halims' furniture.

I was about to give up and go away when a woman came out of a neighboring house. "Why are you looking in the Halims' windows, *Engleezhi*?"

"Oh, I'm looking for Mrs. Halim. Have you seen her?"

She shrugged. "I cannot say for certain whether I have seen her or not."

"Okay." I held up an Egyptian pound note. "Does that loosen your tongue any?"

She tucked the money away in her robes. "Mrs. Halim and the children were there until late last night, when they suddenly left."

"Uh-huh." This was sounding more and more fishy all the time. "What about Mr. Halim?"

"Captain Halim?" She smiled. "Such a noble gentleman, and so very kind to all who know him. I cannot say whether he is gone or not." She held out her hand, and I put another pound note in it. "He is gone as well. He has been gone for many days."

"You know where Mrs. Halim and the children might have gone?" Where had Tareenah been when she'd called me? Was she in hiding or was this some kind of a ruse?

"I am sorry. I do not."

I waited till she left, then let myself in the back door. The inside of the house was cool and dark, and most of the blinds had been drawn over the windows to keep out the fierce heat of the day. Yeah, we used to do the same thing back in Philly when I was a kid: close all the curtains and keep the worst of the heat out, although it made the inside of the house pretty stuffy come the end of the day, but that never mattered to me. I was never inside long enough to care. Either I was playing ball with Frankie, or riding my bike, swimming in the public pool a few blocks over, or getting into trouble with Susie Fitch and her sister, Edith, under the bleachers at the high school football field. Frankie was always up for that sort of thing, always ready to do whatever I wanted to do without complaining. Yeah, Frankie was....

I had to stop thinking about him; I'd grieve for him later when there was time. I couldn't think about him now, propped up in that chair in Jonah Octavian's fancy desert house. It wouldn't have been so bad if he'd looked more natural... if maybe he looked like he was sleeping. You know, people say that sort of thing all the time at funerals and wakes: *he looks real good. Yeah, he looks just like himself.* Because death had the power to change a person's features, make them into someone else entirely.

I went down the hall and found a series of rooms opening off the main corridor: a couple of kids' bedrooms with books and toys, and Sam's study. At the end of the hall there were two matching bedrooms, side by side, joined by a connecting door. The left side of the suite was distinctly feminine, and I found women's clothing in the closet. The right side must have been where Sam slept. This room was decorated in blue and gold, there were books in huge piles on every available surface, and Sam's uniforms hung in the closet. I pulled back the bedspread, exposing the pillows and sheets. It was a ridiculous risk I was taking, but there was nobody around, and nobody knew I was in here. I bent low and pressed my face into each of the pillows in turn. The one on the left smelled mostly of laundry soap and some commercial bluing preparation; the pillow on the right smelled like Sam. I took it into my arms and held it, hugging it like it really was Sam, like he was close enough to touch. *I know where you are, Jack. I always know where you are.*

"How very appropriate." The voice came from behind and above me, and I tensed, but then I heard the click of a gun being cocked. "Do not, I beg you, make any sudden movements, Mr. Stoyles. I should very much hate to splatter your brains over Captain Halim's bed linens."

I turned my head slowly. Yeah, it was Jonah Octavian all right. I'd recognize those cold, dead eyes anywhere. "I wondered when you were going to show up."

His thin lips curved into a smile. "How nice that the suspense has now been broken. Get up, Mr. Stoyles, and don't give me an excuse to shoot you."

I did as I was told. Octavian was a slippery character, duplicitous as hell, and I wasn't about to try and second-guess him. "Been watching me, Octavian?"

"Shut up, Mr. Stoyles. There will be plenty of time for small talk later." The barrel of the gun was jammed into my back, just above my kidneys. "Start walking toward the front door. I have a car waiting to take you to my country home."

"We can skip the guided tour, Octavian. I've been there already. You should hire an interior decorator. That dead guy in the living room doesn't go with the drapes."

He pushed me outside and into a big Mercedes outfitted with a uniformed chauffeur. We pulled away from the curb. The morning sun was now up over the broad, smooth expanse of the Nile, and under any other circumstances it would have been real pretty. "So you're going to take me into the desert and kill me?"

Octavian lit a long Egyptian cigarette and took a drag. "You disappoint me, Mr. Stoyles."

"Brother, you have no idea how often I've heard that."

"I had hoped you would have found me out long before now, but no, instead of following the most obvious of clues, I find you sniffing pillows in your paramour's bedroom."

"Maybe I was looking for the laundry mark. You know how some of these places are, you send in your linens and get back some other guy's dirty socks."

Octavian rolled down the window and tossed out the spent match. His technique was flawless, not once did the gun barrel stray even a millimeter from my side. "I hate to do this to someone like you, Mr. Stoyles. You're a relatively harmless creature, even if you are annoyingly obstinate. If it were up to me, I'd put you on the next plane back to Newfoundland and have done with it."

"But you can't do that."

"No, I'm afraid I really can't. You see, you're one of those people who are simply too much trouble. You attract it like iron filings to a magnet."

"Right. So which one are you, the filings or the magnet?"

He smiled thinly. "You are an inquisitive man, Mr. Stoyles, one who is far too curious for his own good and who doesn't know when to leave well enough alone. I'd kill you myself, except...."

"You don't want to get your hands dirty."

He ignored the dig. "Mr. Missalo was a good friend of yours, wasn't he? What a shame you killed him. I expect the authorities aren't going to take such a brutal murder lying down."

"I killed Frankie." This guy was something else. "*I* did."

"Of course you did, Mr. Stoyles. Frank Missalo had a good scheme worked out with the war contractors back in Newfoundland, one which allowed him to pocket lots and lots of cash, with minimal effort. It couldn't last forever—nothing ever does—and when Sam Halim started sniffing around, your friend Missalo got nervous."

"Like you're nervous now, Octavian?"

The gun jabbed hard into my ribs. "Don't interrupt, Mr. Stoyles. It's bad manners. Missalo got nervous, so he decided the best way to deal with Halim was to remove him. He hadn't counted on you and Halim getting... cozy. That's to my benefit, of course. The authorities will think you came all the way to Cairo to find Frankie Missalo and pay him back for interfering in your perverted little love affair. You killed him in a rage, you know. Beat his head in with a hammer."

"I get it. I'm the fall guy."

"Yes, Mr. Stoyles." Octavian picked an imaginary piece of lint off his shirt. "You are, sad to say, the fall guy."

"Hey, you." I spoke to the chauffeur. From the back he was easily one of the biggest men I'd ever seen. "You okay with this? It's cold-blooded murder, is what it is."

The driver turned his head and said something I didn't understand. "Constantine speaks only Greek," Octavian said. "Appealing to him is rather pointless, I'm afraid."

"Yeah, you got it all fixed." Something about the chauffeur bothered me, but I couldn't put my finger on what it was. There was something not right with his eyebrows or maybe it was his hair. His face looked like he'd suffered a bad burn at some time in the recent past, for it had the smooth, shiny look of too-new skin. I remembered a crack Frankie made once, about a guy we used to knock around with back in Philly: *He looks like he borrowed somebody else's face for the weekend.* Maybe that was it….

Octavian didn't talk much after that; he mostly concentrated on keeping the gun in my ribs and smoking one cigarette after another. He was nervous about something, but I couldn't readily place what that might be. He had no qualms about having his gorillas smack me around, just as he'd had no qualms about getting his little girlfriend, Julie Fayre, to poison me with quinine. In the end, it was Julie who went to the gallows while Octavian slipped quietly away. He probably planned to do the same thing now, once this business was over. He'd make sure I took the rap for Frankie's death, and he'd fix it so I'd never bother him again. Yeah, where I was going, I'd be hard-pressed to interfere with anybody.

Octavian was funneling money and supplies to the Nazis, selling out his own people to the enemy. "I hope you don't make it through the war," I said.

"What does that mean?" He turned his flat, empty eyes on me. "Hm? What exactly are you saying, Mr. Stoyles?"

"I wouldn't want to be in your shoes, Octavian. When this war is over and we've won, the Greeks are gonna knock themselves out getting hold of you." Maybe it was the heat or my imminent demise, but the thought of Octavian being handed over to the Greek Resistance was hilarious. "You'll be lucky if all they do is draw and quarter you."

"Shut up, Stoyles." He grimaced. "You have no idea what you're talking about. After the war I'll be welcomed back to Athens as a hero."

"Is that so?" It might have been my imagination, but the Greek chauffeur's big shoulders moved up and down a notch. "Not after they find out about you, Octavian. The things you've done, the lives you've sacrificed. I think a firing squad is way too good for you. The Greeks are liable to think so, too."

"Oh, Mr. Stoyles, you are so completely simpleminded. I am not so stupid as to openly cast my allegiance with any one body! I do a little here, I do a little there. It really doesn't matter to me who wins the war."

Just listening to him was making me sick. "Yeah. You only care that you get paid."

"And I do, Mr. Stoyles. I get paid very, very well, and I have the satisfaction of knowing my small contributions are put to the best possible use. The Germans have made such rapid progress in Greece. To subdue an entire nation takes careful planning and the very best lines of supply. Can you imagine the satisfaction I feel, knowing it was I who made that happen?"

There it was again: the chauffeur's shoulders moved, and his eyes met mine in the rear view mirror. What the hell was going on? "You're a real inspiration, Octavian. I'm sure your starving countrymen appreciate everything you've done."

"Oh, but you are again mistaken, Mr. Stoyles. In this war, I consider myself a soldier. Unofficially, of course."

"Of course." I could see the white house on the desert, looming ahead of us through the windshield. We'd be there in a matter of moments.

"So I have taken care to"—he smirked—"spread the wealth a little. Sometimes there are clandestine air drops of food and medical supplies to some of the sorely harassed areas, or some surplus clothing, marked, of course, with the logo of my company, Octavian and Weiss. It is easier to be grateful for that which one has received when one is familiar with the giver, don't you think?"

I didn't have to answer. The chauffeur pulled the car up in front of the house, turned, and spoke something in Greek to Octavian. He kept the gun in my ribs while we got out of the car, holding me nice and steady. The big chauffeur walked behind Octavian, just in case I got any ideas about making a break for it. "It's a shame, Mr. Stoyles, that you feel the way you do. I could use a man like you in my organization." He stopped before the door and waited, but the chauffeur didn't move, so Octavian barked something in Greek. The chauffeur turned so quickly, it was impossible to follow, and something flashed silver in the morning sun. Octavian's gun fell away, and he was crouched against the side of the house with both hands wrapped around a gaping wound in his throat. His mouth moved as if he was trying to speak, and then he simply folded to the ground, dead at my feet. The chauffeur moved toward me, pulling at the skin on his face, dislodging his hair and mustache and eyebrows, and Colonel Andros Scala emerged, coolly self-assured. "I did not want to kill him."

I looked down at Octavian's dead face. "You saved my life."

Scala shook his head sadly. "I did not do it for you."

I followed him into the house. Frankie Missalo's body had been removed and some attempt made to clean up the living room. Sam Halim sat in a chair by the window with a Browning 9mm handgun in his lap. He looked at us, Colonel Scala and me, as if he had never seen either of us before. "Is he dead?"

Scala nodded.

Sam's face stiffened, and the hand holding the gun trembled. "It is well." He tried to smile at me, but couldn't quite manage it. "I have done all I could for your friend, Mr. Missalo. I have shrouded his body and said the *Salat al-Janazah* for him. His remains are resting in the bedroom."

"I'll go see him in a minute. Look, Sam, I know Jonah Octavian is your cousin…." There wasn't anything I could say, not really.

Scala shifted his feet. "I will contact the others." He disappeared down the hall and into another room; I heard him talking on the telephone.

"It is over now, Jack." Sam tried to stand but fell back into the chair. His gun clattered to the floor, and I bent to pick it up. "I had hoped to avoid the inevitable, but he left me no choice." He shook his head slowly. "The day I left you in Newfoundland, I knew this could not end until I found him." He pressed his hands against his eyes. "I am so tired, Jack."

I went down on my knees and pulled him into my arms. "Me too, Sam." I kissed his cheek. "Me too."

I left him there for a few minutes while I went and had a word with Frankie. Sam had washed the body and shrouded it in a clean white sheet. I knelt beside him and touched the shroud where I figured his heart would be. "They'll never believe this back in Philly. You and me, huh Frankie?" I didn't need to ask why he'd hooked up with somebody like Octavian; I knew. Frankie was dirty. He hadn't started out that way; he just couldn't resist the money Octavian was offering.

See, Frankie came from a family with too many kids and not enough money, and lived in a falling-down house in a crummy part of Philly. By the time he was twelve, he had three paper routes and was earning extra money by selling apples after school. Mind you, my family wasn't doing too great either, especially after my old man was killed at work, but there was only me and Ma. We didn't have nowhere near the number of mouths to feed that Frankie's family did. I guess growing up that way makes you hunger for all the things you don't have. So when Jonah Octavian came knocking, Frankie took him up on it. He probably found some way to reconcile the things he was doing with the other stuff going on in the world, and maybe he reckoned it wasn't so bad. Maybe all the things he'd done to help me balanced the scales. The way I figured it, Frankie threw in with Octavian because the Greek had money and connections, and because he'd probably made Frankie the kind of promises that are hard to resist.

"Good-bye, Frankie." I didn't know what else to say. I felt a hand on my shoulder.

Sam was there. "He was your friend. I am sorry it ended the way it did for him."

I nodded. Mostly I was trying not to cry, but I could feel the back of my throat closing together. "Yeah." I coughed, just to try and get rid of the awful feeling of wanting to break down and sob my guts out. "So, uh, what happens now?"

Sam brushed my cheek. "Jonah Octavian has been effectively... removed. He is out of the equation. Now we go back to Cairo. My wife and children are staying with relatives. I am anxious to see them."

There was that old, familiar, kick-in-the-gut feeling again. "Sure."

"Jack."

"Mm?"

"If I were to come to your room this evening, would you be available to"—his gaze lingered on my mouth—"receive me?"

"You mean...?"

"Oh, yes." His eyebrows arched. "If you aren't otherwise occupied." He smiled, and something kindled in his dark eyes. "I believe the time is right."

AT QUARTER to eight that evening, there was a knock at the door of my suite. I'd been waiting, trying to read the newspapers, sipping some coffee, but my nerves were jumping all over the place. "Hello, Sam." He was dressed simply, in khaki trousers and a blue shirt; he still looked tired but not as bad as he'd looked at Octavian's place in the desert. I couldn't remember the last time I'd wanted anybody as badly as I wanted him.

"Jack." He looked at me for a moment. Maybe he was thinking the same thing I was, that we were finally alone together, behind a closed door, safe from prying eyes. "My darling."

I took three huge steps toward him and crushed him in my arms. Our mouths found each other, fumbling at first, hot and slippery and wet and so good—oh God, so good. His fists twisted in my shirt, and he walked me backward until we fell down on the bed together. The noises from the open window vanished, and the room went away; there was nothing but Sam's hands and his mouth, his body. I strained toward him, wanting to feel him all over me. I groveled into his shoulder, groaning wordlessly as his lips roamed over my neck, the hard bulge of his clothed erection pressing into my belly as he rubbed himself on me. He stiffened, his whole body taut, his mouth open and his eyes closed. He groaned deep in his throat, a sound that rippled through me like heat, and I caught him to me as the tension left him and he came to rest against my shoulder, breathing hard.

I chuckled. "That good, huh?"

"Oh, Jack." He swallowed hard and tried to catch his breath. "It has been a very, very long time for me. I beg you, please forgive me."

"Forgive you? Sam, I'm flattered." I lifted his chin and kissed him. "It's been ages since anybody wanted me that much."

He propped himself on one elbow and smiled down at me. "You are never going to allow me to forget this, are you?"

"Never."

"Years and years from now, when we are both old men, you will remind me of just this incident."

"Uh-huh."

He kissed me, and my heart just about burst wide open. Goddammit, I loved this man.

"Jack, let us bathe together now, and then we will love each other slowly."

We stood under the shower's warm cascade and kissed, touching and exploring one another with all due consideration. It was strange, because I'd been waiting for such a long time now to have Sam to myself, to kiss him and touch him and make love to him without the fear of prying eyes. I couldn't stop looking at him. He was lean and more muscular than I'd expected, his chest and abdomen beautifully defined. His shoulders were broad, angling down to a narrow waist, and the muscles in his arms stood out in sharp relief. There was a scar on the right side of his chest, perhaps three inches long, evidence of some past surgical repair. The little finger on his left hand had been broken and badly set. He was the most beautiful thing I'd ever seen.

He kissed me and pulled me into his arms, warm and slippery under the falling water. He held my face between his palms and gazed into my eyes. "Jack."

"Sam." I was grinning like a fool.

We turned the shower off and lay down together on my bed, our bodies warm and wet. He pressed me down and kissed my neck and shoulders, licked my nipples and the hollow of my throat. I surged toward him, desire throbbing through me like a rampant heartbeat. He took my cock into his mouth, and I was gone, brother, but good. I cried out and fisted the sheets, groaned and sobbed and begged him to let me come. I told him over and over how much I loved him, how much I wanted him. My release rose in my belly, uncoiling like a snake, and I came so hard my vision grayed out around the edges. When I finally drifted down from it, Sam was there, holding me as the aftershocks rippled through me like jagged lightning.

I reached for him, took his cock into my hand and stroked him gently, varying the speed and pressure, tugging him closer and closer to his climax. He writhed, fisting the sheets, and now and then a powerful shudder would run through him. He whispered to me, little things that lovers say, muted cries and wordless exclamations. He was silent when he came, panting through it, reaching for me and murmuring my name, his hands on my face, in my hair. "Jack." Sam looked at me and smiled. "My beloved."

"Mmm." I didn't know what would happen after this idyll was over, and I didn't want to ask. "Sam. I'm so glad. You know, I didn't think… I didn't think we'd ever get here. Like this." Something occurred to me. "Your wife and children, are they…?"

"They are well, Jack. Thank you for asking." He traced the bridge of my nose. "Jack, I must tell you something, in order to help you understand the way things are between my wife and me."

"Sam, that's not necessary. It's none of my business—" My throat closed together.

"No, Jack. I would have you understand." He sighed. "My wife and I met at Oxford University in England. It is rare for a Moslem man to meet an educated woman of my generation. Tareenah was beautiful and bright, and we felt the same way about so many things. My family had been insistent I marry upon my return from England; I had given my father my word. I knew I could not marry a woman simply to acquire a broodmare. I wanted a mate, a companion. Thus, Tareenah."

"Love at first sight, huh?" There was that feeling again, like I'd been kicked in the gut.

"No, Jack. Not at first sight. That is a Western notion. Your people may think us cold and unfeeling because we regard the sexes differently than you do. We are as passionate as your people, but we choose to enact that passion privately. What passes between a man and his wife is not for the outside world, and we believe love grows slowly, from the humblest of beginnings. I loved Tareenah; I still do."

"Yeah, sure, Sam. I get it." It was almost a physical ache. "I really do."

"No, Jack, you do not." He sighed and kissed the corner of my mouth. "My wife is brilliant. She is beautiful. She is an excellent mother to our children. In that, she has no equal. When our twins were born—Stamos and Tabia—the doctors told my wife another pregnancy would kill her. We have discussed the use of contraceptive devices, but my wife prefers to abstain from marital relations entirely."

"Jesus." I didn't know much about Sam's religion, but I was pretty sure he was expected to have sex with his wife. "There's other things…. Sam, this is none of my business." To say this conversation was awkward was putting it mildly, and I didn't know Sam's domestic situation well enough to comment on it.

"There are other paths to pleasure, you will agree, but…." He sighed. "Tareenah prefers to devote herself to her work. She is deeply involved in the welfare of refugees and others displaced by the war. I respect her decision. She has given me four beautiful children; what more could I ask of her?" He studied me carefully. "You probably cannot understand such an arrangement."

"No, you're wrong, Sam." Suddenly my respect for Tareenah Halim grew by about a thousand degrees, even if I didn't understand her. "I do. I really do. Does your wife… does she know…?" Dammit, how the hell did you say such a thing? "Does she know you have close male friends?"

"Jack." His voice was very gentle. "I have never had any close male friends, as you say." He picked up the gold cartouche and smoothed it between his fingers. "You, my darling, are the first. I sincerely hope you will be the last."

"What will your wife think?" I didn't relish the idea of being Sam's extramarital affair.

"My wife approves of you, Jack. It is with her blessing that I am here. Do you know it was Tareenah who urged me to come here today? *'Go to him,'* she said. *'Do not keep such a man waiting.'* Tareenah's wish is that I am happy. With you, that is possible."

He stayed with me for the rest of the night, and we slept in each other's arms. It was strange, after all these years of being alone, to lie next to someone, close enough to hear his sleeping breaths.

Near dawn, we woke and made love again and drifted back to sleep. When I next opened my eyes, it was nine in the morning and Sam was sitting by my bed, fully dressed. "You're going?"

"I must. Will you come by the police station later this morning and make a report? The details of my... of Jonah Octavian's death must be properly recorded."

"Sam, what's going to happen to us? When I go back to Newfoundland, I mean."

He stroked my cheek. "I cannot answer that, my darling. Let us take each day as it comes." He leaned in and kissed me. "Until later."

"Good-bye, Sam."

I knew I'd see him in an hour or two, but saying it—saying those words—felt strangely and unpleasantly final.

CHAPTER SEVEN

WHEN I arrived at the police station later that morning, Ibrahim Samir was in Sam's office, sorting through papers on Sam's desk. He glanced up but didn't smile. "Captain Halim is not here."

"Good morning to you, too. Where is he?"

Samir shuffled rapidly through a stack of file folders. "He has taken exercise. You will find him in the athletic club on Sharia Soliman Pasha."

"You… you okay, Samir?"

"I have never felt better." His gaze was pointed, his dark eyes as hard as obsidian. "Was there something else you wanted?"

"No. No, I'm good." Whatever the hell was wrong with Samir was his business; I wasn't interested. I found the athletic club on the Sharia Soliman Pasha, as Samir said. Sam wasn't in the sauna or getting a massage, but I did find him in the boxing ring, sparring with some hulking brute of a guy who had fists like hams. I stood by the ropes for a while and watched.

Sam was a naturally graceful boxer, light on his feet and with lightning-quick fists. The big guy moved in, flailing, and a punch caught Sam on the side of the face, but he shook it off. His opponent came at him again, lashing out with both hands, but Sam danced back out of his way, and then feinted a right hook. The big guy struck again, a glancing blow high up on the cheek that opened a cut under Sam's eye. He's going to get pulverized, I thought. I was sure I'd be scraping Sam off the mat when everything was said and done, but he surprised me.

He waited till the other man swung, overreaching himself, and then danced back out of range. The big guy kept on coming, but Sam stayed away from him, leading him around and around the ring like a tethered ox until finally, when he had sufficiently exhausted his opponent, Sam stepped in with an uppercut and simultaneously slammed a left hook into the side of the guy's head. He dropped like a stone. Sam grinned, and then bent over to help the younger man up. I recognized him as one of the policemen from the station.

"Please, Captain Halim, no more." He laughed. "I beg you. No more."

Sam saw me waiting and stepped through the ropes to where I was. "Enjoying the show, Jack?"

I grinned at him. "Remind me never to get on your bad side."

"Oh, that? I like to keep myself in form. It is necessary for my work. You are looking very well this morning."

"You look fine except for that cut under your eye. You should get that looked at."

He dabbed at his face with a towel. "Yes. El Ajat might not be fast, but he is big and strong. Perhaps I'll assign him to the Bulaq district as punishment." He laughed. "Join me in a steam?"

"Sure."

It was early, and most of the club's clientele seemed to be elsewhere, so we had the sauna to ourselves. The hot steam felt good, and I didn't have any problem sitting there admiring Sam's naked body, either.

"Sam?"

"Yes, Jack?" He leaned against the bench, eyes closed.

"What's that scar on your chest?" I touched it lightly. "An operation?"

He cracked his eyelids a little. "It is where they took out my heart," he said solemnly. "At least, that is what the new police recruits are told."

I laughed. I had no trouble imagining that.

"Really, it is where I had a bullet removed."

"Yeah?" The thought made me sick. "Somebody shooting at you?"

"Jack, I am sorry to say there is often someone shooting at me. I am a police officer, and when I am not a police officer, I am—"

"The assistant to the British Consul. Yeah, I remember."

His soft brown eyes were sad. "I regret the deception, but it was necessary."

"Yeah, I know." I thought about my meeting with MacBride that day in the desert. I told Sam what MacBride had asked me.

"What did you tell him?"

"I haven't said anything yet. Sure, I'm as patriotic as the next guy but"—I lowered my voice—"espionage?"

"What Kevin MacBride asked you to do is not, strictly speaking, espionage. It is, rather, information gathering."

I gave him a look. "Come on, Sam. A rose by any other name…?"

"Would smell as—yes, all right, Jack." He huffed out a breath. "Sometimes I wonder if you deliberately set out to annoy me, or if such behavior is merely an inescapable fact of your personality." His hand slid down my arm. "If I did not love you as much as I do, I would probably kill you." He sat back and closed his eyes. "Maybe I will kill you anyway." He rested his head on the bench and sighed.

We finished our steam, and then headed to the showers together. It was really hard to stand under the hot water in the communal shower and not touch him, but I knew better. Sam was taking an incredible chance, and so was I; if the wrong people found out about us, Sam would lose his commission, and I'd be going back to Newfoundland in a cardboard box. Sure, there were guys like me in Egypt, but they were careful about it. Nowadays, more than ever, you didn't know who to trust. "What will you do with the rest of your day, Jack?"

"I dunno. I guess I should probably get ready to go home." I forced myself to smile. "I came here because you were missing. You're not missing anymore." It was like a knife in my chest. I ducked my head under the stream of water and rinsed my hair.

He gazed at me soberly. "And you have your cafe."

"Yeah. Yeah, I got my Heartache." Thanks to Frankie. I owed him a lot, and he was dead, killed by Jonah Octavian or one of his henchmen. Christ, what a sorry mess that whole thing was. I'd jumped out of one frying pan and into a second one, even hotter and greasier than the first. I turned off the water and we stepped out, carefully not looking at each other as we toweled off and dressed. "I guess… yeah." The unspoken words sat in my throat like a lump of ice, and I wanted to throw my arms around him, beg him to come back with me. I knew it would be futile.

Sam finished buttoning his shirt and slid the knot of his tie into place. "Can I give you a ride to the station?"

"Yeah, sure. Thanks." Sam had work to do on a forgery case, and I still needed to give a statement about Jonah Octavian's death. As soon as we arrived, he handed me over to Samir. "Sergeant, if you could take Mr.

Stoyles' statement? It concerns the death of Jonah Octavian. Mr. Octavian, as I'm sure you remember, was…." Something infinitely painful, something disappointed, flickered on Sam's face for an instant, and then was gone. "Mr. Octavian was a Nazi collaborator."

Samir leaped to his feet, taut as a bowstring. "Your command, Captain Halim."

"If Mr. Stoyles has any additional information that we do not, kindly take note of it."

"As you wish, Captain Halim. If I can serve in any other way—"

"That will be all, sergeant."

I followed Samir down the hall to a small room with a desk and a couple chairs. There were minimal furnishings and no windows; the ceiling light buzzed annoyingly, like a fly trapped in a window screen. Samir gestured that I should sit down. "You want to tell me exactly what the problem is?" I wasn't really asking; I knew I'd been a five-star jerk where Samir was concerned, but as far as that went, he owned at least some of the blame. He'd as much as said he had no expectations—that we were keeping each other company, nothing more. "You seem pretty sore." I tapped out a cigarette and lit it.

Samir glared at me. "No smoking is permitted in this room."

"Samir—Ibrahim—it's me, Jack. What's going on? You're acting like I killed your mother."

His mouth tightened. "My family is none of your concern. Now, then. Your statement regarding the death of the war criminal Jonah Octavian. You may begin when ready."

"Still holding on to the guy who killed Pasha Nubar?"

"That is not your affair."

"That's the word I was looking for." I waited, but he didn't take the bait. "We never made any promises, you and me."

A flicker of hurt passed across his features. "Just as you say." He kept his gaze on the desk.

"Ibrahim…."

"Captain Halim asked that I question you. Please permit me to do so."

I didn't know what he was playing at, and he didn't seem real eager to tell me, so I figured I'd better leave it alone. Whatever was up Samir's nose was his business, but I couldn't shake the feeling it had something to do with me. I told him everything I knew up to and including Octavian's messy death at the hands of Andros Scala, and he took it all down without looking at me once.

"Did Scala give any indication why he executed Octavian? Did he say anything to you?"

"No. I got the feeling it wasn't up for debate." It was odd, taken in context, why Scala had killed Octavian instead of Sam. He was Sam's cousin, not Scala's. If anybody was going to kill him—

"Captain Halim is a sworn officer of the law." Samir's voice startled me. I must have been thinking out loud again. "Whereas Scala is an Allied combatant. For Captain Halim to kill Octavian would have been murder, but Colonel Scala could dispatch him with fewer… complications."

"But it's wartime. And Sam—Captain Halim—isn't your average police captain. Surely, there are mitigating circumstances."

Samir sat back in his chair and regarded me with open hostility. "In your country, it is perhaps acceptable to kill a man of one's own family."

"That's a dirty crack, Samir."

"Is it?" The Ibrahim I knew was gone; in his place was the cold and judgmental Sergeant Samir, the same Samir who'd pushed me up against the wall the first day we'd met. "One has only to see an American film to know murder is a way of life with you."

"Samir—"

"I do believe I have everything I need, Mr. Stoyles." He closed the folder. "Good day."

And then he simply got up and left. I waited awhile, and when he didn't come back, I figured that was it. I caught a cab back to my hotel and left things where they were.

I didn't figure I'd hear from Sam or Ibrahim Samir the rest of the day, so I changed into something cool and airy, laced up my walking shoes, and set out to explore Cairo. Everywhere you went in this city, it seemed like there was somebody waiting with his hand out—kids, old men, young men—running alongside you, tugging at your sleeve and begging for baksheesh. Frankie had warned me about this, and although I had no intention of supporting the local beggars' guild, I kept a few piasters in small change in my pocket just the same. Sometimes beggars were the people with the information. They operated on the fringes of society, and they saw and heard things the rest of us didn't. Their information wasn't free, but for a price, you could find out just about anything—if you knew how to ask the right questions.

The whole business with Frankie was nagging me. Sam hadn't said a word about it, except to assure me it was Octavian who'd killed him. If he knew why—and I was pretty sure Sam did—he wasn't saying, or maybe that was classified information. The official story was that Missalo was working with Octavian, and that's why Frankie had gone to Newfoundland in the first place. Octavian had been using the island as his base of operations, which made a lot of sense. Newfoundland was of enormous strategic importance in this war. Octavian's construction company gave him a perfect front, but what did Frankie have? He didn't work for anybody in particular, just sort of bummed around, hiring on for a day or a week as a construction laborer with the choice to punch out whenever he liked. There were lots of jobs, and lots of foremen looking to hire guys who knew their way around a site; if you got bored doing one thing, chances were good you could switch off and do something else.

So if Frankie was working for Octavian, like Octavian had said he was, chances were good he knew all about Octavian's racket. But why follow Octavian to Cairo unless Octavian had given Frankie some kind of job to do? Maybe there was a reason why Frankie had arranged my travel, had set me up in a good hotel—had done everything short of flying me across the Atlantic. Guys like Octavian don't do the dirty work themselves; he'd have had one of his goons take Frankie out into the desert and bump him off, make it seem like Sam had done it. The odds were decent that Octavian had no more use for Frankie, and probably Frankie was tired of doing Octavian's grunt work, or maybe Octavian had given him an order and Frankie had refused. I didn't know the whole story, but I could piece some things together out of what I knew.

Octavian had tried to bump me off back home in Newfoundland, using Julie Fayre as go-between. When that failed—when Sam intervened in time to save me—Octavian had bolted, leaving Julie to take the rap. But he wasn't idle while his girlfriend was dancing her last tango at the end of a rope. He'd arranged to kidnap Sam and bring him to Cairo, knowing I'd come looking for him, that I wouldn't let it rest. Hell, Sam had probably agreed to go with him, on account of family feeling and a shared nostalgia for old times… the same kind of nostalgia Frankie and I had.

How much had Octavian known, and how much had he told? To whom had he told it? I was betting Sam knew more than he was telling, and I was pretty sure MacBride's merry band of saboteurs, or whatever they were, probably had the inside dope as well. It would be pointless to go to either of them, however, and ask for information. Sam would politely stonewall me and MacBride would pretend he didn't know what I was talking about. There was only one person I could ask.

SHE ANSWERED the doorbell on the first ring and invited me in. The house was pleasantly cool and inviting after the heat of the day, and when she offered me a cold glass of orange juice, I didn't refuse. "I am glad you have come. We have just returned from visiting with family in the country." Her dark hair was loose around her shoulders, and she wore a pale blue robe that floated around her slender figure. "I have very much wanted to speak with you."

"I want to talk to you as well." I didn't hesitate; this was no time for niceties. "Since I came to Cairo, I've been caught up in one mess or another pretty well nonstop. Now, I'm not a policeman or a soldier or part of any commando squad. I run a cafe in Newfoundland. I didn't come here looking for trouble, but it seems like I've been getting plenty of it. I think you know more than you're telling."

She avoided my gaze by fussing with her clothes. I let her keep on for a few minutes, figuring she'd talk when she was good and ready. "There is much you do not understand."

"Yeah, you know, people have been saying that to me ever since I came here. You're wrong. I know as much as I need to know. Sam's spying for the Allies, with the blessing of his government, and you—I don't know what to make of you. Ever since day one, you've been playing me for a fool. First you come out with a big sob story to get me on your side. Help me find my husband, you said. Then, when I start digging up some dirt, you get antsy and tell me to back off. I find Sam anyway, which is what he intended, but I'm thinking maybe you might not have wanted him found, that maybe it was better from your point of view if Sam went missing for good, or at least until I was safely out of the picture."

Her cheeks flushed bright red. She stood, her composure vanished. "You will leave my house at once."

"Just what kind of game are you playing, Mrs. Halim? You get me out here to some party you're having, and then you throw Ibrahim Samir at me, hoping I'll be satisfied with him, hoping maybe I won't bother Sam anymore."

She pointed to the door with a shaking hand. "Get out! You get out of here immediately! You do not understand anything! Go back to where you came from and leave me alone."

She advanced toward me, but I caught hold of her wrist and held her there. "Or what, Tareenah? You'll report me to the police? You'll tell Sam I came over here and put my hands on you? That I made you do things? He'll never believe you."

She smirked. "My husband loves me. He will believe anything I tell him."

"You think you're real clever. You thought if Samir and I got nice and cozy, I'd forget all about Sam. Then you could have Sam back again. I wouldn't want him anymore."

"No, that isn't true!"

"Who killed Pasha Nubar? Huh? Who shot a blow dart through the window? A dart that was maybe meant for me? And what's the real reason you don't want to sleep with Sam? Maybe there's no prohibition in your religion against contraception, but you'd rather leave Sam high and dry—" Her hand slammed into my face and I staggered backward. "What did Octavian promise you?"

Her expression was triumphant. "You will die not knowing, Americani. I will never tell."

There was a faint rustle at the door. "Yes, you will." Sam stood there in full uniform, his service automatic pointed at his wife. "Yes, my wife, you will tell. You will tell me everything."

IF IBRAHIM Samir was surprised to see the three of us turn up at headquarters together, he didn't say anything. I figured Sam was angry I'd decided to interrogate his wife in her own house, but he had insisted I come along, "Since you have been involved in this from the beginning." We went into Sam's office and sat down—Sam behind his desk, Tareenah and I in front of him. For a long time, he didn't say anything, simply sat there gazing at Tareenah calmly, as if she were any other traitor. Then, when some ten minutes had elapsed, he took a folder out of his desk drawer and dropped it in front of her. "Open it."

She kept her eyes down, her gaze humble and averted. "I... have angered you, my husband."

"*Open it!*" he roared. I had never heard Sam shout; it scared the hell out of me. "Look through it, my wife, and tell me what you see."

Tareenah murmured something, paging through the papers.

"I'm sorry." Sam lit a cigarette. "I did not hear what you said."

"My husband is displeased with me."

Sam looked at me and laughed. He looked at Tareenah, still sitting with her head bent, flicking idly through the documents. "Your husband is displeased with you." He nodded. "Mm. Have you nothing else to say?"

She shook her head mutely. Sam took the folder from her, turned it so I could see it. "Jack, if you please."

They were telegraph carbons, left over from messages sent to Jonah Octavian in Newfoundland. There were a lot of them, and registered letters with recent postmarks, and reports sent by special messenger. Some of these had gone to Octavian while he was still overseas, and some had been sent here in Cairo; they were obviously coded, and I was willing to bet they didn't say anything good. "Jesus."

"What did he promise you? Hm?"

She slumped in her chair, silent.

"I ask you again. What did Octavian promise you?" Sam pressed the button on his intercom. "Sergeant Samir, come in here." The door swished open; Samir must have been waiting on the other side of it. "Take the woman to a cell." Samir helped her up, and she went away without so much as a word to Sam or a look in his direction. The door closed behind them, and Sam buried his face in his hands. I ached to touch him, to offer such comfort as I could, but I knew now wasn't the time.

"How did you know?" I asked.

Sam raised his head. "MacBride. They'd had her under surveillance while I was overseas. His team reported unusual activity around my house during my most recent absences. When they tracked the source, it led to Tareenah." He shook his head. "My sister will come from Alexandria to care for my children."

"Sam, you aren't… you're not going back to…."

"I must." He laughed humorlessly. "Already Rommel's forces are massing for a second attempt on Cairo. There are numerous reports from partisans loyal to the Allied cause that the Nazis have their sights set on other cities along the coast of North Africa. What can I do? In the face of such rampant destruction, of what significance is a disloyal wife?"

"Sam, are you sure?"

"I am not sure of anything!" He got up and walked several agitated steps toward the filing cabinet, his back to me. "Jonah and I... I had not seen nor heard from him for years and years. Suddenly, a few months ago, he appears as if out of the sky, wanting to renew our childhood acquaintance." His shoulders were raised, his back stiff; he looked like he'd forgotten to take the hanger out of his coat before he put it on. "I am not a fool, Jack." He turned slowly. "He must have known I would take precautions, that I would check. He must have realized that presenting himself to me was dangerous. I have never made any secret of my profession."

"Except to me."

He winced. "That isn't fair."

"You're right. It isn't fair." It occurred to me that maybe Tareenah was taking all the blame for something Octavian had cooked up, and that didn't seem right. "Can I... would you mind if I tried talking to her?"

He gestured at the door. "You may *try*. Ali!" A baby-faced cop appeared at the door, clutching a notebook. "Please take Mr. Stoyles to see Mrs. Halim. That is all."

I started to say something but Sam had opened a thick file folder and was pretending to read it, so I decided to let things lie. I followed Ali downstairs to where the cells were. Tareenah was near the end of the row in the women's block, sitting on the bunk with her head down. Ali unlocked the door, and I slipped inside, sitting down on the opposite bunk. The cell was small and oppressively hot, and smelled overpoweringly of stale cigarettes and old urine and fear. What light there was entered through a tiny, barred window set high up in the wall.

"Mrs. Halim, Sam asked me to come and talk to you." Not precisely true, but I was willing to make a nod to diplomacy. She ignored me completely. "I'd like to hear your side of things."

We sat there in silence for maybe fifteen minutes, and I was beginning to think I'd wasted my time when finally she stirred. "He does not understand."

"Sam doesn't?"

"There are things...." She clenched her hands. "Would you happen to have an American cigarette, Mr. Stoyles?"

"Sure." I fished one out and lit it for her. "What doesn't he understand?"

"This man, Octavian. He is dead?"

"Yeah." I remembered the clean arc the big Greek's knife had made, the spray of Octavian's blood against the white wall of the house. "Yeah, he's dead."

"My husband does not know the full scope of my relationship with Jonah Octavian. He sees me only as a traitor, a betraying wife."

"What was in that file folder was pretty damning, Mrs. Halim, as far as evidence goes."

"I did it, Mr. Stoyles. I will not lie to you. Oh yes, I did it."

"Why?"

She held my gaze and didn't flinch. "He threatened to kill my children if I did not help him." I made a face, but she stumbled on. "No, you can smile if you wish. One day I went to collect Stamos and Tabia at their school. The teacher said my children had already gone—their uncle had picked them up and taken them home. My children have no uncle."

"Octavian."

"Yes."

"Why not seek Samir's help?" I didn't understand why she hadn't gone to the police immediately. "Surely you knew Samir would help you. Why not go to him?" Samir was loyal to Sam; she could hardly compromise her husband by confiding in his subordinate.

"Do you think Octavian is stupid?" She shook her head. "I had reason to believe I was being closely watched. He would know I had gone to the police."

"So you just went along with him." Sam deserved better than this.

"Think of me what you will, Mr. Stoyles, but I did what I had to do in order to protect my children." She drew hard on the cigarette, her expression ravaged. "Now go. Persuade my husband to return to Canada with you, or wherever it is you are going."

"Newfoundland," I said quietly. "Not Canada. It's not quite the same thing." I drew a deep breath, wishing to hell I knew how to proceed. "Mrs. Halim, I understand why you did this. If Octavian was threatening to harm your children—"

"If! You do not believe me either." She shook her head. "It does not matter."

I didn't have to wonder how she rationalized all this to herself; I knew. But I wondered if she really understood the implications of what she'd done. Did she realize there were men out there in the desert, men who would die because of what she'd done? "Yeah, I believe you." I stood up to go. "And I'm trying to understand why you did it. I really am."

I called for Ali. He came and let me out, and I went back up to Sam's office. He was on the phone when I got there, but he motioned me in, so I sat down across from him and waited till he was done. Sam's conversation was in Arabic, and I didn't understand any of it, but he seemed agitated. Finally he put the phone down and looked at me. "What did she say to you?"

"Octavian was threatening the children."

"She claims." Sam's composure wavered for a moment, and he pressed a hand to his forehead, shielding his eyes from me. "Jack, I confess I do not know what to do."

"Sam, are you sure she's safe here?" I saw his look and hastened to explain. "I mean, if Octavian's boys are still around, they're bound to know she's let the cat out of the bag. Don't you think they might come looking for her?"

"Cat?" He tilted his head on one side. "Jack, my wife does not keep a cat. Ah, yes, I see. This is one of your American expressions." He was silent for a moment, stroking his mustache. "There is a chance Aaltonen or someone might come looking for Tareenah, yes." His gaze met mine. "You are familiar, I take it, with the phenomenon of using bait to lure a predator?"

"Uh-huh."

"Your expression says you despise me for using my wife in this manner." He was trembling. "Allah protect me! My back is against a wall, and I swear on the heads of my children, Jack, I do not know what to do."

I shut his office door and turned the key in the lock. Then I went around his desk, knelt down on the floor, and took him into my arms. He was trembling the length of his body, shuddering like a leaf in the wind, and I turned his face and kissed him. "We'll figure it out. We will, Sam. You and I. We'll get through this together."

It was fine and good to make such lavish promises, but in reality, I didn't know a damned thing about espionage, and I sure as hell had no idea where to start.

MY FIRST thought upon waking was that somebody was in the room. It wasn't even a thought as such, just a general and immediate impression.

My body was up and halfway out of the bed before my brain had even registered I was awake. "All right, start talking." I reached for the bedside lamp and switched it on. The man known as Mukbar sat in the chair beside my bed, his arms neatly folded in his lap.

"Did you know, Mr. Stoyles, your snoring is unduly loud for a man of your age and physical condition."

"What the hell do you want? How'd you get in here?"

"To help you. As to how I got in—" He traced the crease in his trousers. "Far too easily, I expect. Even considering the Acacia Court is a first-rate hotel, you would do well to put the chain on your door before retiring." He smirked. "I might have killed you in your sleep."

He was holding a small pistol fitted with a silencer, and it was pointed right at my chest. "You gonna do me in with that, Mukbar?"

"It shoots, Mr. Stoyles. Please, you will get dressed and come with me."

"I'm not going anywhere with y—" There was a sound like a firecracker popping deep down inside a well, and a small hole appeared in the wall next to my shoulder.

"You will get dressed and come with me." His large eyes blinked once or twice, slowly; he was easy in himself, and endlessly patient. "Come with me now."

My watch read half-past three when Mukbar and his tiny gun escorted me down the back stairs to a waiting car. The moon hung above us, huge and ponderous, and immediately I thought of Sam. I'd hoped to have at least one more intimate interlude with him before I went back home, but if Mukbar's intentions were what I thought they were, I could forget about that.

"Go on, get in." He prodded me, and I slid into the back seat beside a tall, thin man I immediately recognized: the Finn, Errki Aaltonen, the same man who'd taken Sam to the bank the day I'd shown up with the key.

"So nice to see you again, Mr. Stoyles. I fear our previous meeting was under less-than-salutary circumstances."

"So you're in on this too, huh? I might have known. How'd you get out? Sam's jail is supposed to be one of the tightest in Egypt. Pay somebody off, did you, for a little inside job?"

He laughed, showing white, faintly feral teeth. "You're a smart man, Mr. Stoyles. Tell me what else you know, hm?"

"You and this creature were involved in killing Pasha Nubar. Where'd you learn to use a blow gun?"

The car jolted into motion, and Aaltonen chose to ignore my question, focusing his gaze on the view through the windshield. Cairo was quiet at this hour, but Mukbar was an indifferent driver, and more than once we nearly ran up onto the sidewalk as he veered away from some obstacle. I started thinking that if only I could distract Mukbar long enough to make him drive into something, I could easily get away from Aaltonen. I wasn't stupid, I knew both of them had guns, but maybe I could escape down an alley and....

And what? Lose yourself in the native quarter? It was almost like I could hear Sam's voice in my head. *Get yourself knifed to death? Strangled?* It was better to stay put, and maybe if I kept my wits about me, I could get to a phone and alert Sam, and he could come charging in and arrest Mukbar and Aaltonen on the spot. That is, if they didn't kill me first, and if they didn't see Sam coming, and he and his men were able to approach without being seen, and thus ambush—

Skip it, my mind said. Keep your mouth shut and your eyes open, and you might still get out of this alive.

We were heading north out of Cairo, toward the desert. That wasn't good. I didn't see any provisions in the car and neither Mukbar nor Aaltonen were carrying water. My guesses might be good or they might be crummy, but it looked like I was being brought out into the desert, where they intended to leave me. Yeah, the heat and thirst would make short work of me, and by the time Sam or his men found me, I'd be nothing more than a shriveled husk. "So what is this, exactly? You boys planning to do away with me, or are you just giving me the scenic tour?"

"Mr. Stoyles, I dislike cliché almost as much as I dislike cheap sentiment, therefore I will be honest with you." Mukbar sighed like he was genuinely sorry for me. "You know too much to be allowed to live. In Egypt, as in much of North Africa these days, knowledge is a dangerous thing. Your knowledge makes you extremely dangerous indeed, as does your ability to, shall we say, assemble the pieces."

"So you are gonna knock me off."

"Why don't you sit back and enjoy the ride, Mr. Stoyles? There will be no need for you to talk."

Mukbar's command was punctuated by a jab in the ribs from Aaltonen's gun, and I did as I was told. My mind kept going back to Tareenah, sitting in her jail cell. What would happen to her? I knew the penalty for treason during wartime, but surely Sam wouldn't condemn his own wife. If Octavian had been blackmailing her, then she'd given him the information under extreme duress, and wasn't there some proof of that somewhere? As it stood, she was being railroaded, and she didn't seem to be doing a lot to defend herself. Why was that?

Eventually my musings and the early hour got the best of me, and I fell asleep leaning against the car door. I dreamed I was on a boat, sailing on some unfamiliar body of water, alone. The boat was fitted with a sail, but there were no oars; I seemed to be drifting in a fathomless fog. I cupped my hands around my mouth and called out, but my voice went nowhere; the fog closed in around the boat, and I was smothering, I couldn't breathe—

"Aaltonen, you fool, not yet." Mukbar and the Finn held me upright between them, and we were moving rapidly down a set of stone steps toward a narrow door set into the side of the hill. The horizon had begun to lighten, and the stars were beginning to go out. I longed viciously for Sam and wondered if I would ever see him or my Heartache Cafe again. "In you go, Mr. Stoyles, I am sure you will find it very comfortable." They shoved me in, the heavy door was swung into position, and the bar dropped across it. I was in utter and absolute darkness, with not so much as a crack showing anywhere. I raised my hands above me and my palms hit solid rock a few inches above my head. This was bad. This was very, very bad. I had no way of knowing how large or small my prison was, and so I couldn't calculate how many cubic feet of air I would have the privilege of breathing before my supply ran out. The important thing, I knew, was to stay calm. Getting excited would increase my heart rate and respiration, hastening my death.

I felt for the floor and lowered myself down, sitting with my back against a rock wall. The air was warm but not uncomfortably so, and I guessed the thick stone insulated the place against the worst of the desert heat. I laid my head back and concentrated on calming myself by taking slow, even breaths. After a while, I began to drift off into that queer place between sleep and wakefulness. I dreamed I was lying in bed beside Sam, and the low rays of the morning sun had just begun to show over the horizon. The room was white, and the bed in which we lay was also white and crowned with a huge mosquito net made of some diaphanous stuff. Sam was naked except for a white silk sheet, and I leaned over him, watching his sleeping face and waiting for him to wake. His dreams swam across his features and fluttered his dark lashes, and his mouth was curved in a smile. He turned his face and, without opening his eyes said, "My beloved is mine and I am his, who is delighting among the lilies...."

Then we were standing at the bar in my Heartache Cafe, and Chris was mixing us a drink; no, that was wrong, Sam didn't drink, he was a Moslem, and I hadn't touched the stuff in ages. "It's all right," Chris said, "there's only soda water in this one." The sun was setting in a blaze of scarlet and gold, lighting up the windows of houses along the South Side. "You have to go now." Chris came out from behind the bar and took me by the arm and walked me to the door of my cafe. "You aren't supposed to be here. You have to go." And then I was standing on the bridge again in Philly, the freezing wind slicing through my clothes and cutting into my skin. The cold was cutting off my feet and hands, sawing through my legs at the ankles—

I woke with a start. I was sitting with my legs folded in front of me, my hands dangling in my lap. I couldn't be sure how much time had passed, and I might have been there for hours or for merely moments. That wasn't what woke me, however. I had registered something in my sleeping state, something different enough for my subconscious mind to remark upon it and thus draw my attention to... what? Dammit, what was it? I had to remember. I was lying with Sam, and he was quoting the Song of Solomon; then we were in the Heartache Cafe with Chris, watching the sun set. I was cold: my hands and feet were cold; the cold was cutting through my legs at the ankles.

I put my hands down and let them dangle for a moment and then I knew: a veritable torrent of cold air was streaming in from somewhere to the right, cooling my feet and hands. I got down on my belly and put my face into the stream and sure enough, it was real. Cold air in the desert usually means there's water somewhere nearby, an underground spring or aquifer. This could mean the difference between life and death, provided I could find the source. I dug my index finger into the earth to the last knuckle and found nothing but dry sand, but I wasn't giving up just yet. I followed the stream of air back farther, always keeping it in front of me, stopping now and then to dig into the soil but so far, I had found absolutely nothing.

After about an hour of this, I sat back to rest. Maybe there wasn't any water. Maybe the cool air was a trick, designed to make me wear myself out looking for a stream of water that didn't exist. Aaltonen had probably rigged it himself, as some kind of sick joke, and I couldn't help thinking that these were the kind of people Frankie had chosen to play ball with. He'd probably signed on figuring he could capitalize on the benefits without getting caught up in the nasty parts, but he'd figured wrong. Guys like Aaltonen and Octavian didn't play fair; they played dirtier than anybody, and they'd kill whoever happened to get in the way, including each other.

"All right," I said aloud, "one more go." I lay down on my belly, put my face into the stream of air, and started forward. I had gone maybe six or seven feet when my outstretched hand touched something—something cold and rubbery and faintly fleshy.

I didn't need light to tell me I was touching a human foot.

CHAPTER EIGHT

I SAT there in the dark for a long time, hunched over and trying not to breathe too fast and use up all the air. My mind was jabbering away a mile a minute, and I spent a helluva lot of energy just trying to make myself shut up. Whoever owned the foot was dead, because they sure as hell didn't move, even when I reached out, grabbed them by the ankle, and shook. I figured this was probably another one of Octavian's operatives, bumped off because they didn't behave like the big boss wanted. I couldn't think who this could be: Mukbar and Aaltonen seemed pretty tight, and as far as I knew, Octavian had no reason to kill Ibrahim Samir. One more Cairo policeman more or less meant nothing much to him or his cronies. It was Sam they were after.

I guess maybe I'm a lot dumber than I give myself credit for, because the other possibility didn't occur to me until a long time afterward. I remembered the conversation Sam and I had in his office before Mukbar showed up in my hotel room to take me for a ride. *If Octavian's boys are still around, they're bound to know she's let the cat out of the bag. Don't you think they might come looking for her?* I reached farther up the leg and felt the unmistakable contours of a woman's hip, the indentation of her waist and then, finally, her long hair. There was no light for me to see, but I knew it could be no one else but Tareenah Halim. How they had gotten her out of jail was one thing—surely Octavian's boys had operatives on the inside, things being the way they were—but did they think Sam would let them get away with this? He was bound to come looking for his wife, and Sam was too much of a policeman to let a trail stand long enough to get cold.

I felt sick. Sam would come looking for his wife, and when he did, Mukbar and Aaltonen would be waiting for him. Yeah, there was still plenty of room in here for one more. They'd wall us up in here together and let us bide our time until the air ran out. They were a nice bunch, Octavian's guys, real loyal to one another.

There was a commotion outside, and then the sound of something scraping against the stone. The thin beam of a flashlight stabbed the darkness, and I instinctively covered my eyes. "Mr. Stoyles, how fortunate that you are still alive. We were worried you would not be able to receive your visitor." Mukbar: I'd recognize that voice anywhere. "In you go, Captain Halim. Mr. Stoyles is waiting for you. I am sure the two of you have plenty to talk about."

"Sam—" I reached for him, caught him as he fell. "Sam, I'm sorry. I don't know what happened but I wish to God I could have stopped it."

The door was closed, and I heard the grating noise as the key was turned in the lock. We were plunged into absolute darkness. Sam felt for my hand and held on. "Well, if we wanted a quiet place where we could be alone, our wish has certainly been granted, don't you think?" His voice was calm and faintly amused; this was the Sam I knew.

"Sam, there's something you should know." How in God's name could I tell him something like this? "We aren't alone in here."

"Not alone." There was a long pause, and when Sam spoke again, some of the vigor had gone out of his voice. "They have brought my— Tareenah is here, isn't she?"

I guided his hand to where the body lay supine against the wall. "Yeah, Sam. She's here."

He was silent then, and for a long time afterward, we sat there in the dark, not saying anything. Maybe an hour passed before he spoke. "The first time I ever saw her was in a graduate seminar on Semitic languages. She sat to one side of the room, taking copious notes, writing very rapidly."

"Sam, you don't have to...."

"I wondered what she could have been writing, that she wrote so quickly. I began to suspect what she was writing had nothing to do with the seminar." He was smiling, I was sure of it. "When the professor invited the students to expound upon the material presented, Tareenah raised her hand. She recited a summary in perfect Aramaic."

An invisible hand closed around my heart, squeezing painfully. "Octavian's boys did this to her, Sam. They probably snatched her from the police station." I told him how I'd woken up to find Mukbar in my room. "Now that Octavian's dead, they're doing a little tidying up. I guess the three of us are just loose ends to them."

"Yes. That is all we are, Jack: loose ends." His voice broke, and I pulled him into my arms and held on to him while he cried, his body heaving with a grief I could not hope to reach or mediate.

I guess I must have fallen asleep, because the next thing I knew, there was a light in my face and somebody was shaking me by the arm.

"Lieutenant Stoyles." Kevin MacBride leaned down and looked into my face. "It's all right. You're safe now. You're safe."

I blinked at him. My head was aching and everything felt wrong, like the world had shifted on its axis. "What time is it? How long have I been here?" I watched two men lift a shrouded bundle up into the light: Tareenah Halim.

"It's morning." MacBride's voice was very gentle. "One of our operatives advised us when Captain Halim was abducted from his office. We've been following you ever since."

"How long—" I cleared my throat and tried again. "How long have we been here?"

MacBride glanced across at Sam. "You've been here for a day."

HER BODY was conveyed through the streets of Cairo on a flower-strewn funerary bier, Sam on one side and his oldest son on the other. I kept a respectable pace behind, walking with Ibrahim Samir. The midday sun beat down cruelly on my uncovered head, and I was sweating ferociously. Sam was in full uniform, standing erect under the weight of his grief. He walked slowly, with measured steps, one hand on the bier, his gaze fixed straight ahead. I don't know what he was thinking—we hadn't had a chance to speak since Kevin MacBride's men had taken us out of that hole in the desert—but I was betting it had nothing to do with me. Watching him, standing straight and tall beside his wife's dead body, I felt like more of an outsider than ever. I didn't belong here. I would never belong here. I had come here to find Sam, and now that I had found him, that part of it was over. The best thing for me to do—the only thing for me to do—was to go home, back to Newfoundland, to Chris and my Heartache Cafe. I'd already spoken to MacBride about travel arrangements, and he'd gotten me a seat on a military transport heading for Newfoundland the day after tomorrow. All that was left was to pack my things and say my good-byes to Egypt.

The procession stopped at a pretty little cemetery not far from the Muski bazaar, and Sam and the other mourners moved to lift Tareenah's body from the bier. Islamic custom dictated that three balls of earth be placed under the corpse by the next of kin: one under the head, one under the chin, and one under the shoulder. Before Tareenah was buried Sam, Ibrahim Samir, and a man I knew only as Sam's cousin Iqbal, stood together and poured three handfuls of dirt into the open grave, reciting a verse from the Koran. Sam looked stricken and physically sick, and I saw Ibrahim Samir lay a hand on his shoulder as they moved to lower the corpse into the grave. There was no loud wailing, no rending of people's clothes—in fact, nobody uttered a sound—but it felt like something had been drained away, something that could never be regained.

My face felt hot and my eyes were burning, and I tried to hold myself together but I couldn't do it, and before I knew what was happening, I was crying, bending forward from the waist, my hands over my eyes. I thought about Judy's death, ages ago in Philadelphia, lying on a bloodied operating table with her legs in stirrups, staring at the ceiling. I thought about my father, killed when I was just a kid, crushed under a runaway locomotive at the navy yard in south Philly, and the guys who came to our house that afternoon to tell my mother. Yeah, I thought about Tareenah Halim, out there in the desert, dead and waiting to be buried, and I hated that I was being so goddamn selfish, and I hated that I couldn't stop crying, and I hated that she had to be dead. None of it made any sense, and what was the point of trying to make things better anyway, if it all just came to this, to dust and ashes?

Someone's arm went around my shoulders, and I was crushed against a hard, lean body wearing a police uniform. Ibrahim Samir pressed his cheek to mine, and his face was wet with tears. "Your grief is most acceptable, Jack. It honors the deceased to weep for her. It honors us all." He drew me toward the grave, where he bent and gathered up a handful of earth, which he pressed into my palm. "We finish the grave together, taking care as we work that we are ever mindful of our own mortality." He knelt and drew me down beside him. "Come. We will work together, you and I."

It took under an hour to fill the hole, to mound up the dirt and pat it smooth. The mourners were returning to Sam's house where his mother-in-law was waiting with the younger children; I understood various distant relatives and members of the community would arrive to offer their condolences. I started back toward the cemetery gate, my hands still grimy with grave dust, but once again Ibrahim Samir came to me. "Please accompany me to Captain Halim's house. You are most welcome."

"I don't want to intrude." I laid my hand on his shoulder. "Ibrahim, the best thing for me to do is to go back to the hotel. I'll be leaving for home in a day or so. I should probably start packing."

His dark eyes were red-rimmed with fatigue and sorrow. Samir was Sam's friend as well as his subordinate; he loved Sam as much as I did. "Please. Captain Halim would want you to be there."

I tried to demur but he was relentless. In the end, I agreed to share a cab with Samir. We sat together in the back seat, and he held my hand between both of his. I watched the Cairo landmarks slip by for what would probably be the last time. "I never did tell you about Pasha Nubar." Samir's hand tightened on mine. "He was killed by a local who had been hired for that purpose, the son of a jeweler in the native quarter."

"Who hired him? And why Pasha Nubar?"

"We are reasonably certain he was hired by the man who calls himself Mukbar—a career blackmailer we have had our eyes upon for some time. Pasha Nubar was killed because he was about to give you information." He smiled. "You have probably already learned that information is a valuable commodity in Cairo."

"You arrested him?"

"Yes. The same day I arrested you, as a matter of fact. Sadly, he did not survive."

My skin prickled. "What do you mean, he didn't survive?"

Samir turned to look out the side window of the cab. "He killed himself in jail. He has been buried in the police cemetery."

"His father didn't claim the body?"

"No. No one wanted him. It is usually the way." Samir shrugged. "Mukbar and his associate, the Finn, are in custody. We expect a swift… resolution to the case."

"Mm." I knew what he meant. Mukbar and Errki Aaltonen would be kicking their heels at the end of a rope before too long. I didn't have it in me to care too much. As far as I was concerned, the world could rotate quite nicely without guys like Aaltonen and Mukbar. "So that's the end of it."

Samir shrugged. "A little police work, a few piasters dropped into the right palms, and we found them. Mukbar was already known to us. He has rather an illustrious reputation as a blackmailer of some note."

"Sam was right about one thing, Ibrahim."

"Oh?"

I squeezed his hand gently. "You're a good cop."

Sam's house was full of people, all of them strangers to me. His mother-in-law—an older version of Tareenah—came bustling toward Samir and me, offering the traditional greeting and herding us toward the food. I suppose you could say death is a hungry business or maybe it was my body's way of reaffirming that I was alive, because I was starving. I excused myself and went to the bathroom to wash up. I should have knocked because when I opened the door Sam was in there, sitting on the edge of the bath with his head in his hands. It didn't take too much imagination to figure out he'd been crying. He looked up, and I turned to go, mumbling an apology.

"Jack." He stood up and straightened his uniform tunic, wiping his eyes on his sleeve. "I wanted to say—"

"Sam, you don't have to say anything." There were so many things I wanted to tell him, and it was all pressing against the back of my throat like unshed tears. "I should tell you…." Goddammit, I wanted to rush to him and fold him in my arms and hold on to him until the pain stopped, until we could both breathe again—but I didn't have that right and I didn't know if I ever would.

He nodded. "You are leaving."

"Yeah." It was me saying the words, but I wasn't really hearing myself, and I didn't quite understand what was going on. My mind was full of a roaring pain that sounded like the sea does when a cold nor'easter is blowing full onshore.

"I suppose that is for the best." He made no move to touch me. I couldn't blame him.

"Yeah, I suppose so." I was going to bawl; I could feel it. "Sam, you once said—"

"Thank you." He took my hand. "For everything." The expression in his eyes, the sorrow he wore like a mask, these things told me what he could not say in words. It was over. Whatever we'd had, whatever we'd figured we were doing, was done. He didn't have to tell me; I already knew.

"I guess maybe we should... what I mean is, uh—" My throat closed, and I turned away. "Good-bye, Sam." By the time I got to the front door, I couldn't see a goddamn thing.

I SPENT the next day packing up my stuff, what was left of it after the hotel room exploded, and getting my affairs in order. I sent a wire to Chris, advising him I'd be home. My flight didn't leave right away, so I lay down on the bed for a while and tried to nap, but all I could think about was the time Sam and I had made love in this room and held each other, and spent the night sleeping in each other's arms. I thought about going downstairs to the bar, but tried to put it off as long as I could. Crawling inside a bottle wouldn't solve a goddamn thing. This just hurt so much, a pain so deep I hardly knew what to do with it. I found myself wondering if maybe I'd have been better off if Sam and I had never met. Would that have made a difference? What if Sam, looking for directions, had walked into some other cafe that day on Water Street, or what if his map had shown exactly where he needed to be? Would I be happier? Would he? *Sam. I'm so glad. You know, I didn't think... I didn't think we'd ever get here. Like this.* But we had, and it was obviously over. I couldn't honestly expect Sam to be with me in the way I wanted, not after everything that had happened. Tareenah's betrayal and her death had taken something out of him, and he would never be the same. Maybe we could be together later on, once the pain had lessened and he could imagine himself living in the world again.

Yeah. Maybe that would happen.

The telephone by my bed rang, and I reached out automatically to pick it up. It was the desk clerk, advising me I had a visitor. I wasn't in the mood to see anybody, but a tiny part of my mind—the part that still held out hope, regardless—said it might be Sam, so I told them to send him up.

"Lieutenant Stoyles?" Kevin MacBride's tall form filled the doorway; the big Greek, Andros Scala, was just behind him. I invited them both in. "I wonder if you've given any further thought to our proposition." MacBride looked tired, as though he hadn't been getting enough sleep lately. Scala looked the same as always: composed and steady, a human colossus with the saddest eyes I'd ever seen.

"Look, Captain, I'm leaving tomorrow morning, as you know. I'd prefer to put this whole thing behind me."

"The news about Captain Halim's wife is tragic." Scala inclined his head. "I offer my condolences."

"Why?" Something in me snapped, something I'd been holding in check for a long time. "You said yourselves you didn't trust her, and now that it's all come out, why should you care? What's it to you?"

"Our sympathies are with Captain Halim." MacBride nodded toward my suitcase, lying open on the floor. "And with you. I understand Captain Halim is your special friend. I'm truly sorry all this has happened."

I sat down on the bed and lit a cigarette. "Yeah. War is hell."

MacBride and Scala exchanged a look. Scala came to sit beside me. "You could be of immeasurable help to us when you return to your island."

"I'm not in the market for whatever it is you're selling—heroism, martyrdom—you can keep it." He had some nerve, asking me this. What the hell were they playing at? "I'm not interested."

Scala nodded. "This is a particular pain you are feeling. Doubtless some would tell you it will fade in time. I do not believe such usual wisdom."

MacBride pretended to gaze out the window, his hands in the pockets of his olive-drab trousers. There was something painful and set in his profile; he seemed to be keeping himself forcibly in check.

"Yeah?" I drew savagely on my cigarette. "You're the only one."

Scala turned so he was looking directly at me. "Early in the war, before the Germans invaded and ravaged my country, I was a happy married man. I had a lovely wife, three beautiful young daughters, and the keeping of my father's olive plantation."

MacBride made a tiny sound and turned away from the window.

"The day the Germans marched into my village, I was away, selling our oil in the city. They went up to where my house was on the side of the mountain, killed my parents and butchered their bodies, and hung them from the rafters of their home by the ankles. They raped and killed my three sisters and set fire to the bodies—"

Jesus Christ.

"My wife, they also raped, and my three daughters, who were three, five and seven years old."

MacBride sat at the table in my hotel room, as unmoving as a statue. His clenched hands lay on the tabletop, knuckles showing white against the skin. I didn't understand how Scala could speak of this and stay so calm, as if it had happened to someone else, someone he didn't even know.

"The Germans hung my children on the front of my house for me to see when I returned from the market that day."

MacBride finally spoke. "When it got dark, Andros, his brother-in-law, and several men went down into the village to find the Germans who had done this." He wasn't looking at Scala or at me; his gaze remained fixed on the table and on his own clenched fists. "It took thirty minutes to kill them all. When it was over, the restaurant where they had been eating and drinking was awash with their blood."

My stomach contracted, and I thought I was going to be sick. "Look, I understand... and I'm sorry. But Captain Halim and I, we—"

"Captain Halim is your special friend... your very best friend in all the world, yes?" Scala's huge hand rested on my shoulder like the paw of a friendly bear.

He could see inside me, I thought, and he knew everything. There was no point hiding from a man like this. "I... Captain Halim and I... it isn't merely friendship, it's not like that. You wouldn't understand."

MacBride moved to where we were. He slid an arm around Scala's broad shoulders and sat beside him. The two men looked at each other and something passed between them, something I'd have had to be blind not to see. "Yes," MacBride said quietly, "I rather think we would."

"You... two?"

"We trained together, early in the war," Scala said. "Sometimes there is great comfort in the most unexpected places."

"I... would have never guessed. I mean... you don't seem—"

MacBride smiled faintly. "Would you? In a place like this?"

I shook my head. I couldn't think straight. "I can't give you an answer, not right now. Maybe in a few weeks, when I've had time to think.... I dunno."

They shook my hand at the door. "Please," MacBride said, "think about it. We need you. And your service would help Captain Halim as well."

I couldn't give him an answer. The only thing in my mind was pain.

CHAPTER NINE

THE PLANE took a sharp, banking turn around the Southside Hills before turning north to Torbay Airport, and something deep inside me told me I was home. It's strange how a place grows on you, and before you know it, becomes the only real haven you've ever known. If I wasn't exactly glad to see St. John's, I was something pretty close to it.

I collected my bags and went through to the main door, hoping to flag down a taxi, but lo and behold, a familiar hand fell on my shoulder, and a voice I knew as well as my own said, "Welcome home, Jack."

"Chris!" I couldn't help myself. I hauled him into my arms and held on. "What are you doing here?" He looked the same as always: tall, dark-haired, and handsome, with those killer dimples that had the power to melt even the hardest of hearts.

"I came to pick you up." He grabbed my extra suitcase. "The car's over this way. I had to close the cafe down for a little while. We're short on staff, and there's nobody to watch the place. Did I tell you Dave Chan quit? Yeah. He went off to enlist in the army, can you believe that?" Chris threw my bags in the back seat of his battered Dodge and we got in. The car started up with a roar, rattling like a battleship; Chris shoved it into gear with difficulty and no small amount of swearing.

God, it was good to see him. Good old Chris, with his warm brown eyes, his ready smile, and the easygoing manner that belied a world of hurt. I wouldn't soon forget the way Julie Fayre had nearly killed us both, or that her crimes had sent her to the gallows. It had taken Chris a long time to find his way back and maybe the scars Julie had inflicted might never fade. It always amazed me how decent people seem to bear the brunt of so much violence in this world.

"You're not saying very much." Chris cast a sidelong glance at me. "Something on your mind, Jack?"

I shook my head. "Naw. It's nothing."

He reached across the front seat and took hold of my hand, interlacing his fingers with mine. "You can talk to me. You know that."

I felt the hot press of tears against my lids and willed them not to fall. I looked out the window, pretending interest in the passing vista. "I sure missed this place." I could just make out the harbor from where we were: the sun was setting over the Southside Hills, burning scarlet and crimson into the land, and the Narrows were a deep, blood red. "It's not the same in Egypt. The sunset, I mean. Oh sure, you've got the Nile—"

This is what I want, as well as you.

"—and the sunset in the desert is pretty damn spectacular, I have to admit—"

That is all we are, Jack: loose ends.

"But it's nothing like this. I never realized before how beautiful this place is. You know, you travel for miles and miles and you think you're looking for something—"

Jack, let us bathe together now, and then we will love each other slowly.

I was voiceless, the unsaid words fluttering in my throat like netted birds. What was the matter with me? Why did I always end up here, in this same lonely place? Why did I keep making these same mistakes?

"Everybody makes mistakes." Chris glanced over at me as we stopped at Rawlins Cross to wait for the light. "It's not just you." He laughed bitterly. "At least Sam didn't try to frame you for murder like Julie did with me."

"Sorry, Chris. I must have been thinking out loud again."

"Naw, it's okay." The light turned; he put the car into gear. "I don't think about her that much anymore." We bumped down over Prescott Street and across Duckworth, navigating a set of streetcar tracks as we turned onto Water. The light from the setting sun lit up the windows on the north side, bathing my Heartache Cafe in a deep orange glow. "There you are, Jack. Home sweet home, huh?"

I sighed, and something loosened inside my chest. "Aw, Chris, it's good to be back."

He took my bags up to my room above the cafe and turned down my bed. He'd kept the place clean while I was gone; there were fresh towels in the bathroom, and the trio of little houseplants on the chest of drawers was doing fine. Obviously Chris had kept them watered while I'd been away.

"You need anything, Jack?" He lingered in the doorway, one hand on the lintel, the other jingling his keys.

"No… no, I'm fine, Chris." I smiled. "See?" Maybe I'd go for a walk, wander around a bit until I got my bearings. "You go on. I'll see you in the morning."

I waited till I heard the downstairs door click shut behind him. Then I lay down on the bed and cried myself to sleep.

"HEY, JACK." Chris waved to me from the end of the bar. A tall, thin man with the kind of beaky nose that always reminded me of a bird was currently our only customer. He had come in earlier in the evening, ordered a double scotch, neat, and preceded to sit there, hunched over like a sack of old clothes. It was a good thing, I thought, we weren't relying on him as our only source of revenue. I left the cash register and went down to where Chris was. The tall man looked up from his drink and I saw, with what amounted to a sort of mental twinge, that he hadn't even touched his scotch.

"Yeah, Chris, what is it?"

He drew me away from the bar, turned his back, and cupped a hand over his mouth. It was like something out of a spy movie, and I couldn't help laughing. "This isn't funny, Jack. There's something strange about that guy. He's been sitting here all night. It's kind of screwy, don't you think?"

"I dunno, Chris. Look, it's pouring rain outside. The poor guy probably just wants a place to get dry." I glanced over Chris's shoulder at the man. He was rummaging through his pockets, picking out little pieces of paper and laying them on the bar. It kind of reminded me of this old guy I once knew back in Philly, Hairy Jim we used to call him, on account of his long, unkempt beard. Hairy Jim was one of these guys you see in just about every city in the world. Nobody knew what he did for a living or how he managed to survive, all on his own. He had no home and spent most of his time hanging around the docks or begging for change in front of the big department stores downtown. Hairy Jim claimed he could tell your fortune, and the way he did this was by printing symbols on tiny pieces of paper and then laying the bits of paper out in a certain order. I never asked him to tell my fortune—I knew pretty well how my life was going to go—but a few of the guys, Frankie Missalo included, said that Jim had told them stuff about themselves he had no way of knowing. That gave me all the reason I needed to avoid him. Maybe the present wasn't too hot, but it was where I was, and I was satisfied to stay there. I didn't need to borrow trouble by peering into the future and trying to figure out what was going to happen past the next day or so. No sir, you could have that hocus pocus; I didn't want any part of it.

"Yeah, Jack, it's been raining all day. That don't mean I got to like it. And it don't mean he can use the cafe like it was the YMCA or something."

I tried not to laugh, but I couldn't help it. "Tell me the truth, Chris. You're just pissed off because of the crummy weather. Is that it? Or is, ah, Sergeant Picco making you work for it?"

"I never saw so much goddamn rain." Chris shook his head, slung the towel over his shoulder, and walked back down to the end of the bar. I heard him asking the thin man if he wanted anything else, but I wasn't paying much attention. The weather was pissing me off, too. When I bought the Heartache, I'd been assured by the real estate agent that the building was sound in every way. But as soon as the heavy September rains began, the whole place started leaking like a basket. At first, we tried to stem the damage by placing buckets under all the drips, but this was only a temporary measure. Pretty soon, little leaks turned into bigger ones, and before we knew it, we had serious water damage. I could only imagine what all the moisture was doing to the electrical system. Yeah, sometimes it's better not to think about things.

I was doing a pretty good job of not thinking about Sam Halim. In the six weeks since I'd come back from Egypt, I'd dreamed about him every night and hardly thought about him at all, except every five minutes. I kept going back to the way he had looked at his wife's funeral: his face sad and drawn, his lean body bent low under the weight of his grief. Sam was tough; he wasn't the kind of guy who cried over every little thing. You could probably set Sam on fire and he wouldn't even flinch. But this—the murder of his wife—had to strike at the very core of the man. If ever Sam Halim needed a friend, he needed one now; if he had asked me, I would have stayed in Egypt, but Sam never asked me. He didn't seem to care one way or the other, and I understood that. I wasn't expecting any heartfelt declaration of love from the man, not at a time like that, but he hadn't even come to the airport to see me off. It was like he was embarrassed by me, and couldn't wait to get me out of the country so he could forget all about me, forget what had occurred between us, whatever that was.

Yeah, I was doing a real good job of not thinking about Sam. I thought about him when I inhaled; I thought about him when I exhaled. I would wake up in the night and roll over, reaching out for him, wanting to touch him, confused when all I found on the other side of the bed was empty air. And all those nice, shiny bottles lined up on the bar, they were doing a real good job of not calling to me. I had already started bargaining with myself, the kind of bargaining you do when you know you're one step away from falling right back into that abyss. I just wanted something to dull the pain.

I had just come out of my office with a handful of last month's receipts when Chris came around the end of the bar again, even more agitated than he had been earlier. "Now there's two of them."

"Chris, I don't have time for this. Leave the man alone. It's not like the Heartache is full of customers tonight." A headache was starting, one of those huge, throbbing ones that sit behind your eyes, banging away like the big drum in a Salvation Army band.

"No, Jack, another guy just came in. And you're not going to believe this." Chris was about as excited as I'd ever seen him, which is saying something. Like most of New Orleans, he's as calm and easygoing as they come. "Just take a look at who's sitting with our friend over there."

"Chris, I'm serious. I got a lot of work to do. Hey, look, if you don't like working here—"

"Jack." He caught hold of my arm and pulled me around so I was looking directly at the two men who were now seated at the end of the bar. At first, all I could see was the thin man, sitting so his body blocked my view of the other guy. But then he bent over to pick up something from the floor, and all the sudden I was questioning my sanity. The other man—the man who had just come in—was none other than Jonah Octavian.

I was around the bar in a literal eye blink and had Octavian's lapels crushed in my hands. "What the hell is this, some kind of a joke? You know as well as I do what happened in Egypt. How'd you end up here, Octavian? You got nine lives like a goddamn cat?"

"Please." He freed his lapels from my grip. "I have no idea who you are or what you're talking about. If I had known what sort of establishment this was—"

"Who are you?" I started for the phone, picked up the receiver. "You got five seconds to gimme an answer I can understand, or I'm gonna call the cops."

Octavian got up; his companion followed suit. "I don't know what is the matter with you, sir, but I think it best I be on my way." He tossed some coins down on the bar and started for the door.

"Oh no, you don't." I got there first and barred his way. "Not until you tell me who you are and how you ended up here."

"Get out of my way." He reached for the door, and I brought my fist down on his arm.

"You're not going anywhere," I said. Chris was standing behind the bar, by the phone. "Chris, get your boyfriend on the horn. Tell him to get over here and bring a couple of constables."

"Jack, maybe—"

"Call the cops, goddammit!" I took my eyes off Octavian for no more than a second or two, but it was enough. He shoved my arm away, ducked around me and out the door, his friend hard on his heels. I took out after them, but they'd obviously mapped out their escape route in advance, since they were nowhere to be seen. I turned left from the Heartache's front door and cut through a laneway that joined Water with Duckworth, just in time to see a flapping raincoat as its owner passed a taxi stand. "Octavian!" I pounded down the pavement, leaping over a cardboard box full of garbage and sloshing my way through a puddle big enough to swallow a tank, but it was no use. I was tired and Octavian was gone. "Fuck." I wanted to yell it at the top of my lungs, but I didn't have the energy. I turned slowly and splashed my way back home in the pouring rain.

THE HEARTACHE Cafe was quiet, so quiet I could hear the raindrops pounding on the roof. It felt like I'd been lying here for centuries with a cold cloth over my eyes, trying to concentrate on breathing and marking time until the pills I'd taken made a dent in my headache. Chris had already locked up and gone home, and even the two bums who sat outside the front door every night had taken themselves away. What I'd seen didn't make any sense to me. Jonah Octavian was dead. I'd seen Andros

Scala kill him in Egypt, kill him as if he were no more than a bug to be crushed underfoot, discarded and forgotten about. I don't know much about ghosts or the spirit world, but I know dead men don't drink whiskey. Dead men don't drink whiskey, and they don't sit at the end of my bar. If you grab a dead man, he slips right through your fingers—but Octavian was as real as anybody. It made no sense.

So if it wasn't Octavian, who was it? The list of likely candidates was pretty short. Octavian was dead, Mukbar was dead, Tareenah Halim was dead, and even Pasha Nubar wasn't alive to tell any tales. The only explanation was a double, but even that sounded like a plot device from some hokey pulp novel.

Far out on Chain Rock, I could hear the slow rumble of the foghorn, and I imagined the dark, sleek shapes of German submarines moving silently underneath the Narrows. I knew the kind of things Sam Halim was up against, back in Egypt, but was there anything at stake for me? Sam had all but said it was over between us, so why was I holding on to something that now existed only in memory? If I held on because I still loved him—because I would always love him—then it made sense. But if I was holding on because I was hoping he'd come back to me, hoping he still loved me? That was just screwy. I lay for hours, trying to make it come out right. Dawn was lightening the windows before I finally closed my eyes. I dreamed I was in Egypt.

CHAPTER TEN

THINGS WERE quiet around the Heartache for a while, and as September melted into October, I forgot all about Jonah Octavian. Maybe I'd been tired that night, and maybe I'd been seeing things. Either way, I wasn't going to dwell on it. I was plenty busy with my cafe, and lately we'd had an influx of servicemen, all eager for a decent sandwich and a real cup of American coffee. The war, previously a distant murmur in Europe, had come to Newfoundland, and there were rumors that U-boats patrolled the waters around the island. Early in September, two ore carriers, moving precious nickel from the mines at Bell Island, had been struck and sunk by a submarine that then escaped into the open sea. A full blackout was in effect in St. John's, and between sunset and sunrise, anything that could conceivably cast light was outfitted with shutters. The sky was full of eyes, and in the evenings, the low drone of warplanes could be heard, moving northward to Conception Bay and across the dark expanse of the cold night ocean. It was only a matter of time before the Germans, emboldened by the success of their recent attacks, launched a full-scale offensive.

I was behind the bar one afternoon near the end of October, polishing glasses and tidying the place up a bit. Chris had a doctor's appointment uptown, so I'd given him the afternoon off, with the provision he'd be back in time for the evening rush. There wasn't much of anything going on, and I liked having the place to myself. It gave me time to think. Sometimes, I'd pour myself a cup of coffee and sit at a table near the window with a newspaper. I enjoyed watching the ever-changing flow of traffic: people walking by, mothers with their children, servicemen in their uniforms.

Sergeant Picco's jurisdiction took in the section of Water Street where my cafe stood, and he often came in for a cup of coffee on his break and to see Chris. As far as I knew, the two of them were still an item; they were just discreet about it. Most of their rendezvous took place at Chris's place and sometimes at the cafe, but Picco had a car and sometimes they'd save up their gasoline rations and go for drives in the country. Once I'd come downstairs late and found them saying good night just inside the cafe's front door, kissing passionately and oblivious to everything but each other. I didn't know if Chris was sleeping with him, and I wasn't about to ask, but it sure looked that way. I was glad for Chris, but seeing them together made me positively heartsick. This particular afternoon was cold and cloudy with a chilly wind out of the northeast and the promise of a heavy rain later in the evening. I was half listening to the radio while I worked, and I must have drifted off into some kind of hypnotic state. I didn't hear the door open, and Sergeant Rick Callan had already spoken to me twice before I even noticed he was in the room.

"I said, you look like a man who really enjoys his work." Callan's Mississippi twang broke into my thoughts, and I started like a man waking from a dream. I had last seen Callan during Jonah Octavian's stint at the construction site at Fort Pepperell, and I guess some part of me expected to see him again.

"Sorry, Sergeant, I didn't hear you come in. What can I get for you?"

He took his hat off and tossed it on the bar before hoisting himself onto a stool. "How about a cup of genuine down-home coffee? You know, the good stuff?"

I kept a small stash of Community coffee hidden behind some boxes in the pantry—Chris brought me a few pounds whenever he got home to New Orleans—and I brewed a pot, poured him a cup, and poured one for myself. "Here you go. On the house."

He drank it gratefully. "You know, it's next to impossible to get a decent cup of coffee anywhere in this town. Mostly, all they drink is tea." He made a face, caught my eye, and grinned, and I realized, not for the first time, that he was a very attractive man: strong and solid, with a becoming touch of gray at his temples, and soft, long-lashed brown eyes. Was Sergeant Callan married? Had he ever been married? Perhaps he had a girl here, some pretty, local woman who'd appreciate the company of a lonely American. "Hot tea. I ask 'em for sweet tea, and they don't know what the hell I'm talking about."

I laughed. "I thought Private Thomas"—the young army clerk who spent his days in Callan's office—"made your coffee."

His gaze skidded away from mine, and it occurred to me I'd said something I shouldn't have. Callan was wiping down the bar with his hat, moving it back and forth under his hand in a distracted fashion that spoke of great inner turmoil.

"I'm sorry." I refilled his cup. "It's none of my business."

He sipped his coffee in silence for a few moments, then shifted on the stool and gazed out the window. "You ever have a really good friend, Jack?"

Sam's face swam before my inner vision. "Sure have."

"I mean the kind of friend that, man, you'd lay down your life for. The kind of guy who really understands you, without having to even say a word."

"Yeah." He was coming to something, and I wanted to let him know it was okay by me. "You know, bartenders are kind of like doctors."

His head jerked up. "Huh?"

"I'm not allowed to repeat anything you say to me." I crossed my heart and held up two fingers in a Boy Scout salute. "Honest Injun."

Callan laughed. "You sure are a crazy one, Jack. Yes, sir, that's for sure." He sighed. "Private Thomas requested priority reassignment."

Something about the way he said it made my stomach lurch. "He did, huh? What happened?"

He searched my face. "I did something I shouldn't have done." Callan pressed the heels of his hands into his eyes. "He was kind enough not to mention it to the brass. I suppose I should be grateful. He could have… it would have been easy for him to make a lot of trouble for me."

I laid my hand on the bar, close enough to touch him. "I'm listening."

"I kissed him."

A flush of heat bloomed in the center of my chest. I forced my features to stillness. "I see."

"That don't shock you? You mean to tell me the idea of one man kissing another man don't bother you one bit, Jack?"

I didn't answer. I wasn't about to incriminate myself. Sergeant Callan seemed okay, but I didn't know him and for all I knew, he'd only made up the kissing story. People do strange things.

"Uh-huh." Callan nodded. "I see. Taking the Fifth, huh? Well, all right." He pushed the hat away from him. "I came in this morning, and he'd packed up all his stuff. Didn't even leave me a note. Just didn't bother to show up. Didn't bother to tell me, either. Just…." He made a swishing motion with his hand, like shooing flies. "Gone."

"I'm sorry." I turned to put on a fresh pot. "Had you known him long?"

Callan laughed, but there was no humor in it. "Long enough. Yeah, I'd known him just long enough to—" He shook his head. "Goddammit."

"I'm sorry." Christ, I was repeating myself.

"Just forget I said anything." He looked like he hadn't slept in days. "Shoulda known better. Anyway, that's not what I came here for. Listen, Jack, there's something you ought to know, and I think maybe you can really help out the Allied cause if you put your mind to it. A man like you, in the position you're in, could be very useful."

Not this again. I'd already had this, in Cairo, from MacBride's buddies. "I don't think I'm what you're looking for."

"You ain't heard what I got to say." He reached across the bar and clasped my wrist, held on. His big hand was warm, a welcome touch against my lonely flesh, and I wondered: what would it be like? Sam and I were definitely through—he'd made that abundantly clear—and maybe it was time to move on. Maybe the best thing to do was find someone else, a friend, someone to fill my off-hours and perhaps warm my bed, if I wanted to take it that far. Rick Callan was free, he was available, he was damn good-looking, and he was as lonely as I was. It would be nice to have someone. It would be nice to have that big, solid body in my bed.

I turned my hand and held on, amused by the sudden flush of surprise in his face. "I'm listening, Rick."

His thumb stroked the palm of my hand, and his dark eyes burned into me. "Jack… you sure?" His voice, suddenly husky, warmed me. Christ, he was sexy.

I gave him a look. "What time do you knock off?"

"Mmph. Six o'clock. I'll come pick you up. Say, seven-thirty?"

"I'd like that."

He grinned. "All right." He straightened, suddenly official again. "Now listen here, boy, what I got to tell you isn't for foreign ears, you mind me?"

"Okay." I was intrigued.

"We've recently received word the Germans had a spy aboard one of their tin fish. They put him ashore at Quebec."

I shrugged. "That sounds like it's Quebec's problem." I wished the French well. So far, they'd had a helluva time this war, or were the Quebecois Canadian? I wasn't really sure. Come to think of it, neither were they.

"No, it's our problem, because the word is there's more of them. All of 'em moving in from Quebec's north shore, down through Labrador, till they get to St. John's."

The back of my neck prickled. Was this what MacBride's team had been trying to tell me, back in Cairo? *Lieutenant, you can be eminently useful to your country and to this cause. Newfoundland is of primary strategic importance to the Allies, as I'm sure you know.* "And when they get here?"

"There's something going on. We dunno what, but there's something. Few of our boys have had their ears to the ground since the start of this whole shindig. Something's gonna happen between now and Christmas."

"So what do you want from me?"

"You get to hear a lot of stuff. Guy like you, standing behind the bar all day long. Yeah, I bet you hear a lot of talk."

"You want me to eavesdrop?" This was too good: it was Kevin MacBride all over again.

"You think it's funny, boy? Just how long you been away from the army, anyhow?" His tone snapped me back.

"Sorry."

Callan huffed out a breath. "Look, Jack. There's innocent people gonna die in this town, maybe a lot of them. Now, you think that's some kind of a joke, we don't got nothing more to say to each other."

"I'm sorry. I'm not laughing at—Jesus, Rick. It sounds serious." I refilled our cups.

"It is serious." He raised the cup to his lips and sipped. "Goddammit, it's as serious as a heart attack."

I reached out and laid my hand over his. "I'll do what I can. If I hear anything unusual, I'll let you know."

He relaxed. "Honest?"

I crossed my heart again. "Honest Injun."

THINGS WERE quiet for about half an hour after Callan left, and then the supper crowd began to arrive. Chris came back from his doctor's appointment and got busy helping me in the kitchen. With Dave Chan gone to war, we'd hired a succession of temporary cooks, but none of them worked out. One guy left halfway through his shift with no explanation, and I caught another one skimming from the till. You'd think in a town the size of St. John's, there'd be plenty of guys looking to make a decent dollar, but it seemed most of them were content to hang around in pool halls or on street corners, picking their teeth and testing their wit on the local yokels. Chris had taken over the cooking until we could find somebody but, as good as he was, his culinary efforts tended to be a bit spicy for the locals. Cajun food didn't exactly go over gangbusters, but I had to give him credit for trying. Still, I worried we were losing trade to the plethora of fish-and-chip shops that dotted the local landscape like pimples on a fat man's ass.

I was so busy from five until about six thirty, I hardly lifted my head, and the whole of my view consisted of bottles and glasses. I handed off the latest round of drinks to Anita, one of my waitresses, and turned to dump some ice cubes down the sink. At first all I saw was a white shirt, a dark jacket, and a pair of slender hands, faintly freckled, resting on the bar. "What can I get you, mister?"

"How about a beer, Jack?"

That voice… there was something—Texan? "Jesus. Tex?"

He grinned, the same old grin I'd come to know in Cairo. "How are you, Jack?"

"Tex! My God!" I came out from behind the bar and grabbed him, hauled him into my arms and hugged him until I felt his ribs creak. "It's good to see you. What the hell are you doing on this side of the pond?"

He shrugged. "Well, I don't rightly know an easy way to say this: I got canned. I knocked around Cairo for a while, but there was nothing, so I figured I'd come over here and look you up." He was momentarily shamefaced. "I was wondering if maybe you might have some part-time work I could do, enough to tide me over until I can find something more permanent."

"Tex, can you cook?" I was already untying my apron.

He nodded. "Sure."

"Here." I handed him the scrap of cloth. "Tie one on. The kitchen's that way. We serve all the usual stuff. Chris—" I pointed him out at the other end of the bar, "and I will take care of the drinks. Think you can handle it?"

He double-tied the apron around his slender waist and grinned. "You won't regret this, Jack." He disappeared into the kitchen, and I'm not sure, but I think he was whistling "Dixie."

"Who's the redhead?" Chris laid a tray of empty glasses on the bar.

I told him. "He's a nice kid from Texas. Go easy on him, huh?"

"Texas?" Chris made a rude noise. "Yeah, I'll go easy on him." He nodded, acknowledging a summons from the far corner of the cafe. "You sure do like to collect strays, Jack."

Tex was as good as his word, turning out sandwiches and hamburgers, french fries, and tuna salad, until the supper rush was over. I found him in the kitchen, stacking plates for the dishwasher. "Hey, Tex, you got a roof?"

"Nothing yet. I'm staying at the Y."

"There's a spare room at the back of the cafe. It's nothing special, but the bed's comfortable and there's a radio. It's yours if you want it."

He stared at me for a moment like he didn't quite believe me. "Well, jeez, Jack… thanks."

"Least I can do." I grinned. "You never know, I might hit you up for another massage."

Around seven, the crowd began to slack off, and I was able to go upstairs to my quarters and get showered and changed. I wasn't sure what to expect—Rick Callan hadn't said where we'd be going or what we'd be doing—but the October evenings were cold, so I wore dark flannel trousers and a sweater, and layered my shearling jacket over it.

At quarter after seven, I went downstairs and saw Rick Callan sitting at a corner table sipping a cup of coffee. He raised a hand when he saw me, stood up, and summoned me over. We shook hands as if this were just an ordinary business meeting instead of what it actually was. For a moment, holding Rick Callan's warm, strong hand, I wondered if I wasn't being too hasty. Sam hadn't actually said it was over between us—I'd only assumed it—and maybe it was too soon to start dating again.

"Good to see you, Jack." Callan was wearing dark trousers and a dark, V-neck sweater over a white shirt. His shoes were buffed to a gleaming shine, and he was clean-shaven. I had the feeling Sergeant

Callan was just as nervous as I was about this whole date business. "I was starting to think you'd stood me up."

I laughed. "Hey, if you want to back out, don't let me stop you."

"Oh, you ain't getting rid of me that easily." Callan looked me up and down briefly. "It's a real nice night out. I figured maybe we could take a drive in the country, maybe head toward Topsail way. Not too cold, if you're dressed for it."

That sounded good to me, so I followed Callan outside. He'd parked his car in front of the Heartache Cafe, a nice, late model Buick. I made to open the door but Callan slipped in ahead of me and tripped the latch. "Never too late to get off to a good start."

I made some feeble joke about how Callan was a romantic, but I was starting to get a little bit nervous. I wasn't afraid of Callan—he seemed like a steady enough guy—but I wondered exactly what he expected out of tonight's date.

We chatted amiably as he turned the car north, heading out of the city and into the dark, wooded valleys of Conception Bay. I didn't do a lot of driving outside the city, and it was weird to see the road in front of us illuminated by the two tiny slits of light emanating from Callan's blacked out headlights. The city and its environs had been under blackout order almost since the war started; it was thought that even the smallest glimmer of light from any of the coastal communities would draw unwanted attention to the numerous Allied warships patrolling the waters around the island. There weren't a lot of other cars on the road, but every one had the same kind of blackout shields over the head lamps. Nobody was taking any chances.

Topsail was only a few miles from the city, and Callan was a good driver, as well as being good company. He kept me entertained and laughing with ridiculous tales of his boyhood spent in rural Mississippi. I gathered his parents' marriage had been an unhappy one. Callan was an only child, and when the union was finally dissolved in divorce, he went to live with his mother. His father became a shadowy figure, seen once or twice a year at Christmas and on Callan's birthday. "He died when I was twenty-one." Callan's big hands gripped the steering wheel tightly, and I sensed that he was struggling with some dark emotion. "Momma didn't hold with how I felt about Daddy." The sergeant shook his head. "Hoo boy! Didn't she carry on when I told her I was going to Daddy's funeral. You'd a thought I stuck a knife in her back."

I told him a little bit about my family, how my father had been killed one day at work, struck down by a runaway locomotive at the Philly rail yard where he'd been employed since he was seventeen years old. "I guess I had to be the man of the family after that. My mother didn't have much, but she did the best she could, and she raised me right."

Callan took a right turn off the main road and for maybe a minute, we bumped and bounced over a narrow, rutted gravel road. The full moon had risen, and I could see a narrow band of gleaming silver on the bay. "There's a real nice beach down here. Doesn't have much sand on it, but there's a trail that goes up over the hill and a place where we can sit down and look out over the water. That okay by you, Jack?"

"Sure. Yeah, I'd like to take a walk."

Callan pulled the car up next to a narrow strip of trees and cut the motor. He rolled the window down and for a moment, we sat in silence, listening to the faraway lap of waves against the shore. "You know, it don't seem to matter how angry or pissed off my life makes me. All I gotta do is come out here and sit for a while and somehow it all just"—Callan waved a hand—"washes away."

He was quiet, lost in some private reverie, and I wondered what he was thinking about, what he was remembering. Maybe he'd taken Private Thomas out here, hoping to make some sort of a connection and never thinking he would be rebuffed. I wondered about that: Callan seemed to be reasonably astute about things. Had he really misread Thomas's intentions? Or had Thomas lost his nerve?

"Come on." Callan opened the car door and got out. "Let's head up the trail a ways, see what we can find."

We walked for perhaps ten minutes, sometimes in companionable silence and sometimes chatting quietly about nothing much. Callan was interesting and educated and funny; there seemed to be no end to the hilarious stories he remembered or the ones he could make up on the spot. "You know, Jack, there ain't a lot of people I can talk to round these parts. My job being what it is, I gotta be careful."

"Yeah, I know what you mean." I'd seen the posters: BUTTON YOUR LIP and SOMEONE TALKED in bold type, with illustrations of screaming, dying men—lurid reminders of what loose talk could cost the Allies. "Everybody's extra careful these days. It's hard to know who you can trust."

"That's for sure. And me, being the kind of man I am, well."

We had been following a narrow path for some distance through the forest. On our right the dark bulk of the mountain hoisted itself head and shoulders over the smooth back of the waiting sea, and I could hear the waves still murmuring in the distance. "But you don't…. You don't talk about that, do you?"

Callan was walking slightly ahead of me, and he stopped, turned back to look at me. "No, Jack, I don't talk about that." There was strong emphasis on the word "that," and I sensed I'd hit a nerve. "How long do you think I'd last in this man's army if everybody knew I was a—"

He didn't say the word, but I knew what he meant. Yeah, I'd heard that word a lot. I hated that word.

"Hey, look." I caught up with him and took hold of his arm just above the elbow, turning him to face me. His face in the moonlight had a beauty and nobility that belonged solely to him, and his big, dark eyes were sad. I cupped his cheek in my hand; his skin was warm, and I sensed the subtle rise and fall of his breath as he struggled to calm himself. "They kicked me out on a blue ticket. You might as well know. That's why I'm here instead of on the front lines with the rest of the boys." Some of the bitterness I felt inevitably spilled over into my voice and it made me sound weak and self-pitying, and I hated that. "You think every goddamn American, every Brit, every Australian—" I thought about Kevin MacBride for some reason, and his friend Andros Scala. "I spend the war serving beer and sandwiches to tourists or topping up coffee cups."

"Blue ticket?" Callan shook his head. "I'd like to get my hands on the sons of bitches who think giving a man a blue ticket is any way to win this war." He leaned in and kissed me, a gentle touch of his lips against mine, but it went through me like a bolt of lightning. I gathered him into my arms as I deepened the kiss, probing his mouth with my tongue, tasting him. It felt so good to hold him in my arms, to feel the heat of his body burning through my clothes.

"Well, boy!" He grinned at me. "Why, you're all about diving right in, ain't you?"

"Sorry." I suddenly felt foolish, like a teenage boy on his first date. "I hope you don't think…."

"What I think is we have reached our destination." He indicated a bench, set in a hollow depression behind a grove of trees. "Come on, sit down here with me." He patted the wooden seat next to him, and I sat down. From this vantage point, the entire expanse of Conception Bay spread out before us, glistening darkly in the moonlight. "Yeah, makes you wonder how many goddamn tin fish are out there right now, waiting to blow this whole island to kingdom come." Callan fished a hip flask out of his pocket, handed it to me. "Drink?"

"No, thanks, I…."

He took a pull. "Don't drink?"

"Gave it up for Lent."

Callan laughed. "You're a funny one, Jack. How'd you come to be running a cafe here, anyway? I mean, why here?"

I shrugged. "Why not here?" I told him about Frankie Missalo, about how I'd left Philly to follow him up here after Judy died. I left out the part about the botched back-alley abortion and about standing on the bridge over the Delaware that freezing cold morning. "Seemed as good a place as any."

"You afraid they were gonna charge you with that girl's murder?"

Something deep inside my gut clenched. "I didn't kill her." I remember how Tex's face had looked when I said it. Was Tex her brother? Had my intuition been right about that? It seemed too close to be a coincidence, when he'd told me about her, back in Cairo. Did he know about me and Judy? Did anybody?

"Ain't nobody saying you did." He studied me for a long moment, and then turned to look at the expanse of shining water in front of us. "Where I come from—little place called Vardaman, in Mississippi—we ain't close to the sea. Well, not this close, at any rate. I used to dream about seeing the ocean up close like this, so close you can taste the salt on your tongue."

I caught the point of his chin and turned his face to me and kissed him. I didn't want to talk. I just wanted this.

Callan groaned as I deepened the kiss, and his arms went around me, pulling me tight against him. The zipper on his jacket was so cold it burned my fingers; I yanked the tab down and slipped my hand inside, under his clothes, my palm flat against his warm skin. His chest was muscular and lightly furred, his nipples exquisitely sensitive to touch.

"You gonna kill me." Callan dragged my face up and kissed me savagely, guiding my hand to the clothed bulge at his groin. I cupped my hand around his hard cock and rubbed, starting slow and easy, pacing him and myself while we kissed, our mingled breath steaming white into the cold night air. Callan's hand made short work of my zipper, slipped into my pants and swiftly negotiated the gap in the front of my shorts, fingers closing around my cock. He bent over me and sucked me into his mouth and the world went away. I was dimly aware of the hard bench digging into the back of my head, of the cloak of stars unfurled above me and the narrow trunks of the trees that obligingly screened us, but my entire universe had shrunk down to a set of sharply defined sensory impressions. He sucked me like an old pro, and within maybe ten strokes, I was coming, but feebly, and what should have been a tidal wave of glorious sensation was instead a mere shudder. An awful sense of guilt dropped over me like a filthy curtain.

"Stop." I pushed him away from me. "Stop. We have to stop." *Jack, let us bathe together now, and then we will love each other slowly....*

He sat up, wiping his mouth on his handkerchief. "What's wrong?"

I was saved from uncomfortable explanations by the sound of voices coming up the path. "I... somebody's coming."

The whirling red beam of a police car stabbed the darkness, and I could hear men shouting. I tucked myself inside my clothes while Rick Callan did the same, and then we started back down the path together, walking side by side but not speaking.

Alphonsus Picco met us halfway up the hill, carrying a flashlight. He swept the beam over our faces. "Mr. Stoyles, I think you had best come with me." It was a measure of Picco's agitation that he didn't ask what I'd been doing up in the woods with Callan in the dark.

"Sergeant Picco. Is something wrong?" One of Picco's constables was asking Callan for identification, which the sergeant provided. The constable looked it over quickly and seemed satisfied; he motioned Callan to go on.

Picco's pale eyes flickered over my face, and he seemed to be barely holding back an expression of disgust. "Your... friend is free to go, but I insist you accompany me back to the city."

Callan touched my arm. "Everything okay, Jack?" There was no recrimination in his gaze. Of course, he assumed we'd merely gotten interrupted by the Constabulary's untimely arrival. It wasn't like he could see inside my head.

"It's fine." I nodded to him. "I'll call you in the morning." I followed Picco back down the hill to the waiting police car. No less than three additional cars had been called out, but I didn't think all this was for me necessarily. Some of Picco's men were searching the beach while others had been deployed along the narrow strip of trees at the base of the hill. "You boys lose your way?"

Picco held the passenger door open for me. "Please, sit in the front. You are not under arrest."

The car's interior was as spotlessly clean as Picco himself, and just as bare of ornament. He got in and started the engine, but didn't put the car in gear. "Mr. Stoyles... Jack." And just like that, all the starch went out of him. He turned to me, as anguished as I've ever seen him. "There was an accident tonight in your cafe."

"What do you mean, an accident?" My gut twisted itself into a knot. "Somebody break one of my windows again?"

Picco gazed out the windscreen, his hands white-knuckled on the steering wheel. "No. I am afraid it is much more serious this time—nngh." This last sound was a strangled whimper, the noise a grown man makes when he's trying his damnedest not to cry. Hearing Picco make it alarmed me like nothing else could. "Please. You must come with me at once. There's no time to waste." He put the car into gear with hands that shook. "There's no more time at all."

CHAPTER ELEVEN

THE HEARTACHE was swarming with uniformed policemen when I got there, most of them grouped around a big, sticky pool of blood just inside the cafe's front door. I saw Tex standing off to the side, talking to a young constable, who noted everything Tex was saying; there was blood on the front of the Texan's shirt, and his amiable, freckled face was white to the lips.

"What the hell's going on here?" I grabbed Picco's arm as we came in through the door. "It looks like—"

"Jack!" Tex saw me and came rushing over. "Did he tell you?"

"No." We'd spent the journey back from Topsail in comparative silence, listening to the swish of the car's tires on the road. "What's with the blood? Somebody get stabbed in here tonight?"

As soon as I said the word "stabbed," everybody got real quiet.

The constable who'd been talking to Tex flipped his notebook shut and slipped out the door. The jingling of the bell sounded like a klaxon. "Chris DuBois was injured."

Picco was holding himself together, but barely; I admired his restraint. If someone had stabbed the guy I was in love with—

Yeah. Better skip it. "Chris? What happened to him?" I fumbled for a chair and sat down, and Anita brought us some coffee while Tex and Picco filled me in.

Tex had been in the kitchen, fixing an order; Chris had been at his usual post behind the bar. The Heartache's bar wasn't visible from the kitchen—in order to see Chris, Tex would have had to come out of the kitchen and past my office—so Tex had no idea what was going on until he heard Chris yelling for him. He'd run out of the kitchen to see Chris slumped on the floor, right where the puddle of blood was, bleeding from numerous stab wounds. Chris wasn't in any shape to talk, but from what Tex could make out, three guys in dark pants and dark jackets had come into the cafe asking where I was. When Chris told them I was out, they'd rushed at him and stabbed him. He'd been taken to St. Clare's hospital in an ambulance not half an hour ago.

THE CHARGE nurse was tall and thin, her lips pressed together in a disapproving frown. I explained to her I was Chris's employer, and I lied and said Picco was his brother-in-law. She agreed to let us in, "But for five minutes only. Mr. DuBois is badly hurt. The doctor wants him to rest."

They had Chris in a room by himself, and as soon as I got closer, I knew why. Whoever had stabbed him had wanted to make a thorough job of it. He had two black eyes, and there were deep cuts in his face, across his cheeks and the bridge of his nose, and down his arms. His palms were cut, probably as he was defending himself, and most of his torso was a mass of bandages. I counted four drains running out of various wounds on his body. "Aw, Chris." I laid my hand gently on his forehead. "I'm sorry." I felt like crying. If I'd stayed at the Heartache instead of gallivanting around with Callan, none of this would have happened.

"Not your fault, Jack." His voice was weak and strained; obviously, he'd sustained some kind of internal injuries, probably from the stab wounds. "M'gonna be okay. Just you wait. Be back at… Heartache. No time."

"Never mind that. Just… concentrate on getting better. Okay? You just… get better." There was so much I wanted to say to him, but I didn't dare, things like *you're one of the best friends I've ever had* and *I'd go to the wall for you, Chris* and *tell me who did this to you so I can run over there and finish the bastards off.* I didn't say any of it. I handed him over to Picco and went out into the corridor.

Rick Callan was waiting for me, standing by the nurses' station with his hands in his pockets. When he saw me, he pushed away from the wall and came over. "I heard what happened at your place tonight. Anything I can do?"

I shook my head. "Naw. I just…. I just want to get out of here."

His dark eyes assessed me with their usual keenness. "Don't like hospitals, huh?"

"Don't like hospitals."

"Come on." We went downstairs and out the front door; Callan's car was parked in the smaller lot behind the hospital. "Is he going to be okay?"

"Yeah, I guess." I rubbed my eyes. "What time is it?"

"Little after eleven." Callan cast a glance at me. "You sure you're okay, Jack? You don't look okay—now, that's just my impression. Having one of your guys get all cut up like that's a hard thing for a man to take, especially if he's a friend." He pulled onto Ricketts Road, heading for Cashin Avenue and downtown.

"I don't know who would do this. I don't know why." I searched my memory for a list of likely candidates but kept coming back to the man with Jonah Octavian's face I'd seen in the Heartache. Maybe Octavian wasn't really dead, and what I'd seen in Cairo had been a carefully constructed ruse meant to throw me off the scent. No…. I had seen Andros Scala kill him, and I didn't think Scala was the type to make a mistake.

Callan sighed. "Jack, there's a lot I can't tell you—a lot I don't have clearance to tell you—but I can tell you this…." We stopped for a red signal and Callan turned to me, his features lit by the eerie glow from the car's dashboard lights; it almost looked like he was on fire. "There are people in this town who are here for no good reason… enemies, plotters, and saboteurs. They'd target you simply because you're an American." The signal changed, and he let out the clutch, easing the big Packard sedan forward. "Now, don't smirk. You mind me when I tell you something, son."

I smiled. It had been a long time since someone had called me that. "I'm listening."

"There is a lot of stuff going on in this town you don't know nothing about." The brakes squeaked as the big car slowly navigated the steep incline of Patrick Street. "You got guys coming off of ships in the harbor, sneaking ashore to do God knows what. Maybe it was you they were looking for—you think about that?"

"Yeah." Maybe I'd been followed to Cairo by men who knew what Sam really did for a living, and who were part of the gang that had kidnapped him in the first place—kidnapped him and killed Tareenah Halim. It was just possible they'd come here to find me and finish me off. "Thank you for… this." I was suddenly and absurdly grateful for his steady, solid presence. "You've been real swell to me tonight." Looking at him in the dim light of the car's interior, I was forcibly reminded, again, of how handsome he was and how much I liked him—and reminded, too, I didn't want to be alone tonight. "Rick?"

"Hm?" He turned left onto Water Street, heading toward the Heartache.

"What time are you on duty tomorrow morning?"

"I am off tomorrow morning." He grinned at me. "Why?"

"Would you...." Christ, this shouldn't have been so awkward. The man had blown me on a park bench, for chrissakes. It wasn't like we were strangers.

"Don't feel like being alone?" His gaze was knowing. He saw right through me, and I didn't know what to say. "Look, Jack. I ain't asking you for nothing. I don't expect nothing." He shrugged his big shoulders. "No strings, son. Just in case you ain't heard, there's a war on. Ain't none of us can make long-term plans."

"Do you want to… uh, come over to my place?" I was close to tears, and the damnedest thing was, I didn't know why. I wanted comfort. I didn't want to be alone, and there was something about Callan that I wanted to be near. He was safe.

"Yeah." He reached across and took my hand. "You bet."

Callan parked the car in the alley behind the Heartache, and we went up to my quarters above the cafe. Tex, I knew, was bunking at the Y tonight, so we had the place to ourselves. I shot a glance at the spot where Chris had been stabbed: someone—probably Tex—had cleaned up the blood. I reminded myself to give the kid a raise. Callan stopped just inside the door to my rooms and looked around. "You got a nice place here, Jack. You've made a real home for yourself."

I went to him and slid his coat off his shoulders. He sighed and leaned back against me. *Stop thinking about Sam. Sam is over. This is now.* "I want you to feel welcome here." I pressed my mouth against the nape of his neck, wrapped my arms around his waist.

"I do." He turned in my embrace so we were facing each other. "I do feel welcome, Jack." We were of a height, and he rested his hands on my shoulders. "As long as you're comfortable, I'm comfortable."

I put out all the lights except a little *oud* burner on the mantelpiece, a souvenir of my time in Cairo. I'd bought it the morning of Tareenah's funeral, from a tiny stall at the edge of the Muski bazaar, intending to give it to Sam as a sort of mourning gift, only I'd never gotten around to it. I undressed Rick Callan by the light of its tiny, flickering flame, drawing my hands down his naked chest and pulling him into my arms. He was warm and beautiful and alive, solid and real, and when we moved to lie down together on my bed, I knew I wanted this, needed it.

"Put your hands on me," he murmured, and I did. I smoothed his naked flesh and kissed him, laying a trail from the hollow of his throat to his navel. He groaned quietly when I leaned in and licked the head of his swollen cock, and his strong hands moved to rest against the nape of my neck. "Oh, sweetheart." He sighed when I drew him into my mouth. "Oh, darling."

His warm skin tasted like salt, and I worked him slowly, taking him up one peak and down another, until he bucked and twisted under me, seeking his release. He was quiet when he came, his big hands fisting the sheets, his body straining in every muscle and tendon, and I held him in my mouth until his release spent itself and he was still. We lay together afterward, and he was so very gentle with me as we loved each other slowly. He wrapped one leg around my waist and pulled me to him, enfolding me in his arms as our kisses grew torrid and the slow pulse began to beat inside me. There was nothing in my mind besides what we were doing, and how he was making me feel, a primitive throb thundering along my veins, filling me up inside. He was a hot mouth and a pair of warm hands and a soothing voice in the dark, and before I knew what was happening, I was sobbing my release into his shoulder as wave after wave crested and crashed over me, dragging me under.

I didn't know too much for a little while after that: I was a sated body and a pair of eyes staring into the dark while my muscles shivered and twitched, and a thousand tiny aftershocks sizzled along my nerves like captive sparks. I heard the scrape of a match as Rick lit a cigarette, and then the brief flare illuminated his face. "Thank you." His voice was hushed, as if in deference to the night, or maybe this—whatever this was—had evoked the same feelings in him as it had in me. "That was… real nice." We shared the one cigarette, smoking it down to the end, and then he crushed it out. "Well. Guess I should get going."

A needle of panic pricked my heart. "Why? You said—I mean, you're not working tomorrow. I don't open the Heartache till noon."

"You want me to stay?"

I cupped my hand under his chin and rubbed his full lower lip with the ball of my thumb. "Yeah."

He lowered his gaze. "What's your guy gonna think? That young red-haired fella?"

"He's not my guy. He just works for me, and anyway, Tex understands this sort of thing."

"Oh." He leaned close to me. "He does, huh?" He kissed my bare shoulder, his lips warm and soft. "You really want me to stay?"

I turned my face and kissed him. It was a real nice kiss, and maybe that decided him. He sighed and lay back down, and I moved to lie in his embrace, my head on his shoulder. "Thanks, Rick."

We were quiet for a long time, listening to the various night sounds of the city, the far-off moan of the foghorn out on Chain Rock. "You don't like hospitals, huh?"

I had been drowsing, drifting close to sleep, but his question brought me immediately awake. "No. No, I hate hospitals."

"Ever been in one?"

I sat up quickly, my face turned from him; it took a few moments before I could speak. "Yeah, I have."

"I thought so." He sighed. "Yeah, I thought so." He sat up and pulled the blankets around us both. "They did it to you, didn't they? When they gave you the blue ticket."

"Yeah." I couldn't help myself; I shuddered. It wasn't something I liked remembering and truth be told, I'd done my level best to banish the memories of that time to the furthest reaches of my mind.

"You poor kid." He wrapped his arm around my shoulders and held on to me. "Those sons of bitches. I hope they burn in hell."

I had never told anybody—not even Judy—about my stint in a military hospital, nor had I mentioned it to Chris or even to Sam. It wasn't part of my life now, and I saw no reason to keep remembering my stay there and the things they had done to me, the battery of tests to which I'd been subjected. *You are being discharged from the army, Lieutenant, on what is known as a blue ticket.* I'd been naive enough to think it meant I could pack up my things, clean out my footlocker, and go. I'd imagined myself disappearing into some small town somewhere and doing some ordinary job. I'd be okay, I reasoned, as long as I kept my head down. Nobody would ever need to know. *In order to release you from the army, we request that you undertake a series of tests—oh, nothing serious. It's merely for administrative purposes.*

"They took me to a VA hospital." I had begun to shiver, so violently it seemed my bones were shattering. The room was suddenly too large, and the dark was coming down on me and there was no escape. Rick murmured I should lie down, and he heaped the blankets over us both and held me close, warming me with his body. "They said it would be just for overnight, but I think I was there a week, maybe longer. I don't really remember. They gave us stuff, and then they asked us all these questions." *Just a little needle prick, it's nothing. Don't look at the needle, Lieutenant. It's just a sugar solution. This is just for experimental purposes. Don't bother yourself about it.* "They asked us all these questions, over and over again, the same questions, and I couldn't remember what I said to them."

I'd like you to look at some photographs, Lieutenant. "Pictures of men… ordinary pictures to start with, men working on cars, men walking with briefcases, men flying planes or reading books and magazines." Four men standing near the hull of a huge ship, three of them together and the fourth leaning against it, possibly smoking a cigarette; a group of men on a beach, cooking something over an open fire; a bunch of guys sitting on the deck of a destroyer, wearing life vests; Lady Cavendish in a Red Cross uniform, talking to a group of soldiers. The pictures started out general, then became more and more specific: two men, both naked, standing on a beach holding strategically placed volleyballs; a group of German soldiers bathing naked in a stream; a muscular man crouching on a suburban lawn, holding a basketball. *What do you feel when you look at these pictures, Lieutenant? Please try and be as specific as you can.* Then more explicit images: a young man seated nude on a narrow wooden pillar; a soldier sprawled on a beach, legs apart; two men lying together under a tree, nude except for a picnic blanket, their arms around each other.

As soon as I began to get aroused, they'd shoot something into me, some kind of drug that made me vomit. *Do you still find these photographs appealing, Lieutenant?* I made up lies, told them they meant nothing to me, asked them if they had any pictures of naked girls for me to look at, that was the sort of thing I liked. Then they injected something into my other arm and the lies got all tangled up so I couldn't remember what I'd said. They showed me a picture of a young, dark-haired man lying on his back, touching himself, and asked me what I felt. *Nothing. I don't feel anything. Honest. I don't feel anything at all.*

Eventually they left me alone, but whatever had been in those needles was messing with my mind: time became strangely dilated as I lay there in the dark, still strapped to the bed. I was convinced that hours had passed when in reality it had been merely minutes. I flushed hot and cold, and sometimes felt as though insects were crawling under my skin. I kept wondering what I'd done to merit this sort of treatment. I was a commissioned officer, which ought to count for something. Why were they doing this to me?

"They threw me in the stockade." My voice sounded hoarse even to my own ears, and my face was wet, although I didn't remember crying. Rick lay beside me, holding me in the dark, not speaking, just listening. "There were three other guys in there, one of them just a kid. He'd only joined up the week before. He'd lied about his age so he could join, and this was what they did to him."

"This why you don't drink?" Rick's voice was close to my ear. He reached out and brushed away my tears.

"Yeah. I... hit the bottle pretty hard after that. Trying to forget, you know?"

"Yeah. I know." He wrapped his arms around me, holding me, and I must have drifted off because the next thing I knew, there was daylight seeping into the room and Rick was gone. I found a handwritten note propped up on the nightstand: *If you need anything, you know where to find me.* I'd be lying if I said I wasn't grateful: after last night's confession, I wasn't sure I could face him in the full light of day.

By the time I got downstairs, it was half-past eleven and Tex had been in the kitchen for a while, prepping for the lunch crowd. He was anxious to know how Chris was doing, and I told him everything I knew. "Tex, do you remember what the guys looked like?" Picco's men had been intently searching the shoreline of Topsail beach. What had they been looking for?

I waited while he searched his memory. "Gee, Jack, everything happened kinda fast. There were three of them. One guy came in first. He was the tallest one—I mean, he was real tall, taller than normal. They were dressed in black, and they all had scarves on their faces, like blindfolds or masks."

I was making mental notes as he spoke. "Yeah?"

"One of 'em went behind the bar and grabbed Chris—he must have, because when I came out of the kitchen, he was holding the knife to Chris's throat—and the other two were driving people out of the place, telling 'em to go on home. I tried to stop them, and this one guy came rushing at me with the knife and cut me."

"He cut you? Where?"

He pulled aside the placket of his shirt, revealing a jagged, red weal across the base of his throat. "Aw, it ain't nothin'. He just sliced me a little. It's not serious."

"Tex, you should get that looked at."

"It's fine. I took care of it. Honest, Jack!" He waved away any further entreaties I might be planning to make. "They dragged Chris toward the door. It kinda looked like they were thinking of kidnapping him or something. One of them—yeah, the tall one—kept asking where you were."

"What'd he tell them?"

Tex was laughing. "He told 'em to fuck off."

That sounded like Chris. "Look, Tex, do you think you could hold down the fort for a little bit? I want to check in with Sergeant Picco, see if he's got any leads."

"Sure, Jack. You can count on me." Suddenly his grin turned sly and knowing. "So, had some company last night, Jack?"

I had to laugh. "Yeah. And it's none of your business."

Tex gave me an exaggerated shrug. "Good looking guy. Military, is he?"

"Hey, Tex?" I cupped a hand behind my ear. "Don't I hear the carrots calling you from the kitchen?"

THE MAIN office of the Royal Newfoundland Constabulary was plenty crowded by the time I got there. I asked for Picco at the desk, was told he was busy and directed to a straight-backed wooden chair in the waiting area, which was filled with loud-mouthed dock workers and hard-faced prostitutes, some of them sporting a black eye or other facial contusions. I flipped through a copy of the *Evening Telegram* while I waited, but the only news was that Good Luck brand margarine was on sale at Jackman and Greene.

The place was warm and overcrowded, so I put my head back and closed my eyes for a bit. I felt pleasantly sated and a little bit sore, and, as I played back the events of the previous night, I wondered if maybe I shouldn't have told Callan about my Section 8 experience. I'd never told anyone, not even Sam, about that part of my past. But really, who was Callan going to tell? I no longer had any ties to the military, and it wasn't like they had the power to court martial me. Anyway, Callan didn't really seem the type to go blabbing: as far as one-night stands went, he was the steadiest I'd ever seen. No expectations and no regrets, no questions asked, he lived entirely in the moment. I envied him that. It was something I'd been trying to master for most of my life, without any luck. Maybe Callan knew something about the future the rest of us didn't.

After about an hour, Picco appeared from an inside room and nodded to me. I got up and followed him down a narrow hallway and into a small, dark room with barely enough space to contain Picco's desk and chair. The only natural light came from a tiny window set high up in the wall and shielded with a sturdy set of iron bars. "What's that for?" I pointed to the window. "They afraid you're gonna escape or something?"

"You're some funny, you are." Picco squared his desk blotter and arranged his pencils. He was trying to be nonchalant, but I could see that Chris's injuries had taken a toll on the young sergeant. "That all you came here for, or did you want something?"

I got up and closed the door. "Sergeant, I want some information from you."

He straightened in his chair. "Is that right?" He tossed a copy of the *Telegram* across the desk at me. "You can get Good Luck on sale with the coupon on page five." He was trying to be his usual acerbic self, but the tense lines bracketing his mouth and eyes said otherwise.

"Phonse." I reached across the desk and took hold of his wrist. "How is he?"

His face crumpled and all his carefully tendered reserve vanished. "Jesus, Jack, how do you think he is, boy? He's lying over there in St. Clare's all cut up."

"I know." I squeezed his hand. "I know, and that's why I'm here. I want to try and do something about it, find the bastards who did this."

"It's a police matter." He pulled his hand away on the pretext of adjusting his uniform tunic. "Best thing for you to do is to stay out of it."

I ignored him. "Look, Phonse, the other night when you came to get me, a bunch of your boys were nosing around Topsail beach. What was that all about?"

He assumed an official expression. "I'm not permitted to comment on an ongoing investigation."

"Right. Sure. But this is me, remember? Maybe I can help you find out who did this."

He gazed at me for a moment with his strange, pale eyes, then got up and went to the filing cabinet in the corner. "I'm going to get a drink of water." He drew out a folder and tossed it onto the desk. "I might be a while. But I expect you'll be gone when I get back?"

He didn't have to tell me twice. "Sure."

"Right on." He pulled the door closed behind him.

The folder contained Picco's notes on the investigation, and they were extensive. His report of the stabbing jibed with what Tex had told me about there being three assailants, but added that they had fled in a waiting sedan, which his men had tailed to the Topsail area. The car had been found abandoned on a dead-end road half a mile from the beach—that would explain why Picco's men had been scouring that area—but as yet, no one was in custody. Farther down the page I saw something that really piqued my curiosity: Picco had noted the arrival of the S. S. *Chandris* at St. John's harbor a week before and contacted the harbor master to search the ship, "acting on information received from a noted police informant." The ship had been seized by harbor authorities and towed into port, but the men on board had been allowed the freedom of the city, simply because the harbor master didn't know what else to do with them. The constabulary had probably been real pissed about that one. No doubt that same harbor master was looking for another job.

I flipped back through the folder and turned up a copy of Octavian's mug shot; nothing new there. But just underneath it was a picture of a younger man, perhaps thirty, with dark hair combed straight back. He was handsome, but there was something debauched and languid about the dark, heavy-lidded eyes and a certain cruelty to the mouth. He looked like a man who was capable of anything, but I didn't know him, and there was nothing written on the reverse side of the picture.

A Greek ship in international waters was cause for concern. Greece was currently under Nazi occupation, so the only way the *Chandris* could have left Greece was with German approval, which meant she was as good as a German ship. No wonder she'd been seized. Had the three men who'd attacked Chris initially arrived on the *Chandris?* I was amazed that they'd even gotten into the Narrows—how the hell had they pulled that off? With the *Kreigsmarine*'s latest incursions into Conception Bay—

It hit me like a big, cartoon hammer, and I sat up straight, everything else forgotten. Of course Picco's men were searching Topsail beach. It fronted directly on the bay, and everybody knew German submarines regularly patrolled the waters around Bell Island. Before the war, German ships had often arrived to pick up precious iron ore from the Island's mines, so they'd know every nook and cranny of Conception Bay. Callan had mentioned reports of "tin fish"—German submarines—in Newfoundland waters and how this was a cause for concern. Only a couple weeks before, the passenger ferry, the SS *Caribou,* was sunk by U-69, killing a hundred and thirty-seven people.

Maybe the Greek ship was intended as a diversion, something to keep the Constabulary busy while the Germans sent their men ashore from a concealed sub, but Picco wasn't that stupid. He'd have sent a man or two down there, possibly to do some investigating, but mainly to make it seem like he'd taken the bait. It wasn't hard to launch an inflatable raft from a submarine, and as a mode of transportation it was quick and quiet. Pick yourself a night when there's no moon, get your raft and your men in the water, and nobody's the wiser. Picco knew this, and he probably knew or suspected a whole lot more, which meant only one thing: I had some work to do.

I left the folder on Picco's desk and went out the same way I'd come in. The wind was steady out of the northeast, and tiny snowflakes were fluttering out of a steel-gray sky. I left Fort Townsend and headed east toward Barnes Road. It was hardly the sort of day for a leisurely stroll, but I needed time to clear my head before I went back to the Heartache. Callan had told me there were rumors of enemy saboteurs in the city, and I'd heard it said by more than one customer the Germans were planning something nasty. I'm not the sort of person who puts much stock in rumor or innuendo, but my investigation of Picco's case notes pointed past the rumors and toward a singular truth: something bad was coming, something big. The men who'd attacked Chris had come looking for me, which meant somebody saw me as a threat, so the quicker I could sort this thing out, the better.

I had just crossed Rennie's Mill Road into Bannerman Park when the tiny hairs on the back of my neck started to prickle, and not because of the cold wind, either. It's the kind of feeling you get when you're sure somebody's looking at you. I did a quick survey of the park, and sure enough, a man in a long, dark coat was standing by the southwest corner of the Colonial Building. I wasn't close enough to make out his features, but there was something oddly familiar about his stance and the set of his shoulders; I could have sworn I'd seen him somewhere before. I couldn't puzzle out why he was just standing there like that: he didn't have a dog with him, and on such a cold day, there was nobody else in the park. He could have been waiting for someone, but most people would have chosen a more prominent spot—the front steps of the Colonial Building, say, or the fountain that fronted on Military Road. He stood very still until I was maybe five feet away from him. Then he took his hands out of his pockets and started forward.

"Chilly morning for a walk, Mr. Stoyles."

He was waiting for someone, all right. He was waiting for me. The man standing in front of me, his hand outstretched in greeting, was none other than Jonah Octavian. Again.

CHAPTER TWELVE

I'M NOT ashamed to say I turned and ran like a scared kid, all the way back to Constabulary headquarters. I'd be damned if I let that bastard get away again. I found Picco sitting at his desk, drinking a cup of tea and talking on the phone. He held up a hand when he saw me, so I waited till he'd laid down the receiver. "Jonah Octavian's alive. I just saw him in the park."

Picco's eyebrows climbed toward his hair. "Jonah Octavian is dead. Are you drunk?"

"No, dammit, I'm not drunk. Listen to me, would you? He even greeted me by name." I told him how Octavian had been standing there, almost like he'd been waiting for me. "He was killed in Egypt. I saw him die myself."

Picco gazed at me for several long moments. "Sure he did. And he somehow came back to life and was waiting for you in the park."

"Not just in the park. He showed up in the Heartache one night, with some guy."

Picco shuffled some papers on his desk. "Stoyles, don't be wasting my time with your foolishness. I got enough on my plate. I did what I could for you, now go on home out of it."

"You have to listen to me. Goddammit, Picco, put that down!" I yanked the folder out of his hand so hard it cut him. "I'm sorry."

He sighed and reached for a Kleenex. "Stoyles, look. You're not a bad sort of fellow. Sure, you're a Yank, but unlike the rest of 'em around here, I like Yanks." He sucked the blood away from the cut, watching me over the edge of his hand. "But you got no respect for proper protocol."

"Picco—Phonse—this is the same guy who snatched you off the street and stuck you in a cave over on the Southside. You know how dangerous Octavian is."

"Octavian's dead." He sat back in his chair and regarded me wearily. "Do you think we haven't been keeping an eye on him? I know everything that's happened to him since he left last year. He is dead—I didn't need you to tell me that, by the way—so whoever you saw in the park, it wasn't Jonah Octavian."

"Phonse, you gotta listen—"

"Jack!" He stood up, and we were suddenly eye to eye and toe to toe. "That's enough. Octavian is dead. I got a copy of the signed death certificate from the Egyptian officials, forwarded here by priority air post the day after he was killed. I even contacted the head of the Cairo police force and had him check the teeth. Octavian is dead, and that's the end of it."

"Yes, but couldn't there have been some mistake?" I was, I knew, grasping at straws, but the sight of whoever that was in Bannerman Park had shaken me to the core. It was starting to feel like Octavian's ghost was chasing me. "Maybe the Egyptians got something mixed up. Maybe they only thought Octavian—"

"Good-bye, Mr. Stoyles." Picco stepped away from his desk, took my arm in his strong policeman's grip, and steered me to the door.

"You're making a mistake." The door closed and I was on the outside of it. I heard the key turning in the lock. "Fine, if that's the way you want it." I waited to see if Picco would change his mind, but there was no sound from behind the door. It was already well after twelve, so I used the phone at the front desk to call a cab and waited outside until it pulled up: a rickety black-and-white number with a skinny guy at the wheel.

"Where to, buddy?" His graying hair was combed straight back and secured with something that looked and smelled like axle grease. His face was seamed like a crumpled paper bag, and he was chewing a toothpick so old it was probably a sliver of the True Cross. He reeked of old booze and too many cigarettes—the kind of guy who'd benefit from a strong gargle and some good, thorough dentistry.

I gave him the address of the Heartache and sat back. The inside of the cab hadn't been cleaned since the horse-and-buggy days, but I didn't have time to be picky. I'd left Tex alone to prep for the lunch crowd, and with Chris out of commission, I needed to get back before the afternoon rush. "You can head straight down Prescott if you like—that'll probably be the fastest." But he bypassed the hill and kept going east, toward the Newfoundland Hotel. "Hey, wait a minute! I'm already late as it is."

"Don't worry, my son. I knows a shortcut. You'll be there in plenty of time."

Something about this was making me very, very nervous. I'd grown up in Philly, and I knew cabbies often tried to take the rubes for a ride by going the long way around, but this was just weird. He swung around the hotel, heading south toward the waterfront, past the long line of red brick houses on Devon Row, and down the steep incline of Temperance Street. "Hey! Where are you going?"

He caught my eye in the rearview mirror and nodded at me. "Don't worry, Stoyles. This way you'll beat all the dinnertime traffic."

"How'd you know my name?" I reached for the door handle. "Put the brakes on. I'm getting out." The handle wouldn't budge: the door was jammed shut. "Stop this car! I want to get out."

He turned around to face me, giving me the weirdest, most disturbing smile I'd ever seen in my life. "I'm going to get out, Mr. Stoyles, but you won't be going anywhere. See, I got 'er rigged so she gets 'er gas even if I'm not pressing on the pedal."

The view out the front windscreen was chilling: a wide expanse of dark, dirty water. We were heading for the harbor unless I managed to stop this thing in the next few seconds. "Hey! You can't just leave me here!"

He wasn't listening to me. His narrow shoulders jerked as he yanked on the handle, trying desperately to get the door open. "It won't come open. Why won't it come open?"

"Put the brakes on, dammit! Put the brakes—"

There was a loud thump as the underside of the car struck the dock, and then we were airborne, the sea and the sky hurtling around me in a sickening kaleidoscope. We hit the water, and as the car began to sink, I remember thinking this was a stupid way to die.

WHEN I woke up, it hurt to swallow and I had the worst headache of my life; I tried to talk but there was something down my throat.

"Rest. Do not try to speak. You are in Grace Hospital. You have been through a terrible ordeal, Jack." Sam Halim looked about the same as always—perhaps a little older, perhaps a little wearier, and there were new lines around his eyes. "My darling. Why do you do this to yourself?"

Sam. My eyes were full of tears, and I reached for him with both hands: he was real. *I missed you.* I wanted to talk to him and couldn't; whatever was down my throat was getting in the way, and I tried to get at it.

"You mustn't take out the tube." He stroked my cheek, leaned in, and kissed my forehead. "It's very late. Sleep now, and I will come to you when I am able."

Don't go. The darkness was clawing at me, pulling me under. I tried to fight it, but my eyelids felt like garage doors, and before I knew it, I was out.

When I woke up again, it was later, and a trim young nurse in a starched white uniform was yanking open the curtains with the kind of grim efficiency you only ever see in such places. She picked up my wrist and felt for my pulse, then lifted my open eyelids and peered into my eyes.

"Mr. Stoyles, you have had a very close call. A very close call indeed. The next time you decide to go swimming in the harbor, I recommend you wait till at least July."

"It wasn't my choice." They'd apparently removed the tube sometime earlier, which explained why my throat felt like I'd been gargling with broken glass. "Can I have a drink of water?"

She came around the other side of the bed and fluffed my pillows. "Nothing by mouth until the doctor's seen you. You had nearly half the harbor down your lungs."

"Any of it get into my stomach?"

She wasn't amused. "Nothing till the doctor's seen you."

"You're no fun, sister." I lay back on my pillows and tried to figure out why a cab driver, a stranger to me, would want to kill me by driving into the harbor. I'd developed a theory or two when Sergeant Picco arrived, looking like he hadn't been to bed for ages. Since this was an official visit, I lost no time in telling him my version of events.

"Why would Rocky Power—the cab driver—want to kill you?" Picco sat on the edge of the hardbacked hospital chair, trying desperately to convey an image of self-assured command. "Did you do anything to him?"

"No. I never saw him before in my life."

"Hm. So how come he wanted to kill you?" His expression said he wondered why more people didn't try to kill me.

"I don't know, but he did."

Picco scribbled something in his notebook. "Mm."

"You sound like you don't believe me. Goddammit, Picco, they fished me out of the harbor." I still didn't remember anything that happened after we hit the water. Everything after the accident, from then until I'd woken up in hospital, was a complete blank.

"I never said I didn't believe you," he said tiredly.

"Then put me in touch with this Power guy. I'll get the truth, supposing I have to beat it out of him."

"That's hard to do. As far as we can tell, you somehow managed to free yourself from the car before it went to the bottom. Power wasn't so lucky. He's dead."

"Huh." That probably hadn't been part of his plan. "How'd I get here?"

"You were found lying on the American army docks, soaking wet and suffering from exposure. An anonymous call came through our switchboard, saying a man had been fished out of the harbor. Sounds like someone was looking out for you, Stoyles."

You have been through a terrible ordeal, Jack. No, it wasn't possible. Sam was in Egypt. He'd been nowhere near the American docks when the cab went over. His supposed presence in my room the night before was probably nothing more than the aftereffects of my near-drowning. "Hey, Phonse, how is Chris doing?"

He brightened. "Good. He had a bit of a fever and they were afraid he mightn't make it, but he's all right now."

"You stayed with him?"

He nodded shyly, his pale cheeks suddenly flushed with hot color. "I was there all night. He was sitting up having his breakfast when I left to come over here."

That was good news. With any luck at all, Chris would make a full recovery. I was about to say something when the nurse came back. "Sergeant Picco, there is a telephone call for you, from a Mr. Scala, I think he said. Long distance."

Scala? Andros Scala?

Picco stuck his notebook back into the breast pocket of his tunic and got up. "Thank you, nurse. Jack, I have to go."

"Phonse, wait—do you think this taxi driver, this Rocky Power guy, could have been hired by someone?"

He seemed reluctant to answer. "It's possible. Don't go getting any ideas."

"Right. Well, I'm not going to lie around here waiting for them to come and kill me." I threw back the bedclothes and put my feet on the floor. The room swung around me, and I swayed. Picco caught me and sat me down on the bed. "Thanks." My attempt had left me shaky, sweating, and nauseous. It almost felt like a repeat of the quinine poisoning episode a few months ago. "Just need to get my bearings and I'll be fine." God only knew what was in the harbor water: on a clear day you could smell it for miles. I'd probably ingested some horrible bacteria that would kill me. Well, that'd save Octavian the trouble.

"Get back in bed, Stoyles, you friggin' fool."

I held on to his arm for a moment longer. "I'll be fine. Just got up too quick is all."

"Look, if there's somebody after you, the safest place you can be is here in the hospital." Picco helped me lie down and pulled the blankets over me. "I'll even send a constable to stand watch on the door, just in case." He patted my shoulder. "Stay here. Now, you mind me. I'll come back later on and see how you are."

Picco meant well, but his suggestion that I stay where I was didn't make any sense to me. Maybe Octavian was dead and maybe he wasn't, but this whole situation was cockeyed from beginning to end and lying flat on my back in a hospital bed wasn't doing me any good. I dug my clothes out of the closet and got dressed. It seemed to take twice as long as usual, and I was exhausted by the time I'd finished tying my shoes.

I'd just slipped into my coat when the nurse came back. "Mr. Stoyles! Get back into bed right this instant."

"No, thanks. I'm getting out of here." I slipped past her and out into the hallway. A door at the end of the corridor had a big, red Exit sign over it, and this drew me like a magnet draws iron filings.

"Mr. Stoyles! You can't leave this hospital!" The nurse followed me, but I wasn't interested. I had no idea how long I'd been here, but I'd already wasted too much time. She shouted at me that she was going for the doctor, and I shouted back that was fine, and hurried down the stairs. A door at the bottom let out onto LeMarchant Road, and from there it was easy to find my way back to the Heartache. Twenty minutes later, I was hauling myself in the front door.

Tex, a towel slung over his shoulder, came running to greet me. "Jack, what the hell are you doing out of bed? That cop was here—what's his name with the gray eyes—and he said you were fished out of the harbor." He guided me to a chair. "We didn't know where you were. Anita came in here crying, saying something about how you were drowned and all that. Shoot. You scared the life out of me."

"I'm okay. Just a bit shaky, you know, kind of tired." I felt like I'd been dragged backward through the wringer of an industrial washing machine.

"Yeah, you look it. Hell, why don't you go on up to bed? Me and Anita can handle the lunch crowd. It's been nonstop in here ever since your accident. I guess some people got a taste for that sort of thing, huh?"

"Yeah." My head was spinning, and I rested it in my hands for a moment. "How long was I gone?" My sense of time was horribly distorted: it could have been a day, or I might have been gone for a week.

"Day before yesterday." Tex regarded me with concern. "You're lucky to be alive. From what I've heard, most people who go into that harbor don't come out again. Oh, hey—" He fished in his pocket. "I almost forgot. This came yesterday, special delivery. Normally, I wouldn't open your mail, but I was afraid it might be something important. There was only this card." He handed it to me. It was an ordinary-looking calling card, with nothing except a name printed on pale cream card stock: JONAH OCTAVIAN.

"Tex, where's the envelope this came in?" Seeing that name made me sick to my stomach.

"It's around here somewhere." He went to my office at the rear of the cafe and returned bearing a pale blue envelope. The postmark indicated it had been sent from St. John's, but there was no return address and no way of knowing who had sent it or why.

"Hm. Yeah, that's about what I figured." I crumpled the envelope in my fist. "Goddammit." I got up.

"Jack, where are you going?" Tex came around the table and started buttoning up my coat; it was a cute and curiously tender gesture, and it made me smile like an idiot. "It's freezing out there, and besides, you just got out of the hospital."

"I need some information on this Rocky Power guy."

"The cab driver."

"Yeah." I squeezed his shoulder to show him there were no hard feelings between us. "You okay to handle the lunch crowd?"

"You know it."

THE CITY directory showed a Rocky Power at 74 Signal Hill Road. This was a modest wooden house attached on one side to a row of similar houses and with an open field on the other side. I knocked on the door and waited, but nobody answered, so I knocked again, a little harder this time. After half an eternity, a middle-aged woman came to the door with her hair in curlers. "Oh, excuse me. I didn't mean to bother you. You're obviously getting ready to go out."

She stared at me. "Wha'?"

"Your… curlers, there." I pointed. "I said you're obviously getting ready to go out."

"No, my son, that I'm not." She stood back and held the door open. "I might go to Bingo tonight with my sister, Margo, but then again I might not. Are ye coming in or what? I'm not heating up St. John's."

I stepped into the entryway, which was absolutely filthy, even to the handmade rag rugs on the floor. The walls were made of sagging ten-test, painted an improbable pink, surmounted with numerous holy pictures and religious relics. A cross-eyed Jesus, squeezing the Sacred Heart in his clasped hands, ogled me from the opposite wall. The house smelled like boiled cabbage and dirty socks. "I'm looking for a cab driver named Rocky Power. Are you Mrs. Power?"

"No, I'm not Mrs. Power. I'm Mrs. Cahill. He used to board here." She peered up at me through a pair of filthy cat's eye glasses. "How come you're asking about him? He's dead, sure."

I still felt pretty crummy, and I didn't intend to get into it with her. "Is there anybody here who knew him?"

"His brother came in from Gambo yesterday for the funeral. The poor bugger's getting buried this afternoon. You want to talk to him?"

"Sure." The brother might be a waste of time, but since I'd come all this way, I might as well see something for my efforts. I followed Mrs. Cahill into the next room, stepping over empty milk bottles and discarded foodstuffs in varying states of decay. A pair of angry yellow eyes watched me from under a chair, and a set of needle-sharp claws slashed at my ankles as I went by.

Mrs. Cahill stopped at the foot of the stairs and bellowed for Rocky Power's brother. "Here he comes." A shadowy figure appeared in the semidarkness at the top of the stairs. "You can talk to 'en in here if you wants to."

Rocky Power's brother looked nothing like Rocky Power. First of all, he was a good deal younger and a lot better-looking, but there was something hard about him, something sinister. I'd gotten a similar feeling once before, in Philadelphia, when Frankie Missalo and I had done some construction work for a friend of Frankie's father, a big, burly man with a cigar stuck in his face and expensive rings for every finger. He'd been nice enough, but something told me not to turn my back on him. I found out later he was the number one button man for the Sbarro crime family, and he was personally responsible for at least a hundred deaths.

He came downstairs slowly, walking on his heels and letting his body's weight sink noiselessly down under its own impetus. He was very well-dressed, in dark trousers and a silk shirt open at the neck. His face was narrow and watchful, and his heavy-lidded eyes were obsidian dark, with thick, almost feminine lashes. The nose was thin and sharp, like the beak of some predatory bird; the lips, in contrast, were full and fleshy, a little oversensual for my taste. He could have been the man in the photograph, the one I'd seen in Picco's folder. He stopped in front of me and looked me up and down. "Good day. I am Nicholas Power. How can I help you, Mr....?" The accent belonged to Newfoundland about as much as I did.

"Stoyles. Jack Stoyles. I was in the cab your brother was driving."

"Ah." The muscles of his face flexed, drawing up the corners of the mouth while the rest of his face remained utterly still. It was a chilling spectacle. "I am glad you were not killed, as Rocky was."

"Yeah, well, so am I. That's not what bothers me, though."

"Oh?" He drifted closer. "What bothers you?"

Time to drop the bomb. "I think someone hired your brother to kill me."

"Mm." His expression didn't change. "That is rather a strong accusation."

"You have an interesting accent for someone from Gambo. I've never heard a Newfoundland accent that sounds like yours."

"Hmph." It might have been laughter. "I have been working overseas for many years."

"Is that so? Sounds Turkish to me... or maybe it's Greek."

"How interesting."

"So if you are Greek…." I left it hanging. "You know, you remind me of a picture I saw recently. You familiar with a guy named Picco?"

"Mr. Stoyles." The smile came and went. "Is there a purpose to your visit? Apart from pointless accusations, I mean."

"Listen, I'm not interested in your brother. There's nothing I can do about him. What I am interested in is who hired him."

He laid a cold, reptilian hand on my shoulder; it was all I could do not to shrug it off. "Mr. Stoyles, I cannot condone what my brother did, but I think he has paid for his crimes." He gazed deeply into my eyes. "You, on the other hand…."

"Hey, wait just a minute!" I shoved his arm down. "Your brother almost killed me, and I think maybe you know something about it."

"That may be." He shrugged with one shoulder. "A few evenings ago, a man came to see my brother." A dark red easy chair, piled high with dirty laundry, stood nearby; he shoved the clothes onto the floor, folded himself into the chair, and lit a cigarette. "My brother didn't want me in the room, so I went out for a walk along the waterfront." He drew on the cigarette till the end glowed bright red.

"Did your brother say what the man's name was?"

"Mm. I don't recall." He sighed. "He was about your height, perhaps a man of middle years, but extremely well-groomed, manicured fingernails, fine clothes. He had curling dark hair going gray at the sides, and he spoke with some sort of European accent. He told my brother he had been involved in the construction industry for many years."

Construction. Yeah, it sounded like Octavian all right, right down to the manicured fingernails. I didn't need him to tell me anything else; I could put the pieces together just fine. "Thanks." I did my best not to sound sarcastic. "You've been a lot of help."

He made a noncommittal noise and waved the cigarette at me. "I hope so, Mr. Stoyles. You can show yourself out?"

I threaded my way back through the mess and found the front door without too much trouble. Mrs. Cahill was nowhere to be seen, but I couldn't feel too sorry about that. I was too busy wondering how the hell Jonah Octavian had managed to rise from the dead.

I SPENT an hour in the public library on Duckworth Street, paging through recent newspapers. The *Daily News* had a small piece on the front page, as well as an obit—*Local businessman Jonah Octavian murdered overseas*—but declined to elaborate. The *Evening Telegram* coverage featured a small, black-bordered box on the lower right-hand side of the front page, but said mostly the same thing. A thorough search of the obituaries revealed nothing more than the usual: Octavian had died in Egypt, presumably murdered, burial had already taken place, *Mr. Octavian is survived by his brother Nicholas.*

Whose last name, I knew, wasn't Power. This put a whole new slant on things—but the effects of my impromptu swim in the harbor had begun to reassert themselves, so I left the library and headed down the hill to Water Street and the Heartache Cafe. The walk was only about a block, but by the time I made it through the front door, I was weak and sweaty. Tex and Anita were cleaning up after the lunch crowd; they both hurried over when they saw me, and Anita fetched me a hot cup of coffee, which tasted like ambrosia. "Do you guys think you can hold things together? I'd like to go upstairs and lie down for a little while."

"You shouldn't be up going around." Anita looked like she was about to cry. "You almost died, and me and Janice thought you were after drowning in the harbor, and here you are, dragging yourself all over God's half-acre and for what, I don't know." She pressed the hem of her apron to her eyes.

"Aw, come on, now." I pulled her into my lap; she was no bigger than a minute. "I'm fine. You can't kill me with a meat axe—just ask Tex. Isn't that right, Tex?"

He made a face. "Yeah, I guess so."

Anita bounded up off my lap, swatting at me. "Go 'way, you foolish bugger. I got work to do. Go on up and lie down. I'll bring you up a plate of supper now the once."

"Uh, Jack?" Tex drew me aside. "Take a look out the window, there."

I glanced toward the front of the cafe. "Guy across the street, in the dark overcoat and hat?"

"Uh-huh."

The man in question was standing near the corner of Water Street and Bishop's Cove. He wasn't real tall, but carried himself with authority. He was walking up and down, stopping now and then to glance toward the Heartache. The dark coat was obviously camouflage, as was the hat pulled low over his face. "Watching us?"

"Sure looks that way."

"Never mind!" Anita tugged at my arm. "You're not well. You should be up lying in the bed, never mind what buddy across the street is doing. Sure, he could be anybody." She pushed me toward the stairs. "Go on, now. If anything happens, you'll be the first to know."

I did as she told me—Anita might be little, but she's fierce—and anyway, I felt like I'd been dragged behind a barge. I undressed and got into bed but sleeping was hard, and every time I closed my eyes I could see water flooding into the car. I was drifting in that in-between place that isn't sleep and isn't quite wakefulness, and I kept trying to open the car door, but no matter how much I tugged on the handle, it wouldn't let go. This action was repeated a dozen times over: my hands reaching for the handle, trying and failing to open the door, and then sinking back with the dull acceptance that this was it. I would die here. And then the darkness parted and a pair of hands reached down, as if from a long way off, and I was moving through the murky water, floating upward as if pulled on a string. My head broke the surface, and I was dazed but alive, and looking up into a face I knew as well as I knew my own.

I sat bolt upright in bed, gasping for breath, and suddenly I knew what I was seeing wasn't a dream. Standing over my bed in the uncertain light of a late October afternoon was the sickly smiling face of Jonah Octavian. I shoved the covers off me and surged toward him, and just then, I felt a sharp prick at the side of my neck and the unmistakable sensation of falling. I fumbled with suddenly uncoordinated hands for the gun in my night table. I managed to get the gun out and squeezed off three rounds but Octavian was already gone, fleeing down the stairs toward the cafe. "Get him!" I scrambled to the door and started after him but crumpled, and I fell as blackness filled my world and everything—the gun, the stairs, Octavian and me—went away.

CHAPTER THIRTEEN

IT WAS morning when I opened my eyes, and I was alone in my room with the tentative October sunlight slipping through the gaps in the venetian blinds. Had my experience been merely a bad dream, or had Jonah Octavian actually risen from the dead? No, it was too fantastical to be true and anyway, what could he hope to gain from it? There was a war on, for chrissakes. We didn't need to manufacture bogeymen.

I'd decided to go back to sleep when the phone rang. "Stoyles, Heartache Cafe."

"Is yer awake? I didn't mean to get you out of bed." The voice, believe it or not, was Mrs. Cahill, she of the boarding house, the holy pictures, and the filthy carpets. The clock on my nightstand said it was a little after ten.

"What is it, Mrs. Cahill?"

"That feller you was asking about, Rocky Power."

"Uh-huh."

"His brother left here last night and never even bothered to pay me."

"Mrs. Cahill, don't you think that's a matter for the police?"

"Never mind that. I heard him talking on the phone. They were talking about you, because I heard him mention your name three or four times." She paused, and I could hear the crackling sound of paper being unfolded. "I wrote it down. He said you were going to queer the works unless they did something about you. I don't know what that means, but I figured I'd tell you anyway."

I was suddenly and absurdly grateful. "Mrs. Cahill, thank you. I really appreciate this."

"Oh, that's all right, my son. Listen, now: you don't know anybody who's looking for a room to rent, do you?"

I shaved and dressed as quickly as I could and caught a cab to Fort Townsend. If I knew Picco, he'd been at his desk since daybreak. Driving east on Water Street, I noticed the same man who'd been watching me the night before, still standing at the corner. I wondered if he'd stay put or follow me to the police station. Picco wasn't in yet, but he was expected, so I waited in his office. There was a stack of folders on his desk, and I spent some time paging through them. They were the usual stuff: police records of drunken fights, break-and-enters, car accidents, and then I saw something that made me stop short: a folder with my name on it. The contents were mostly what you'd expect: a photograph of me, pictures of the Heartache, copies of business permits and my liquor license, but nestled in the middle of the folder was something altogether different. Oh, I'd seen telegrams before—but why Kevin MacBride of the Long Range Desert Group was in contact with Alphonsus Picco was anybody's guess. The telegram was cryptic enough, but that didn't surprise me. It contained maybe ten words: MIDDLE DECEMBER -- STOP -- GET BARN DANCE STARTED -- STOP -- STOYLES KEY

"Having a good read, are you?" Picco stepped into the room and closed the door behind him. Despite his rancorous tone, he seemed to be in good spirits.

"Been to see Chris?"

"I have."

"How is he?"

"He's well." Picco reached across and took the telegram from me. "He should be out of hospital by the end of the week. It's amazing, really, considering his injuries." He seemed to be insinuating that, if Chris meant anything to me, I'd have gone to visit him.

"I'm glad he's on the mend. I'd hate to lose him. He's been a good friend to me."

"Stoyles, is there something you want? Or are you just here to torment me?"

"What does this mean?" I indicated the telegram. "What 'barn dance'? Picco, what do you know about this?"

"That is official police business, which means it's none of yours."

"Official police business?" I sneered. "You even know what that means, Picco? I've been nearly killed, and then last night, I wake up and guess who's standing over me? Jonah Octavian." I pressed my hand to the side of my neck. "He did something to me, shot something into me, some kind of drug. My guess is a blow dart, something like that." It was too much like what had happened to Pasha Nubar in Cairo to be merely coincidence.

"A blow dart." Picco nodded. "So now we are in a Tarzan film?"

I'd had about as much as I could take. "Goddammit, Phonse! I almost drown in the harbor and then Octavian's in my bedroom. Somebody's trying to kill me! And there's some guy in a dark overcoat who keeps following me. I saw him outside the Heartache the other day. Five'll get you ten he's out there now."

"Outside… in the street?" Picco got up to look. "That man out there?" He pointed. Dark Overcoat was standing at a bus stop, looking the other way.

"Yeah, that's him."

Picco smiled—it was genuine, which surprised me. "Calm down, my son. He's one of ours. After you went into the harbor, I figured you could stand some watching."

"Oh." I digested this for a moment. "Yeah. I didn't think of that."

"I expect you say that a lot. Look, Stoyles, go on home out of it. Or go over and see Chris. Just stay out of my way."

"What about the telegram? What 'barn dance' is he talking about? Is there something going on I should be aware of? I mean, apart from crazy cab drivers and Octavian's younger brother."

"Never mind the telegram." Picco looked distinctly uncomfortable and made a show of being suddenly busy. "Let us handle it from here, all right? You stay out of it, and the quicker we can get this cleared up. And by the by, don't get any ideas about playing cop. I'm watching you, Stoyles. You set one foot wrong and I'll be all over you. Mind I'm telling you."

"Yeah, you're all the same, every one of you. You don't give a damn." I slammed out of there and caught a cab over to St. Clare's hospital. Chris was sitting up in bed reading the newspaper when I arrived; I leaned in and hugged him.

"You look terrible, Jack." He held on to my hand. "Phonse told me about the cab smash-up. Jeez."

I filled him in on what had happened, especially the part about the man in the photograph, and the blow dart. For some reason, Chris seemed to find the whole thing funny. "Jack—stop—don't make me laugh. I'm busting my stitches here." Sensing I wasn't nearly as amused, he immediately sobered. "Look, you almost getting killed isn't funny. But honestly, Jack, don't you ever ask yourself why you seem to get into these scrapes? You're like one of those fancy metal detectors that can pick up coins underground." He grinned at me, and my anger evaporated. It should be illegal for a grown man to have dimples like Chris's.

"Keep laughing," I said. "You realize, of course, I'm docking your pay for every day you spend in here?"

He stretched his arms in front of him and leaned back in the bed. "Dock away, brother. I'm living the high life here." He gazed at me. "Uh… Phonse said they never caught the guys… the ones who did this." He gestured at his bandaged torso. "It kinda makes me wonder." His features were pinched with anxiety. "Jack, do you think…."

"Anybody tries it, I'll kill 'em with my bare hands." I cupped his cheek in my palm. "You got my word, Chris."

"Jack…." He sighed. "Okay, this is gonna sound crazy, but I figure you and me are friends, so I'm gonna say it anyway."

We were a bit more than friends, Chris and I. I remembered the dark days earlier this summer, when Chris's girlfriend, Julie Fayre, had been executed for murder, and I had taken him to bed. "Okay."

"The night it happened, when those guys stabbed me…. I was pretty shaken up when the ambulance brought me in. The doc says I lost a lot of blood and I dunno, maybe I wasn't thinking straight." He took a deep breath. "Anyhow. After I came out of surgery I wasn't feeling too good. Maybe it was the anesthetic or something."

My heart sped up, thundering in my chest. "Yeah?"

"This is gonna sound crazy but… I coulda sworn there was somebody in the room."

I let out my breath in a whoosh. "What did they look like?"

Chris shook his head. "I couldn't get a good look at him. It was a man, maybe half a head shorter than you. He wasn't a doctor, I know that much. This guy was wearing a dark suit, and he had a foreign accent. I couldn't really place it. He was saying something to me, but I don't remember much."

My skin prickled. "Was he Greek, maybe?"

"Maybe." He laid one hand across his bandaged waist. "Think it was one of the guys who stabbed me?"

"Chris, at this point I'm not sure of anything." I patted his shoulder. "I'm gonna get back to the Heartache."

It was heading for noon by the time I left Chris, and too close to the lunchtime rush for me to get any further with the whole Octavian thing. The usual crowd—school teachers, bus drivers, government workers—had begun to filter in when I made it back to my cafe, and against Anita's protests, I grabbed an apron and got busy. Tex was up to his eyeballs in the kitchen, and I didn't feel like leaving the two girls to handle all the traffic.

Anita seemed to take my presence as a personal affront and wasted no time in telling me what she thought. "I think it's shocking. You're a sick man, Jack. You should be up lying in that bed, not down here scoating your guts out."

"Scoating my guts out?" The local idiom never failed to amuse me; this was the weirdest saying yet. "Is that good or bad?"

Anita paused to pick up a tray of drinks. "Alls I'm saying is, you shouldn't be out of bed."

The girls seemed to have most of the tables covered, so I spent my time behind the bar, mixing drinks. Around half past one, the crowd started to slack off, and I was able to catch my breath and pour myself a cup of coffee. I had just turned around to replace the pot when I caught sight of someone in the big bar mirror. He was standing with his back to me, so all I could see was his head and the dark overcoat he wore, but something about that figure, the set of the shoulders, was disquieting. My breath seemed to come hard in my lungs, and the cafe began to get dim around the edges. He turned around, and I was looking at Jonah Octavian.

"Tex! Get him. Don't let him—he's—stop him!" I stumbled back, crashing into a row of half-empty glasses, knocking them to the floor. I reached out, instinctively grabbing for a handhold but came up with a lot of air. Octavian pushed past three women and was out the front door, disappearing into the street. I scrambled to my feet and took out after him, but it was too late. He'd vanished like a puff of smoke.

"Where'd he go?" Tex was suddenly at my elbow. "Did you see him?"

"Naw, he took off." This was getting me nowhere. I didn't care what Picco thought, or what he figured I should do. It was time for the charade to stop. Octavian—or somebody in Octavian's employ—wanted me dead. Well, first he'd have to find me. I was going to make sure he did.

Valley of the Dead

THE BAR was little better than a rat's nest: a rickety pile of rotting wood tacked onto the back of a fish-and-chips place that fronted on Water Street, complete with the usual set of growling scoundrels, prostitutes, and greasy-haired corner boys down on their luck. I'd put the word around that I was looking for a man named Octavian, and then I waited for the underground network to do the rest. A lucky tip from the bartender at the Bosun's Whistle had brought me here, to Necker's Bar on George Street.

I took a corner table, ordered a drink, and sat back to wait. It was a little after nine when I arrived, but I knew I could be waiting awhile. The jukebox was playing a selection of the latest tunes and some I wasn't familiar with, mostly local stuff. I could never understand the local love for accordion music; to me it sounded like somebody jumping on a bag of cats, but they went crazy for it here. The air was blue with tobacco smoke, which was a blessing, because the place smelled like the back end of a horse. I couldn't be sure, but it seemed like one of the toilets might have backed up.

After a while, a girl singer came on, flanked by a short, fat guy with a guitar and a tall, skinny guy with the ubiquitous squeezebox. Someone pulled the plug on the jukebox, and it died with a yelp just as the girl launched into "Sliding Down Signal Hill" with gusto. She sang with a wonderful Irish brogue, playing it up for the audience, who mostly ignored her with the exception of one old guy, seated near the raised dais that served as a stage: now and then he'd lean forward and thump his hand on the boards, throwing his head back and bellowing something unintelligible to me but which the rest of the crowd greeted with enthusiastic applause. An hour later, the girl went off and a small man in a greasy tweed cap and worn corduroys mounted the stage, carrying a wooden chair and a pair of kitchen spoons, which he played by banging them on his knees and elbows and, by way of a farewell, on his buttocks. He was followed by a young woman in a diaphanous pink dress, high heels, and opera-length gloves. By now the smoke was so thick, I could barely see the stage, but I had a pretty good idea what was going on, and it made me laugh. The military brass and the local clergy alike were tripping over themselves to keep the good American boys away from this sort of thing, an imprecation that greatly benefited the strip clubs and burlesque houses of St. John's.

She started peeling off her gloves one finger at a time and flipping her hair around like she was the star attraction in a burlesque revue. By the time she got to the stockings, the locals were whooping it up, and one old fisherman climbed onto the stage and tried to embrace her, but a couple of muscle boys picked him up by the elbows and hustled him outside. The girl, for her part, kept dancing like nothing happened, her unbound breasts bouncing gently under her see-through dress.

Touch me like this… oh, don't be shy. That's what we're here for, isn't it?

Years ago, Frankie Missalo and some of the boys had all chipped in to buy me a girl for my seventeenth birthday. They'd even paid to put me up in a hotel room and everything: the kind of run-down, fleabag place you can find in just about any city in the world, with broken windows and dead cockroaches on the bathroom floor. I was green as grass and eager, and the girl was pretty and still young enough that her profession didn't really show. She was kind to me, and she knew exactly what to do, but I got so carried away, I came in my shorts before she'd finished undressing. *It's all right. It happens to a lot of guys. Don't feel bad. Here, put your hand on me.* I was clumsy and embarrassed, glad when it was over and I could put my clothes back on. I never told anyone, but I got through it by pretending: I closed my eyes and imagined she was a handsome, dark-haired man who loved me, who wanted me, and whenever Frankie or one of the other guys asked, I made sure to brag about how hard I'd banged her. I guess that should have tipped me off that maybe something was up with me, that maybe I wasn't like the rest of the guys.

The thick fog of cigarette smoke was making my eyes water and the girl hadn't even taken off her dress. I turned toward the door, thinking maybe I'd step out for a moment, and there he was, standing in the doorway. I bolted out of my chair and started after him and, just like before, he did the same disappearing act—only this time I watched where he went and was able to follow him down the narrow laneway stairs to Water Street. He paused on the sidewalk for a second, then headed west with me on his heels. I chased him toward the dockyard, but he made a quick right off Water Street, kicking open a cellar door. I thought I recognized it, some kind of warehouse for wines and spirits. I'd bought port from them before, and if I remembered correctly, this door was the only way in or out.

The warehouse was windowless, pitch black under a low ceiling. I cautiously felt my way forward. "Come on out, Octavian! I'm not leaving, so you'd better show yourself."

That got a response: the sharp retort of a pistol and a bullet whizzed past my face, grazing my cheek. "I like that you are so suggestible, Stoyles. I could lead you anywhere and you'd follow, wouldn't you?"

Trying to see him in that place was like looking for a priest in a whorehouse. "I'm not interested in chitchat. I know you hired Rocky Power to kill me, and you made sure to take care of him, too, so he couldn't talk. It's all over. You might as well come out now and give yourself up."

"Or what?" A match flared in the blackness, illuminating a face as pale as a mask. Dark eyes glinted at me, but the expression remained neutral. "You'll kill me?"

"Something like that." There was water dripping somewhere behind us, and in the confinement of the warehouse, it sounded eerily like footsteps.

"You can't kill me, Jack." The figure's head tilted to the side. "I'm already dead." He raised the gun and there it was, right in front of me, and there was nothing I could do. I just stood there, staring dumbly into the barrel of an ugly little snub-nosed gun. His finger squeezed the trigger and everything slowed to a crawl. *So this is how it's gonna be.*

The hammer clicked on an empty chamber, and brother, that was enough for me. I lunged for him and slammed his forearm across my upraised knee as hard as I could. Octavian yowled as something inside the limb snapped, and he collapsed on the floor, yelling.

"Git up, you sumbitch." Someone reached past me, hauling Octavian by the collar and standing him on his feet. "You okay, Jack?"

I'd recognize that voice anywhere. "Jesus Christ."

"Not even close, boy."

I shivered, and then I was laughing, as giddy as a schoolgirl. "Rick? What the hell are you... how'd you know...?"

"That little cop of yours dropped a word in my ear. He don't miss a trick. Said you were fixing to do something stupid, and maybe I'd best keep an eye on you."

We marched Octavian out into the light and stood him up against the wall. He looked sick, his arm swollen to three times its normal size. His head lolled back against the bricks, and I saw something I hadn't noticed until then: a thin seam under his chin. "What the hell...?" Octavian struggled but Rick kept hold of him while I got my fingers under it and pulled. It came off in one piece and I saw it for what it was: a lifelike rubber mask. Not the cheap kind that kids wear at Halloween—this was a custom job, made by somebody who really knew his trade. The man wearing it was the dead cabbie's supposed brother, but I knew better. "Octavian. You're his brother. You're the man in the picture."

Picco was waiting for us at Constabulary headquarters when we arrived, and he lost no time taking Octavian the younger into custody. Rick waited in the anteroom while I gave Picco my statement. When I finished speaking, he looked up at me. "I didn't believe you when you said Octavian was after you. I figured you were a bit sick in the head, after the accident and all that." His brows knit, and he shook his head. "I'm an idiot."

"No. You had no evidence. You couldn't very well proceed on just my say-so." I laid my hand on his shoulder. "You're a good cop, Picco. You listened to your instincts. If Rick Callan hadn't been following me...." Something occurred to me. "Hey, how'd you know Rick Callan and I...?"

Picco smirked. He stood up and yanked down on the hem of his uniform tunic. "Because I'm a good cop."

I left Nicholas Octavian in Picco's able hands and went out into the night. Callan was waiting by the main door, smoking a cigarette. "All taken care of?"

"You could say that." It occurred to me, what I had to say, and I drew a deep breath, nerving myself like someone getting ready to dive into cold water. "Listen, Rick, there's something I have to say."

He was smiling. "Yeah, I guess maybe there is." There was something bleak there in his eyes, and I knew he'd already figured it out. "Just my luck, huh. Who is he?"

"He's...." Sam's face swam before my inner vision: gentle, dignified, and handsome. "It's over. He's someone I knew in Egypt." It felt like something that had happened years and years ago, long before I'd ever come to Newfoundland or opened the Heartache.

"Egypt, huh." Callan nodded. "Yeah, that's a long ways away, for sure."

"Come on back to the Heartache with me. I'll fix you a drink."

Callan dropped the cigarette and stepped on it, shook his head. "No, thank you, Jack. I do thank you but no, I think it is best if I just go on home now." He couldn't or wouldn't look at me.

"Rick." I felt lower than dirt. "Let me—just one drink, huh?"

"I said no." He spoke quietly but with an authority I didn't dare question. "Now, you mind when I'm talking to you, all right?" He yanked down his uniform jacket. "Colder'n a witch's tit out here. I'd best be going."

He turned and walked away and that was that. I knew there was no point in arguing with him. He knew, even if I didn't, that as long as I clung to the memory of what I'd had with Sam Halim, there could be no possibility of anything between us but friendship. I simply wasn't available to him.

It was late when I got back to the Heartache; Tex had already closed up and gone home. He'd left the light burning over the back door for me, and Anita had put by a plate of sandwiches in the icebox, but I wasn't hungry, so I went upstairs, stripped off my clothes, and got into bed. The wind rose, howling out of the northeast hard enough to shake the building, and I wondered if the old structure would hold. Of course it would, I mused; it had been here for a long time and would remain a long time after I was gone. It was like the Great Wall of China or those giant heads on Easter Island or the pyramids at Giza….

It seemed I was lying or half-sitting against some kind of natural stone pillar that shielded me. Someone else was there, and it was as though we had been there together for a long time—hours, perhaps. My companion was a warm weight against my shoulder, his body—I somehow knew instinctively that he was male—lying close beside my own, so that we touched at several different places. *You must not think of that other.* The voice—his voice—might have come from outside me or from inside my own head. *Be here in this moment only. That is all. Simply rest.* I struggled to open my eyes but it was like my body wouldn't obey me, and then his hand was on my face, drawing me to him, and we kissed: eager, open-mouthed, sensual and slow.

I woke suddenly with the conviction that someone was in my bedroom. I sat up slowly, feeling under the pillow for my gun. "Who's there?" The wind howled around the eaves and the radiator near the window ticked. For several long moments, I listened while my heart thumped so hard it was almost painful. "Hello?"

I lay awake until dawn with the gun in my hand.

CHAPTER FOURTEEN

FOR A long time, things were quiet around town and around the Heartache. Chris got out of hospital and came back to work, along with a few new scars. Tex stayed on in the kitchen, but Anita found herself in the family way and had to get married, which left me with one waitress. I put a want ad in the local papers, but it was hard finding decent staff, and the idea of training another girl to do what Anita could do with her eyes shut was a ready-made headache.

Toward the end of November, it started to get cold and the rains were unrelenting—until they changed into snow. By the second week of December, we had enough snow underfoot that it was starting to look like Christmas, and I was busy getting the Heartache ready for the holidays. Chris and Tex moved the piano out of its usual corner and put up a tree, which we decorated with the usual tinselly frou-frou, and I strung a few lights around the windows. It was bitterly cold, which was good news for me as it drove people indoors; I added some cakes and muffins to the menu and ordered in as much strong English tea as the ration board would let me.

"Hey, Jack, would you take a look at this?" Tex handed the *Daily News* to me across the bar. I'd been attempting to fix a leaky tap that dripped incessantly, but so far all I'd done was make the problem worse.

"What is it, Tex? I'm kinda busy." I was trying to keep tension on the pipe wrench I had fastened around a leaking copper washer; if I could just twist the little sucker into place....

"Isn't that your friend? The sergeant?"

I leaned over to peer at the photograph on the front page. There was Rick Callan, standing on the steps of the Knights of Columbus hostel on Harvey Road. He was flanked on either side by smiling government officials, one of which was shaking his hand. SERGEANT NAMED HOSTEL CHARGE OFFICER, the headline read. "Looks like he's gotten himself a promotion, or at least a change of orders."

"Well, good for him." Tex tapped the photo. "You seeing him tonight?"

I grimaced. "No." I twisted the wrench, felt the washer give a little. "No, that was over ages ago."

Tex watched me working on the faucet. "Still hung up on Sam, huh?"

I glanced up at him. "Something like that."

"Think you'll ever see him again?"

I shook my head. "No." The wrench slipped off the washer and clattered on the floor. "Fuck."

"I got it." Tex handed it to me. "Have you tried writing to him?"

"Who?" I cranked the wrench closed over the washer and started the whole process over again. "Sam? He wouldn't want to hear from me."

"How do you know?"

I glared at him. "Is this going to be Twenty Questions? Because there are some dirty glasses in the kitchen—"

Tex threw up his hands in mock surrender. "All right, okay. I won't mention it again."

"I'd appreciate that." I leaned on the wrench, easing it forward, and felt the corroded washer give way. Tex had left the newspaper on the bar, and I found myself drawn to the photograph of Callan on the hostel steps. Something about it bothered me, but I couldn't put my finger on what it was. The hostel was the sort of place you see wherever American servicemen are stationed: a combination dormitory and social club with a reading room, a restaurant, toilets and showers, a recreation room with various games, an auditorium for dances and variety shows, and a dormitory upstairs. From what I'd heard, the food was okay, and the entertainment was generally good, and if you were too tanked to stagger home, you could always crawl upstairs and sleep it off.

A shadow fell across the bar, and I found myself looking at a small man, perhaps five feet in height, with protuberant blue eyes set flat in his face and a wide, almost piscine mouth. His brows were thin and arched and so fine they appeared to have been drawn on his forehead. There was something wrong with his features—no, with the face generally—that I couldn't immediately identify. "Can I help you?"

"This is the Heartache Cafe?" His voice was low, cultured, with what sounded like an eastern European accent—Bulgaria, maybe, or Rumania.

"Yeah. What can I get you?"

"I would like a cold glass of lemonade. Please serve me at that table over there." He pointed to a table in the far corner of the room, partially hidden behind a huge potted fern.

"Cold weather for lemonade, don't you think?" I didn't usually keep any in the fridge, not this time of year, but if he wanted it, I'd make it for him. "Don't you want a cup of coffee instead?"

His strange, flat eyes focused on me, and I had the impression of gazing down a tunnel. "I never consume hot beverages."

"Your funeral," I muttered. I went into the kitchen and told Tex to make a pitcher. The little guy with the fishy face was looking through the copy of the *Telegram* I kept for customers: licking his thumb and finger before catching hold of the page, then turning it slowly and deliberately, like a child might. It was a disconcerting spectacle. I laid the lemonade down and turned to go.

"Mr. Stoyles, is it not?"

"Yeah?"

"I am...." He paused, reached to sip the lemonade delicately. "How to put it? A stranger to your town. I wonder if you could direct me to… ah, Parade Street?" He folded his hands on top of the table and gazed at me, and I realized, with a start, that he had no eyelashes.

"Parade Street? You want the top end or the bottom end?"

This seemed to amuse him, although I had no idea why. "The bottom end, if you please."

I thought about it for a minute. "Let me see… best way is to turn left out of the door. Keep going till you see Bowring Brothers up ahead, on your right. Before you get there, you wanna turn left onto George Street, then on up Bates Hill. Turn right at the top of Bates—that'll be Queen's Road. You're gonna walk up there till you see a long, steep hill with a cathedral at the top—that's the Basilica. Go up to the top, turn left and you're on Harvey. Keep walking till you see the Knights of Columbus hostel. Parade's just around the corner." If I kept this up, I might as well get a job as a tour guide.

"Thank you, Mr. Stoyles. You are most kind."

Just then a group of lady Christmas shoppers blew in through the door, and I went to see to them. When I turned back, the little man had gone, leaving most of his lemonade untouched. I didn't have too much time to think about him, however: the parade of Saturday shoppers kept us on the hop till well past five and it was five thirty before we started dressing the tables for the supper crowd. I'd taken a handful of reservations for dinner, but knew the following week would probably be busier. Besides, the popular local band known as Uncle Tim's Barn Dance was playing at the K of C hostel tonight, and they were supposed to be a real big deal. Around nine, Tex asked me if he could use the phone in my office; he was in there a good half hour, and when he came out, he seemed more preoccupied than usual. I didn't have time to question him about it: we had a sudden, last-minute flurry of customers and from then until closing, the only things I thought about were seating arrangements, drink orders, and the customary gratuities. It was eleven on the dot when I closed and locked the front door, and turned the sign in the window. "God, I feel like I've been run over by a train."

Chris lifted a fresh pot of coffee off the burner and poured us all a cup. "Here you go, boys. A good night's work in anybody's books, I'd say." The radio behind the bar was tuned to a local station; tonight they were broadcasting live from the K of C hostel and just then some guy was giving his all to "Moonlight Trail."

"Goddammit, I hate that song," Tex moaned. "And he's murdering it. Why the Sam Hill do they try and sing country songs around here anyway? It's not like—"

Chris shushed him. "Jack, turn it up."

I got up and twirled the radio knob, but there was nothing on except static—a faint crackling sound, very dim and faraway. It was almost like the signal had gotten interrupted between there and here. Then we heard a series of thumps, a girl screamed, and far away in the background, I heard a man yelling there was a fire, the building was on fire, and then the signal died.

We stared at each other, wondering if what we'd just heard was real, wondering if we ought to go and do something. Rick, I thought, Rick Callan was there, and he would know what to do. Rick was good at taking care of things. He would have matters under control immediately, and the band would come back on and everything would proceed as normal. This wasn't Brooklyn or the slums of Philadelphia; this was Newfoundland, and it was safe and there was nothing here that could hurt anyone....

The man with the face.

"Huh?" Chris was looking at me strangely. "You say something, Jack?"

"The man... lemonade. The man with the face, he had no eyelashes." No lashes, and no eyebrows, either. They'd been painted on, drawn on, something. The skin of his face was too tight, and shiny, as if.... "He was here. This afternoon. He sat in here. He asked me for cold lemonade."

Tex nodded. "Yeah, I remember him. Lemonade. You think...?"

I didn't have time to answer him because somebody was pounding on the door. Dan O'Hagan, my old pal from the *Telegram*, was there, his cameras slung around his neck like bandoliers. "The K of C hostel's on fire! I'm going up there now. Come on! They might need help."

We threw our coats on and followed him out into the freezing cold. There were hardly any people about, and the only cars we saw crept along at a snail's pace, their headlights showing just a thin beam through the slits in the blackout covers. The cold was already biting my nose and the tips of my ears. I'd shoved my feet into winter galoshes but my toes were numb, and my fingers tingled painfully; it hurt to breathe. "Dan, slow down."

"Come on." Tex caught hold of my sleeve and towed me forward. "You stand around too long, you'll freeze in place."

We had just reached the top of Long's Hill when we saw the blaze: red, enormous, leaping up into the blackness of the winter night. My heart lurched. Rick Callan was there. Rick Callan was in there. I waded through ankle-deep snow, crossing as close to the hostel as I dared. At this proximity, the heat was intense, searing my naked face, burning my lips and eyelids. A line of fire hoses had been linked to the hydrants and ran across Harvey Road and up Parade Street, and a group of firemen were doing their valiant best, but it was already too late. The building had by then been reduced to a pile of flaming rubble, burning with the intensity of hellfire. It was no use. There was nothing I could do. There was nothing anyone could do—not now, not ever again.

"I'M SORRY to have to do this, Jack. We tried to locate someone else who could positively identify him, but most of his friends all died in the fire." Picco's hairline was singed, and his eyebrows were completely gone, but he was otherwise unscathed. Fort Townsend's proximity to the hostel meant a great many Constabulary officers turned out to assist during the fire; Picco had been one of them. "You can take a minute if you want. There's no rush."

"No, it's fine." I swallowed hard. The room—an empty parade hall in the CLB Armoury building—had been pressed into service as a temporary morgue, the city morgue having been overrun with corpses of the recently dead. The bodies here were laid out in neat rows, each one covered with the requisite white sheet. "I'm all right." Picco peeled back the part of the sheet that covered the head, and I looked, then nodded, and stepped away. Callan's face was as unblemished as it had been the last time I'd seen him alive. "How did he...?"

Picco replaced the sheet. "I don't know, Jack." He sighed. "The body isn't burned as badly as some of the others. He may have been hit by falling debris. He was found outside the structure, lying face-down on the ground; two soldiers took him to a medic, but he couldn't be revived." His pale eyes searched my features—for what, I didn't know. I felt nothing even remotely like grief, or sorrow, or regret, or any of the things you usually felt at a time like this. I felt nothing, nothing at all, as if some invisible force had come along and stolen my capacity to react to something like this. "I'm sorry," Picco added. "I know he was your friend."

"Yeah." The room was of necessity cold, and I shivered. "Yeah, he was. Come on. Let's get out of here." We went out to where Picco's car was parked. I'd walked up from the Heartache, despite the cold, and he had offered to drive me home. The first of the funerals for the fire victims would take place today, and local churches had pushed aside whatever holiday season business they might otherwise have had to make room for the dead. It seemed to me that I spent an inordinate amount of time doing that myself. First with Judy, then with Frankie, then with Sam's wife Tareenah and now there was Rick. Maybe I was a bad luck charm, a jinx or something: brush up against me and you die.

Picco stopped for the traffic cop at the intersection of Duckworth and Prescott. "You all right?" He reached across and touched my arm. "I'm sorry, Jack. I really am." He sighed. "Listen, I'm not supposed to tell you this, so if you say anything to anybody I swear to God I'll gut ye." The cop waved us through and Picco's car tipped down over the hill, turning right onto Water Street. "There's significant evidence to suggest the fire wasn't an accident."

I might have said something, but I'll be damned if I remember what it was.

"A Bulgarian agent was put ashore in Conception Bay back in October. You remember that night I found you and Callan out in Topsail?"

"Yeah, I remember. I felt like you were my mother, and I had to hide my dirty magazines under the mattress."

"We received a tip that lights had been spotted offshore in Conception Bay, so we went out to check. We didn't find anything."

"So how'd you know... Bulgarian?" *I wonder if you could direct me to... ah, Parade Street?* "There was a man in my cafe that same day, the day of the fire. He was little, not much over five feet tall, and he had an accent. There was something strange about his face, too. I remember he had no eyelashes."

Picco gazed at me while we waited for the traffic ahead of us to move. I thought I saw anxiety flit across his features, but it was gone almost immediately. "You didn't tell me? Jesus, Jack."

This was new; Picco never, ever swore. "What was I supposed to do? Call you up and report it? 'There's a man here with no eyelashes. I think you ought to arrest him.'"

He dragged his gaze away from me. "Either way, if this... eyelashless man in your cafe is who we suspect he is, he may well have started the fire. His name is Yosif Tzvetanov—"

"I'm impressed. Say it again."

"Yosif Tzvetanov, and he is a Nazi collaborator. He was probably working with Jonah Octavian."

A Greek working with a Bulgarian? "Uh-huh."

"The fire was deliberately planned as an act of sabotage." Picco pulled up in front of the Heartache. "Stoyles, be careful. Octavian's buddies know all about you. You better watch yourself. Carry a gun if you got one."

I opened the door and put my foot on the sidewalk. "Thanks for the ride. Come in for a coffee?"

Picco raised his nonexistent eyebrows dismissively. "I'm on duty."

I got out, but leaned back in and grinned at him. "Seeing Chris tonight?"

He kept his gaze fixed on the front windshield. "None of your business."

"Where do you guys do it, anyway? You live with your sister—"

Picco put the car into gear and pulled away from the sidewalk so fast I nearly went down, but his reaction made me laugh, and I was grateful. If

Picco was still a jerk, then some things were definitely right with the world. I went inside, stopped long enough to say hello to Tex and Chris, and went through to my office. Normally, I wouldn't abuse the telephone lines, this being wartime and all, but I'd decided upon a course of action, and I needed to carry it out before I lost my nerve. The hostel fire had set some things in motion, things I was powerless to stop. The only thing I could do now was strap in and hope I survived the ride.

I got Kevin MacBride's line on the first try, but there was a wait since Cairo was four and a half hours later than Newfoundland and the young woman who took my call said she believed the captain was at supper. It took about fifteen minutes for them to locate MacBride and get him to the telephone; the first thing he did was apologize for the wait. "So you've decided, then?"

"Yeah." I pushed away the crossword puzzle I'd been working on. "Yeah, I'll do it. What we talked about—" I wasn't dumb enough to say it over an open wire. "I'll do it."

MacBride let out his breath into the transcontinental silence. "Right. Good on you." He laughed. "Great to have you aboard. Someone will be by to see you in a day or two and give you some instructions. That all right?"

"Sure. After the year I've had, I'm game for anything."

I'M NOT sure exactly when it was, except I know it was noon and the sun was shining, even through the December cold. The Heartache was empty of customers, and I was working behind the bar, sorting through the previous night's receipts, when I became aware of someone standing in front of me, waiting patiently for me to look up. I guess I'd expected a lot of things: maybe MacBride himself would come, or maybe Tex would turn out to be my contact, or Chris or Picco. I took my time before I gave him my attention and in retrospect, I'm glad I did.

"I wonder if you might help me. I am looking for a particular building."

Maybe he said something else; I don't know. It seemed like the cafe, the street, the sun through the windowpanes, the world—all of it vanished into meaningless chaos, and there was only him. "Sam."

"*Salam alekum*, Jack."

I was trembling so much, I had to hold on to the bar to keep from falling. "Sam, you… why… I mean—MacBride said—did you come all the way from Cairo?"

He laughed, the laugh I loved so much, and reached out a hand to steady me. "No, Jack. I regret even I am not capable of spanning the globe in a mere eye blink." His gentle gaze took me in. "After Tareenah…." There was a long silence, while he composed himself. "No, I have been here for some time now, helping out your Sergeant Picco and lending a hand wherever I might. It was me you saw that day, outside your cafe, watching you from across the street. I hope you didn't mind too much. Are you glad to see me?"

"You have to ask?" I wanted to rush to him, to leap over the bar and grab him, tell him how much I loved him, how much I had missed him, but I was afraid. "H-how are… I mean, your children, how are they?"

"My children are well, thank you. My sister came from Alexandria to care for them. They are… managing, as am I." His elegant mouth curled up at one corner. "Is that all you have to say to me, Jack?"

"Well, I think—"

I came out from behind the bar and there he was, standing in front of me, so close it would have been impossible to insert a hand between us, and he was gazing up at me and smiling. "Do you know what your problem is, Jack?"

It was suddenly very hard to speak. "No."

"You think too much."

And I took him in my arms and kissed him.

J.S. COOK was born and raised on the island of Newfoundland. She holds a B.A. and an M.A. in English Language and Literature and a B.Ed in post-secondary education. She makes her home in St. John's, Newfoundland, with her husband Paul and Lola, her spoiled rotten dogter.

J.S. Cook also writes as JoAnne Soper-Cook.

By J.S. COOK

But Not For Me
Come to Dust
Famous Last Words
A Little Night Murder
The Lovely Beast
Oasis of Night
The Quality of Mercy
Sixteen Songs About Regret
The Stranger at My Door
The Winter Dark

Published by DREAMSPINNER PRESS
http://www.dreamspinnerpress.com

Stranger at the Door

By J.S. Cook

South Carolina lawyer Calvin Amos is confident he can gain Thomas Basinger his freedom on appeal. Thom was convicted of a murder during an armed robbery gone bad. But Basinger's case proves more difficult than Cal anticipated, and the battle he assumed he'd win turns into a devastating failure. Remorseful over the personal defeat, after Basinger is executed, Cal throws himself out of his office window.

Bizarrely, the fall doesn't kill him. Even stranger, Thom Basinger rings Cal's doorbell looking for a job. Both men are drawn to each other. Before long, the two forge a unique, heartfelt connection that transcends the boundaries of life and death.

Calvin Amos always imagined himself in possession of some great love or other. He didn't know he had to die to find it.

http://www.dreamspinnerpress.com

Famous Last Words

By J.S. Cook

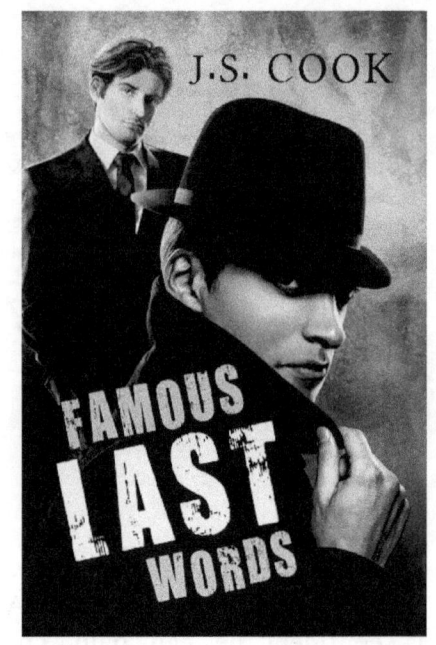

When former Indiana farm boy William Henry Rider goes on a bank robbing spree in Benedict Fouts's corner of Depression Era Illinois, it's up to Ben to bring him in. But Rider is no ordinary criminal. Famed for robberies that happen in the blink of an eye, Rider becomes a folk hero who steals from the rich and burns the mortgage papers of poor farmers teetering on the edge of financial ruin.

Intrigued to learn that Fouts has been assigned to his case, Rider approaches him in a darkened movie house with a unique proposition: "We'll have ourselves a game of Cops and Robbers. I'll run, and you catch me. The clock starts right now, Ben."

Ben knows he's the only one who can stop the Bureau from murdering Rider, but he's soon struggling with another reason to chase the enigmatic fugitive.

http://www.dreamspinnerpress.com

http://www.dreamspinnerpress.com

www.ingramcontent.com/pod-product-compliance
Lightning Source LLC
Chambersburg PA
CBHW070055030726
47506CB00002B/471